Paul Doherty was born in Middlesbrough. He studied History at Liverpool and Oxford Universities and obtained a doctorate at Oxford for his thesis on Edward II and Queen Isabella. He is now headmaster of a school in north-east London and lives with his wife and family near Epping Forest.

Paul Doherty is the author of the Hugh Corbett medieval mysteries, the Sorrowful Mysteries of Brother Athelstan, the Canterbury Tales of mystery and murder, the Ancient Egyptian mysteries, the Journals of Roger Shallot, THE SOUL SLAYER, THE ROSE DEMON, THE HAUNTING, DOMINA, THE PLAGUE LORD and MURDER IMPERIAL, all of which have been highly praised.

'Extensive and penetrating research coupled with a strong plot and bold characterisation. Loads of adventure and a dazzling evocation of the past' *Herald Sun*, Melbourne

'An opulent banquet to satisfy the most murderous appetite' *Northern Echo*

'Paul Doherty has a lively sense of history . . . evocative and lyrical descriptions' *New Statesman*

'Teems with colour, energy and spills' *Time Out*

'Vitality in the cityscape . . . angst in the mystery; it's Peters minus the herbs but plus a few crates of sack' *Oxford Times*

'As always the author invokes the medieval period in all its muck as well as glory, filling the pages with pungent smells and description. The author brings years of research to his writing; his mastery of the period as well as a disciplined writing schedule have led to a rapidly increasing body of work and a growing reputation' *Mystery News*

Also by Paul Doherty and available from Headline

The Rose Demon
The Soul Slayer
The Haunting
Domina
The Plague Lord
Murder Imperial
An Evil Spirit Out of the West
The Assassins of Isis

The Canterbury Tales of mystery and murder
An Ancient Evil
Being the Knight's Tale
A Tapestry of Murders
Being the Man of Law's Tale
A Tournament of Murders
Being the Franklin's Tale
Ghostly Murders
Being the Priest's Tale
The Hangman's Hymn
Being the Carpenter's Tale
A Haunt of Murder
Being the Clerk of Oxford's Tale

The Sorrowful Mysteries of Brother Athelstan
The Nightingale Gallery
The House of the Red Slayer
Murder Most Holy
The Anger of God
By Murder's Bright Light
The House of Crows
The Assassin's Riddle
The Devil's Domain
The Field of Blood

Ancient Egyptian mysteries
The Mask of Ra
The Horus Killings
The Anubis Slayings
The Slayers of Seth

Hugh Corbett medieval mysteries
Satan in St Mary's
Crown in Darkness
Spy in Chancery
The Angel of Death
The Prince of Darkness
Murder Wears a Cowl
The Assassin in the Greenwood
The Song of a Dark Angel
Satan's Fire
The Devil's Hunt
The Demon Archer
The Treason of the Ghosts
Corpse Candle
The Magician's Death

The House of Shadows

Paul Doherty

headline

First published in Great Britain in 2003
by HEADLINE BOOK PUBLISHING

First published in Great Britain in paperback in 2004
by HEADLINE BOOK PUBLISHING

5

ISBN 0 7553 0777 1

Typeset in Trump Medieval by
Palimpsest Book Production Limited, Polmont, Stirlingshire

Printed and bound in Great Britain by
Clays Ltd, St Ives plc

HEADLINE BOOK PUBLISHING
A division of Hodder Headline
338 Euston Road
London NW1 3BH

www.headline.co.uk
www.hodderheadline.com

In loving memory of William (Wills) Walford-Grant

Beloved son of Michael and Annie

of South Woodford

Born 2 March 1989, tragically killed 8 November 2002

The tavern is the Church of the Devil where his disciples wander to serve him and where he works his miracles.

Le Menagier de Paris, a medieval sclf-help book (edited by J. Pichon, Paris, 1846), Volume I, p.48

Prologue

Eve of the Feast of St Matthew, 1360

The courtesan known as Guinevere the Golden crouched amongst the headstones of St Erconwald's cemetery. She had concealed her lustrous golden hair beneath a tight-fitting hood, and put on a dark cloak to cover her finery. She had taken off her ring and placed it in the small casket beside her. The autumn night was bright with a full moon, which bathed the cemetery in a silver glow and illuminated the dark mass of the church. Guinevere was fearful. That sombre pile of masonry was God's house. The preachers claimed angels trod there, and wouldn't the good Lord see into the very recesses of her soul? Guinevere just wished her comrades would come. She wanted an end to this fear, to give way to the excitement which made her heart skip and her blood tingle. She settled herself more comfortably. The night sky was beautiful; she watched a faint cloud drift, as if following the moon

1

across the night sky. She started as an owl, silent as a ghost, swept above her, feathery wings beating the air as it plunged on its victim, scurrying through the high grass of the cemetery. The door to the death house creaked. A chilling sound in the darkness.

Nevertheless, Guinevere felt safe. The old church had no priest, and very few people would come to the cemetery at night. Guinevere recalled the old story of how each cemetery, each portion of God's Acre, possessed a watcher, the ghost of the last person buried there. He, or she, had to stay on guard in the cemetery until replaced by the spirit of the next person buried. Guinevere swallowed hard; she mustn't frighten herself. She closed her eyes and tried to think of the cheery tap room at the Night in Jerusalem. All her friends and acquaintances would be there. A fiddler would stand by the log fire; perhaps a travelling songsman would chant a lay. The tambour and the rebec would strike up, a pulsating sound which marked the beginning of the dance. Guinevere so loved to dance; that was how she had met him, the man who had promised her wealth beyond all reckoning.

'A chest full of treasure!' he had whispered.

At first, Guinevere had been reluctant. She'd blinked her eyes prettily and claimed she had given her heart to another, but those words, 'a chest full of treasure', had so enticed her. She would be rich, a princess, a great lady, like those who swaggered through Cheapside with their gauze veils and fur-lined cloaks, jewellery glittering at their throats, soft bodies smelling of sweet perfumes. She would wash her hands in golden bowls and sit before a piece of polished silver to examine her beautiful face.

The wind moaned amongst the headstones, the breeze was strengthening; soon the fleet would sail. Guinevere clenched her fists in excitement. She had done her part. She opened the casket and took out the gold ring, turning it over in her fingers, examining it carefully. What did it matter? She slipped the ring on her finger and leaned back against the headstone. What would be happening now? Surely the alarm would have been raised, yet she had just come slipping through the streets of Southwark and seen no excitement. Nothing wrong, no torchlight flickering against the night or mailed men tramping through the streets to the clash of armour.

'Guinevere!'

She raised herself up and stared across the cemetery. She saw the signal, a shuttered lantern being opened and closed like a beacon flashed from a clifftop. Guinevere stood and moved across the cemetery. A dark shape detached itself from the death house and came towards her. The lantern was raised, the shutter slightly open. Guinevere sighed in relief. Lifting the hem of her gown, she ran towards him. The lantern was lowered. Guinevere the Golden was so excited she didn't even hear the hiss of steel. So eager to hear the news, she almost ran on to the dagger point. She felt the fiery stab of pain, but it was too late. She was trapped, drawn close, pressed further and further on to the blade thrusting deep inside her.

Guinevere groaned and slipped, the life light fading from her beautiful eyes.

Chapter 1

The hideous murders began on the Night of the Great Ratting, the eve of the Feast of the holy martyr St Wulfnoth, who had been boiled alive by the heathen Frisians. The inhabitants of Southwark, their tattered purses full of crocards and pollards, those battered and clipped coins rejected by worthy tradesmen, these denizens of the slums, hoods pulled up against the freezing cold, made their way to the spacious tavern, the Night in Jerusalem, which stood on the broad thoroughfare which swept down to London Bridge. The night was bitterly cold; the season of Advent was only a month away. The seers had prophesied snow, but the night sky was cloud-free and the stars brilliant. A full moon bathed the reeking alleyways and lanes in its ghostly light. The day's business was done, windows were shuttered, doors locked and barred. The cats slunk away whilst the rats, as if they sensed what was going to happen, kept well clear of the frozen rubbish heaps.

Everyone knew about the Great Ratting. Those who liked to gamble or play hazard had already laid their wagers. Others were just curious as to see what would happen. Of course, every thief could smell a profit. There'd be purses to be cut and pockets to be picked whilst enjoying a good night's entertainment. The news had spread across the swollen black Thames, attracting the more well-to-do and genteel from Cheapside, Farringdon Ward, and even as far north as Clerkenwell. Moleskin, the boatman who sailed out of Southwark Steps, was promised a roaring trade. The Thames, however, was choppy, the river breeze sharp as a dagger, so many just slipped under the chains at London Bridge, scampering along the narrow lane between the houses and the great selds, or warehouses, built either side of the bridge. All excited, they ignored the frozen midden piles containing every type of waste heaped high along the middle, nor did they pause to stare at the severed, mouldering heads of traitors placed high on spikes on either side of the bridge. They showed a similar lack of pity for those caught stealing from stalls during the previous day's trading; these malefactors were now fastened in the stocks by hand, head or leg, or shut up in the cages at each end of the bridge, where they would stand all night and suffer the freezing cold.

The petty traders and chapmen, the sellers of figs and apples, the tallow chandlers, the wax chandlers, the fleshers and the tanners all forgot their trade rivalry, flocking to the Great Ratting. They were joined by doxies and the whores in their gaudy rags from Walbrook and Hounsditch. These ladies of the night hid their charms behind cowls, hoods, shabby cloaks, and masks with gaps for their eyes and mouths. Once they reached the spacious tap room of the Night in Jerusalem they removed such disguises.

The tap room's tables and chairs were ringed by row after row of barrels, each table being lit by a yellow tallow candle or a bowl of oil with a burning wick floating in the centre. Even though the champions hadn't arrived, the wagering had begun, encouraged by the good silver and gold brought by the young men of the court, garbed in their tight hose, puffed jackets, protuberant codpieces and high-heeled boots. In the view of many of those who flocked to the tavern, these popinjays with their high-pitched voices, soft hands and faces, and curled, crimped hair were the real reason for the evening. They carried purses and wallets openly for all to see, and the fingers of many itched to be so close to such wealth. A few arrivals brought their own dogs, bull mastiffs, terriers, and even the occasional greyhound or whippet so as to measure up the opposition.

They all crowded in, gathering around the grease-covered tables or going to stare at the stuffed corpses of other prized dogs who had won the title of 'Champion Rat Killer'. Pride of place was given to the embalmed corpse of a white bull mastiff with black patches around its protuberant glass eyes. A collar about its neck proclaimed the dog as 'The Greatest Champion of all times'. In the centre of the tap room stretched the great pit, still covered over, a broad and very deep whitewashed hole ringed with lanterns and hour candles, the flames of which were already approaching the eleventh ring. Soon the games would begin. Mine host, a great tub of a man who rejoiced in the name of Master Rolles, was already enthroned in his chair of state on a velvet-covered dais overlooking the pit. He sat there like a king, bawling for more lights to be brought. Link boys hurried up with lantern horns they'd filched from the doorsteps of houses in the wealthier parts of the City. Once these were in place, Master Rolles, his fat, greasy face shimmering in the light, stared petulantly round, small lips pursed, greedy black eyes gleaming, ready to make his power felt. The tavern was filling up. Master Rolles quietly congratulated himself on making a handsome profit. Once the game was over, he'd visit Mother Veritable's House of Delights and, in the morning, light more candles before the Virgin's altar in the Priory Church of St Mary Overy.

Dishes of burning charcoal were also brought up with incense strewn on top. The taverner liked this touch – the incense gave the tap room a holy smell and helped to hide the reeking odours of the slops-strewn floor. Master Rolles felt a little guilty. One of his maids had stolen the incense from the Priory Church but Rolles quietly promised himself that, in time, he would make compensation. Glowing braziers, their tops capped, were wheeled in from the scullery and placed around the room. More logs were thrown on to the roaring fire, building up the flames under the mantled hearth. Master Rolles bellowed an order and the carcass of an entire pig, only its head and trotters removed, was spiked on a spit and placed on the wheels on either side of the hearth to be turned and basted with spices. The pig had been killed because it had trespassed into Master Rolles' yard. In truth, two of his stable boys had enticed it there, and Master Rolles, knowing the law of the City, had been only too happy to slit its throat. The taverner watched his cooks place the spit carefully, ladling over the spiced oil whilst giving careful instruction to the dwarf who had been paid a penny, told to ignore the heat, and to turn the spit until the pig was cooked.

'Don't go to sleep!' the taverner roared.

The dwarf, who had once been a jester until he had been mauled by a bear, nodded and sat down, turning his face against the blast of the fire. The air turned sweet with the smell of spiced, roasted pork. Customers were now shouting for ale and beer. Scullions and slatterns hurried across with brimming tankards, stoups and blackjacks filled by tap boys from the great barrels. The taverner rubbed his stomach. In an hour, most of his customers would be too drunk to tell how much water he had added to the beer and wine.

The Night in Jerusalem was now almost full. In the

garish light it looked like some antechamber of hell. The underworld was there; the taverner knew each and every one of them: the pimps and the pickpockets, the quacks, the dice-codgers, house-breakers, bully boys and roaring lads. Where they went, prostitutes of every age and description followed, their hair dyed, faces painted, garbed in cheap finery and smelling richly of the perfumes they used to cover their ill-washed bodies. The taverner promised himself to keep a sharp eye on these, as he would the tinkers and petty traders, those who dared to make a profit in his tavern: the sellers of bird eggs, horse bread, old fish, or whatever else they had filched from the stalls in the market across the City. The cranks and the counterfeit men had also arrived. The professional beggars, all surprisingly nimble as they washed off their scars; the leg they had claimed to have lost now miraculously appeared as they undid the straps and heaped their crutches in a corner.

The taverner's own keepers, ruffians from the alleyways armed with cudgels and knives, moved amongst what Master Rolles called his 'congregation' to ensure the peace was kept; ankles were kicked, fingers rapped, and shoulders punched as a warning to observe the proprieties. A relic-seller, who had become drunk and attempted to urinate in the middle of the tap room, was given a beating and thrust into what the taverner termed 'outer darkness'. Customers lined up for a strip of pork, served on a piece of wood and garnished with stewed leeks and a piece of hard rye bread, liberally covered in a cheap hot pepper which Master Rolles hoped would inspire their thirst.

The 'congregation' clustered around the pit. A roar went up as Ranulf the rat-catcher from the parish of St Erconwald, where Brother Athelstan the Dominican was parish priest, appeared in the doorway, carrying his two favourite ferrets, Precious and Pretty, in a reed basket. Ranulf was accompanied by fellow parishioners: Pike the ditcher, Basil the blacksmith, Crispin the carpenter, Mugwort the bell clerk, Mauger the hangman, Moleskin the boatman, Bladdersniff the bailiff and finally, in all her glory, her blonde hair falling around her face like a halo, Cecily the courtesan, one hand resting on Huddle the painter, the other on Crim the altar boy, who was Pike the ditcher's son. The rear was brought up by Pernel the Flemish woman, her hair dyed a garish black and red. Cecily was greeted with catcalls, whistles and lecherous offers; she just curtsied prettily and made an obscene gesture in the direction of her tormentors.

Ranulf walked to the edge of the pit and sat on a stool whilst the rest of the tavern gathered about. Ranulf the rat-catcher had a pinched, narrow face with bright button eyes, a sharp nose and bloodless lips. Some whispered there was more than a passing likeness between him and the rodents he hunted. Now he sat like a prince, black-tarred hood pulled close to his head, under which his oiled black hair was neatly combed back and tied in a queue. This self-proclaimed scourge of London's rats cradled the basket in his lap, whispering to the two ferrets inside. Another roar echoed as Master Flaxwith, with his two mastiffs, Samson and Satan, entered the tap room. He too was greeted like a conquering hero, those who had wagered on his dogs crowding round to offer encouragement and advice. Mine host watched the proceedings. He had to be careful with Flaxwith, who was chief bailiff of Sir John Cranston, Lord Coroner of the City, a man with a fearsome reputation for fingering the collars of those who broke both the King's law and the City ordinances.

'That's certainly happening tonight,' the taverner whispered to himself.

Master Rolles had crossed swords on many occasions with Sir John, an old soldier but a fierce one, with his red face, piercing blue eyes and luxuriant beard and moustache which he would comb with his fingers whenever he questioned the likes of Master Rolles. Cranston acted the bluff, hearty old soldier, the pompous City official, but he had nimble wits and a sharp brain. He was just as quick with sword and dagger, even though he seemed to spend most of his life drinking the best claret from his miraculous wineskin. Even more dangerous was the small, dark-faced Dominican Friar Athelstan, with his soulful eyes and searching looks. Athelstan was Cranston's secretarius, or clerk, and often accompanied the coroner to his investigations of hideous murders, subtle thefts or, indeed, any infringement of the King's Peace along the dark lanes and alleyways of Southwark.

Master Rolles glanced quickly around the tap room; he just hoped and prayed nothing would go wrong tonight, no mistake occur which might provoke the curiosity of those two sharp-eyed hawks of the law.

'Let the festivities begin,' Rolles roared.

The pit was uncovered. First there were the usual diversions. A juggler attempted to spin five cups in the air, but when he dropped one, he was pelted with scraps of food and soiled rushes from the floor. He was followed by the farmyard player, a man who could imitate the quack of a duck or the bray of a horse. He only lasted a few minutes, and was followed by a French dancing master, an old man with straggling grey hair and a nasty cough. His dogs were frightened and refused to dance, so he too was driven from the pit. Crim the altar boy, who had been given a blackjack of ale, silenced the clamour with a beautiful song in his vibrant carrying voice.

Behold Mistress Sweet,
Now you may see that I have lost my soul to thee.

The words were haunting, and the French dancing master, who had agreed to accompany the boy on a flute, created a heart-wrenching sound. For a moment, just for a measure, a few heartbeats, the customers forgot their own ugliness and the hideous circumstances of their lives.

Crim was followed by Pike the ditcher, and Master Rolles was not pleased. Pike was suspected of being a secret member of the Great Community of the Realm, a mysterious society flourishing across London and the surrounding shires. The Great Community was said to be plotting rebellion, to bring about sweeping changes where the noble lords would be pulled down and the Poor Worms of the Earth, as the Community called the peasants, allowed some respite from the incessant demands of both the King's tax collectors and the Great Lords of the Soil. Pike, his narrow, sallow face flushed with ale, immediately launched into the rousing verses,

> *When Adam delved and Eve span, who was*
>   *then the gentleman!*
> *When Adam delved and Eve span, where was*
>   *then the pride of man!*

Such words provoked roars of approval, until the taverner's bully boys hustled Pike from the pit.

Master Rolles had had enough. He snapped his fingers at the ostler standing next to him, and the fellow lifted a horn to his lips and blew three long, carrying blasts, which stilled all the clamour and noise.

'Why can't we have more singing?' someone bawled.

Master Rolles glowered at his congregation.

'We are not here,' he shouted back, 'to plot rebellion! Who here wants to dance in the air at Smithfield, a rope round his neck, the other end fastened securely around the branch of an elm?'

His words chilled the fevered crowd. They all knew

14

what he was hinting at. The young King, Richard II, son of the famous Black Prince, grandson of the war-like Edward III, was under the protection of his uncle, the Regent John of Gaunt. A sinister man, Gaunt, with a finger in every pie and a host of spies swarming all over London; even here in this tap room there might be men and women prepared to sell a name or a man's life for a piece of silver or a paltry groat.

'Let the rats be brought,' Rolles shouted.

The crowds stood hushed as the door leading to the stable yard was flung open and the great boxes were brought in. They were taken to the edge of the pit and the lids lifted, and the whitewashed hole came to life with swarming rats, black, grey and brown, some scarred and lean, others young and plump. Many tried to escape, scampering round, desperate to hide from the light and noise. A few of the bolder ones stood up on their hind legs and began to wash themselves, oblivious to their gruesome future. Everyone crowded around the pit, people climbing on tables or up the great wooden pillars supporting the ceiling, eager to catch a glimpse of what would happen next.

Flaxwith went first; he unmuzzled the mastiff Satan and released the dog into the pit. Satan, hungry and ferocious, began a hideous slaughter amongst the rats even as Master Rolles turned the hourglass over whilst his assistant, the horn man, counted slowly under his breath. It took ninety seconds for Satan to reduce the swarm of rats to a mess of bloody corpses. Samson followed. Fresh rats were brought, and the air quickly turned foul with the smell of their corpses and the gruesome tang of blood. Samson was more swift and deadly, accomplishing his task by the time the horn man had reached eighty-five. The tavern crowd watched with bated breath; now it was the rat-catcher's turn.

The ferret, Pretty, was released into the pit to meet a fresh horde of rats, and Ranulf's disappointment was obvious when the horn man counted ninety-five before Pretty had finished his bloody work. Those who had wagered on the rat-catcher growled and mumbled under their breath. Everything rested on Precious. More rats were brought. Precious was released and the air was riven with the squeal of the vermin and the scampering of their paws. Precious was a master killer, a true slaughterer, one of the litters of the great Ferox, Ranulf's prize ferret. He completed his massacre before the horn man had even reached eighty. For a moment there was silence, then Master Rolles rose to his feet as if he were a Speaker in the Commons in St Stephen's Chapel.

'Master Ranulf has won!'

His proclamation was greeted with shouts of joy and distress. Some who had wagered on the mastiffs tried to leave furtively, but the windows were all sealed whilst the taverner's bully boys guarded the doors. No one was allowed out into the yard until all debts were settled.

Master Rolles turned in his great chair and stared around the tap room. The contest over, the customers were drifting back to the tables, shouting for drink and food. A pet monkey had broken loose; it had been chased by a greyhound and now sheltered in the rafters, chattering noisily down at its tormentor. The taverner didn't fear a raid by the constables; in fact, Master Rolles had paid them well to look the other way. He just wanted to make sure that everything was as it should be. Ranulf the rat-catcher was now being brought tankard after tankard by his numerous supporters, and the taverner drew comfort from this. The rest of the night must pass smoothly. He glimpsed Beatrice and Clarice; the two sister whores looked happy enough. Rolles only hoped their friend the Misericord did not become involved in any mischief and have to flee. Absent-mindedly he took the goblet of wine a pot boy brought and sipped at it. The Knights were there, and the Judas Man? Rolles slouched in his chair. Ah yes, he thought, the Judas Man!

In a small chamber two floors above the tap room, the Judas Man sat waiting for his orders. He was of middling height, with a beetling brow, close-cropped hair and wary, shifting eyes in a lean pockmarked face. Many would describe him as pitiless, a man of little mercy, but the Judas Man didn't care. It was many years since he had darkened the church and mumbled his sins whilst crouched in the shriving pew. Some whispered that he came from Dorset, a farmer whose family had been massacred by the French when they had raided the villages along the south coast. How such bloody deeds had turned his mind, killed his soul, and so he had become a hunter of men.

The Judas Man sat, his Lincoln-green hose pushed into black boots to which the spurs were still attached, his brown leather jerkin unbuttoned to reveal a clean white shirt and round his neck a silver chain bearing a golden ring, allegedly belonging to his dead wife. His cloak, war belt, and small crossbow lay on the truckle bed. They were within easy reach as the Judas Man contented himself, squatting on a three-legged stool playing softly on a penny whistle, a jigging tune, more suitable to a May Day dance than this sombre chamber rented for him. He lowered the whistle; he did not know the name or identity of his hirer. He had simply followed instructions – now he had to wait. He had gathered, from the roars below, how the ratting had ended. Now the raucous sound of a bagpipe echoed through the ceiling.

The Judas Man picked up his wine goblet and sipped carefully. He wanted to remain calm but wished the stranger would come. He felt trapped in London. He did not like its narrow, winding, reeking streets. He preferred to work out in the shires, bringing in the outlaws and wolf heads – those who had been proclaimed 'utlegatum' – beyond the law. He would hunt them down and drag them, at the tail of his horse, into some market square before the Guildhall. He would hand the prisoners over to the sheriff's men and claim the reward. What happened to his captives afterwards was not his concern. Now he had been hired by some mysterious stranger, a generous advance in good coin, with a promise of more to come, once he had captured the Misericord. The Judas Man knew all about the Misericord, a clever thief – the most cunning of men. Rumour had it he was a former priest; they had forgotten his real name. He was called the Misericord because of the small dagger, clasped in a velvet sheath, worn round his neck. The misericord was the dagger used by archers to dispatch a wounded enemy. The Misericord used it to cut purses and prise open locks. He was also an infamous trickster, a man who could sell soil and claim it was gold. No wonder he was wanted dead or alive in numerous towns and shires around London.

The Judas Man had been at Coggeshall in Essex when he had received the letter, written in a clerkly hand, with a generous purse of silver coins. The instructions were quite simple. He was to be in London by the eve of St Wulfnoth and take lodgings at the Night in Jerusalem in Southwark. Once he had arrived, the Judas Man realised that a trickster like the Misericord would try his luck on the night of the Great Ratting. Nevertheless, he had to wait for the signal. He rose to his feet and walked across the room, staring out of the needle-thin window. He gazed down into the stable yard of the inn; here and there a pitch torch, lashed to a pole, gave off a pool of light, shadows flitted across. The Judas Man didn't like his chamber. When he had climbed the stairs he had seen how luxurious the rest of the tavern was, but Master

Rolles had been very particular. This was the chamber which had been hired so this was the chamber he had been given. Suddenly the door behind him rattled. The Judas Man hastened to pick up his war belt; he strapped this about him and walked carefully across as the door rattled again.

'Who is it?' he called.

Again the door rattled. The Judas Man pressed his ear against the wood but he could hear no sound. He loosened the bolts at the top and bottom, lifted the latch and looked out. Nothing, except a lantern horn glowing on the high windowsill at the top of the stairs. The wind rattled a shutter, the floorboards creaked; the Judas Man glanced down and saw the leather pouch lying there. He picked it up and stepped back into the chamber. The pouch contained a scrap of parchment with the scrawl 'The Misericord is below' and a small purse of silver coins. The Judas Man counted these out carefully. They were good – freshly minted, ten pounds sterling. He put the pouch carefully inside his jerkin and finished his preparations.

He had left his chamber and was halfway down the stairs when the group at the bottom made him pause. Four knights in all, dressed like Hospitallers in their black and white cloaks, the golden falcon emblem sewn on the left shoulder; next to them a fifth man in the garb of a Benedictine monk. They were preparing to climb the stairs to the palatial chambers on the Oaken Gallery, which ran along the front, back and one side of the tavern. Luxurious rooms with feather-down beds, turkey carpets on the floor and exquisite draperies and tapestries adorning the walls. One of the knights looked up the stairs, staring full at the Judas Man.

'By the Cross,' he breathed, 'and St Veronica's veil!'

The Judas Man came down the rest of the stairs to be greeted by the knights, who clasped his hands. He knew them all: Sir Maurice Clinton, Sir Thomas Davenport, Sir Reginald Branson and Sir Laurence Broomhill. They asked the same question he asked them.

'What are you doing here?'

'It's our anniversary.' The smooth-faced Benedictine pushed his way through, pulling back the cowl of his robe. 'I'm Brother Malachi,' he smiled. 'Their chaplain.'

The Judas Man grasped his hand, even as he remembered how these important knights, all great landowners in the shire of Kent, were accustomed to come up to London every year to celebrate how they had once sailed from London to fight under Lord Peter of Cyprus, the Great Crusader who had captured Alexandria in Egypt almost twenty years ago.

'Of course!' the Judas Man exclaimed. 'You are the Falconers.'

'That is the standard we fought under,' Sir Maurice, the leader of the group, replied. He was harsh-faced, tall, and thin as a beanpole, iron-grey hair parted down the middle. 'And we lodged at this tavern before we sailed. But what are you doing here?'

'Business,' the Judas Man murmured, staring hungrily past the knights at the shaft of light pouring through the doorway leading into the tap room. He stepped aside. The knights had apparently been enjoying the ratting and drunk much. Brother Malachi supported Sir Thomas Davenport, who was rocking backwards and forwards on his feet. The Judas Man made his farewell to the knights. He heard their laughter behind him and tried to recall what he knew of them. Ah yes! The five noble Falconers, all Kentish men; the sixth, the monk, had also been a soldier until he'd taken his vows. Wasn't there some mystery about them? And where was the fifth? The Judas Man put such questions aside as he stepped into the tap room.

Customers sat round tables. Scullions and slatterns fought their way through with tankards. The great fire was beginning to die, the candles were fading, the bowls of oil drying up. The Judas Man hastily stood aside as a boy pushing a wheelbarrow carted out the corpses of the rats killed in the pit, which was now being washed clean with tubs of scalding water. A sea of faces greeted the Judas Man, some disfigured, others pretty. A whore came sidling up; the Judas Man pushed her away as he walked like a cat round the edge of the tap room, looking intently for his prey. People jostled and shoved, pedlars and tinkers tried to sell trinkets. He was invited to sit in on games of hazard, whilst a pretty slattern asked him what he wanted to drink. The Judas Man ignored all these, eyes ever shifting, moving from face to face. He was looking for a man of medium height with a shock of red hair and a misericord dagger on a lanyard round his neck. At last he found him, seated just near the door, throwing dice with two others. There was no mistaking the silver sheath or that shock of red hair, though the pallid face and scrawny beard and moustache hadn't been in the description. The misericord dagger, though, was unmistakable. The Judas Man pushed his way through, placed his hand on his victim's shoulder and squeezed tightly. The man looked up.

'You are to come with me,' the Judas Man whispered quietly in his ear. 'You, sir, are under arrest.'

His words had an immediate effect. The other two gamblers shot to their feet, pulling out knives even as Red-Hair shrugged off the Judas Man's hand and, as fast as a whippet, kicked the stool back into his legs. Then he sprang up, drawing the knife from the battered belt around his waist. The crash of stools, the shouts and curses, created an immediate silence in the tap room. Master Rolles' bully boys came lumbering across, as the Judas Man drew his own sword and dagger.

'Put up your weapons,' one of the bully boys shouted. 'I'll call the Watch.'

'No you won't.' The Judas Man shook his head. 'I have the law on my side. I carry a commission, sealed warrants from the sheriffs of Essex and Kent as well as those of London. I am empowered to bring in criminals, and this man,' the Judas Man pointed his sword at Red-Hair, 'is under arrest.'

The bully boys stepped back, gesturing for everyone to stay out of this confrontation. Red-Hair's two companions also faded into the crowd, leaving their comrade, much the worse for drink, swaying backwards and forwards on his feet, knife still out.

'I . . . I . . . don't know,' he stammered, 'the reason . . .' He cleared his throat. 'I've only stolen petty things.'

As the man spoke, the Judas Man noticed how his teeth were blackened, his gums sore. He looked closer, a prick of doubt. This man looked unwell; his face was pockmarked, eyes red-rimmed – was this the Misericord? The subtle, cunning man? He lowered his sword, eyes fixed on that silver sheath.

'You are the one known as the Misericord?' he asked.

Red-Hair shook his head.

'You are under arrest,' the Judas Man said gently, taking a step forward.

The other man panicked, a mix of ale and fear. He lunged drunkenly, his knife speeding for his opponent's face, but the Judas Man just stepped aside and drove his own sword in, thrusting deep into the man's stomach . . .

The two whores, Beatrice and Clarice, had left the tap room a short while before the Judas Man appeared. They heard the first clamour and outcry but they had other business. Beatrice and Clarice were sisters and served in one of the most luxurious brothels amongst the stews near the Bishop of Winchester's inn. They had won their reputation by beauty and skill and been given a special invitation to attend the Great Ratting. They had arrived in all their gorgeous finery, gowns of red sarcanet over milk-white kirtles, stockings of pure wool and ankle-high leather boots with silver buckles. They had combed their blonde hair carefully and arranged their jewellery around neck, wrists and fingers. They'd bathed carefully, anointing themselves with perfumed oil, and had delicately painted their faces. They were twins, the daughters of the famous Guinevere the Golden, one of the greatest courtesans of Southwark until she had mysteriously disappeared some twenty years ago. They had been raised by Mother Veritable, one of the most notorious brothel-keepers south of the river. They had been taught how to read and write, and every other skill a courtesan should acquire. They were proficient on the rebec and the lute and could sing the sweetest carol as well as understand Norman French. They had been given places of honour that night and, after the Great Ratting had finished, been told to go to the hay barn which lay at the far side of the stable yard. Beatrice and Clarice had drunk deeply of the coolest, sweetest wines from the Rhine. Master Rolles had been quite insistent.

'I have been given orders,' he murmured to them, 'to look after you well. When the Ratting is over you will have a customer,' he winked lecherously, 'in the barn.'

'And where will we go?' Beatrice had asked, light blue eyes all innocent.

'I don't know.' The taverner had pressed silver coins into their hands. 'Perhaps a bishop's palace, or the silken-hung chambers of some Lord of the Soil.'

The two sisters now clung to each other, laughing as they walked across the yard. They pulled open the door and stepped inside. A lantern horn had been lit, carefully hooded and placed on top of a barrel, well away from the straw and hay. Clarice wished the band round the veil on her head wasn't so tight.

'Was that a fight?' Beatrice asked, sitting down next to her sister.

'I don't know,' came the slurred reply. 'I feel so sleepy.'

'I wonder who it is?' Beatrice lay back and stared up at the rafters. She tensed as she heard a noise outside, a light footfall. The door swung open. A figure dressed like a monk stepped inside. The brown gown covered the new arrival from neck to toe, while the cowl was deep.

Beatrice climbed to her feet and swayed from side to side. She hoped the paint on her face hadn't run, or the carmine round her lips become smudged. She heard the clink of coins and turned to help her sister up. As she did so, there was a sound like a whirr of wings, and her sister fell away as the crossbow bolt struck her full in the chest just beneath the neck. Beatrice turned, mouth opening to scream. The stranger hurried across, knife in hand, burying it deep into the young woman's stomach, pulling her head forward and pressing it against that brown robe to stifle any screams.

Chapter 2

'*Hoc est corpus meum.* This is my Body.'

Athelstan breathed the words of consecration over the host, then genuflected. Behind him his parish council, much the worse for wear after the previous night's revelry, coughed and spluttered as they knelt just within the rood screen. Athelstan looked over his shoulder. Crim the altar boy, half asleep, suddenly started awake and shook the hand bell.

'And taking this excellent chalice into his hand . . .' Athelstan continued with the Mass, trying to concentrate on the mystery of the God who became man now becoming present under the appearances of bread and wine. From beyond the rood screen he heard Brother Malachi, celebrating the Eucharist in the Chantry Chapel, draw his Mass to a close. Athelstan turned and lifted the chalice with the host above it.

29

'Behold the Lamb of God, behold Him who takes away the sins of the world.'

Athelstan always translated the Latin for the benefit of his parishioners, but this morning he was wasting his time. They all looked half asleep. Watkin the dung collector was actually dribbling, his head on Pike the ditcher's shoulder. Pike's sour-faced wife Imelda was pretending to pray but her head kept jerking backwards and forwards. Ursula the pig woman, who insisted on bringing her large fat sow into the sanctuary, was clearly snoring. That precious pig, which Athelstan had secretly vowed to slaughter because of the damage it wreaked in his vegetable patch, looked as sottish as its owner. The rest were there in all their dubious glory, Ranulf the rat-catcher with his wicker-work basket on the floor beside him. As Athelstan went down to give the Eucharist, both ferrets squealed and tried to push open the lid of the basket.

'I think you should wake.' Athelstan's voice carried around the sanctuary. His parishioners all shook themselves awake, forcing their faces into expressions of false piety, clasping their hands as Athelstan distributed the Eucharist.

Athelstan was relieved when Mass was ended. He swept from the sanctuary into the sacristy and took off his vestments, the chasuble and stole, placing the sacred cloths back into the red oaken vestment chest. Crim came staggering in with the cruets bearing the remains of the water and wine.

'God bless you, Crim!'

The altar boy blinked his red-rimmed eyes.

'It's not my fault, Father,' the lad blurted out. 'I did remind them that today was parish council day, but Ranulf—'

'Yes, yes,' Athelstan interrupted, 'I know all about the great victory.' He touched the lad gently on the head. 'And you drank ale last night?'

The boy nodded.

'So you won't be stealing any altar wine?'

'I never—'

'Hush now.' Athelstan pressed a finger against the boy's lips. 'The angels will hear your lie. Now clear the altar while I . . .' Athelstan knelt down and tightened the thong on his sandal. 'I will just wait awhile until my parish council wake up.'

Athelstan left by the side door. A sharp hoar frost still whitened the grass and gorse, the twisted yew trees in the cemetery; even the battered wooden crosses had a silver coating. Athelstan followed the narrow pebbled track up to the small death house. Outside it, the goat, Thaddeus, mournfully cropped at the grass. The animal lifted its head as Athelstan approached, chewing so lugubriously that Athelstan couldn't help laughing. The goat trotted across, nuzzling Athelstan's hand.

'Mercenary,' Athelstan whispered. 'But I have no apples for you this morning.'

'Come in, Brother.'

Athelstan stopped and went into the darkness. God-Bless, the beggar, squatted on the ground attempting to fan the fire he had built on the makeshift hearth. Athelstan joined in, sprinkling dry twigs and crushed charcoal over the flames, then helped the beggar man fashion a grille, laying out the fatty pieces of pork he had given God-Bless the previous evening. All the time the beggar man whispered, 'God bless, God bless.'

'You weren't at Mass this morning?' Athelstan asked.

'God bless you, Father, I was at the Great Ratting.'

God-Bless blew once more on the flames and knelt, watching the pork sizzle on the wire grille.

'Did you drink too much?'

'God bless you, Father, I did, but there was a killing last night.'

'A killing?'

'At the Great Ratting, Father. A man was stabbed. But now I am hungry.'

Athelstan left the beggar and walked across to his own house. The fire in the hearth had burned low. He looked around; everything was in order. He would break his fast after the meeting. His feet brushed feathers. He stepped back and stared down at a mauled pigeon. Bonaventure must have brought it in.

'For what we are about to receive . . .' Athelstan picked up the carcass and took it out to the yard. Of the great one-eyed tom cat there was no sign. Athelstan smelt the roasting pork, God-Bless's cooking, and knew where the cat had gone. He entered the stable built next to the house. Philomel, the old warhorse, was chewing slowly on its oats, and lifted its head as Athelstan came in. The Dominican sketched a blessing in the air and left, then walked round up the front steps and into the church.

His guests, the Falconers, were clustered around Brother Malachi, who warmly greeted Athelstan and introduced his companions: Sir Maurice Clinton, Sir Thomas Davenport, Sir Reginald Branson, Sir Laurence Broomhill and Sir Stephen Chandler. Athelstan had met them all before and welcomed them back to Southwark for their annual visit.

'I thank you for the loan of your church.' The Benedictine's smooth, cherub-like face creased into a smile. He gestured down the nave at the wooden screens; Crispin the carpenter had erected these against the transept wall to form a small chapel with an altar beneath the window and a statue of St Erconwald on a plinth where the wooden screen met the wall. The Benedictine congratulated Athelstan on the carvings along the wooden screen as well as the beautiful sculptured statue of the church's patron saint. Athelstan nodded in bemusement. He had met Brother Malachi on previous occasions and was both flattered and surprised at the Benedictine's interest in this crumbling old church.

'You have done wonders.' Sir Maurice Clinton, the leader of the group, gestured at the vivid wall paintings depicting scenes from the Bible.

'I recognise some of your parishioners.' Sir Stephen Chandler, small and fat, mopped his face with the edge of his cloak.

'Yes, yes.' Athelstan stared at his parishioners gathered in a gaggle further up the nave. He wondered what they were discussing so heatedly. 'Mind you,' he added absent-mindedly, 'I wish Huddle our painter wouldn't use his fellow parishioners as models for his scenes.'

'I don't know.' Sir Thomas Davenport spoke up. 'Cecily the courtesan makes a lovely Mary Magdalene.'

'I was thinking,' Athelstan retorted, 'of Pike the ditcher's wife being cast in the role of Jezebel.'

His remark provoked laughter and the knights drifted away to look at the painting on the wall near the baptismal font. Brother Malachi began to explain the scene in detail. Athelstan adjusted the cord round his middle, fingering the three knots symbolising his vows of obedience, chastity and poverty. He studied the group of knights intently. Sir Maurice was tall, thin, and harsh-faced, Sir Stephen round and red as a ripe apple; the rest all looked like brothers, dressed as they were in their black and white cloaks with the golden falcon emblem embroidered on the shoulder. He reckoned most of them must have seen their fiftieth summer. They walked and looked like the warriors they were – men who had fought in Outremer, strong, muscular soldiers, bodies hardened, faces darkened by years of military service under the blazing sun of the Middle Sea.

Athelstan knew little about their background: knights from Kent, landowners who, some twenty years ago, had gathered in Southwark to join the great expedition of

Peter of Cyprus against the Turks in North Africa. They had served under the Golden Falcon standard and every year gathered at the tavern, the Night in Jerusalem, to celebrate their achievements and talk of old times. Brother Malachi was their chaplain: the Benedictine had served with the crusading army, even had his fingers shorn in the fighting, and returned to England settling in a small monastery outside Aylesford. Each year was the same: they'd gather for Mass at St Erconwald's, then return to their tavern to continue their celebrations. Athelstan hardly gave them a second thought, yet wasn't there some mystery attached to it all? Hadn't Sir John Cranston told him about a great robbery, some scandal, before the crusading fleet left the Thames? Athelstan felt immediately apprehensive. Whenever he thought of Sir John Cranston, the larger-than-life coroner always appeared. Athelstan quietly prayed that Sir John, Coroner of the City of London, would not need his services, that he would not arrive to drag him from his parish to investigate some gruesome murder. Yet hadn't God-Bless mentioned a man being killed last night during the Great Ratting?

'Brother Athelstan.' Sir Maurice led the knights back from the painting. 'Once again you have kindly allowed us to use your church for Mass and our devotions.'

He turned to the Benedictine.

'Well,' he barked, 'give it to him!'

Malachi drew his hands from the voluminous

sleeves of his habit and handed over a small velvet-covered box. Athelstan undid the silver clasp, pushed back the lid and carefully picked up the gold ring, very similar to what a man would use in swearing his troth. He could tell, by the thinness of the gold, that the ring was ancient.

'Do you like it?' Sir Stephen asked, his fat face laced with sweat.

'Of course.' Athelstan put the ring back.

'It belonged to St Erconwald,' Malachi explained. 'It was his episcopal ring. I bought it from a merchant in Canterbury. I have had it tested, it is genuine. There are marks on the inside.'

Athelstan lifted the ring up against the light, studying it intently, and saw the small Celtic crosses etched on the inside of it. He put the ring back, closed the box and slipped it into the wallet which hung from his cord. He was only halfway through his speech of thanks when the door crashed open. For a moment Athelstan thought it was Cranston, but it was Benedicta the widow woman who slipped into the church, apologising profusely for giving the door such a vigorous push.

'I am sorry, Brother.'

Athelstan smiled at her; even the knights forgot what he was saying as they stared at this beautiful woman, her pale face framed by hair black as midnight.

'I am sorry, Brother,' she repeated, 'but I thought I would be late for the meeting.'

Athelstan squeezed her hand, and thanked the knights for their gift, saying that he and his parish council would have to reflect carefully about where it should be kept. He didn't dare mention that most of his parishioners, given half a chance, be it holy relic or not, would steal the ring and sell it in the markets across the river.

Once Brother Malachi and the knights had left, Benedicta began to explain why she was late, only to be interrupted by Watkin the dung collector, leader of the council, who came striding down the church. Athelstan immediately called the meeting to order. Pike the ditcher brought out the stools and the priest's chair from the sanctuary. Athelstan made the sign of the cross and the meeting began. Mugwort the bell clerk sat at his small desk taken from the bell tower, feather quill poised ready to take down what was decided. Athelstan showed them the ring; this was greeted with oohs and aahs. The Dominican despaired at the greed in some of their eyes and the twitch in their fingers.

'We have to decide,' he declared, 'where such a precious relic should be kept.'

'And?' Ursula the pig woman asked.

'Every altar,' began Athelstan, kicking away the sow which came lumbering over to sniff at his sandals. Benedicta hid her smile behind her hand. 'Every altar,' he repeated, 'has a relic stone. It can be taken out and cemented back in again. We'll put the ring there. I'll keep an imitation one to show any visitors.'

Athelstan's smooth, olive-skinned face grew serious. He raised himself up in his chair.

'It would be a most hideous sacrilege to steal such a ring. I would refuse absolution to any such thief.'

Most of the parish councillors stared down, shuffling their feet.

'Anyway,' Athelstan decided to move quickly to other matters, 'Ranulf, I believe you are to be congratulated, your ferrets were victors of the game. Although I think it is a dreadful way for any of God's creatures to die.'

'I've seen rats attack babies in a house near Mary St Bethlehem,' Ranulf retorted. 'Four of them sucked the blood out of—'

'Yes, yes,' Athelstan agreed, 'but your ferrets did well.'

'Can they be baptised?' Ranulf asked.

'Father has already told you,' Imelda screeched. 'You can't baptise animals.'

'Ursula's pig drank the holy water,' Watkin pointed out.

'There'll be no baptisms of animals,' Athelstan declared, 'but I promise you, on the Feast of St Francis . . .' Athelstan couldn't stop himself, even though he recalled the confusion of last time, when one of Ranulf's ferrets had attacked Ursula's sow and sent it squealing around the church. He just hoped that Ranulf had kept the basket secure; the ferrets had smelt the sow and were becoming excited.

'Yes, Father?' Pernel asked.

'On the Feast of St Francis I will bless all animals. Now, let's move to other business.'

Mugwort picked up his quill, dipping it ceremoniously into the inkhorn as Athelstan led his parish council through the various items of business. There was the cleaning of the cemetery, the digging of a ditch, Huddle wanted to paint a new scene from the life of St John the Baptist which provoked a fierce discussion about whether the saint was crucified or beheaded. Athelstan suspected this was a warning of what was to come. Cecily the courtesan, in a light blue robe, sat next to Benedicta, smiling flirtatiously at Pike while making obscene gestures with her fingers at the ditcher's wife. Athelstan hurried on. There was the business of church ales, the levying of tithes, the possibility of a small market in the cemetery and the greening of the church for Advent.

'Now,' Athelstan closed his eyes and offered up a silent prayer, 'we come to our pageant for Christmas, the birth of Christ.'

He paused for breath.

'Crispin,' he pointed to the carpenter, 'we have decided you will be Joseph, Watkin, you can be Herod . . .' The roles were assigned; they even included Bonaventure the cat. Philomel would stand in for the donkey, whilst Athelstan ruefully conceded that Ursula's sow could be the oxen.

'Well,' said Watkin, 'who will be the Virgin Mary? I think it should be Benedicta.'

'So do I,' Imelda agreed, glaring at Cecily, who

pushed her chest out and straightened herself up on the stool she was sitting on.

'I disagree,' Pike the ditcher responded, always ready to oppose Watkin.

'We think it should be Cecily,' Ranulf declared.

A bitter war of words broke out. Imelda, her face mottled with fury, fists beating the air, would have attacked Cecily if Athelstan hadn't intervened. The Dominican let the dispute continue, hoping their pent-up fury would soon exhaust itself. Instead it grew worse, so he had to gesture at Mauger to ring his hand bell. No sooner was silence imposed, with members of the parish council glowering at each other, when there was loud shouting outside, cries and yells of 'Harrow! Harrow!' followed by the sound of running feet. The door to the church burst open, and a man, cloak over one arm, a stick in the other, scampered around the stools and fled up the nave under the rood screen and into the sanctuary. He was followed by a man in black leather, spurs jangling on his boots, a drawn sword in one hand, a crossbow in the other. Athelstan sprang to his feet as he realised what had happened.

'Go no further,' he ordered.

The man carrying the crossbow paused, hands hanging as he fought for breath.

'He's the Judas Man,' Pike shouted. 'He was at the Great Ratting last night.'

'He is also an officer of the law.'

Bladdersniff the bailiff came into the church, clearly

out of breath, leaning on his staff of office, water dripping from eyes, nose and mouth.

'He carries the King's commission, he's in pursuit of a felon.'

'I demand,' the Judas Man rasped, 'that the felon who calls himself the Misericord be handed over to me.'

This proclamation was greeted by cries of derision from the parish council.

'You know the law,' Athelstan stepped in front of the Judas Man, 'and so do you, Bladdersniff. Any man who reaches a church and grasps the altar may claim sanctuary.'

'Which means,' the Judas Man retorted, pointing up the church, 'that the malefactor cannot leave this church for forty days, and when he does I will arrest him: that, too, is the law!'

Athelstan was repelled by the malice in the Judas Man's eyes, the violence of his speech.

'It's against canon law,' Athelstan pointed at the sword, 'to carry a naked weapon in church. I ask you, sir, to sheathe it and get out.'

Athelstan insisted that the Judas Man, the bailiff and all the parish council leave immediately. Pike made to protest; Benedicta intervened and gently shooed the ditcher and the rest out on to the church porch. Athelstan followed. The Judas Man was already in the forecourt, ordering the bully boys he had brought with him to guard all the doors of the church. Athelstan had met such bounty-hunters before and recognised their ruthlessness. An outlaw's head could be worth fifteen pounds sterling, attached to its body; severed, the price was reduced to five. The Judas Man, skilled in the hunt and invoking the law, stared malevolently at Athelstan standing on the top step. He ordered Bladdersniff to include some of the parish council in the comitatus, or posse, he was forming.

'What do you want me to do, Father?' Benedicta pulled up the hood of her cloak.

'Don't be anxious, Benedicta. I would be grateful if you would serve Bonaventure a dish of milk.' He gestured at the priest's house. 'Dampen the fire whilst I see what is happening.'

Athelstan strolled back into the church, slamming the door behind him. He walked up the nave. He was distracted by the gargoyle faces staring down at him from the top of the pillars as if they were the harbingers of ill news. Yet, Athelstan sighed, the day had looked so promising. He went under the rood screen and into the sanctuary, genuflected towards the sacrament lamp and then walked over to the Misericord, who was sitting on the top step, one hand on the high altar. He was tall and red-haired, his pallid, clean-shaven face, slightly pointed ears and slanted green eyes gave him an elfin look. He was dressed in dark blue matching jerkin and hose; his boots were of dark red Spanish leather. He had a knife pushed into the top of one of them and a war belt strapped across his shoulder which carried a Welsh stabbing dirk. Around his neck hung a silver misericord sheath on a black cord lanyard.

'I claim—' the Misericord began.

'Shut up.' Athelstan pulled across the altar boy's stool and sat down, staring up at the Misericord. 'I know the law,' he continued evenly. 'You are a fugitive. You have claimed sanctuary, you can stay here for forty days. I will supply you with food and drink.'

He pointed across the sanctuary to the sacristy door.

'Go through there; outside is a makeshift latrine near a butt of water. You can relieve yourself there, but make sure you leave it clean. Oh, by the way,' Athelstan stretched out his hands, 'I'll take your weapons, which, as you know, must be kept near the Lady Altar.'

He pointed to his left. The Misericord cleaned his teeth with his tongue whilst he swept the sweat from his face.

'Stay there.' Athelstan left the church by the corpse door. Benedicta was still in the kitchen, busy brushing the floor. Bonaventure had sipped his milk and was staring at the steaming cauldron where the freshly cooked oatmeal still bubbled hot. Athelstan explained he was in a hurry. He filled a maplewood bowl full of oatmeal, added some honey, took a pewter spoon from the buttery and drew a tankard of ale. He put these on a wooden board and took them back to the church.

The Misericord ate and drank, gulping the food

down, using his fingers to clean the bowl whilst draining the tankard in one swig. Athelstan collected the fugitive's weapons, including the misericord dagger, and placed them behind the Lady Altar.

'Very good, very good.' The Misericord wiped his fingers on his jerkin.

'I'll have the bowl back and the spoon. The tankard you can keep, for a while.'

'Did you brew it yourself?'

'No, Benedicta did.'

'Ah yes, the widow woman, with hair as black as night and the face of an angel. Do you love her, Father? I thought you were a priest and friar?' The Misericord's green eyes glinted with mischief.

'Benedicta is an honourable widow, her husband was lost at sea. She brews ale, cooks me some bread and, not at my bidding, keeps my house clean.'

'But not your bed warm?'

Athelstan half rose threateningly. The Misericord held up both hands in a sign of peace, his pale, mischievous face all solemn.

'*Pax et bonum*, peace and goodwill, Father. I was only joking.'

The Misericord scrutinised the priest. Whenever he moved into an area, be it a village or one of the wards of London, he always discovered which was the quickest way out, where he could hide, who was to be trusted and which men or women exercised power. He had learnt a great deal about this slim, dark-faced friar with his soulful eyes and wary manner. He had also laid a great wager on Ranulf the rat-catcher, though now he regretted coming to Southwark.

'What is your real name?' Athelstan asked.

'John Travisa, former clerk from the halls of Oxford, a troubadour, a poet, a chanteur, a lady's squire . . .'

'And a thief and a boaster,' Athelstan finished for him.

The Misericord shrugged.

'Hard times, Father. Outside in the shires, the harvests fail and what's left is pecked up by the tax collectors. There's no work for an honest man.' He pulled a face. 'I apologise: even for a dishonest man.'

'What have you done?' Athelstan asked.

'Well,' the Misericord crossed his arms and leaned back against the altar, 'I have been a relic-seller. Do you want to buy a piece of the True Cross, a portion of the baby Jesus' nappy, some hairs from Joseph's beard, one of the Virgin Mary's shoes?' He cleaned his teeth with his fingers. 'I can supply it. I even took a severed head from one of the pikes on London Bridge. I cleaned it up, dried it in spices and sold it to a merchant in Norwich as the head of St John the Baptist.'

Athelstan kept his face straight.

'And why does the Judas Man pursue you?'

'There's a reward of twenty-five pounds on my head. He has been dogging my footsteps through Essex, Middlesex, across the river and into Southwark. I don't know why he is so persistent. I tried to leave

Southwark this morning but he had his spies on both the bridge and the quayside.'

The Misericord pulled a loose thread on his jerkin. 'I had no choice but to flee.'

'But why?' Athelstan became intrigued.

'I don't know,' the Misericord sighed. 'I expect he has been hired by a private citizen. Someone who seeks vengeance.'

'For what?' Athelstan demanded.

'I don't know! I have played so many games. There is one, perhaps that's it. I took the name Dr Mirabilis and offered to sell a powder which would . . .' The Misericord clicked his tongue. 'Let me put it this way, Father, I said it would make a man perform like a stallion in bed, so I wouldn't have offered it to someone like you.'

'And of course,' Athelstan replied, 'it did nothing. What did you claim it was?'

'The ground horn of a unicorn.'

'And the truth?'

The Misericord pressed his lips together. 'A mixture of camomile and valerian.'

'But that would have the opposite effect,' Athelstan said. 'Such a mixture would slow the mind, make the body relax; it's nothing better than a sleeping potion.'

'I know, Father.'

'How did you sell it?'

The Misericord was about to reply when the door of the church crashed open.

'Sir Jack Cranston,' Athelstan whispered.

The Misericord crept back into the shadows. Athelstan sat listening to those hard, heavy boots ring out across the paving stones of the nave.

Sir John Cranston, former soldier, Coroner of the City of London, father of the poppets, as he called his twin baby sons, and devoted husband of the Lady Maud, swept into the sanctuary like the north wind. He had a beaverskin hat pressed down on his unruly grey hair, his great body and heavy paunch were masked by the military cloak pulled halfway up to his face, yet there was no mistaking that bristling white moustache, the vein-flecked cheeks and the piercing blue eyes.

'Good morning, Brother Athelstan.' He peered through the gloom. 'Aye, and morning to you, Master Misericord.'

Cranston undid his cloak, clasped Athelstan's hand and advanced threateningly towards the fugitive now crouching beside the altar. He rested one foot on the second step and leaned forward.

'The Misericord! Also known as John Travisa, also known as Walter Simple, also known as Edward Bowman, also known as God knows what. Wanted dead or alive in the shires of Suffolk, Norfolk, Hertfordshire, Essex and Kent. Oh, this time you'll hang, my boy.' Cranston gestured down the nave. 'I know that Judas Man. You placed your wager on Ranulf's ferrets? Well, he's a ferret in human form. He'll hunt you down, though I'll be the first to deal with you. You killed a man last night.'

47

'No I didn't,' the Misericord yelped.

'Yes you did!'

Cranston suddenly remembered where he was and snatched off his beaverskin hat. He hurriedly made a sign of the Cross, one of the fastest Athelstan had ever seen, then fished beneath his cloak and unhooked the miraculous wine skin which never seemed to empty, unstoppered it and took a mouthful. He offered it to Athelstan, who refused, though the Misericord grabbed it greedily and took a generous swig. Cranston snatched it out of his hands.

'Now, my lovely boy,' Cranston breathed. 'You killed a man last night, or had him killed. You went to Master Rolles' for the Great Ratting, and I will see mine host about that. You knew you were being hunted, so you paid some unfortunate who had a passing resemblance to you to wear that misericord dagger around his neck, a man with red hair and pale face. The Judas Man went to arrest him, and Toadflax—'

'Toadflax?' Athelstan queried.

'Toadflax,' Cranston explained, 'was a dog collector. He took the corpses of dead animals from the streets; now and again he became involved in petty thievery.'

Cranston jabbed a finger in the fugitive's face.

'He was the one you bribed. What did you give him for his life? A penny? A groat? Some numbskull who wouldn't know his right hand from his left; now his corpse is stiffening in an outhouse.'

Cranston turned swiftly to Athelstan.

'Will you bury him, Father? Will you anoint him with oil and put his body in the ground?'

Athelstan nodded.

'Now we have business to do.' Cranston pointed threateningly at the fugitive. 'You stay here, you understand? You only leave here to go to the jakes. That Judas Man is in a fair temper; he will have your neck.'

The Misericord, all courage drained, nodded quickly. Cranston took Athelstan by the elbow and steered him out of the sanctuary.

'Well, good morrow to you, Sir John.'

The coroner beamed down at this friar whom he loved more dearly than a blood brother.

'You look well, Sir John, in fine fettle.'

Cranston stroked his moustache and beard. 'The Lady Maud and I,' he whispered, 'we had a celebration last night, downstairs and upstairs.' He winked knowingly.

'So the Lady Maud is in good health?'

'Aye, but there are three corpses at the Night in Jerusalem!'

'Three!' Athelstan exclaimed.

'You know the tavern? It's owned by one Master Rolles, a true sicarius who harvested rich plunder in France.'

'I know of Master Rolles and his tavern, Sir John – but three corpses?'

'Two flaxen-haired whores and poor Toadflax,'

49

Cranston explained, the smile fading from his face. 'I need you Brother, you are my secretarius.'

Athelstan bit back his disappointment. He'd planned to do so much today: visit the sick, scrutinise the accounts, and he dearly wanted to read a new commentary on Ptolemy. The manuscript had been copied by scribes in his own order, and Athelstan had been loaned it by Prior Anselm, allowed to take it away from its great oaken shelf in the library at Blackfriars.

Heavy-hearted, Athelstan returned to his house, collected his writing satchel, which he hooked over his shoulder, and donned the heavy cloak Cranston had given him as a gift last Michaelmas. The kitchen looked clean and scrubbed, everything in order. Bonaventure was sprawled in front of the dying fire. Athelstan murmured a quick benediction that all would be kept safe, then he grasped his walking stick and joined Sir John, now standing on the steps of the church like a Justice come to judgement. It was obvious that the Judas Man intended to stay, his bully boys now bolstered by members of the parish council: Pike, Watkin, Ranulf and others eager for mischief. They had ringed the cemetery, keeping every window and door under close scrutiny. The Judas Man had even hired a couple of braziers, where the charcoal and wood crackled merrily, as well as supplying his comitatus with bread, meat and wine.

'He is being well paid,' Cranston murmured, staring across at the Judas Man, who sat on the cemetery wall gazing coolly back.

'Who's hired him?' Athelstan asked. 'Not the Corporation?'

Cranston shook his head. 'The Corporation won't do it any more, not unless they have to. It's too expensive. Yet I tell you this, Brother, and I swear by Satan's tits.' He gestured with his head towards the Judas Man. 'He's well named, an evil bastard! He doesn't care if he brings his quarry in dead or alive. There's more compassion in Ranulf's ferrets than in one hair on his head. Well, let me upset him.'

Cranston strode down the steps, Athelstan hurrying behind. They were halfway across the forecourt when Cranston stopped and bellowed at the Judas Man to join him. The man slowly, insolently climbed down from the wall and strolled across, sword scabbard slapping against the top of his boot. He bowed mockingly and stretched out his hand.

'Sir John Cranston.' The coroner grasped his hand and pulled the Judas Man close, such a powerful jerk that the Judas Man nearly missed his footing. Cranston steadied him.

'There, there.' He tapped a finger against the Judas Man's cheek. 'You are not going to touch that dagger, are you?'

The man's hand fell away from the hilt.

'Good.' Cranston smiled. 'Now, sir, you killed a man last night.'

'I am an officer of the law, I carry a commission,' the Judas Man retorted. 'Toadflax pulled his dagger, I had no choice. I have a score of witnesses.'

'Aye, I am sure you have.' Cranston pushed his face closer. 'But I couldn't care if it was St Ursula and her ten thousand virgins. You're accompanying me back to that tavern. I have questions to ask.'

'I have business here.'

Athelstan stared across at the bailiffs. They had forgotten the braziers, the cheap food and ale, and were staring fearfully across. They all knew Cranston by reputation, if not by sight.

'I, too, carry a commission,' Cranston's voice rose to a shout, 'signed by John of Gaunt, Protector of the Realm.' He lowered his voice. 'You can either come freely or I'll have you arrested.'

He pushed the Judas Man away, and walked out of St Erconwald's into the narrow, tangled streets of Southwark. Athelstan had to run to keep up. The Judas Man shouted orders at his bailiffs and, cursing under his breath, was left with no choice but to follow. As they turned and left the church, Cranston was joined by his master bailiff Flaxwith, his two mastiffs Satan and Samson bringing up the rear. Cranston teased Flaxwith over Ranulf's victory last night; the bailiff remained surly whilst his two dogs, as if aware of the disgrace they had brought upon their master, trotted mournfully behind.

The streets of Southwark were now busy, the traders and hucksters, the chapmen and the tinkers had set out their tawdry stalls, piled high with trinkets, second-hand clothing, soiled footwear, cheap buckles and buttons. Some had brought meats and bread, discarded by the cookshops in the wealthier parts of the City, to make a profit from the poor in Southwark. Whores and prostitutes stood at corners and in doorways, guarded by their pimps holding cudgels. These all disappeared, melting away like snow under the sun, at the appearance of Cranston hastening down the centre of the street like a cog of war under full sail. Apprentices and journeymen dashed out of doorways, ready to grasp would-be customers by the sleeve. They never accosted Cranston. Now and again the coroner would stop and stare up past the creaking signs to the narrow strip of sky between the overhanging houses. Matins had already rung, so no slops could be thrown from the windows, but the coroner was ever wary. He had many enemies in Southwark and, as he had confided to Athelstan, there were those who would like nothing better than to empty a jakes pot over him. Dogs and pigs scurried about, chased by screaming, half-naked children. On the corner of Weasel Lane, a travelling leech was shouting his remedies.

'For gut-griping, goitres, lethargies, cold palsies, raw eyes, dirt-rotten livers, wheezing lungs and bladders full of pus . . .'

He kept waving his arms, pointing at the tray slung by a cord around his neck; apparently new to the ward, he tried to entice Cranston. The coroner stopped.

'Why, sir,' he said sweetly, freeing his arm from the man's fast grip, 'what remedy do you offer for so many ills?'

'The juice of the mandrake,' the man gabbled, eyes all greedy at the prospect of a sale.

'The juice of the mandrake?' Cranston replied. 'And you have a licence to sell?'

The man stepped back. Cranston grabbed the tray and plucked up one of the leather pouches tied with yellow twine. He opened this, sniffed, and passed it to Athelstan.

'Mandrake, Brother?'

Athelstan sniffed too.

'No, Sir John, chalk mixed with mint, and thanks be to God.' Athelstan emptied the contents on to the ground. 'If it was mandrake it would truly cure you of all those ailments.'

The leech half smiled.

'You'd be dead within a day, and free of all pain,' Athelstan stated.

Cranston stepped back and, swinging his cudgel, smashed the tray, jerking it loose from the cord, then began to grind the pouches under his boot. Flaxwith's two mastiffs growled. The bailiff himself joined in, squeezing the pouches under his muddy boot into the dirt and ordure, before kicking them towards the sewer which ran down the centre of the street. The travelling leech, aware of his hideous mistake, tried to flee, but Cranston grabbed him by his shabby jerkin.

'You'll be gone from the City within the hour, or I'll have you whipped the length of London Bridge,' he shouted.

The cunning man bolted up an alleyway whilst

Cranston and his small retinue continued apace. They passed the gate leading to St Thomas' hospital and down the busy thoroughfare which led to the Night in Jerusalem. Athelstan had been here before. The tavern was a stately four-sided mansion, built on a stone base with white plastered walls stitched with black timber. A place of contrasts. Some of the windows high in the wall were mere arrow slits, but others lower down were protected by sheets of horn, or treated linen set in strip panels, with an open lattice framework and shutters on the inside. For the grand chambers on the second floor, the windows were of mullion glass and, in some places, even decorated with small pictures of leaping white stags, red hearts or yellow shields. Athelstan knew Master Rolles by reputation. He had only met him when begging for alms, and the taverner had been most generous. They found him in the spacious stable yard, talking to a group of ostlers. As Cranston swept into the yard, Master Rolles dismissed these: he treated Sir John as an equal, grasping his hand and nodding at Athelstan.

'Master Henry Rolles,' Cranston exclaimed. 'Squire to Sir Walter Manny. How well you have prospered!'

Cranston stared around the yard.

'I understand you had the Great Ratting last night. I'm sure you had a licence from the Corporation?'

'The City has no power here, Sir John,' the taverner replied, 'and you know that. If I have broken the law then I shall be summoned to the Guildhall. Yet who cares about licences when there's been gruesome murder?'

He beckoned them forward.

'I do pay taxes, Sir John, for the King's peace to be upheld.'

Cranston ignored the jibe at his expense. Rolles led them all, including the Judas Man, across to an outhouse, pulled back the doors and ushered them in. Two lantern horns hung on hooks suspended from the rafters. In the pool of light below lay three corpses on wooden pallets. Athelstan immediately recognised Toadflax. He had seen him collecting the corpses of dogs; now his own corpse sprawled, eyes staring blindly, blood-encrusted mouth gaping, the front of his shabby jerkin soaked in gore. The other two Athelstan did not recognise, but he felt a deep pang of sadness. Alive, these two young women must have been vibrantly beautiful, with their ivory skin and golden hair, which not even the horror of death could disguise, but now they too lay sprawled, eyes open, heads to one side, faces encrusted with splatters of blood. One had been stabbed, a knife thrust to the belly; the other had had the top half of her chest crushed by the iron-hard crossbow bolt still deeply embedded there.

Athelstan knelt down and gently moved the blonde hair from each of their faces. He began the prayer, '*De profundis* . . . Out of the depths I cry to thee, O Lord . . .'

'Lord, hear my voice!'

Athelstan turned round. Brother Malachi had entered the outhouse.

'I have already recited the death prayers,' the Benedictine explained. 'I have whispered the words of absolution and anointed their hands and faces with holy water.'

Cranston, standing in the shadows, came forward and Athelstan introduced the two men. The coroner glanced down at the corpses. 'Wherever their souls have gone,' he murmured, 'their bodies lie murdered, and someone, Master Rolles, will have to answer for that.'

Chapter 3

Sir Stephen Chandler didn't know he was going to die. After his return from St Erconwald, he had decided to bathe in a tub of hot water, and sip a deep-bowled cup of claret. Chandler liked to bathe; his wife and retainers laughed at him. Most men of his station only bathed on the eve of the great feast days of the Church. Sir Stephen, however, had fought in Outremer, he had swum in the cool fountains and ponds of the Caliph of Egypt's palaces. He had never forgotten that. Once the palaces had been taken, their treasures ransacked, the men slaughtered, the women raped, to swim in the ornamental pools and to smell the exquisite scent of the lotus flowers floating there was pleasure indeed. He was a man who liked his comforts, Sir Stephen, a great landowner in the shire of Kent, owner of Dovecote Manor on the road to Canterbury, a fine red-bricked building with its pastures, meadows, hunting rights, streams and well-stocked carp ponds.

Sir Stephen sat in the leather-backed chair and sniffed appreciatively at the steam curling from the scented hot water the slatterns had poured in. He had insisted on crushed rose juice being added; it always made him relax, and Sir Stephen, if the truth were known, was deeply agitated. He hated these journeys to London every autumn, the gathering, the Masses and, above all, the memories. Sir Stephen picked up the wine cup and sipped carefully. He didn't like that priest, the dark-faced Dominican; wasn't he clerk to Cranston the coroner? Chandler knew Cranston personally – they had fought together on the borders of Gascony. Chandler pulled off his boots, undid his jerkin and stripped himself naked. He stared down at his podgy white body, the red scars and purple welts of ancient wounds, the way his forearms and the lower parts of his legs were still burned dark by that fierce sun.

Sir Stephen waddled across to make sure the bolts on the door were pushed across and the lock turned. He absent-mindedly patted the coffer on the table just within the door and crossed to the bath tub. He would have liked two of the maids to bathe him, but he had to be careful, especially of that self-righteous monk Malachi. He had to hide his secret pleasures. Sir Stephen moved his wine cup to a small table near the tub and stepped gingerly in. He flinched at the heat but lowered himself carefully into the water. He had been quite explicit – the bath tub had to be sturdy and take his size, the finest oak, bound by hoops of iron. Master Rolles, as usual, could not do enough for him and his other companions. No wonder, Sir Stephen reflected, they'd paid the greasy taverner generously enough over the years. He stared appreciatively around the chamber. Master Rolles did look after them! These chambers were luxurious, whilst they dined not in that filthy tap room, but in the comfortable solar at the rear of the tavern. No dirty rushes covered that floor; instead, the oaken boards had been polished to shine like a mirror whilst carpets of soft turkey had been carefully nailed down to deaden the sound and keep in the warmth. The walls were hung with exquisite tapestries of blue and gold depicting scenes from the legends of King Arthur. Each chamber had its own theme, and Sir Stephen had been given the Excalibur chamber. Accordingly, all the blue and gold tapestries described incidents relating to the famous sword, from its discovery in a stone to its return to the Lady of the Lake.

Sir Stephen leaned back, gazing up at the black rafters and the Catherine wheel of candles which could be lowered, lit and hoisted up again. In each corner of the chamber were capped metal braziers, the charcoal now red and spluttering, exuding not only warmth but also the fragrance of the herb packets placed carefully amongst the coals. Sir Stephen smacked his lips; he would bathe, dress, perhaps sleep, before joining the rest for his midday meal. Master Rolles had promised them fresh pheasant, served in the tavern's special oyster sauce, with newly baked white loaves. Sir Stephen sighed. These pilgrimages to London might be difficult but at least they were comfortable. He stared across at the coffer with its three locks. He always checked to ensure it was secure. He bathed his face in water, and even as he did so, the memories came flooding back. He must not forget that he was a soldier of the Faith. He had borne the Cross against the infidel; surely that was reparation enough? How many men had fought in the hot sands around the Middle Sea, the sun beating down, harsh and cruel as any war club? The excruciating thirst, when the tongue became swollen, and the mouth was dry as the sand you trudged through! The foul food aboard the war cogs, the salt of the sea stinging your eyes and worsening your thirst. The long marches during the day, watching your comrades die! The freezing cold of desert nights, and above all, the enemy, dressed in white, astride nimble horses, appearing out of nowhere with ululating war cries, so swift a man had hardly time to arm. The patter-patter of arrows, the sudden surprise of a night attack, the hideous embrace of hand-to-hand combat as you fought for your life and tried to silence the enemy gasping beneath you.

Sir Stephen moved uneasily in the bath, his feet feeling strangely cold. And the sieges! The long ladders against the wall, the dizzying climb, rocks being hurled down, the splash of boiling oil, worsened by fire arrows which turned comrades into living, screaming human torches. Oh yes, Sir Stephen told himself, he had done his duty, he had received the blessings of popes and bishops, so now he should comfort himself and forget past sins. He moved his legs, becoming alarmed. The feeling of coldness was creeping up his body. He wanted to get up but his legs felt paralysed, as if encased in the heaviest steel armour. He stretched out for the wine cup and took a deep draught, not realising he was swallowing his own death.

He began to panic. Pains fired in his lower stomach, and he felt as if he was slipping away, as if the bath water was turning cold and rising to swallow him. He thrashed about, but in vain. His throat felt strangely dry, the chamber seemed to be moving, the tapestries on the wall rippling as though shaken by some unseen hand. He caught one scene, the arm of the Lady of the Lake coming up to grasp Excalibur. The water was turning black and swollen, like the water on the river so many years ago. He made one last effort to rise, only to slip back, his head hitting the side of the wooden tub. Sir Stephen Chandler, Knight of the Golden Falcon, landowner of Kent, knight of the shire, and former Crusader, slipped quietly to his death . . .

Cranston was holding court in the outhouse. Athelstan had made himself comfortable on a stool. The leader of the knights, Sir Maurice Clinton, had joined them. He had come looking for the taverner and stayed out of curiosity. The Judas Man was at first reluctant to answer Cranston's questions.

'You can, sir . . .' Cranston took a swig from the miraculous wine skin and popped it back beneath his cloak. 'You can, sir, either answer my questions here or at the Guildhall. You arrived at Master Rolles' tavern yesterday and three murders occured.'

'Two murders,' the Judas Man answered. He pointed to Toadflax's corpse. 'I killed him in self-defence.'

'Right.' Cranston went across and sat down on a bale of straw. 'Master Rolles, do the same for yourself and for him.' He pointed at the Judas Man.

'Is he always like this?' Brother Malachi whispered to Athelstan.

'Sir Jack has his own way,' the Dominican murmured. 'Like the Holy Spirit,' he smiled, 'he works secretly, his wonders to behold.'

'I heard that, Brother.'

Cranston took off his beaver hat and threw it down between his feet. Loosening his sword belt, he made himself comfortable. Once the Judas Man was seated on the bale of straw, the questioning was resumed.

'You were hired to capture the Misericord. By whom?'

'I don't know. Look.' The Judas Man held up a hand. 'Whilst working in Essex I received a letter along with a purse of silver. I was given the Misericord's name and a slight description. I was told to be in London at this tavern by the eve of the Feast of St Wulfnoth.'

'Why were you hired? To capture the Misericord or kill him?'

'The Misericord is an outlaw – he is wanted dead or

alive. I would have given him the chance to surrender.'

'Why were you hired?'

There was a pause as Sir Maurice Clinton went over and secured the outhouse door, which was banging in the cold breeze.

'I've told you,' the Judas Man retorted. 'The Misericord is a villain, he is wanted dead or alive. He has probably offended someone who is tired of dealing with sheriffs and coroners and wants to see him hanged at Smithfield.'

'So you came here. Oh, by the way,' Cranston jabbed a finger, 'I would be grateful if you would treat the office of coroner with more respect.' He jabbed his finger again. 'You lodged at this tavern?'

The Judas Man shrugged in agreement.

'How did you know the Misericord was in the tap room?'

'I received a message, left outside my chamber along with another purse of coins.'

'Who brought it?'

'I don't know. I went downstairs – I met Sir Maurice and his comrades. I went into the tap room looking for a red-haired man with a misericord dangling around his neck. I thought I had found him. I questioned him. I gave him the chance to surrender. He attacked me, so I killed him.'

'I can vouch for that.' Master Rolles undid the top clasp of his boiled leather jerkin. 'My bailiffs saw what happened.'

'Did they now?' Cranston took another slurp from

his wine skin but didn't offer it to the others, a sign of his growing annoyance. 'Master Rolles, you will have to vouch for many things. These corpses were found in your tavern. Two beautiful women, one killed by a crossbow bolt, the other by a dagger. I understand they were found in the hay barn?'

'Yes, it is just across the yard.'

'What were they doing there? Come on,' Cranston barked. 'Who hired this Judas Man's chamber, who brought the message to his chamber? Who told these two girls to leave the tavern and go to a hay barn in the dead of night?'

The taverner wiped his sweat-soaked palms on his woollen hose.

'Sir John . . .'

'Don't Sir John me. I am not Sir John or Sir Jack to you, but the Lord Coroner of London. In your eyes you must regard me as God Almighty on horseback. Answer my questions.'

'We all have visitors at night,' the taverner murmured. 'About two weeks ago, on the Feast of St Hedwig, a customer brought me a message, told me I had a visitor outside—'

'Of course,' Cranston interrupted. 'I am sure, Master Rolles, knowing what I do of you, you have many visitors at night: the cask of Bordeaux brought in without paying customs, the cloth from Bruges, farmers prepared to sell their meat without paying London tolls, fishermen who sell their catch without handing over any of their profits to the Guild.'

'You can't prove that,' Rolles retorted.

'Oh, one day I will! Sooner than you think, if you don't answer my questions. This visitor . . .'

'I went out to the yard,' Rolles confessed. 'There were three of them, all cloaked and cowled. I told them my time cost money. A silver coin was tossed at my feet. I asked them what they wanted. One man stepped forward, he was hooded and visored. I couldn't recognise his voice or make out any emblem or sign. He asked me when the Great Ratting would take place. I told him. He said he wished to hire a chamber for a thief-taker, known as the Judas Man. He gave me a description and said he would arrive here, as he did, the afternoon before the Great Ratting. I was to give him safe lodgings, food and drink.' The taverner spread his hands. 'Why should I refuse good custom? I was paid in advance and given every assurance that more would be paid. After all, the Judas Man is a law officer. He is hardly likely to steal away in the dead of night. He arrived, and that's all I know.'

'You don't know who brought the message?' Athelstan asked.

The taverner twisted round. 'Brother Athelstan, isn't it? I know all about you.'

'Do you now?' the Dominican replied. 'Then you are a better man than I. The message?'

'Do you know everyone who comes to your church?' Rolles taunted. 'People come in and out of my tavern, every sort and ilk on a night like the Great Ratting.' He pulled a face. 'I cannot say.'

Rolles turned back to the coroner.

'I've answered your questions.' He gestured at Sir Maurice. 'I have meals to prepare.'

Cranston lifted his foot, and pressed so firmly down on the toe of the taverner's boot that the man winced in pain.

'Master Rolles,' Cranston shook his head, 'you are only halfway through your story. I knew those beautiful girls.' He gestured at the corpses. 'Two sisters, Beatrice and Clarice, hair like the sun, eyes as blue as the summer sky, impudent and mischievous; now they lie cold, two of the most accomplished courtesans in Southwark. What were they doing in your hay barn?'

'They came for the Great Ratting. They were looking for custom. Ouch!' The taverner yelped, as Cranston pressed his foot back down.

'They didn't have to look for custom,' Cranston declared. 'Custom went looking for them, men greedy for their soft flesh and expert ways. Why were they in your hay barn?'

'The stranger,' Rolles gasped. Cranston took his boot away. 'The stranger who hired the Judas Man paid me very well, silver coins, this year's batch, freshly minted at the Tower. He told me that, on the night of the Great Ratting, I was to hire two accomplished whores, Beatrice and Clarice. Of course I knew their names. I told them they would be my guests.'

'And?' Cranston asked.

'The stranger said that when the Great Ratting was over the whores were to meet him in the hay barn. I was simply told to tell them that they would be lavishly paid. I did what he asked. I sent the usual message to their keeper, Mother Veritable.' Rolles forced a smile. 'I put the message to be collected in the Castle of Love; it's a pocket on a tapestry in the solar, the usual way I tell Mother Veritable to send her girls for customers who have a need. Mother Veritable—'

'Oh, that cruel-hearted hag,' Cranston broke in. 'You haven't met her yet, Brother Athelstan? Mother Veritable, with a face as sweet as honey and a soul of sour vinegar. I will be paying her a visit soon. Well, continue, Master Rolles.' He lifted his boot.

'The two whores turned up,' Rolles gabbled on, 'dressed in all their finery.'

Cranston stretched out his hand. 'I noticed their jewellery was missing.'

'I have it in safe keeping.'

'I'm sure you have,' Cranston grinned, 'and I'll take it before we leave. Brother Athelstan can sell it for the poor. But, Master Troubadour, do continue with your tale.'

'After the Great Ratting was over, I told the girls to go to the hay barn. I'd lit a lantern horn. They would be safe, warm and dry. That's all I know, Lord Coroner. I had forgotten all about them until early this morning, when an ostler discovered their corpses.'

'And I suppose nobody saw anything?'

'We didn't,' exclaimed Sir Maurice, who was leaning

against the door. 'We always stay at the Night in Jerusalem. We have never known such excitement! The Great Ratting, the fight in the tap room, the whores being cut down in the hay barn. Like the old days, Sir Jack.'

Cranston looked sharply at him.

'I have been standing here watching you,' the knight explained. 'I remember Master Rolles from the war years, but now I recall you. You were in Sir Walter Manny's expedition out of Calais. Do you remember?'

Cranston smiled and brushed back his mass of grey hair.

'Of course, days of glory, eh? I was freshly knighted. I was handsome then, slim as a whippet, fast as a falling hawk, but I don't recall you, sir.'

'I was a lowly squire,' Clinton replied.

'So many different memories,' Cranston mused.

He got to his feet, walked over and, crouching down, pulled back the sheet covering the corpses of the two women.

'I knew these two girls,' he smiled over his shoulder, 'though not in the carnal sense. I also knew their mother, a very famous whore! A woman of mystery. She was famous throughout Southwark. One night ...' Cranston paused, 'Satan's tits,' he whispered, 'one night she disappeared.'

Athelstan felt a prickle of cold on his back. The coroner had recalled something significant.

'Guinevere the Golden,' Cranston murmured.

His remark brought a gasp of surprise from Brother Malachi, who was sitting beside Athelstan. The Benedictine sprang to his feet, fingers going to his lips, his agitation so obvious Athelstan became alarmed.

'What is it, Brother?' Cranston re-covered the corpses and got to his feet. The Benedictine looked as if he was about to faint. Athelstan put down his writing satchel.

'I don't know.' Malachi scratched his forehead. 'I don't really know.' He glanced quickly at Athelstan. 'I don't want to talk here.'

'You can use the solar,' Rolles offered. 'I'll take you there myself.'

'And me?' the Judas Man asked. 'Are you finished with me, Sir John?'

'No, I am not finished with you, but you can return to your post. On no account leave Southwark without my permission.'

'The corpses.' The taverner stopped at the door. 'They'll begin to ripen.'

'Flaxwith,' Cranston roared.

The bailiff, followed by his two dogs, came hurrying across the yard.

'Have these corpses removed. They are to be taken across the river and buried in the strangers' plot outside Charterhouse. The Corporation will bear the cost.'

Athelstan and Cranston left the outhouse with the others and crossed the muck-strewn yard. A faint drizzle had begun to fall, so the passageway into the tavern seemed even more warm and sweet-smelling.

71

They passed the tap room, still being vigorously cleaned after the previous night, and into the more comfortable part of the tavern, the solar, a large chamber which overlooked a well-laid-out garden.

'I grow my own herbs and vegetables,' Rolles explained. 'So visitors don't come at the dead of night,' he continued sharply, 'to offer me leeks and shallots for sale.'

Cranston laughed and patted him on the shoulder. The taverner shrugged this off and pointed to the polished wooden table which ran down the centre of the room.

Cranston sat at the top, Athelstan on his right, with Malachi and Sir Maurice on his left. Athelstan placed his writing satchel on the floor. What he learned today he would write up later. Brother Malachi still looked pale. The taverner's offer of a jug of Rhenish wine and a plate of comfits was eagerly accepted by Cranston. Athelstan believed the taverner wished to eavesdrop, so he nudged Sir John under the table. The coroner took the hint and loudly began to praise the solar's furnishings, pointing at the mantled hearth, where a log fire spluttered, the coloured drapes above the wooden panelling, the glass in the windows. Despite the taverner's obvious annoyance, the coroner heaped praise upon praise and continued to do so until Rolles had served the wine and the silver dish of marchpane, and left the room. Even then Cranston got to his feet, still talking, opened the door and slammed it firmly shut.

'Well done, Brother, well done.' He smiled, tapping the side of his nose.

Malachi's colour had returned, and he drank greedily at the wine but refused to eat anything. Athelstan wondered what had so alarmed the Benedictine. He was, Athelstan reflected, a youngish man, yet he appeared to have aged. His usual cheeriness had crumpled, the furrows around his mouth were more obvious, his skin was pasty, his eyes tired, his mouth slack.

'Brother Malachi need not tell you. I shall,' Sir Maurice offered, patting the Benedictine gently on the arm. 'Twenty years ago the French signed the peace treaty of Bretigny, and the war with France ended, at least for a while. I and my companions . . . well, Sir Jack, you know how it was, young knights with little land and no wealth? We all came from Kent, we'd fought across the Narrow Seas, but none of us had taken any plunder or ransoms. We became mercenaries. The Crusader, Peter of Cyprus, organised an expedition against the Turks in North Africa. He hoped to seize Alexandria and free the trade routes in the Middle Sea.'

'I remember it,' Cranston nodded. 'An army assembled in London. The King loaned ships, a squadron, berthed here in the Thames, cogs and merchantmen.' He dropped his voice. 'Sir Maurice, I think I know what you are going to talk about. The treasure, the Crusaders' war chest?'

'The Lombard treasure,' Sir Maurice agreed. 'Peter

73

of Cyprus raised a huge loan from the Bardi in Lombard Street. Now the Crusader fleet lay at anchor in the Thames, taking on men and supplies. It became common knowledge that the Lombard treasure was to be taken aboard. It was decided the treasure should be moved by night, and as few people as possible would be told when and how it was to be transported to the flagship, *The Glory of Westminster*. The leader of the English force, Lord Belvers, a Kentish man, apparently arranged for two of our company, two knights, Richard Culpepper and Edward Mortimer, to receive the Lombard treasure and transport it by barge to the flagship.' He coughed. 'We learned all this later.'

He paused as Brother Malachi lifted a hand.

'My monastic name is Malachi, a famous Celtic saint, but I am Thomas Culpepper by birth. Sir Richard was my brother.' He sipped his wine. 'We all came up to London, excited by the prospect of war, glory and plunder. The Pope had promised a plenary indulgence for all those who took the Cross. We called ourselves the Company of the Golden Falcon – that was our emblem – eight of us in all, led by Sir Maurice here, whilst I was their chaplain. We all hoped to achieve great things, to win glory for God and Holy Mother Church. Only afterwards did we discover that two of our company, my brother included, had been chosen for a special task.

'We all lodged here, not so luxuriously as we do now.' He smiled weakly. 'Master Rolles had just bought the tavern from his profits. You, Sir John, were not coroner, and there was no priest at St Erconwald's. Richard was young and vigorous. He loved to dance, he thrilled to the sound of music. While we waited for the army to assemble and the fleet to sail, he and the rest caroused in the fleshpots of London. We stayed here for some time. Richard became infatuated with a whore, a courtesan.'

'Guinevere the Golden?' Athelstan asked.

Malachi nodded. 'He had known her for months. Lord Belvers had often sent him to London on this errand or that. Guinevere became pregnant, twin daughters. Richard suspected . . .' Malachi's voice trailed off.

'God in Heaven!' Athelstan whispered. 'Are you saying those two corpses were your brother's daughters, your nieces?'

'Possibly.' Malachi spat the word out. 'But there again, Guinevere had many admirers; those children could have been anybody's. Now the Lombard treasure arrived, it was taken from the Tower by barge and apparently handed over to my brother. He was to transport it by boat to the flagship.' Malachi fell silent.

'But neither the barge nor the Lombard treasure ever reached the flagship,' Sir Maurice explained.

'Impossible,' Athelstan said.

Sir Maurice shook his head. 'Believe me, both the river and the city were searched. Of the boatmen who brought the barge, or the two knights, not a trace was found, nor of the treasure they were transporting. They all vanished off the face of the earth.'

'I remember this.' Cranston refilled his wine cup. 'I was in Calais at the time and returned to London just before Christmas. A thorough search was organised.'

'And nothing was found?' Athelstan queried.

'Nothing.' Malachi shook his head. 'My brother and Edward Mortimer . . . well, it seemed as though they'd never existed. For twenty years I have searched. What is worse is that both were proclaimed as thieves. On the same night the Lombard treasure disappeared, Guinevere the Golden also vanished. Every year we come up to London, every year I make enquiries, but nothing.'

Athelstan rose to his feet, seemingly fascinated by the tapestry mentioned by Rolles, which hung just within the doorway. Costly and heavy, the stitching was exquisite, its red, green and blue thread streaked with gold. The tapestry described the famous fable, the storming of the Castle of Love. Armed knights, displaying the device of a heart, were preparing to swarm into the castle, their catapults and trebuchets full of roses with which to shower the lady custodians, who were ready to defend themselves with baskets of brilliantly coloured flowers. Athelstan ran his hand down it and found the heavily concealed pocket in the bottom right-hand corner of the tapestry.

'I have seen that device before,' Sir John called out. 'In the well-to-do taverns and hostelries of France, a place where favourite customers can, anonymously,

leave a letter asking for the services of a courtesan.'
Sir John smacked his lips. 'Or whatever their heart
desires.'

Athelstan dug his hand deep into the pocket. It was
empty. He returned to the table.

'Has any trace of the Lombard treasure ever been
found?'

Sir Maurice shook his head. 'Everything disappeared. Our two comrades, the treasure, not to mention the whore Guinevere.'

'No, that's wrong.' Malachi spoke up. 'I discovered
many years later that the barge had been found in the
mud and slime further downriver.'

'How did you discover that?' Athelstan asked.

'Two bargemen had been hired; both were married,
both left widows, who petitioned the Exchequer for
compensation. Of course the barons of the Exchequer
replied that the men could still be alive, so the widows' kinsmen organised a search. You see,' Malachi
spread his hands, 'the fleet sailed three days after the
robbery. We had to leave. So the search for the treasure
and the others was left to the City authorities. Only
many years later did I hear about the barge.'

'That's true,' Sir Maurice murmured.

Athelstan was about to continue his questioning
when there was a knock on the door. Master Rolles
entered carrying a tray of herbs, bowls of saffron, mace,
nutmeg, cloves and cinnamon. Athelstan breathed in
the refreshing smells.

'I've brought these to sweeten the room,' the

taverner explained. 'If you are finished, sirs . . .'

He paused at a loud hammering and knocking from the gallery above, followed by shouts.

'If you are finished,' Rolles repeated, choosing to ignore the clamour, 'I would like to prepare for the midday meal.'

'Certainly, sir.' Sir John rubbed his stomach. 'And what are you offering, Master Rolles?'

'Frumenty soup, sprinkled with venison and saffron, Tuscany broth with rabbit and almond milk, garnished with nutmeg and galingale, followed by pike stuffed with lampreys and eels. Pheasant . . .'

Sir John groaned in pleasure.

The taverner placed the tray on the table. As he did so, Sir Laurence Broomhill hurried in.

'Sir Maurice, Master Rolles, you must come.' He paused to catch his breath. 'After we returned from Mass this morning, Sir Stephen asked for a jug of wine and a goblet. He said he wished to bathe . . .'

'I remember.' Rolles wiped his fingers on a napkin and stuffed it into the belt round his waist. 'What's wrong?'

'We cannot rouse him. We've knocked and shouted, but there is no reply.'

'The door?'

'It's bolted and locked.' Broomhill clawed at his beard. 'He may have had a seizure.'

Sir Maurice sprang to his feet and, followed by Brother Malachi and the taverner, hurried from the solar. Cranston and Athelstan glancing sharply at each other quickly followed. They went out along the passageway and up the broad corner staircase. On the gallery above, a throng of people had gathered outside the third door along. Athelstan noticed the muddy boots outside the door placed in a reed basket. He grabbed Rolles' arm and pointed at these.

'A tap boy was meant to clean them.'

The taverner pushed Athelstan's hand away and, shoving a path through the throng, pounded at the door.

'Sir Stephen Chandler,' he bellowed. 'I beg you, sir, open up.'

The clamour brought more servants and grooms up the stairs. Cranston ordered one of these to fetch a bench from the passageway below and asked the knights to step away. At first there was confusion, but under Sir John's direction, the bench was used as a battering ram, swinging hard against the door until it buckled on its leather hinges, the locks and bolts at the top and bottom snapping back.

The room inside was warm. Athelstan noticed how the windows were shuttered, and peering round the rest, he glimpsed the pale body sprawled in the iron-hooped bathtub. Cranston, roaring at everyone to stand back, pushed his way through, almost dragging Athelstan with him. Once inside, he kept everyone else back, insisting no one should enter the room or touch anything. Athelstan quickly examined the body. Sir Stephen was beyond all help. The Dominican quickly recited the requiem and, pressing his hand against the dead man's neck, once again made sure there was no blood beat. He crouched down and murmured the words of absolution in the hope that the soul hadn't immediately left the body, trying not to concentrate on those half-open, staring dead eyes, the slack jaw, the bloodless lips and liverish face. The water was ice cold. Athelstan glimpsed the small overturned stool and the fallen wine cup which had stained one of the turkey carpets. He plucked a napkin from the lavarium, picked up the cup and carefully sniffed. It had a heavy, unpleasant odour, rank and foul, like rotting weeds, though when he tested the wine in the jug it smelt wholesome.

'God rest him,' Athelstan murmured. 'He is dead, murdered, poisoned.'

Sir Maurice, standing next to Cranston, tried to push forward but the coroner restrained him.

'It can't be!' Sir Maurice shouted. 'Who would poison poor Stephen?'

'I don't know, but poisoned he is. The jug of wine is wholesome, but the cup is tainted. Was Sir Stephen taking any potions or powders?' Athelstan asked.

'None, none.' Sir Maurice's agitation was obvious. 'Sir John, Brother Athelstan, can't this room be cleared?' He gestured at the corpse. 'Must he be left sprawled like that?'

'A murder has been committed.' Cranston stood, legs apart, his enormous girth blocking any further entry into the room. 'A murder has been committed and I am the Lord Coroner. Master Rolles, take your guests away – oh, and send for a physician.'

Cranston shooed them all back into the gallery, blocking the view by pulling across the unhinged door. Then he turned, mopping his face with the hem of his cloak.

'Athelstan, you're sure it's murder?'

'Poison, Sir Jack. I would wager a year's collection, and by the coldness of the water, he has been dead at least an hour.'

Whilst they waited for the physician, Cranston and Athelstan surveyed the room. The Dominican noticed the small coffer with its three locks and started to search for the keys. Cranston, however, was much taken with the luxury of the chamber: its glowing tapestries, the dark blue gold-fringed hangings around the four-poster bed, and the carved oak and walnut furnishings. Athelstan half listened as Sir John described the scene on one of the tapestries, Excalibur being taken down to the Lady of the Lake.

'Ah, I've found them!' Athelstan moved a candle on the small table beside the bed to reveal a thick silver key ring. He was about to try the keys in the small coffer when there was a tapping and Master Stapleton the physician edged his way round the broken door and came into the room.

Cranston and Athelstan had done business before with this cadaverous-faced leech: his ever-watery eyes and constantly dripping nose always tempted Athelstan to whisper the words 'Physician heal thyself', but

Master Stapleton had no sense of humour. He came shrouded in his customary food-stained robe, sniffing and spluttering as he stood staring disdainfully down at the corpse. He pressed his hand against the neck, felt the stomach, peered into the mouth and pulled up an eyelid.

'Good morrow, Master Stapleton.' Cranston leaned down as if trying to catch the physician's glare. 'You do know who we are?'

'Of course I do, Sir John; in your case, once seen, never forgotten. Good morrow to you too, Brother Athelstan,' he declared and poked a finger at the corpse. 'This man's dead. My examination will cost you five shillings.'

He picked up the wine goblet and sniffed at it.

'Oh, he has been poisoned, so that'll be seven shillings.'

'I know he's dead,' Cranston roared. 'What of?'

'Now, now, Sir John, do not disturb your humours. You know how the black bile of anger warms the blood.'

'Shut up!' Cranston snapped.

'Very well.' Stapleton clasped his cloak with both hands, head going back like a judge about to pass sentence. 'I suspect he died of water hemlock, probably mixed with henbane. I can tell that by the offensive smell, and before you ask, Brother, the wine would hide both taste and smell, at least for a while. Now henbane flowers in late July, so the poison was probably a dried powder, very potent. The cup's polluted but the wine jug is free of any noxious smell. So,' Stapleton held out a hand, 'either he, or someone else, put poison in that cup. He drank and climbed into the bath. Death would follow fairly swiftly. The victim is fat, like you, Sir John; perhaps his heartbeat was not too strong.'

'And the symptoms?' Athelstan asked.

'A stiffening of the limbs.'

'You mean paralysis?'

'That's right, Brother, feet and hands first. It's the same poison Socrates drank. So,' Stapleton wiped his nose with the back of his hand, 'for coming here, four shillings, one shilling for inspecting the corpse, and two for discovering a murder.'

Cranston pulled the door aside.

'Master Stapleton,' he smiled sweetly, 'put your bill into the Guildhall, no more than five shillings, mind you. It was Brother Athelstan who discovered the murder.'

The physician sighed heavily and, hitching his robe, went out into the gallery to continue his argument with Master Rolles, loudly demanding he be given food and drink for his trouble.

'I doubt if it was suicide,' Athelstan mused. 'Sir John, pull back that door. I want Master Rolles and the rest in here now.'

Cranston pushed the door to one side, and strode out bellowing names. Athelstan went and sat on the great chest at the foot of the bed. Rolles and Sir Maurice led the knights back in. Cranston sat down on the heavy

83

oaken chair against the far wall, taking a generous slurp from his miraculous wine skin.

'Can't the corpse be removed?' Sir Maurice protested. 'It seems as if Sir Stephen is lying there staring at us.'

A short discussion followed. Athelstan agreed to the request and Rolles organised some of his bully boys, who stripped the bed of a sheet, lifted the corpse out, wrapped it up and removed it.

'Put it with the others,' Cranston shouted, ignoring the gasps of the knights.

'I object,' Sir Maurice declared.

'Don't object, sir,' Athelstan replied. 'You've read your Scripture: leave the dead to bury the dead. Sir Stephen's body will be given an honourable burial wherever you choose, but his soul has been dispatched to God before its time, and God, not to mention the Crown and our Lord Coroner, would like to know the reason why.'

Rolles stood near the doorway, whilst the knights resigned themselves to Athelstan's questioning. Some sat on stools and chairs. Sir Maurice stood by the door, his hand on the small coffer. Brother Malachi, having accompanied the corpse downstairs, returned with an ale pot in his hand.

'I believe Sir Stephen was murdered,' Athelstan began. 'The poison was offensive and strong. It wasn't in the wine jug but in the cup. Who brought that up?'

'I did,' Rolles declared. 'And before you mention it, I had nothing to do with that man's death. Ask my servants in the kitchen. Sir Stephen came back from Mass, he was complaining he felt hot, he had the rheums, and a slight fever.'

'Sir Stephen often suffered from them.' Sir Laurence Broomhill, a narrow-faced man clearly agitated by his comrade's death, played with the Ave beads wrapped round his fingers.

'So he had a fever?' Athelstan confirmed. 'His nose was full of mucus?'

'He was coughing,' Sir Maurice agreed.

'So,' Athelstan chose his words carefully, 'Sir Stephen comes back to the tavern, orders a hot bath and a jug of claret. The tub is brought up and filled with hot water. You, Master Rolles, brought a tray with a jug of wine and a cup?'

'Yes.' The taverner nodded.

'And when you came in here?'

'Sir Stephen had begun to strip. He had complained about his boots being muddy. I told him to leave them in the basket outside, one of my pot boys would clean them.' Rolles spread his hands and blinked. 'Brother Athelstan, Sir John, I swear the cup was clean. The wine was the best Bordeaux. If I meant to poison Sir Stephen I would hardly have brought it up myself, would I?'

Athelstan agreed, but his searching stare disconcerted the taverner, now fearful of this quiet friar with his sharp eyes and pointed questions.

'Did that cup of wine leave your care?' Athelstan asked.

'Never, I took the cup from the shelf, I rinsed it out with clean water, dried it with a napkin, put it on a tray and brought it up. I placed the tray on the table, talked to Sir Stephen about his boots and left. I heard him draw the bolts and turn the key behind me.'

He paused as Cranston gave a loud snore. The coroner's head was going down. Athelstan quietly prayed that Sir John was not going into one of his deep slumbers. One of the knights laughed quietly.

'Did anyone come into this chamber?' Athelstan asked. 'After Master Rolles had left?'

Sir Maurice and the rest shook their heads.

'We wouldn't,' one of them declared. 'If Sir Stephen was having his bath, he was most particular about his comforts.'

'So, here we have Sir Stephen,' Athelstan summarised, 'alone in his chamber. When the cup and wine are left here there is no trace of poison in them. So someone must have come into this room and, whilst Sir Stephen was distracted, poured poison into that goblet. There's no secret passageway, no one could come through the window and we have no reason to believe that Sir Stephen would take his own life. Now the claret was rich, it has a strong smell.'

'A fragrance all of its own,' Cranston abruptly declared, shaking himself and blinking.

'Sir Stephen also has the rheums,' Athelstan added, 'mucus in his nose, so his sense of smell would not be so sharp. He climbs into the tub, drinks the wine and dies.'

'He must have opened the door again,' Cranston interposed.

'Of course.' Athelstan smiled. 'Master Rolles, the boots weren't placed outside when you left?'

The taverner shook his head.

'So, it must have happened afterwards. There are two chambers, one on either side,' Athelstan continued. 'Who occupies them?'

'One is a storeroom,' Rolles replied. 'Sir Maurice occupies the other.'

Athelstan sat staring down at the floor. He could only accept what the taverner had said; Rolles had no obvious grievance or grudge against Sir Stephen, and if he was involved in the poisoning, he certainly would have not brought up the wine himself. He asked Rolles again about the cup and jug never leaving his care. The taverner was adamant. Athelstan was convinced of his innocence, especially as Rolles made no attempt to pass the blame on to anyone else.

'Was Sir Stephen in good humour? Was he anxious about anything?'

Athelstan's questions only provoked a chorus of denials.

'I must search the chamber,' Athelstan declared. He was surprised by the reaction his statement provoked.

'Sir Stephen is a lord,' Sir Thomas Davenport shouted, 'not a common criminal; his goods are not being distrained.'

'I must search this chamber,' Athelstan insisted.

Cranston rose to his feet and was glaring at the knights, challenging them to question his authority. In a moment of taut silence, Athelstan walked across to the coffer with the three locks.

'What is this for?'

'Private papers,' Sir Maurice spluttered. 'Keepsakes. Brother Athelstan, is this necessary?'

Athelstan patted the wallet which swung at the end of the cord around his waist.

'Sir Maurice, I have found the keys. I wish you to leave now.' He smiled thinly. 'I have kept you long enough from your midday meal. Sir John and I still have business here.' Athelstan paused. 'Now, as for this casket, Master Rolles, have two of your men deliver it into the sanctuary of St Erconwald's Church.'

'Will it be safe there?' Sir Maurice demanded.

'I have the keys,' Athelstan answered, 'and not even my parishioners will steal something I place in the sanctuary.'

Sir Maurice and the other knights left, Cranston shouting out that he would not join them at table.

'What do you think?' the coroner asked once they were alone.

'I don't think anything, Sir John, except that I must search this chamber.'

They went through the dead knight's possessions, which were stored in the great chest at the foot of the bed, as well as the aumbry built in the far corner, but found nothing remarkable except finely cut clothes, jerkins, hose, boots of cordovan leather, spurs, a sword and two daggers in decorated scabbards attached to an embroidered war belt. Beneath the table, beside the bed, Athelstan found a psalter and leafed through it. The parchment pages were of the finest quality. Athelstan was intrigued that the psalter book was not regularly used except for one page, where Chandler had copied the words of a prayer. This page was well thumbed, the parchment black and shiny due to constant use. Athelstan read the first line aloud.

'Have pity on me as you had pity on the possessed whom you saved from the power of the Devil.'

He glanced up. 'I wonder what sin weighed so heavily on Sir Stephen's soul that he had to recite this prayer time and time again?' A question he posed to himself as much as Sir John Cranston.

Chapter 4

Cranston and Athelstan left the tavern. The coroner went into a scrivener's to peer at an hour candle and came out loudly declaring for all to hear how it was past two in the afternoon and he was very hungry. Athelstan wanted to go back to his parish, but Cranston plucked at his sleeve claiming it was time to meet Mother Veritable, the Whore-Queen of Southwark. They made their way through needle-thin, filthy streets under the jutting storeys of houses which leaned so far out they blocked the sky and seemed about to crash into each other. Athelstan kept a wary eye on the windows as well as the creaking shop signs hung so low they were as dangerous as any axe or club. The streets were busy, packed with thronging crowds; they also reeked of sulphur as the scavengers were out, clearing the lay stalls, the Corporation's refuse tips. The stench of the rubbish, which included the rotting corpses of animals, was so offensive Cranston bought two pomanders from a passing tinker. They held these to their noses, Athelstan firmly gripping his walking stick in his other hand as the poor of Southwark swirled about them, eyes and fingers ready to filch. Prostitutes, pimps, cunning men, the naps and the foists slunk back into doorways or alley mouths at Cranston's approach. Now and again a piece of refuse was thrown – thankfully it always missed – followed by a curse or shout.

'Watch out, watch out! Fat Jack's about!'

Cranston growled deep in his throat but chose to ignore such taunts. The King's justice was also very apparent along these grim streets. Cranston and Athelstan had to stand aside as a moveable gallows, a scaffold on a huge platform fixed on wheels, was pulled by oxen down one broad lane. Bailiffs guarded each side of the cart. On each branch of the four-legged gibbet hung a corpse, pitched and tarred. A placard nailed to the back of the cart proclaimed that the dead men were river thieves, hanged on the quayside just after dawn. After these came four women, wearing striped hoods, who had been caught playing naughty. They would be taken down to the stocks until their menfolk collected them and gave guarantees of future good behaviour. This macabre procession was followed by the bell man, dressed in the colours of the city livery. Every so often he would pause, ring his bell and proclaim how Miles Sallet, a cobbler, was to forfeit twenty-two pairs of shoes of good calfskin leather for knocking down a City beadle, and refusing to pay the fine.

Eventually Cranston led Athelstan off this broad thoroughfare and down Darkhouse alleyway. At the bottom of this, across a strip of common land, rose a fine but rather decayed mansion, its tiled roof, lead piping and red bricks peeping above a high grey curtain wall. Cranston marched up to the gatehouse and pulled at the bell rope, hidden by a screen which looked curiously like a penis. He pulled at the cord again. Athelstan read the proclamation nailed to a piece of wood hanging from one of the gate pillars which declared that the 'Garden of Delights' beyond offered grapes, apples, pears, cherries, quinces, peaches, mulberries and apricots. Above the notice was a painting of a pale swan nesting, its long neck turned.

'To the uninitiated, Brother,' Cranston laughed, 'that appears to be what any coster would sell from his stall. Take my word for it, you've never seen the type of gooseberries this house grows.'

Cranston hammered on the gate. The small grille opened, and eyes peered out.

'Piss off,' a voice snarled.

'Is that you, Owlpen? Open up. It's Jack Cranston. Either open up or I'll return with warrants.'

The gate swung open and a little man with rounded eyes in a rounded face, two tufts of hair sticking up like the ears of an eagle owl, peered fearfully up at the coroner.

'Oh! Sir John.'

'Never mind that,' Cranston snapped.

He pushed Owlpen aside and walked up the pebble-dash path. The garden on either side was cordoned off by a latticework fence. They went up some steps, through a half-open door and down a twisting passage-way. The walls were lime-washed, the paving stones scrubbed clean. Owlpen tried to catch up but Cranston knew where he was going. He turned right and entered a small solar with two large windows overlooking a lovely garden. Athelstan glimpsed a lawn and raised herb patches as well as a small dovecote at the far end. The solar itself was more like a nun's cell, plain with white plastered walls, dark furniture, no tapestries or pictures except for a great Crucifix above the mantled hearth. A woman sat beside the crackling fire, deep in a throne-like chair, feet resting on a small stool. She was busy with a piece of needlework, and hardly raised her head when Cranston doffed his beaver hat and gave a most mocking bow.

'I thought you'd come, Cranston, like a fly from the dung heap.'

The woman looked up. In the poor light from both window and fire, Athelstan could not determine her age. She had a pale, hard face, quite beautiful, if it wasn't for her glittering eyes and the slight twist to her mouth. She was dressed in a dark blue kirtle, with front lacing, a low girdle, and over this a velvet cloak lined with embroidered silk. Her dark hair was hidden by a headdress of fine gauffered linen cut in semicircles to hang down on either side of her face. Around her neck hung a gold chain with a jewelled cross, with a matching ring on the little finger of each hand.

Cranston didn't reply to her insult. Instead he just stood over her, like some sombre shadow.

'Roheisa,' he whispered, 'don't make me act the bully boy.'

'Mother Veritable to you, Sir Jack.'

She put down the embroidery on a side table, picked up a hand bell and rang it vigorously. A maid came in. Mother Veritable asked for two stools to be brought. Ignoring Cranston, she looked Athelstan over from head to toe.

'A Dominican,' she sneered. 'Ah well, it takes all types. In this house, the cut of a man's cloth means nothing. Why do you stand there, little priest? I've heard of you, with your sharp wits,' she laughed, 'and your snouting nose.'

'God bless you, Mother Veritable.' Athelstan sketched the sign of the Cross; she just made a dismissive gesture with her hand.

Owlpen and the maid returned with stools. Cranston and Athelstan made themselves as comfortable as they could.

'I won't offer you refreshment.' Mother Veritable kicked the foot rest away. 'You'll take nothing in this house, will you, Cranston?'

'I'll take the truth.'

Mother Veritable sighed and raised her eyes heavenwards.

'Here we go, my Lord Coroner, back into the world of men, eh? Two of my girls were killed last night, Beatrice and Clarice.'

'Guinevere's golden daughters.'

'I remember Guinevere.' Mother Veritable's eyes looked sad, her face lost some of its hardness. 'As I said, Sir Jack, the world of men, sharp and cruel. I loved Guinevere. Oh! She had a heart as black as her face was fair, but perhaps I loved her because of her treachery. You knew us both then, Jack.'

Cranston coloured with embarrassment and shuffled his feet. Mother Veritable leaned forwards and placed her jewelled white fingers over Cranston's great paw.

'You remember the glory days, Jack?' Her voice was soft and sweet. 'Guinevere loved, I loved, you loved, the City was full of young knights with their fair damsels. It wasn't so hard then. My heart hadn't turned to stone. I hadn't accepted the world for what it is, cruel and harsh. Do you remember the man I loved, Jack?'

'Killed,' Cranston replied. 'Killed outside Bordeaux, wasn't he?' He withdrew his hand as if suddenly remembering why he was here.

'Beatrice and Clarice?' The woman sat back and shrugged. 'Master Rolles, as usual, had sent for them, left a message in the tapestry of the Castle of Love; somebody wanted to hire them both. So they bathed and perfumed themselves, donned their best robes and went off to the Great Ratting. Oh, by the way, I've destroyed Rolles' message.'

'And you agreed?' Athelstan asked. 'To send two of your women out into the night?'

'I had already received a silver coin, a token of what was to come.' She held Athelstan's gaze. 'They didn't come back. I thought they had been hired for the night. This is the only place they know. They would have returned and brought their silver with them.'

'Every penny?' Athelstan asked.

'Little priest—'

'Friar,' Athelstan corrected. 'I'm a Dominican friar.'

'Whatever you are,' she snapped, 'I tell you this: woe betide the girl who returns here and holds back what she owes.'

Her gaze shifted, staring at a point behind Athelstan's head. The Dominican turned: two great oafs dressed in leather jackets, hose pushed into high-heeled boots, sword belts strapped round their waists, stood silently at the door grasping cudgels.

'Tell your lovely boys to go away,' Cranston demanded. Mother Veritable gestured with her head. Cranston heard the door close behind him.

'Master Rolles sent a message this morning. How the two girls had been found in the hay barn. Killed by a cross-bolt and dagger, wasn't it? I went down to view the corpses,' Mother Veritable continued matter-of-factly, as if describing a visit to a market stall. 'Still beautiful, but dead.' She half smiled. 'Master Rolles had taken their jewellery.'

'I had forgotten that.' Cranston snapped his fingers.

'I meant to take the jewellery for Brother Athelstan to sell and distribute the money amongst the poor.'

'I don't want it.' Athelstan spoke up. Despite this woman's apparent harshness, he wondered if she was trying to make sense of the horror she had witnessed. 'Sir John,' he turned to the coroner, 'have the jewellery returned here.'

Mother Veritable smiled with her eyes. 'The singer not the song,' she murmured and winked at Athelstan. 'Not many priests would have said that. Did you pray for them, Brother?'

Athelstan nodded.

'Do you know what happened?' Cranston insisted.

'From what Rolles and the others described,' Mother Veritable sighed, 'the two girls enjoyed the evening, and quietly left to meet their customer in the hay barn.'

'And you do not know who this was?'

'Sir John,' she glanced coyly at the coroner, 'if I did, my beautiful boys would have visited him by now. Master Rolles didn't know. Nobody saw anything.'

'Did Master Rolles ever . . .' Athelstan searched for the words.

'Sample such wine?' Mother Veritable teased. 'At his tavern? Not to my knowledge.' She tapped the tip of her nose. 'But he's always welcome here.'

'You know who resides at the Night in Jerusalem?' Cranston asked. 'The Judas Man.'

Mother Veritable shook her head and pulled a face.

'And the Falconers, the Knights of the Golden Falcon.'

Mother Veritable rested her elbows on the chair and stared down at the floor.

'Did they ever come here? Maurice Clinton, Thomas Davenport, Reginald Branson, Laurence Broomhill, Stephen Chandler? Did they come here?' Cranston repeated. 'Do their names mean anything to you?'

Mother Veritable turned her face away, staring into the fire. She coughed as if clearing her throat, her shoulders shook and Athelstan realised she was crying. The room had fallen deathly silent, the only sound the flames crackling, and the spluttering from one of the braziers. Mother Veritable rose, grasping a cane, and limped over to a side table on which a chaffing dish stood. She opened a small pot and sprinkled herbs, then came back to the chair, wiping the tears from her cheek.

'My leg was broken.' She sat down carefully, clutching her stick. 'Sir Jack will tell you about it, Brother Athelstan. A man I didn't please came visiting with his bully boys, but to answer your question, yes and no. No, those knights have not been here . . . well, not recently. Yes, I know their names.' She wiped her tears with the back of her hand. 'As I said, in the glory days . . . They were friends of Culpepper, weren't they, and the other one who stole the Lombard treasure and fled.'

'What makes you so sure they stole it?' Athelstan asked.

'Because at the same time Guinevere disappeared. She and Culpepper were smitten with each other,

her beauty had turned his head.' Mother Veritable rested on her stick, a faraway look in her eyes. 'Glory days,' she whispered. 'London was full of young soldiers, knights and squires, preparing for the Great Expedition. The Thames brimmed with ships, cogs from Hainault, war vessels from Flanders, galleys from Venice – all the young lords ready to take the Cross and go out and kill the infidel for sweet Jesus' sake.' She paused. 'Culpepper and the rest stayed at the Night in Jerusalem. He and Guinevere met. Of course the men came here, including Sir Maurice Clinton, who was much taken with me, at least in those days.'

'Did Guinevere ever tell you about what was planned?'

Mother Veritable shook her head. 'Oh, she hinted that this life was not hers, that one day things would change, that her knight, like some hero from Arthur's court, would come galloping along and scoop her up into his arms. Culpepper was deeply in love with Guinevere; she thought she was in love with him.'

'Thought?' Athelstan asked.

'Guinevere's heart was as fickle as the moon. All she dreamed of was bettering herself, becoming the Grande Dame.'

'And the father of her daughters?'

Mother Veritable chuckled. 'It's a wise man who knows his father. Guinevere made a mistake but, there again, she had many admirers. You've been kind, Brother, so I'll tell you this. On the night she disappeared, well, the afternoon beforehand, she packed all her belongings and stole away. She was all excited. I asked her where she was going.'

'And?'

'Why, to your church, Brother.'

'St Erconwald's?'

'That's what she said. She was never seen or heard of again.'

Mother Veritable leaned over and nudged Sir John, who was beginning to fall asleep. The coroner stirred.

'What do you think happened, Roheisa?' He smacked his lips.

'I've heard reports,' she confessed. 'And you can check the records, Sir Jack, that a woman fitting Guinevere's description was seen boarding a cog, a Venetian ship, three days after the crusading fleet left for Alexandria.' She pulled a face. 'But that is all.'

'And her two daughters?'

'I reared them, two peas out of the same pod. They were so much like their mother. Sometimes I thought Guinevere had returned.' She put the stick down beside the chair.

'Can we search their chambers?'

'I've done that already. There's nothing much.'

'Can we see it?' Athelstan insisted.

'Will their jewellery be given back to me?' she asked.

'You have my word,' Cranston assured her.

Mother Veritable got to her feet and, leaning on her cane, walked towards the door. She whispered to the servants outside and returned to her chair, sitting serenely like an abbess in a convent. A short while later a young woman entered the room, her auburn hair caught up behind her. She was dressed in a Lincoln-green smock, a white girdle around her waist. If Mother Veritable was the abbess, this young woman acted as comely and coy as any novice. She brought a stool over and sat beside her mistress, cradling a small leather bag.

'This is Donata,' Mother Veritable explained, 'a close friend of the two dead girls.'

Donata lifted her pale face; her almond-shaped eyes gave her a serene, calm look.

'Donata is resting at the moment,' Mother Veritable continued, 'which is why her face and lips aren't painted. She is also in mourning.' She touched the black ribbon tied round the girl's swan-like neck. 'Donata, this is Sir John Cranston and Brother Athelstan. No, don't be afraid, Sir Jack has no authority here.' Mother Veritable smiled. 'Whilst I have powerful patrons. Tell them what you know.'

'Beatrice and Clarice . . .' Donata began.

Athelstan detected a West Country accent. He noticed how long and slim the girl's fingers were. He wondered what such a beautiful maid was doing in a house like this, until he recalled the droves of young men and women who trudged in from the countryside looking for work.

'What about them?' Brother Athelstan asked.

Donata took a deep breath, her beautiful butterfly eyes dancing prettily.

'We are meant to give every penny we earn to Mother Veritable who looks after us so well,' she added hastily. 'But one night, in their cups, they said, well, they said they could earn more gold and silver than I could imagine, that's all they'd say.' She shrugged. 'I thought it was a jest, wine words.'

'Who were their customers?' Athelstan asked.

Donata stared serenely back.

'Brother Athelstan,' Mother Veritable laughed, 'our customers don't wear placards around their necks, they come and go like shadows.'

'That's all they said,' the girl pleaded. She handed the small sack over to Athelstan. 'They kept their precious things in there.'

Athelstan undid the cord and tipped out the contents: some jewellery, trinkets, gewgaws, buttons, hair clasps, a lock of hair and a small roll of parchment, rather dirty and yellow. Athelstan placed the sack down and unrolled the piece of manuscript. The writing was in a deep black ink. The hand looked clerkly, the letters clearly formed; it was a poem written in Norman French, imitating the troubadours of Paris. Athelstan read the opening lines.

Le Coq du Couronne Rouge est Maigre
Comment le grand Seigneur, Monsieur Le
    Coq . . .

Athelstan realised it was one of those poets' clever conceits: the references to a 'cock' and a 'red crown' were sexual allusions. The writing was cramped, of little significance, so he rolled it up and put it back.

Cranston made to get up, but abruptly his hand shot out and he grasped Donata's wrist. The girl started.

'The Knights of the Golden Falcon?'

Mother Veritable tried to protest; Cranston pressed the fingers of his other hand against Donata's mouth.

'I'll have you arrested, girl, and questioned if you do not tell the truth!'

Athelstan was surprised at Sir John's roughness. He could tell from Donata's face how Sir John had stirred up a hornet's nest.

'They come here?' Sir John asked. 'Those great lords from Kent, not together, but perhaps singly. They do, don't they?' He tightened his grip. Donata, eyes rounded in fear, nodded. 'And they asked for Beatrice and Clarice, didn't they? Which ones?'

The girl, terrified, shook her head.

'Let her go, Sir Jack.'

Mother Veritable picked up her stick and beat it on the floor. Cranston released his grip. Donata snatched the sack back. She got up so quickly she knocked over the stool, and fled through the door, slamming it behind her.

'You were too harsh.'

'I told you, I came for the truth,' Cranston retorted. 'Do you really expect me to believe that five great lords of Kent who have come up to London to celebrate, fill their bellies with wine, ale and good food, do not satisfy their other hungers? That they wouldn't visit a brothel which they frequented in their youth? Oh, they'll do it differently now they're important, won't they? They won't come swaggering up the path, carousing, singing a ribald song, but, as you might say, like a thief in the night. Now, if you want, Mother Veritable, I can have this place searched. I can whip up Master Flaxwith.'

'I've told you more than I should, Sir John. You know the rules of this house about secrecy! Yes, you are correct. They've all been here, one at a time. They all asked to see Beatrice and Clarice, sometimes one, sometimes both together.'

'Ah!' Cranston sighed. 'And so it's not beyond imagining that, on the night of the Great Ratting, one, or two, or all of those stalwart knights asked for Beatrice and Clarice?'

'But why meet them in the hay barn?' Athelstan asked.

'Mother Veritable knows the answer to that, don't you?' Cranston rose and stood over the brothel mistress. 'Whoever hired them wouldn't dare take them up to their chamber; they didn't want such stories going back to Kent. Who knows, perhaps in the hay barn itself, some other tavern, or even your cemetery, Brother Athelstan.'

Cranston leaned down and pressed Mother Veritable's shoulder.

'Which of the knights favoured both girls together? Don't glare at me! Which of the knights?'

Cranston plucked up the piece of embroidery and

held it out as if he was about to drop it in the fire. 'Two young women were brutally slain!'

'They all did,' Mother Veritable conceded.

'And what did the girls report? Come on,' Cranston growled. 'You collect tales about your customers.'

'They are as old as you, Sir Jack, so they have their difficulties, particularly the small, fat one, Sir Stephen Chandler.'

'You know he's dead?' Athelstan asked.

Mother Veritable made a rude sound with her lips.

'So, another man has died, Brother. I don't care! Yes, they've all come here. They always asked for Guinevere's daughters. They liked that. They saw the girls as a link with the past.'

'And something else?' Cranston taunted. 'If Guinevere was so smitten by Culpepper, unobtainable to them, they might think that the daughters were sufficient compensation.'

'You know the ways of men, Lord Coroner, better than I do. Now, you must be finished.'

'This custom,' Athelstan demanded, 'of Master Rolles sending for girls?'

'It's very profitable to us both.'

'And they always come back with silver?'

'Usually they do. Sometimes there are disappointments, a rare occasion.'

'And the Benedictine?' Athelstan asked. 'Malachi?'

Mother Veritable shook her head. 'I know nothing of him.'

A short while later Cranston and Athelstan left the house and went up Darkhouse Lane, now well named as the day drew on and a faint river mist began to boil up the alleyways and runnels. Candles glowed in windows and, already, lanterns were slung on doorposts outside houses. The main thoroughfare, however, was still busy. The crowds, in their motley-coloured garb, were eager to buy; trading was drawing to an end, so meat, fish and vegetables were reduced in price. The bailiffs were also busy, parading a set of steps through the streets, proclaiming how a washerwoman, busy with her clothes on the Thames, had slipped off these steps and drowned. The bailiffs declared the steps had been estimated at a third of a mark and, because of the accident, the wood would be sold and the profits go to the Crown. Behind them came a wax chandler sitting backwards on a horse, a leaking pitcher on his head, the dirty water trickling out, the penalty for drawing off water from a public conduit. The bailiffs were accompanied by a set of bagpipe players, their noise deadening all sound. Two madmen, attracted by the noise, cavorted wildly, dirty rags streaming in the stiff breeze from the river.

'Where are we going, Sir John?' Athelstan asked.

'Where do you think?'

Cranston turned to the right and Athelstan groaned as he realised they were going back to the Night in Jerusalem, though he quietly conceded that such a visit was necessary; those gentlemen of Kent were not as innocent and high-minded as they appeared.

They reached the stable yard, Cranston striding across, bellowing for the taverner. Athelstan stared around the open cobbled expanse. The tavern must have been a lordly mansion, with stables, outhouses, granges and barns. These had now been converted for the use of travellers. The hay barn, its doors now concealed by a huge high-sided cart, stood at the far side. Athelstan realised it could be approached from the main doorway of the tavern as well as through the side door and kitchen door, not to mention the various windows. At night the yard would be pitch dark, perhaps lit by a cresset torch, or a brazier, but he could imagine someone slipping through the blackness, crossbow in hand, dagger thrust into his belt, sliding like the Angel of Death through that half-open door and into the hay barn. Inside, a capped lantern would provide the assassin with sufficient light. Beatrice and Clarice would be tired. They would have drunk deep . . . How long would it take to release the cord of the crossbow to send the bolt whirring through the air? At such closeness death would be immediate. The other girl would be confused, the assassin could stride across thrusting the dagger deep. Athelstan pulled his hood up and stared down at the mud-strewn cobbles, shining in the light drizzle which had begun to fall. The murderous act would take no more than a few seconds, faster than a priest pattering through his psalter.

'Well, Athelstan.'

Cranston stood in the tavern doorway, beckoning him over. Athelstan hurried across, grateful for the sweet warmth of the inn. Rolles was busy in the kitchen, but the coroner was most insistent on meeting the knights, and a short while later, Cranston sat at the head of the long walnut table in the solar, Master Rolles, Brother Malachi and the four knights ranged down either side. Athelstan sat at the far end. He brought his writing tray out, uncapped the ink horn and had a sharp quill ready.

'I must protest.' Sir Thomas Davenport spoke up. 'My Lord Coroner, we intended to visit Trinity, guests of the Aldermen at the Guildhall.'

'I couldn't care if the Lord God Almighty was your host,' Cranston snapped. 'I have more questions for you.'

Davenport pulled a sullen face. Sir Reginald Branson, with his long grey hair tied in a queue, made to leave, scraping back his chair, his black and white cloak draped over one arm.

'If you leave, sir, I'll have you arrested for murder.' Cranston pounded the table with a ham-like fist. 'And the same goes for you, Master Rolles, busy as you claim, even if you had Mary and Joseph in the stable outside, though, knowing you, you wouldn't even give them that!'

Cranston's anger stilled all protest.

'Master Rolles, you hire girls from Mother Veritable?'

'I've told you.' The taverner's fat face glistened with sweat; his piggy eyes screwed up in annoyance, he

109

breathed noisily through his nose and gestured at the tapestry. 'A letter left there, a silver coin with the name of the girl wanted.' He drummed his fingers on the tabletop. 'Sometimes that's just left for me, other times I put it there for Mother Veritable's messenger—'

'How many coins?' Athelstan interrupted.

'Whatever the arrangement, it's a deposit of two coins; one for me, one for Mother Veritable.'

'Isn't that against the City ordnances?' Athelstan asked.

'Tell him, Sir John.'

'Southwark lies beyond the jurisdiction of the Corporation. As long as Rolles doesn't actually house the girls in question, he is breaking no law. So, these wenches simply arrive and their customers are waiting?'

'Yes,' Rolles agreed. 'The note will designate where they are to come, to the tap room or to a chamber.'

'Or a hay barn?' Athelstan asked.

'Where is your note,' Cranston asked, 'inviting Beatrice and Clarice?'

'I understand Mother Veritable has destroyed it.'

'You saw them arrive?'

'Yes,' Rolles agreed. 'On the night of the Great Ratting they came into the tap room. They were to meet their customer once that was over, about the second hour after midnight. There are hour candles in the tap room. The girls wouldn't miss such an assignation. I saw them there until just before the fight, when the Judas Man killed Toadflax thinking he was the Misericord.'

'Why are we here?' Sir Laurence Broomhill, slightly shorter than the rest, leaned over the table and glared down at Athelstan.

'You know full well. Would any of you here,' Cranston stared around, 'take an oath that they have never lain with either or both of those slain women?'

Sir Laurence sat back.

'Answer the question.' Cranston pounded the table. 'You come up to London to celebrate what you call the "old days", when you gathered here as Crusaders under the banner of Lord Peter of Cyprus. Every year you return. You lodge here and have Mass said at St Erconwald's. You also visit the brothel, and always ask for Clarice or Beatrice.'

'Is this true?' Brother Malachi asked weakly. 'You still consort with whores?'

'You cannot come to Mass,' Athelstan spoke up. 'You must not take the Eucharist, until you stop such sin, confess and receive absolution.'

The knights were clearly taken aback and stunned into silence.

'In fact,' Athelstan continued, 'I do not want you in my church. You have committed fornication.'

'More importantly for me,' Cranston remarked, 'one, two or all of you may have committed murder. Where were you on the night these girls were killed?'

'We left the tap room.' Sir Maurice Clinton spoke up. 'We left after the Great Ratting. We returned to our chambers.'

'All of you?' Cranston asked.

'Tell the truth,' Brother Malachi said. 'Go on, Sir Laurence.'

The knight rested his elbows on the table, running his fingers through his thinning hair.

'We all returned to our chambers. Brother Malachi came to mine, alarmed by the sound from the fight below. He wanted to know if I would share a cup of wine with him, but I'd gone back downstairs to see what the fray was all about.'

'And so?' Athelstan asked. 'What did you do, Brother Malachi?'

'I went downstairs, to see what had caused the tumult. By then the man was dead, his corpse laid out in the tap room. I went to take the night air in the stable yard. I saw Sir Stephen come back, his cloak all about him. He appeared agitated.' The Benedictine glanced quickly around the table. 'I do not want to betray my comrades. But we must tell Sir John what happened in the tap room.'

'Well?' the coroner demanded.

'During the Great Ratting,' Sir Maurice replied, 'Chandler parted company with us. I saw him arguing with the two whores.'

'You mean he solicited them?'

Sir Maurice nodded. 'They would have nothing to do with him,' he continued. 'They were laughing,

112

pushing him away. He came back sweating, cursing under his breath.'

'Oh *Domine, miserere*! Lord have mercy,' Sir Laurence whispered.

Cranston spread his hands on the table.

'Is it possible,' Davenport asked, 'that Sir Stephen was insulted by those two whores? He may have invited them here but they refused him because they had another assignation.'

'I must confess,' Sir Maurice broke in, 'we have been through Sir Stephen's possessions. He owned a small arbalest, which is now missing.'

Athelstan scrutinised these knights of Kent, powerful lords, men who owned rich estates, warriors of the Cross, who lived secret lives, coming up to London – Athelstan curbed his anger – to roister and carouse. They'd sin secretly in the dark of night then swagger into his church to eat and drink the body and blood of Christ. Oh yes, Athelstan reflected, Sir Stephen, indeed any of these men, would kill a whore in the blink of an eye, out of rage, frustration, or a sense that their famous honour had been besmirched! He stared down the table at Sir Jack, who was also lost in thought; he recalled that the coroner had told him how knights like these, lords of the land, were flinty-eyed, hard of heart and grasping. Little wonder the poor peasants in the shires round London seethed with discontent. Men whispered how there would soon be a rising, led by the Great Community of the Realm. Cranston claimed the revolt would begin in

Kent, no surprise with narrow-souled hypocrites like these lording it in the shire.

'Did any of you go to that barn?' Cranston asked.

'What would I have to do with whores?' The Benedictine raised his right hand and displayed his stunted fingers. 'The work of a scimitar, Sir John. I could not handle a crossbow. Ask any of these good men here.' Malachi's voice was rich with sarcasm. 'I am more a danger to myself with such a weapon than to anyone else.'

'And you, Master Rolles. Where were you?'

The taverner got to his feet and went to the door. He shouted for Tobias who served as cook and cask-man and returned to his chair. A short while later a young man with spiked red hair, a leather apron wrapped about him, came into the solar.

'Tobias, tell the gentlemen here where I was after the Great Ratting.'

The man scratched his face with bloodied fingers, then played with the flesher's knife in the pocket of his apron.

'The fight broke out,' he mumbled. 'Yes, that's right, the fight broke out, but you were busy in the kitchen. By the time you returned, Toadflax was dead. You had the corpse laid out in the tap room, then you returned to the kitchen.'

'Yes,' Rolles declared exasperatedly, 'and what happened then?'

'You told me off for letting some of the pork burn, for not removing it from the spit.'

'And then?'

'You stayed there. Something had gone wrong with the tourt, the brown bread,' Tobias explained. 'It hadn't risen in the oven.'

'Thank you, Master Tobias,' Cranston snapped. 'You can go!'

For a while, the coroner just sat drumming his fingers on the table, watching Athelstan, head bowed, his quill racing across the parchment held down by weights at each corner. The friar was now chronicling everything that had happened. Cranston was glad, for he could make no sense of this chain of events.

'Sir John,' Sir Maurice asserted himself, 'you have mentioned our failings, but what about Sir Stephen? His corpse lies cold and stiffening in an outhouse.'

'For all I know, Sir Stephen could be a murderer,' Cranston retorted. He stopped himself just in time from openly speculating whether Chandler had gone out to the yard last night of his own accord or been sent by his comrades.

'Talking of who was where,' Rolles squirmed in his chair, 'Mother Veritable has been very truthful with you, Sir John. Did she tell you she was here, in the tavern this morning, when Sir Stephen died?'

Athelstan's head came up, his eyes narrowing. Rolles was obviously losing his temper, quietly seething, alarmed at how much Mother Veritable's girl Donata had confessed.

'What are you saying?' Athelstan asked.

'Two of her girls were slain here.' Rolles couldn't

keep the spite out of his voice. 'It was well known that Chandler had custom with them. He was soliciting both last night, whilst she was in the tavern this morning when he was killed.'

Athelstan returned to his writing.

'And there's someone else.' Rolles licked his lips. 'The man sheltering in your church, who calls himself the Misericord.'

'You know him well?' Cranston asked.

'He's a merry rogue,' Rolles conceded. 'He was at the Great Ratting last night. He often comes to this tavern.' He paused, collecting his thoughts. 'He, too, had words with Beatrice and Clarice – that was before he tricked Toadflax into wearing that sheath.'

Athelstan returned to his writing, making careful note of what he heard. Cranston pushed back his chair, rose to his feet and walked down to the window overlooking the garden. The day was dying, the darkness creeping in, the river mist thickening.

'Sir John, are you finished?' Master Rolles called out.

'Is it true,' Cranston asked, not turning round, 'that there were sightings twenty years ago of Richard Culpepper and Guinevere the Golden?'

'As many as leaves on the tree,' Sir Maurice replied. 'A lavish reward was offered. Nothing substantial ever came of it.'

'On that afternoon,' Cranston asked, 'when Culpepper disappeared, did he pack all his belongings?'

'Yes, everything.'

'Including the truth,' Cranston snapped back. 'Gentlemen, we are finished, but none of you are to leave this tavern or Southwark without my permission. Oh.' He smiled falsely at Rolles. 'The dead women's jewellery is to be handed back to Mother Veritable.' He waved a hand. 'As for Chandler's corpse, do what you want.'

They left the Night in Jerusalem. Cranston wanted to go to a cookshop, loudly proclaiming he wished to eat in good company and not with a coven of hypocrites.

'Sir John,' Athelstan pulled up his cowl, 'I would like to go down to the riverside. I want to see the place where the great robbery took place. Do you know it?'

'The Oyster Wharf,' Cranston replied, 'or so common report had it. I also know where we can eat.'

They set off through the streets, now emptying as night fell and a freezing river mist swirled in. Stalls were being put away; only a few egg-sellers, carrying their baskets, shouted 'Ten for a penny!' Cranston led Athelstan through a maze of alleyways and streets, murky and dirty, reeking of all sorts of offal, and back on to the thoroughfare which wound down to the river. They went along Mincing Lane, past a small chantry chapel which, Cranston explained, had been built in memory of the Earl of Pembroke, who had been killed in a tournament on his wedding day. The streets grew noisier as they approached the riverside. The rippers, the gutters of fish, were still trying to sell what produce was left. The weigher of the beam or tron was busy checking the weights and measures for cheese, butter and wax. At last they reached the Oyster Wharf. Further down stood a great windmill; even so, the air reeked with the stench from the nearby tanneries. Fishermen in their hures, shabby caps of sheepswool, were preparing for a night's fishing. Near the steps, the boatmen had brought in their catches of oysters, whelks and mussels, laying their baskets before the Serjeant of the Whelks and the Assayer of the Oysters, two officials who guaranteed the quality of each catch before they were sold at fourpence a bushel.

The officials stood under a leather awning. Cranston and Athelstan joined them, eating oysters and onions, a hog's head serving as a table, whilst the coroner shared out his miraculous wine skin. Further down, young boys with baskets ran about offering salmon, mackerel, haddock, eels and herring at only tuppence a catch. The boys stopped to ridicule a fishwife who had been forced to stand in the stocks for selling whitebait, which had now been draped around her neck. Whilst Cranston chattered to the officials, Athelstan wiped his mouth and walked to the steps leading down to the river. He tried to forget the sounds and smells, so as to imagine this quayside on the night of the great robbery. He went as close as he could to the edge. The river was ebbing, the mist blocked off all view, except for the glow of a torch or lantern horn as some barge made its way down to Westminster. The mist tendrils curled like the cold fingers of a ghost.

'Be careful, Father!' one of the boys shouted.

Athelstan stared down at the green-slimed steps.

'The Lombard treasure arrived,' he murmured. 'It would be unloaded, probably left on the quayside. Culpepper and his companion, helped by the two bargemen, would . . .' He stopped his whispering. 'No,' he reflected, 'Culpepper would have waited until those who had brought the treasure had left. He and his accomplice would then kill the bargemen, load their bodies with stones, and arrange . . .' Athelstan chewed on the corner of his lip. 'No,' he whispered. 'This is all nonsense, I must find out more.'

'What are you thinking, Brother?' Cranston came up beside him, sucking on an oyster.

'I can think of nothing, Sir John, nothing now.'

'I don't think I'll go home,' Cranston declared.

'But the Lady Maud will miss you.'

'I'm going to stay at the Night in Jerusalem, but only after a few more oysters.'

Athelstan patted Sir John on the hand. He made his farewells and, grasping his writing satchel and walking stick, left the quayside.

When he reached St Erconwald's, he found his parish a hive of activity. The Judas Man had lit braziers and his comitatus were grouped round these, warming their hands as they roasted strips of bacon. Athelstan knew better than to object. They had every right to food and warmth on the Crown's business, yet, he smiled to himself, the men hadn't had it all their own way. Apparently the women of the parish had decided to do their washing and, as usual, had laid the wet clothes over the tombstones and the walls of the cemetery. He glimpsed the Judas Man standing near the lychgate and raised a hand. The Judas Man popped a piece of meat into his mouth and turned away. Athelstan shrugged. He entered the cemetery by the small wicker gate at the side and glanced around. The soil here was very thin and it was not unknown for some of the children to play skittles using bones for pins and skulls for balls. He walked along the winding path around the church to the death house. Thaddeus was picking at the grass, whilst God-Bless must have joined the comitatus.

Athelstan went inside to make sure everything was safe. He unlocked the mortuary chest; the parish pall, pickaxe and shovel were still there, as was the rammer used to press corpses down into the soil. He relocked the chest and patted each of the three parish coffins stacked on the three-wheel trestle. God-Bless was keeping everything tidy. As he left the death house, Athelstan noticed two chickens busy pecking at the earth and wondered if God-Bless had stolen them or if they had just wandered in. He went across, unlocked the coffin door and entered the church. The usual smell of ancient walls, incense and candle wax greeted him. In the sanctuary a candle glowed, as did tapers before the small Lady Chapel. Athelstan walked carefully round. The scurrying of mice echoed from shadowy corners.

'You shouldn't be here, little ones,' Athelstan murmured. 'Bonaventure the killer will find you!'

'Who is it?' the Misericord called, all alarmed. 'Who's there?'

'*Pax et bonum*,' Athelstan called back. 'Do not concern yourself, it's only Brother Athelstan.'

He walked back up the nave through the rood screen, and paused. The wood smelt freshly polished and he remembered how the previous day five of his parishioners, who called themselves the 'Brotherhood of the Rood Light', had cleaned and polished the oaken screen. The sanctuary lay in darkness, except for the candle on the high altar and the red lamp which showed where the pyx containing the Sacred Host hung from its silver chain. A shadow moved beside the altar.

'You can come out, sir.'

The Misericord stepped into the light and sat on the top step.

'I'm hungry, Brother, I thought you would never return.'

'I'm sorry,' Athelstan replied. 'I was longer than I thought. Murder is a vexing business. So stay there, sir, and I shall come back with food, a good jug of wine, some meat and bread, not to mention a piece of cheese. Afterwards we shall talk about what part, if any, you played in these terrible killings.'

'Brother . . . !'

'Oh!' Athelstan came back. 'I believe a coffer was brought here from the Night in Jerusalem?'

'What's happening?' the Misericord pleaded. 'I heard rumours. When I went out to relieve myself, Pike the ditcher said there'd been hideous murders.'

'Did he now? But where's the coffer?'

'Watkin put it over there. He and Ranulf brought it in.'

Athelstan walked across the sanctuary. The coffer was under the offertory table. He drew it out and, ignoring the Misericord's demands for his food to be brought quickly, walked back down the nave and out through the open door, where he put the coffer down. The Judas Man was sitting on the bottom step. He turned and pointed at the chest.

'That was brought earlier. I hoped it would be safe in there.'

'It has three locks,' Athelstan replied, 'and the Misericord is no fool, and neither are you. If a sanctuary man steals from the Church, or interferes with anything, the law says he can be handed over to the sheriff's men.'

The Judas Man bit at the quick on his thumb. 'I'll have him soon enough.'

'Are you always so zealous in hunting men down?'

'You preach, I hunt,' came the tart reply.

Athelstan pointed to the gold ring on the chain around the Judas Man's neck.

'The keepsake of a lady?'

'My betrothed.'

'She died?'

'No, I found her with another man. I killed them

122

both.' The Judas Man drew his head back, staring at Athelstan from under heavy-lidded eyes. 'She meant everything to me. I found them out in the woods. He drew a knife, I claimed self-defence.'

'And since then you have been a hunter? And your soul, Judas Man?'

'I leave such things to the likes of you and God. Now, you have not come to question me about a ring.'

'Are you sure you know nothing about those two women murdered at the Night in Jerusalem?'

The Judas Man shook his head. 'I know nothing about that. I was fighting for my own life.'

Athelstan stared across the cemetery. He noticed how the Judas Man had divided the comitatus to keep the entire outside of the church under view, his own parishioners were now clustered around a makeshift brazier, enjoying the meat and ale.

'Will you join us, Father?' the Judas Man asked.

Athelstan picked up the coffer and shook his head. 'Will you pray, Judas Man?'

The hunter of men made to turn away, then paused and glanced over his shoulder.

'I'll talk to God, priest, when He talks to me.'

Chapter 5

Sir Laurence Broomhill was half asleep. He was drowsy yet aware of being in his chamber at the Night in Jerusalem. He heartily wished he was back in his comfortable manor house on the road to Gravesend, but then again, none of them could have anticipated what had happened. Sir Laurence, like the rest, had drunk deeply that afternoon and lurched back to his chamber, La Morte D'Arthur, with its coloured tapestries exuberantly depicting the Great Hero's struggle with the black-armoured Mordred. The picture of knights helmeted and visored, swords and shields raised, provoked vivid memories of the battles in Outremer, outside Alexandria.

For a while Sir Laurence recalled those arrows, wrapped in flaming cotton, shooting through the air. Scaling ladders all ablaze, the men on them, small black figures trapped by the inferno, dropping like pieces of soot to the ground below. The hideous song of the mangonels, catapults, the ominous battering of the rams, the creak of siege towers and that chilling climb to the parapets . . . Sir Laurence had been there, one of the first, eager to seek the absolution promised, in the heart of the fight, all around him the hiss of the sword, the clang of the axe and the dire music of those arrows let loose against the fiery sky before dropping like a deadly rain. On either side of Sir Laurence men went down as they fought to advance the great white banner with its red cross further along the battlements. They were all maddened, the noise of battle pulsing fiercely through their blood, made worse by the fever brought on by the pitiless heat and myriad flies. Their opponents, men in turbans and billowing cloaks, fell like scythed corn before them, blood splattering out.

Sir Laurence opened his eyes. Even now he could recall their snarling faces as well as those of the innocent, cut down as the Crusaders advanced deeper into the city: the young, the women, left broken with sightless eyes and blood-dripping mouths. Sir Laurence would never forget the exquisite beauty of those fountain courts, all awash with red water. Gardens, heavy with scent, turned into battlefields, the blood-chilling screams, and afterwards? Sitting on ebony-inlaid chairs, sleeping on low-cushioned divans, drinking sherbet and wine, stuffing his mouth with dried dates, and clothing himself in the soft fabrics found in the chests of the treasure houses of their enemies. Sir Laurence sighed deeply. Whatever the bloodshed, he, and the other Knights of the Golden Falcon, had taken that victory as a sign of God's favour. They had all survived, returned home to enjoy the fruits of their endeavours.

Sir Laurence stiffened at the knock on the door. He pulled himself up and swung himself off the bed He walked across the room. He was about to draw the bolts when he glimpsed the scrap of parchment pushed beneath the door. He snatched it up, read it quickly and paled at what was written. He strode across and swiftly pushed the small scroll deep into the brazier, losing it amongst the burning coals. For a while he paced up and down, wondering whether to rouse the rest, only to reject this idea. The note had been quite explicit, promising to reveal the truth behind Chandler's death and warning him to come alone. Sir Laurence pulled on his boots, fastened on his war belt, took his cloak and went out down the stairs. The passageways were fairly deserted. The tap room had yet to fill for the evening revelry, whilst it would be some time before he and the rest of the knights gathered in the solar for a feast of roast swan and whatever other delicacies the taverner could offer.

Sir Laurence paused. He stared across the tap room, watching a scullion mop at a table. All pleasure had gone out of this visit, with Chandler's death, and that olive-skinned Dominican and his harsh remarks about sin and absolution. He reached the cellar door, lifted the catch and went down into the musty darkness.

Candles glowed in the gaps between the old red brick-work. It was still frighteningly dark, made worse by the scampering and squealing of vermin. Sir Laurence reached the bottom step; all was dark, except the candle which was glowing at the far end. He screwed up his eyes; was it a lantern or a lamp? He could make out the tuns and vats stacked at either side, and the wine-soaked path between.

'Who's there?' His voice echoed. His hand fell to his dagger. Perhaps he should go back? The cellar had now fallen very silent. The rats and mice were cowering in the dark, as if they too were aware of what evil might lurk there. Sir Laurence stepped down, and his booted foot hit something hard. In a few heartbeats he heard a click, a snap, and his leg shattered as the cruel claws gripped and dug deep. He screamed as tongues of pain shot up his leg, forcing him back, coursing like flames through his body. He tried to move but could not, and in his agony he recalled the lush papyrus groves along the great river near Alexandria, those huge water beasts with their long snouts and cruel teeth which could drag a man down, sever a limb with a snap of their jaws. Was this happening? Sir Laurence found he couldn't move at all. The pain was intense. That dreadful chill, the words of the Dominican echoing about sin . . . Had the past leaped forward like a panther to punish him? Sir Laurence screamed as a fresh wave of excruciating pain swept through him . . .

*   *   *

Athelstan returned to his house to find the kitchen and scullery scrubbed and cleaned. Benedicta, who had a key, had also left a pie and freshly baked doucettes. The fire was banked, fresh green logs on the top to keep the flames down, but the heat from the charcoal beneath was refreshing. Bonaventure, stretched out, lifted his head disdainfully as the Dominican came in. Athelstan cut the pie and took pewter, tranchers, horn spoons and napkins across to the church, telling the Misericord to wait a little longer. Then he visited the stables where Philomel, belly full, was snoring loudly.

Athelstan locked his house and stared up at the church tower. The mist was spreading, rolled in by a biting breeze from the river. In a few hours it would hang like a thick blanket, shrouding everything. He looked up at the sky. The stars seemed so distant. He would have loved to go up and spend the last hours of the night watching the stars wheel and wondering if that comet he'd recently glimpsed would be seen again. Athelstan loved to spend such evenings suspended, as he had described it to Cranston, between heaven and earth, watching the glory of God, whilst Bonaventure sprawled out beside him. Did the earth move? Athelstan wondered. Or was it the stars? He had read certain new treatises collected by his mother house at Blackfriars. Was Aristotle right? Did the planets give off music as they turned? What force, apart from the power of God, held stars in their position? Yet why did comets fall?

He felt a movement against his leg and stared down at Bonaventure. 'Great assassin of the alleyways,' he whispered. He stood for a few seconds watching the fire of the braziers and half listened to the men crouched around him. Their raucous singing made him smile. Watkin must have drunk deeply. He would only sing when his belly was full of ale. Athelstan hurried back to the church. He arranged the firing of a small brazier and filled two chafing dishes with burning charcoal. Once they were warming the sanctuary, he and the Misericord sat either side of the rood screen door, leaning against the wood as they shared out the food and wine. The Misericord ate ravenously, gulping the pie and two doucettes even before Athelstan had finished Grace. Afterwards, one hand over a chafing dish, the other holding a goblet, the Misericord stared down the nave.

'How old is this place, Brother?'

'Some say two, others three hundred years old. A few even claim it was built before the Conqueror came.'

'Does it hold anything valuable?'

Athelstan recalled the ring and quickly felt his wallet, his fingers brushing the small case.

'It contains very little,' he conceded. 'According to canon law we should only have a missal, a complete set of vestments, a fine linen cape, a pyx on a silver chain and a corpus case.'

'What's one of them?'

'The leather pouch in which you put the pyx. You have never stolen from a church?'

The Misericord shook his head. He was about to say something but changed his mind.

'Look.'

The Misericord pointed at the mist now curling under the doorway.

Athelstan had lit two of the wall torches but, with the mist seeping in and the shadows shifting, they made the church even more sombre.

'Do ghosts walk here?'

'Perhaps,' Athelstan teased.

The Misericord gave a low groan.

'Don't worry,' Athelstan assured him. 'Ghosts can't come into a church. Watkin claims that sometimes, early in the morning, a young man with dark red-rimmed eyes in a snow-white face can be seen on the top step outside, one arm around a dog. The parishioners claim it was a young apprentice who hanged himself on a yew tree in the cemetery. And of course,' Athelstan continued, 'a former parish priest dabbled in black magic. He was called Fitzwolfe. I met him once, a tortured mind with a soul as black as midnight. Oh, and by the way,' Athelstan pointed further down the church, 'over there, see the leper squint? Once upon a time a leper hospital stood nearby. The poor souls who lived there were not allowed to come into church, so if they wanted to hear Mass, they looked through the squint holes in the church wall from outside. The ghost of a poor leper woman is sometimes seen kneeling there. She has fiery red hair and liverish scaly skin. She is supposed to have mocked the Mass, but

I think that is only a story meant to frighten the children.'

The Misericord refilled his goblet.

'And what ghosts do you harbour?' Athelstan asked. 'I know you are a scholar and a singer, so what brings you here?'

'I was a member of the Society of Pui. The name comes from the French town Puy-en-Vale. It is a society dedicated to music. Its purpose . . .' The Misericord screwed up his eyes. 'Oh yes, that's what its charter says: "For the increasing of joy and love and, to that end, the spreading of mirth, peace, harmony and joyousness, that they all be maintained."' The Misericord opened his eyes. 'I hail from the Halls of Cambridge. I was a good singer, a poet . . . The society used to meet in St Martin's in the City. You had to pay sixpence for admission, and every year you had to compose a new song. A contest was held, and the winner would be crowned with a gilded chaplet.'

'And what happened?'

'Well, when we met, one of us was given money, to buy a fifty-pound candle of pure beeswax. On one occasion I was given the money, but I had fallen on hard times so I bought a cheap candle and filled the centre with fat, turpentine, cobbler's wax and resin.'

'Oh no!' Athelstan groaned.

'Oh yes!' the Misericord declared. 'I brought the candle back and gave it to our leader. When he was halfway down the nave of the church, the candle . . . well, the flame reached the turpentine and fat, and it all disappeared in a shower of flame. I was expelled from the society.' He shrugged. 'And one thing led to another: thievery, trickery, filching, clipping coins. At first I was successful, until the sheriff's men discovered who I was. I was proclaimed a wolfshead and went into hiding.'

'Why?' Athelstan asked. 'You have a keen mind and nimble wits.'

The Misericord put his face into his hands. He muttered something inaudible.

'Why are you hiding now?' Athelstan asked.

'I don't know.' The Misericord took his hands away. 'I'm a cunning man. I have deceived many. It's happened before. Some powerful official whose wife I have bedded, or a merchant I have tricked. It's not the first time that I have had the hunters of men tracking me as if I am a deer.'

'And this time?'

The Misericord shook his head.

'Whoever it is,' he confessed, 'the malice runs deep. The Judas Man has pursued me all over Southwark. I know him by reputation. He had two of my friends hanged.'

'And last night?' Athelstan asked. 'At the Great Ratting?'

'I had to be there. I know all about your parish, Brother Athelstan. Amongst those who live in the twilight world, Ranulf the rat-catcher has a fearsome reputation. I decided to wager on him and won a good purse.'

'But you suspected the Judas Man would follow?'

'Oh yes, that bastard is worse than a hunting mastiff. So I decided to play a trick. I looked around the tap room and glimpsed poor Toadflax, with his red hair and pale face. He had more than a passing resemblance to me, so I paid him a coin and gave him one of my misericord daggers. I didn't intend the poor man to be killed. I thought he would delay the Judas Man.'

'Did you see the Judas Man enter the tavern?'

'I knew he was there but I hid in the shadows. I was determined about my wager.'

'Did you see him speak to anybody?' Athelstan asked. 'You must have wondered who had hired him.'

'I don't care who hired him. Whoever it is cannot catch me. It's the dog he's hired which worries me.'

'And you saw the fight?'

'I saw it begin, but then fled.'

'Do you know Master Rolles?'

'Know him? He is a distant kinsman. He often shelters me. He told me to be careful.'

'So you often stay at the Night in Jerusalem?'

'Yes, out in the stables or the hay barn.'

'And the two girls who were killed?' Athelstan pressed on with his questioning. 'Beatrice and Clarice?'

The Misericord glanced away and shrugged.

'I know them by sight. Rumour has it that they were garrotted.'

'No, they were killed by crossbow and dagger.'

'I did see them talk to that fat knight.' The Misericord glanced at Athelstan out of the corner of his eye.

'Pike's a good source of knowledge – there's been another killing at the tavern, hasn't there? Anyway,' he continued, 'that pricked my memory. The fat knight was talking to the two girls. They were teasing him how they had enough custom for the night, and he would have to wait.' The Misericord blew his cheeks out. 'That's all I know, Brother. I watched the Great Ratting, collected my purse and fled. I tried to cross London Bridge but the Judas Man had his spies there. The hue and cry was raised . . .' His voice trailed off.

Athelstan rose and cleared away the tranchers and spoons. Bonaventure slid through the half-open corpse door to begin his night's hunting. Athelstan was about to retire when a clamour broke out at the main door. He hurried down and removed the bar. Two women stood there. Behind them, some distance away, the Judas Man and the bailiffs watched carefully.

'Good evening, Brother.' The voice was cultured and sweet-sounding. 'May we come in?'

Athelstan stepped back. He thought the two women were cowled and hooded, but as they came through the doorway, he realised they were both dressed in the heavy brown robes and starched white wimples of nuns. The speaker was young and comely, smooth-faced, with wide-spaced gentle grey eyes. She wore a silver Celtic cross around her neck, a plain white girdle around her waist. The other was much older, wearing a ring on her vein-streaked left hand. Athelstan realised the younger was a novice, whilst the older was a fully professed member of the Minoresses from the

Franciscan convent to the north of the Tower near Poor Jewry. The younger one gestured to her companion to stay near the door, whilst she stretched out her hands to exchange the kiss of peace with Athelstan.

'My lady?' Athelstan gently kissed her on each cheek.

'This is Sister Catherine.' The grey eyes smiled. 'Whilst I am Edith Travisa.'

'I beg your pardon?'

'I am Edith Travisa.'

Athelstan suddenly recalled the Misericord's true name.

'You are . . . ?'

'Edith!'

The Misericord came running down the church. Athelstan hastily closed the door and pushed the bolt back. He turned around. Edith and the Misericord were clasped in a tight embrace. The novice held the young man like a mother would a son, her white fingers gently patting him on the back.

'Edith, you shouldn't have come.' The Misericord stepped back. 'Brother Athelstan, this is my sister.'

'I think we had best leave the doorway,' Athelstan urged. 'Sister Catherine, are you comfortable?'

The old nun gave a gap-toothed smile.

'I'll stay here,' she said in a sing-song tone. 'Mother Superior gave us an hour. We have left our porter outside. He'll see us safely back.'

'Do you want something to eat or drink?'

'There's no time, there's no time.' Edith's voice was stern and the old nun nodded in agreement.

Athelstan escorted the brother and sister back up into the sanctuary. He brought a chair for the novice whilst he and the Misericord sat on the rood-screen step.

'I heard you were taken,' she began.

'I'm not taken,' the Misericord declared, 'and you shouldn't have come here. I'll escape, something will happen.'

'I've brought you some—'

'There's no need,' the Misericord interrupted. 'Brother Athelstan, would you leave us alone?'

'Only if you tell me what this is all about?'

'Edith and I,' the Misericord's haste was apparent, 'are full brother and sister. Our parents lived near Cripplegate. They were clothiers. They died when the plague returned. Other relatives, too, perished. I have to look after Edith. Now, she was betrothed to Henry Sturny—'

'Ah, yes!' Athelstan interrupted. 'They are cloth merchants in Cheapside.'

'Henry loves Edith, Edith loves Henry, but there was the question of the dowry.' The Misericord took a deep breath. 'I wasted my parents' wealth. Now, Brother, you know the reason for my mischief. I placed Edith in the care of the good Minoresses, and have spent every waking moment of the last three years trying to raise her dowry. Five hundred pounds sterling in all.'

Athelstan could tell by the way this cunning man

was staring at his sister how much he loved her. He made to go away, but turned back.

'Do you know any of these knights, with their rather grand title of the Golden Falcon? They'd be known to you by their name and status in the shire of Kent.'

The Misericord blinked and cleared his throat. 'I have,' he chose his words carefully, 'done business with them.'

'You mean you've tricked them?'

'What is this?' Edith interrupted.

'Your brother's usual depredations,' Athelstan explained. 'You do realise he is well known to every law officer south of the River Trent?'

Edith coloured with embarrassment.

'Well, sir,' Athelstan continued. 'Answer my question and I'll leave you alone.'

'I have taken a hare for the pot and a pheasant from their fields,' the Misericord confessed. 'I have also sold all manner of things to their villagers and tenants.'

'Do they have a grievance against you?'

'They may have.'

The Misericord's eyes shifted, and Athelstan knew there was more meat to his admission than the few scraps he had thrown. The Dominican leaned down.

'You think you're safe,' he warned, 'but you are not. Those are very powerful men, warriors, land owners, who would see you swinging from a branch and not blink an eye. Are any of them your enemies?'

'I had a dalliance with one of their daughters.'

'And?'

'Some of their womenfolk, but I forget who. It was some years ago. Brother, that is all I shall say.'

Athelstan sketched a blessing in his direction and walked down the church. He talked to Sister Catherine, a kindly, garrulous old soul, about her own girlhood, how she had been raised in Southwark and had often visited St Erconwald's. Oh yes, she certainly remembered Fitzwolfe, the demon priest, and talked in a hushed whisper about his dabbling in the black arts. Athelstan, with his back to the sanctuary, half listened, ears strained. The echoes in the church were very good, a fact Athelstan always tried to remember when he listened to his parishioners' confessions. Edith and her brother had begun their conversation in whispers, but their discussion had spilled into a quarrel, and their voices were raised. Athelstan was sure he heard the name Mother Veritable mentioned. Sister Catherine chatted on about how Fitzwolfe was supposed to have sacrificed a black hen at night and had committed other blasphemies in the darkness of the night. Athelstan smiled and nodded his head. The conversation at the top of the church had now returned to whispers, and eventually Edith, eyes sparkling, cheeks flushed, came tripping down the aisle, hands concealed in the voluminous sleeves of her gown. She stopped before the friar and bowed.

'Brother Athelstan, I thank you for your kindness to my brother and myself. Now I must leave, as the night is drawing on . . .'

Distracted, she stepped around him. Sister Catherine caught her by the arm, and when Athelstan unbarred the door, they both slipped through and down the steps. Athelstan closed and locked the door behind him. He returned to the rood screen, eager to question the Misericord, but the fugitive was now lying in the sanctuary fast asleep, or pretending to be. Athelstan crossed himself, left by the side door, locking it behind him, and walked into the night.

'Who was that?'

Athelstan spun round. The Judas Man was standing almost behind him.

'This is God's Acre,' Athelstan snapped, 'church land. You should not be slipping about like a thief in the night.'

'Who was that woman?'

'None of your business,' Athelstan replied, stepping closer. 'You are truly determined to bring that man to justice, aren't you?'

'I'm being paid well.'

'By whom?'

'I don't know,' the Judas Man grinned. 'If I did, I would certainly ask for more. By the way, where's your cat?'

'In the church,' Athelstan gestured with his head, 'hunting for mice. He can leave by the sacristy door.'

'Your cat and I have a lot in common.'

'No, sir, you do not,' Athelstan replied. 'My cat hunts to eat. You . . .' Athelstan played with the cord around his waist. 'You, sir, you love it. It helps fill the dark void in your own soul, doesn't it? A way of exorcising your demons. I bid you goodnight.'

Athelstan returned to his house, locking the door behind him. It had fallen cold. He built up the fire, plucked some of the charcoal from it, filled the warming pan and took this up to the bed loft. He pulled back the blankets and the linen sheets beneath. The straw mattress underneath felt cold, icy cold. Athelstan put the warming pan carefully under the blankets and went back down the ladder. He felt agitated and restless. He had spent the day dealing not only with hideous murder, but with people who hid their sins behind lies and conceits. The Misericord had been less than truthful, whilst the presence of the Judas Man was oppressive and menacing.

Athelstan went to the scullery and, from the small pantry, brought out a loaf, some cheese and a pot of butter. He half filled a cup of wine and sat in front of the fire, trying to make sense of the day's happenings. He recalled the small coffer taken from Sir Stephen's bedchamber. He unlocked this and emptied the contents on to the table, and was about to examine them when there was a knocking at the door.

'By St Michael and all his angels,' Athelstan whispered, 'is there no peace?'

He drew back the bolts, half expecting to see the Judas Man; instead, a young woman, hood pulled over her head, stood just beyond the light, and beyond her another figure hidden by the darkness.

'What is it?' Athelstan kept the door only slightly open.

'Brother, don't you recognise me?' The cloak was pulled back.

'Why, it's Donata!' Athelstan greeted the young woman he had met at Mother Veritable's.

'Brother,' she pleaded, 'may I come in? I am freezing cold and frightened. I mean you no harm. Look.' She turned to the person behind her, then came towards Athelstan carrying a small coffer. 'I've brought you a present. I didn't want to leave Beatrice's and Clarice's prized possessions with that old harridan.'

Athelstan took it. 'And who is that with you?'

'My name is Jocelyn.'

The young man stepped out of the darkness. He was tall and thin, but his face was open and kindly under unruly black hair. Athelstan caught the smell of sweaty leather.

'I'm a journeyman from Colchester,' Jocelyn explained. 'I deal in leather goods.' He pointed back into the darkness. 'I have tethered my sumpter pony just outside the lych gate – one of your parishioners said he would guard it.'

Athelstan liked the look of the young man, whilst Donata was clearly agitated.

'You had best come in.'

They stepped into the light. Athelstan barred the door behind them and ushered them to the table, where he served them some oatmeal, already prepared for the morning, and two small pots of beer drawn from the barrel in the scullery. They were both hungry. Athelstan sat at the top of the table between them. Bonaventure scratched at the door and was also let in to bask in front of the fire.

'A busy night,' Athelstan murmured, 'but why are you here?'

'I'm fleeing Mother Veritable's,' Donata splurted out. 'Jocelyn loves me and I love him. We are going to Colchester. We shall be married in St Luke's Church.'

'No, you are not going to Colchester,' Athelstan smiled, 'you are fleeing to Colchester; you're indentured to Mother Veritable. Though,' he added hastily, 'I agree with what you are doing. But why?'

Jocelyn stretched across the table and grasped his beloved's hand.

'I can see you are in love,' Athelstan remarked, 'and what you are doing is right.' He stared at the journeyman. 'I have your word that you will act honourably?'

'On my soul, Brother. We shall be married before Advent. We will exchange vows at the church door.'

'I want to go,' Donata explained. 'Mother Veritable is truly wicked. She takes our souls and sells our bodies. Oh, we live in comfort, but we are at the beck and call of any man with his belly full of ale and his heart full of lust.'

The young woman rubbed her eyes.

'I'm tired of the violence,' she whispered, 'of the searching fingers and foul mouths.'

'What made you decide now?' Athelstan asked.

143

'Beatrice and Clarice's deaths – murders.' She looked directly at him. 'I love Jocelyn, Brother, I want children,' she clutched her stomach, 'here, in my womb. I don't want to drink Mother Veritable's potions and powders. I don't want to grow old raddled with disease, or die in some hay barn, my throat slashed from ear to ear, or stabbed in some stinking alleyway. I don't want the silk and the costly perfumes, or men looking at me as if I am a horse at Smithfield.'

'You are in love but you are also frightened?' Athelstan asked.

The young woman nodded.

'Mother Veritable found out about Beatrice and Clarice. How they had some secret plan to amass their own wealth and flee her house.'

'Just like their mother?'

'Yes, just like their mother,' Donata agreed. 'Mother Veritable was all in a rage – shouting dire threats.'

'What was this plan?' Athelstan asked.

Donata shook her head. 'I don't truly know, but I think that cunning man the Misericord was involved.'

'That's not what Mother Veritable said this morning.'

'She was lying. Those knights lusted after the two girls. I have seen them visit the house. It was always the same, Beatrice and Clarice, either individually or together.'

'So Mother Veritable hates the Misericord?'

'I think so, Brother, but I don't know why.'

'Could she have hired the Judas Man?' Athelstan

asked. 'You've heard of him. He's outside guarding the doors of my church.'

'Everybody knows about him,' Donata agreed. 'Mother Veritable may have hired him.' She gave a great sigh. 'That's why I was allowed out tonight. I was sent to comfort him, invite him to Mother Veritable's solar. So I arranged to meet Jocelyn.' She pulled back her cloak. 'I left in what I was wearing. I had to seize this opportunity. I shall not return.'

'Was Mother Veritable at the Great Ratting?' Athelstan asked.

'It's possible.'

'Could she have killed those two girls?'

'Mother Veritable is violent.' Jocelyn spoke up. 'I visited her house, that's how I met Donata. I have seen her with cudgel and knife. Brother, she is ferocious as any mercenary.'

'So why have you come to me?' Athelstan asked. He took the young woman's hand, still cold, and gently caressed her fingers.

'I want your absolution, Brother. I want to confess my sins.'

Athelstan let go of her hand.

'You already have.' He raised his own hand in blessing. 'And I absolve you in the name of the Father, the Son and the Holy Spirit.'

'Is it as simple as that, Brother?'

'As simple as that,' Athelstan agreed.

'Aren't you supposed to give me a penance?'

'You've already done that,' Athelstan pushed back his

chair, 'but I'll give you a fresh one: leave Southwark, never come back. Cling to Jocelyn, love him, close the door on the past, lock and bolt it . . . But there's something else, isn't there?'

The young woman gnawed at her lip.

'You've left in your shift,' Athelstan joked, 'with just a cloak and a pair of sandals. You need money, don't you?'

'I have some,' Jocelyn spoke up, 'but Donata was insistent that she ask you for help. She said your eyes were kind.'

'Is that why you brought the coffer?' Athelstan asked.

Donata shook her head. 'No, that's my gift. Beatrice and Clarice were my friends, that's all that is truly left of them. They loved this casket, I don't know why. Mother Veritable shouldn't have it.'

Athelstan stared at the small coffer with its faded blue leather cover and the black Celtic crosses painted there. It was certainly old, its locks broken, the lid not too secure, whilst the painted leather covering was faded and chipped. Athelstan tipped back the lid; the coffer was empty.

'Why were Beatrice and Clarice so attached to this?'

'I don't know, Brother. They said it was a keepsake and entrusted it to me. They must not have wanted Mother Veritable to know they had it, but,' she rubbed the side of her head, 'if they had it so long, she must have known.'

Donata blinked away tears.

'Brother, I'm sorry, but you can help me more than I can help you.'

Athelstan got to his feet, went up to his bed loft and, from its hiding place, brought out a small purse. He came back down and thrust this into the young woman's hand.

'Can you tell me, before you leave, how Beatrice and Clarice intended to escape Mother Veritable?'

'I don't know, I truly don't. All I know is that the Misericord may have been involved.'

'Would Mother Veritable resort to murder to keep such girls?'

'Of course, Brother, she said they were worth more than a bag of gold.'

'And she would kill them as a warning to the rest?'

Donata got to her feet. 'Brother, I thank you, and to answer your question, yes, that's why I am fleeing now. I must go,' she pleaded. 'Time is short.'

Athelstan opened the door and the lovers slipped into the night, whispering their farewells and thanks. Athelstan closed the door and bolted it, crossed himself and said a small prayer that both would be well.

He returned to the contents of Sir Stephen Chandler's casket and eagerly sifted amongst them. There was a smell of mint from the quilted sachets placed there. The contents were personal possessions, relics of Sir Stephen's past: a dark blue pennant, neatly folded, displaying a golden falcon, wings outstretched, talons curved to strike; a key; a Turkish dagger with a jewelled hilt in a purple silver sheath; a small reliquary, allegedly containing a piece of the True Cross; a velvet purse, heavy with gold and silver coins; a small Crucifix; a pouch of sand; two exquisite mother-of-pearls; scraps of parchment; a calf-skin-bound ledger and a cream-coloured roll of parchment. Athelstan scrutinised these. The first contained the accounts of Sir Stephen's estates, showing income and expenditure, all neatly entered alongside each other. A quick survey proved how prosperous Sir Stephen was – the sale of livestock, corn, hay, fish and timber, not to mention the income from rents and leases as well as certain mercantile investments.

'Truly a finger in every pie,' Athelstan murmured.

The expenditure was equally lavish: offerings for Masses; the foundation of a chantry chapel in a Canterbury church; gifts to retainers at Christmas, spring, midsummer and Michaelmas; precious cloths brought from Flanders; furnishings, the work of craftsmen in London, Canterbury and Dover. The beautiful roll of parchment, soft and wrapped in strips of red silk, was a draft of Sir Stephen's will. The writing was that of a professional scribe, the Latin that of a scholar, and its clauses, Athelstan concluded, the work of some high-ranking lawyer. According to this, Sir Stephen had left most of his estate and wealth to his children. Only one thing was left to his colleagues, namely this very coffer and all it contained.

The Dominican pushed the documents away and stared at Bonaventure, curled up comfortably on the floor. 'Why,' he murmured to himself, 'would

Sir Stephen bring these documents with him? His accounts, yes, but why his will?'

Athelstan cleared the table and took out his own writing tray. He studied the memorandum he'd written so quickly during Sir John's interrogation at the tavern. From outside echoed the muffled cries of the Judas Man's retinue, now settling down for the night.

Athelstan marshalled his thoughts.

Item Toadflax's death? An unfortunate accident, death by misadventure Cranston would rule. But what does that prove? That the Judas Man had not been given the fullest description and so was easily confused. A subtle trick by the Misericord which showed both how cunning and suspicious he was.

Item The murder of the two whores.

Athelstan paused – he felt guilty. He crossed out the word 'whores' and wrote 'women'.

Who invited Beatrice and Clarice to the Great Ratting? The way they were summonsed was well known, so the girls were neither suspicious nor wary. Accordingly, they must have known that if they were invited to Master Rolles' tavern they would do business, otherwise they would have not refused Chandler. But who had asked for them? One of the other knights? The Judas Man? Master Rolles? Even the Misericord? But why should the Judas Man or Master Rolles murder them? The Misericord? Had these two young women tricked him and so paid the price? Most unlikely; the Misericord was a rogue but hardly a killer. Mother Veritable? A woman with a midnight soul, cruel and ruthless; was she so angry at these two young women plotting to escape that she killed them? But why should the whore queen remove the source of such rich profits? The knights?

Athelstan rubbed his nose with the end of the quill.

All of these, or one of them, could be the killer, but why? Are the murders of these two young women linked to the mystery of their mother's disappearance?

Athelstan suppressed a shiver. 'Like time repeating itself,' he whispered. Guinevere the Golden had tried to escape, only to disappear. Athelstan nursed a deep suspicion that the poor woman had been killed. Now the same fate had befallen her daughters.

Item The death of Sir Stephen Chandler? He was a fat, prosperous knight preparing to bathe himself and enjoy a cup of claret. Who poisoned that wine? Not the jug, but the cup. Which means that the assassin must have entered that chamber and mixed a powerful poison either just before or just after the wine was poured. Master Rolles? No, too obvious. So who?

Athelstan closed his eyes and tried to imagine that chamber. If someone came in, they would have to act very quickly to place powder in a goblet whilst that sharp-eyed knight was preparing for his bath. One mistake, the smallest of errors, and the murderer would have trapped himself.

So how was it done? And what did Sir Stephen feel so guilty about? Did he kill those young women? Had he been out in the yard with his crossbow, which has now gone missing? Did his quarrel with Beatrice and Clarice during the Great Ratting spill over into violence?
Item The great robbery which took place twenty years ago. Was that just history or did it play a vital role in these grisly occurrences?

Athelstan was beginning to believe there was a connection. He looked up, and from outside came the haunting cry of an owl. The Dominican recalled a lecture given by Prior Anselm on how unforgiven sin, ancient and reeking, never died, but lurked in the undergrowth of life, ready to trap you, to bring you down. Was that happening now? Some twenty years after the Lombard treasure disappeared, along with the boatmen and those two young knights from Kent? Were such ancient sins flocking back like carrion crows to pick over the bones of the present?

Athelstan put his quill down and carefully reread what he had written. One thing did puzzle him about that robbery so many years ago. Why had only two knights been chosen to guard the treasure? And why those two? He rose from the table, stretched and went to kneel beside Bonaventure. The cat hardly stirred. Athelstan crossed himself and, looking up at the Crucifix nailed to the wall, began to recite his evening prayers, concluding with the De Profundis for his brother Francis and his parents. Athelstan tried to ignore the sins of others as he concentrated on his own, and strove to make reparation for them: the meeting with those knights who had fought so many years ago reminded him of how he had lured Francis into the armies of the King and taken him to France only to be killed, coming back to break his parents' hearts with the news about the death of their beloved younger son. Athelstan leaned back on his heels. Such sins, forgiven or not, never left him.

His mind drifted back to the Oyster Wharf and the night the treasure had been stolen, when so many lives had changed for ever. Athelstan prided himself on his logic, on the way he argued a case based on evidence. He was wary of so-called mystical theories and spurious spiritual feelings. Nevertheless, although he fought the temptation, he could not avoid the conclusion that now, in Southwark, at that tavern the Night in Jerusalem, the sins of the past had lunged back to haunt the living.

Chapter 6

Sir John Cranston, Coroner of the City of London, sat in his court chamber at the Guildhall overlooking Cheapside. He had arrived just before dawn resplendent in his grey hose and quilted jacket of dark murrey lined with silver piping over a cambric shirt laced high under the chin. He sat in his throne-like chair behind the great oaken table on the dais at the far end of his chamber. On his left, a copy of the *Statutes and Ordinances of the City*; on his right, his broad leather war belt. The writing tray in front of him contained sheets of vellum, sharpened quills, a razor-edged knife, pumice stone and a shaker of fine sand. Just below the dais, sitting on a high stool stooped over his writing desk, sat Simon the scrivener, Cranston's clerk. The day's proceedings were about to begin and, beneath his straggling white hair, Simon's lined, chalky-white face was severe. Nonetheless, he kept his head down to hide his enjoyment. Simon liked nothing better than to regale his wife and large family with the doings and sayings of Sir John Cranston. Today promised to provide fresh amusement, Cranston seemed in fine fettle and some of the cases were set to be highly disputatious.

'Did you send to the Chancery of Secrets,' Cranston barked, 'and tell those lazy buggers I want that document?'

'I did, Sir John,' Simon answered mournfully, shaking his head. 'But you know these Chancery clerks – it's sign this and sign that and by whose authority?' Simon waved one ink-stained hand. 'And so on and so on.'

'Good, good,' Cranston murmured. He scratched his head, his hand going under the table for the miraculous wine skin.

The murderous business at the Night in Jerusalem had perplexed him so much he had decided not to stay there but to return home to the loving embrace of the Lady Maud and the welcoming screams of the two poppets.

'Lovely boys, lovely boys,' the coroner breathed.

'Sir John?'

'Nothing.'

Cranston straightened up in the chair, took a swig from the miraculous wine skin and, as usual, offered it to Simon, who, as usual, politely refused.

'Right,' Cranston declared, 'let's begin. Tell Flaxwith to bring up the first.'

Simon rang the hand bell. Flaxwith, breathing heavily, and escorted by his two ugly mastiffs, marched a line of prisoners into the room, a group of roisterers who had become drunk, attacked the watch and urinated into the Great Conduit in Cheapside. Cranston fined them a shilling each and sentenced them to a morning in the stocks with a small bucket of horse piss to be tied round their necks. The next case was a petty trader, guilty of 'evecheping', selling goods after the market horn had sounded and the day's trading had finished. However, he looked so pathetic and hungry that Cranston gave him sixpence, offered him a swig from the miraculous wine skin and dismissed the case. Two women and a man came next: Eleanor Battlewaite and Mary Dodsworth, followed by a garish-looking man dressed in a black cape decorated with silver stars and golden half-moons. Cranston leaned back in his chair and listened to Simon, who tried to keep his voice level as he read out the indictment.

'Wait a minute,' Cranston shouted. 'What's your name?'

'Peter the Prophet,' the man replied in a squeaky voice.

'Go on,' Cranston said.

Simon described the case – how Eleanor had accused Mary of stealing a yard of silk, Mary had hired Peter the Prophet, told him secrets about Eleanor and bribed him to get close to her to persuade her that Mary had not stolen the silk. The case went on and on, Eleanor and Mary screaming at each other, Peter the Prophet protesting his innocence. Cranston at last grew tired of it all and beat the table.

'So, you say you are a prophet?'

'Yes, my lord.'

'So, you know how much I am going to fine you then?'

'Er . . .'

'Tell me,' Cranston asked sweetly, 'what's going to happen here?'

Peter the Prophet decided silence was the best defence.

'Very well.' Cranston banged the gavel again. 'Mary Dodsworth, you are fined five shillings for stealing the silk and hiring the prophet. Peter the Prophet, you are fined the same for being a charlatan. Eleanor Battlewaite, two shillings for being stupid enough to believe him and for wasting my time.'

Cranston promptly dismissed them, and they were followed by another fortune-teller, Richard the baker, who believed he could predict events by cutting up a loaf. He was fined and dismissed, as were two pastry cooks who had tried to sell pies as venison when they contained rancid beef. Flaxwith cleared the room and Cranston sank back in his chair.

'Satan's tits! I've had enough of this. I am going to pray.'

'The usual church, Sir John?'

'Yes,' Cranston replied. 'The usual church.'

The coroner went down the stairs and out across the courtyard into Cheapside. It was a fine day. The clouds had broken, the sky was blue, and the clamour in the marketplace was almost drowned by the clear tolling of church bells. For a while Cranston stood at the entrance of the Guildhall courtyard. He loved this scene. The market horn had sounded and another day's trading had begun. On either side of Cheapside's great thoroughfare, stalls and shops were open and apprentices were already shouting, eager to catch the eye of citizens who flocked in for the day's trading. The cookshops were busy and the sweet smell of baked pastry and spiced meat curled everywhere, mixing with the more unpleasant odours of horse dung, wet straw, and the piled midden heaps awaiting the dung carts. A group of knights rode by, sitting arrogantly in their high peaked saddles, a glorious array of colour, gleaming harness and the glint of spur, dagger and the bits of their horses. Alongside them ran huntsmen and dog whippers leading the hounds out to the fields to the north of the City. Troops of prisoners were being escorted by bailiffs of the Corporation eager to deposit their charges at the Fleet, Marshalsea, or the prison barges waiting on the Thames to take them downriver for trial at Westminster.

Cranston walked across Cheapside. Stall owners shouted and boasted; already a quarrel had broken out regarding a barrel of salt from Poitou, whilst further down Cheapside, the Pie-Powder Court, which governed the marketplace, was arbitrating over whether a piece of leather was bazen, sheepskin or, as the trader claimed, from Cordova in Spain. People were being fastened to the stocks or led up to stand in the cage above the Great Conduit. Two ungainly figures hobbled towards Cranston. He groaned and tried to quicken his pace but his pursuers were relentless and blocked his passage.

'Good morrow, Sir John. And how is the Lady Maud?'

Cranston glared at these two professional beggars, Leif the lame, who had one leg but could move swifter than many a man with two, and Rawbum who, many years previously, drunk as a sot, had sat down in a pan of burning oil and lived never to forget it.

'Sir John, we have composed a new song.'

Cranston stared unblinkingly, and without further invitation, Leif, one hand on his chest, scarred face staring up at the sky, began the most awful singing, while Rawbum played a tune on a reedy flute.

'Very good, very good,' Cranston intervened, thrusting a coin into each of their hands. 'I've heard enough, now bugger off.'

The two beggars, chorusing their thanks, would have pursued Sir John even further, but the coroner turned threateningly, and they took the hint and headed back towards a pastry shop, whilst Sir John, like an arrow from a bow, sped across Cheapside and into the welcoming warmth of his chosen tavern, the Lamb of God. Once ensconced in his favourite window seat overlooking the herb garden, Sir John welcomed the loving ministrations of the ale-wife, who placed in front of him a tankard of frothing ale and strips of bread covered with honey. He drank and ate staring out into the garden, its bright greenery hidden by a sharp frost. The broad carp pond was still covered with a skin of ice and Cranston realised that it would be some time before the sun's warmth was felt. He chatted about this to the ale-wife as he stared around the tavern. A second tankard was brought. Sir John sipped this whilst listening to a boy in the street outside sweetly singing a carol, 'The Angel of the Lord Announced to Mary'.

'I wonder,' Cranston reflected, 'if God's good angel will reveal the truth to me?'

He sat back in his seat cradling the tankard and recalled the events of the previous evening. He had left Athelstan and returned to the Night in Jerusalem for a cup of warm posset, where he had engaged Tobias the cask man in conversation. Tobias had been full of horror at the hideous murder of Toadflax, Chandler and the two whores. Cranston sipped at the tankard, distracted by the cowl-cloaked individual who sat huddled in the inglenook. The coroner prided himself on knowing everyone who came into the Lamb of God, but he marked that one down as a stranger and returned to his reflections. Tobias had also been angry on behalf of Master Rolles.

'He was in the kitchen all the time with me,' the cask man had protested, 'and I know who did it.' He had tapped his nose knowingly.

Cranston had bought him a drink, and Tobias

159

confessed how he had seen Chandler, plump as a plum, coming in from the yard.

'More importantly,' he whispered, 'I glimpsed blood on his hands.'

Tobias then went on to explain how his curiosity was so provoked he visited the tavern washerwoman, responsible for the linen in the guest chambers. They had both sifted amongst the cloths and found napkins from the dead man's chamber with stains which looked suspiciously like dried blood. The washer-woman was not certain; she pointed out how Chandler had tried to wash the napkins himself. Tobias immediately reported his findings to Master Rolles. The tavern keeper was gleeful, crowing like a cock on a dung hill, exclaiming that, according to an ancient law, he could not be fined the 'murdrum', an ancient tax levied on all hosteliers and taverners on whose premises a mysterious death occurred. Rolles, still happy with this news, had also joined Cranston, repeating what Tobias had said and tri-umphantly producing the stained napkins. Cranston examined them carefully and concluded that both Rolles and Tobias were correct. The stains did look suspiciously like dried blood. So had Chandler killed those two whores, hidden his crossbow and returned to his chamber to wash his hands? But why should a powerful landowner, who could more than pay for the likes of Beatrice and Clarice, murder them in such hideous circumstances? And Chandler's own death? Was that revenge? Was Chandler feverish that morning because of what he had done? Had he taken that bath to wash away any evidence of his crime? Sir John absent-mindedly ordered another ale pot.

'I'll pay for that.'

The figure crouched in the inglenook rose and, taking off his cloak, walked across to join Sir John.

'Well I never!' Cranston's hand went out to shake his visitor's. 'How did you know I would be here?'

Matthias of Evesham clasped the coroner's hand and slid on to the bench next to him, turning slightly to face Cranston, his beringed fingers laced together like some benevolent priest waiting to hear confession. The ale-wife brought two further tankards. Matthias lifted his, toasted Cranston and sipped carefully. The coroner moved slightly away so he could study the newcomer more closely. Matthias of Evesham was newly appointed as Master of the Chancery of Secrets in the Office of the Night, which had its chambers in the Tower. With his round, cheerful face, sparkling blue eyes and pleasant, smiling mouth, he assumed all the appearance of a benevolent monk, an impression he deliberately fostered with his soft speech and ever-present good humour. The only obvious betrayal that he was no ascetic was his love of jewellery: the gold collar around his neck, the costly rings which bedecked every finger, not to mention the gold bracelet on his left wrist.

A man of secrets was Master Matthias, a scholar of logic and philosophy who had lectured in the schools of Oxford and Cambridge, even those of Paris, before entering the service of the Regent John of Gaunt. Many mistook him for a priest, but Master Matthias was married – a good match – with the Lady Alice, who owned a pleasant mansion between the Temple and Fleet Street. Married or not, he was still a man for the ladies, as well as a great ferreter of secrets. He organised Gaunt's spies both at home and abroad and advised the Regent privately as well as at the Great Council meetings at Westminster.

'You're well, Sir John?' Matthias broke the silence. 'And the Lady Maud?'

'I am fine,' Cranston replied. 'My lady wife is fine, my children are well, my dogs are well, my cat is well, the fish in my stew pond are well. You haven't come sailing along the Thames to ask me that?'

'No, I haven't.' Matthias laughed and put his tankard down. 'You asked for a schedule of documents, for the searches made after the Lombard treasure was robbed some twenty years ago.'

'A reasonable request,' Cranston retorted. 'I want to know what searches were made, what was discovered.'

'Very little.'

'So why not let me see the documents?'

'They've been destroyed.'

Matthias looked so sorrowful Cranston burst out laughing.

'You expect me to believe that?'

'No, I don't,' Matthias grinned, 'but they *were* destroyed, because they furnished us with nothing.'

'Us?' Cranston asked.

Matthias ran a finger around the rim of his tankard. 'Let me make it very clear, Sir John, nobody would love to find out more than my master, John of Gaunt, what happened to the treasure. I will answer any question you want and you'll learn much more from me than anyone else.'

Cranston simply stared back.

'Twenty years ago,' Matthias began, 'the Crusading army which left here negotiated a massive loan from the Lombard bankers, in return for which the bankers were promised certain trading concessions in both the Narrow Seas and the Middle Sea. They were also assured of a percentage of any plunder. The Lombards sent the treasure to the Tower. At the time, my master, John of Gaunt, was Keeper of the Tower.'

'Ah!' Cranston exclaimed. 'Now we come to it.'

'On the eve of the Feast of St Matthew, the twentieth of September 1360,' Matthias continued, 'the treasure was taken out of the Tower, placed on a barge and dispatched to a secret place.'

'Why wasn't it taken directly to the ships?'

'The Admiral of the Fleet decided that was too dangerous. He wanted the treasure sent across the river to Southwark then transported secretly to the flagship. For reasons best known to himself he thought this was safer, and so did John of Gaunt.'

'Why all this stealth?' Cranston asked.

'To keep the treasure safe. You see,' Matthias wiped his mouth on a napkin, 'if anyone had heard what was happening and wished to steal the treasure, they would expect it to be brought by land along the north bank of the Thames, past London Bridge and across to the flagship or by royal barge downriver in the direction of Westminster. Sir Jack, when the Crusader fleet was at anchor, every river pirate and outlaw who had heard about the treasure would watch the flagship. They might have attacked when the treasure was being transported, they would certainly know when it arrived and where it had gone. So, John of Gaunt and the Admiral of the Fleet decided the treasure should be taken by barge, during the night across river and along the south bank of the Thames. This meant the route of the treasure barge, its destination and the time it arrived would remain a secret. Barges from the Tower go back and forth across the river to Southwark all the time. Once across the Thames, it was to be collected by two knights and transported to the flagship. Now the bargemen handed that treasure over to two knights whom Gaunt trusted.' Matthias pulled a face. 'Well, at the time they were: Richard Culpepper and Edward Mortimer. Ostensibly they were chosen by Lord Belvers, but John of Gaunt really made the decision.'

'Why,' Cranston asked, 'didn't they have a military escort?'

'To attract as little attention as possible.'

'Why were Culpepper and Mortimer chosen?'

'Because,' Matthias sighed, 'they were trusted by everyone, especially His Grace.'

Cranston bit on the skin of his thumb. Like everything which came from the Regent, Cranston sensed Matthias' story was a mixture of truth and lies. The coroner gazed quickly around the tap room and edged closer.

'Master Matthias,' he whispered, 'let's cut to the chase. How do I know that the treasure wasn't stolen by the Regent himself?'

Matthias smiled. 'His Grace predicted you might say that. Two things.' Matthias held up his hand. 'First, the captain of his guard brought back to the Tower an indenture, signed by Culpepper. Second, for months after the robbery, the finger of blame was pointed at my master. He took a great oath that he knew nothing about the great robbery.'

'In a word,' Cranston replied, 'your master was furious.'

'Yes, and he still is,' Matthias agreed. 'He has not forgotten what happened twenty years ago, and still makes careful enquiries, yet he has found nothing.'

'The woman,' Cranston declared, 'the courtesan known as Guinevere the Golden. They say she was glimpsed here and there.'

'Rumours.' Matthias shook his head. 'Stories, people eager for the reward. A large reward, Sir John, a hundred pounds, not to mention a pardon for any crime.'

Matthias sniffed.

'His Grace the Regent has heard about the killings at the Night in Jerusalem, the sudden and mysterious death of Sir Stephen, so his curiosity is pricked. He

165

wants to know if these events are somehow connected with the Lombard treasure. He asks me to ask you to remember that.'

'Whom does he suspect?' Cranston asked.

'He often wonders where Culpepper and Mortimer fled, or where they may have hidden the treasure.'

'Whom does he suspect?' Cranston repeated, gripping Matthias' arm.

'There's a man sheltering in St Erconwald's Church, protected by your secretarius, Athelstan the Dominican. Did you know that twenty years ago the Misericord's father and Master Rolles were the closest of friends? That the Misericord often absconded from his school master at St Paul's to frequent Rolles' tavern? His Grace wonders if the Misericord, a born rogue, knows anything of this twenty-year-old mischief. Is that why someone hired a hunter as ruthless as the Judas Man to track him down and bring him to justice? Is it because the Misericord knows something about the Lombard treasure?'

Matthias got to his feet and picked up his cloak; he pointed at the bread and honey.

'You should eat that, Sir John. It would be a sin to waste it,' he leaned down, 'as it would His Grace's favour.'

When Matthias had left, Cranston picked up the bread and honey and chewed it thoughtfully. He wondered how much of what he had been told was the truth. The ale-wife came over. Cranston absent-mindedly thanked her, paid the bill and left the tavern, going down to the river to hire Master Moleskin's barge for passage to Southwark . . .

Athelstan had risen early to collect bracken for the fire from the small copse at the far end of the cemetery. He greeted his parishioners and other members of the posse as charitably as he could, and tried to distract himself by admiring the wind-washed sky, which promised a fine day. He acknowledged their shouts of greeting, although he noticed Watkin and Pike kept their backs to him. He returned to the kitchen, built up the fire, washed his hands and settled down to compose himself for the morning Mass. With Bonaventure crouching beside him, Athelstan recited the 'Adoro te devote' of Thomas Aquinas, the great Dominican theologian. A knock on the door interrupted him and, praying for patience, he answered it. However, instead of the Judas Man or one of his parishioners, Brother Malachi stood there in his black Benedictine robe, hood back, and over his shoulders a set of leather panniers.

'Brother!' Malachi stepped back. 'You do not seem pleased.'

'Brother,' Athelstan quipped, 'I thought you were someone else.'

They exchanged the kiss of peace and Athelstan ushered him into the kitchen. Due to the fast before Mass, he could only offer a cup of water, but Malachi shook his head, saying he was only too pleased to warm his fingers above the fire.

'Did you stay at the Night in Jerusalem?' Athelstan asked.

'No.' Malachi spread his hands out to catch the warmth. 'I've had enough of my companions. I left late in the afternoon, I was ashamed of what they said, those two poor girls lying murdered! Sir Maurice and the rest acting all righteous during the day but slinking out like sinners at night!'

'Are you shocked?' Athelstan asked.

'Yes, yes, I am,' the Benedictine replied. 'Oh, I understand the feasting and the drinking. I can understand them being smitten by a tavern wench, but singling out those two girls, it's callous, cruel, especially as they knew their mother. I am not being self-righteous,' Malachi made himself more comfortable on the stool, 'but I do not think I will join them next year. The past is gone, it's finished.'

'You have searched for your brother?' Athelstan raised his hand in apology. 'I know, I have asked you before.'

'I have done what I can,' Malachi replied. 'My order has houses the length and breadth of Christendom, all manner of travellers rest there. It also does business with both the great and the lowly so it is well positioned to hear things. Oh, I have heard reports, but I know in my heart my brother is dead.'

'And Guinevere the Golden?'

'The same.'

'Did your brother ever hint at what was planned?'

'He was much younger than I. He was full of

knightly dreams and chivalry, of beautiful women, of jousting and tournaments and brave deeds. Oh yes, he could act the merry rogue, but he truly lost his heart and soul to Guinevere. He didn't see her as a courtesan or a whore, but a beautiful damsel in distress, trapped in a life she was desperate to escape from.'

'And was she?'

'She had a face as beautiful as an angel, not an evil heart but a greedy one. Fickle of mind, changeable in mood, yet I might as well have asked your cat to sing the Ave Maria than make my brother realise the truth. The last time I saw him was the day before the treasure arrived. He seemed distracted, perhaps excited.' Malachi pushed back the stool and got to his feet. 'But after that, nothing.'

'And why was he chosen?' Athelstan asked.

'I've told you. Lord Belvers, his commander, trusted him. John of Gaunt also played his part; Mortimer was his man.'

'Do you truly think he stole that treasure?' Athelstan asked.

'In my heart no, but the evidence seems to point otherwise. I'll pray for him at Mass.'

'As will I, at mine,' Athelstan replied. 'You know my story, Brother Malachi?'

'I've heard about it,' the Benedictine replied. 'How, when you were a novice, you and your brother joined the levies bound for France. He was killed there, wasn't he?'

'And I came back,' Athelstan agreed. 'My order

made my novitiate twice as long, every humble task was given to me.' He opened the door. 'Let me put it this way, Brother, I know everything there is about the latrines and sewers of Blackfriars.'

They left the house and entered the church by a side door. Athelstan walked to the rood screen, stopped and gasped.

'Brother?'

'Where is he?'

Athelstan hastened across into the sacristy. He opened the side door which led out to the small latrine built over a sewer. Across the cemetery, members of the posse were staring at him. Athelstan returned to the church and locked the door.

'It's the Misericord,' Athelstan gasped. 'He appears to have vanished. Come, Brother, help me.'

They searched the church, the chantry chapel, the sacristy, even the small disused crypt, but of the Misericord not a sign, nothing to mark his stay, except an empty ale pot and a trancher with some stale crumbs. He had vanished along with his weapons. Athelstan scratched his head. He didn't want to shout the Misericord's name or raise the alarm. He was surprised, yet slightly relieved. How had the rogue managed to escape? Once again he searched the church, sending Brother Malachi out to walk the perimeter of the cemetery and visit God-Bless snoring in the death house. The Benedictine returned shaking his head.

'Gone,' he said, 'like the snow in spring. Neither hide nor hair of him.'

'We'll not raise the alarm,' Athelstan declared. 'Not until I've celebrated Mass.'

They busied themselves preparing the altar, lighting the candles, filling the cruets with water and wine. Athelstan vested and celebrated his Mass alone in the small chantry chapel, whilst Malachi did the same at the high altar. Athelstan tried to think only of what was happening, of the Great Miracle, of bread and wine changing into the body and blood of the unseen God, but as he confessed to Malachi afterwards, he was distracted by another miracle. How could a criminal like the Misericord vanish from his church, walk through a ring of armed men ever vigilant to catch him, without let or hindrance?

'Well,' Athelstan crossed himself, 'I might as well proclaim the good news for all to hear.'

He walked down the nave, opened the main door and, ignoring the protests of Pernel and Cecily the courtesan, who had been waiting for Mass, though they confessed they had arrived late, called across the Judas Man from his usual position by the lychgate. This hound and scourge of criminals came swaggering across, sword slapping against his thigh.

'Good morrow, Brother.'

'Good morning to you, sir.' Athelstan forced a smile. 'I must inform you that our sanctuary man, the Misericord, has disappeared.'

'What?'

The Judas Man bounded up the steps, almost knocking Athelstan aside, and throwing back the door with a crash ran up into the sanctuary. Athelstan followed, protesting. The Judas Man took the small horn hanging from his belt, opened the corpse door and blew three long blasts. Soon the nave was filled with men milling about, Pike, Watkin and other parishioners included. Athelstan decided to let them have their head. Once again the church was searched but no trace could be found. The Judas Man, chest heaving with fury, came and stood before Athelstan, sweat coursing down his unshaven face, the smell of wine heavy on his breath. He went to poke Athelstan but the Dominican pushed his hand away. The Judas Man stepped away at the threatening murmur from Athelstan's parishioners.

'For God's sake, man,' Athelstan urged, 'think about where you are! This is a church; I am its priest. I have nothing to do with the escape of your prisoner. You know that.'

The Judas Man opened his mouth to protest but stopped himself just in time. He brushed by Athelstan and stormed out on to the porch, shouting at the others to join him.

'An exciting start to the day,' Malachi murmured.

'Aye, and it's only begun.'

Athelstan returned to the house, where he and Malachi broke fast. Athelstan was still distracted and puzzled by the Misericord's disappearance. He excused himself and returned to the church, where Pernel the Flemish woman was trying to place a chaplet of flowers on the statue of the Virgin in the Lady Chapel. Athelstan helped her. The woman stepped back, fingering her strangely coloured hair, tears running down her parchment-coloured face.

'Father, will you hear my confession?'

'Oh no, Pernel, not again,' Athelstan said.

'But I've slept with men, dozens of them!'

Athelstan grasped her face in his hands, staring into those wild, frenetic eyes.

'Pernel, it's all your imaginings. You are a good woman.'

'Do you think I'll go to heaven, Father?'

Athelstan let her go. 'Well, if you don't, Pernel, no one will.'

'The ghost has been back at the squint hole.'

'What?' Athelstan said.

Pernel pointed down the church.

'Go outside, Father. When I couldn't get into church this morning I walked round to have a look. She must have carried a candle.'

Athelstan, intrigued, left by the sacristy door and went along the side of the church. He found the diamond-shaped squint hole, crouched down and peered through. He could see Pernel standing at the entrance to the rood screen, and his fingers touched the piece of wax on the edge of the squint hole. He peeled it off, stared across the cemetery and laughed quietly. He recalled the novice in her voluminous gown coming into the church last night, Pike and Watkin in the cemetery, the darkness, the heavy mist. Athelstan went back into the church.

'Pernel, please do me a favour. Go and tell Watkin, Pike and Ranulf that I want to see them now.'

'Why, do you want to hear their confessions, Father?'

'Yes,' Athelstan murmured. 'Just before I hang them!'

The old Flemish woman scurried off, and a little while later the three miscreants entered the church. Athelstan told Pernel to stand outside and guard the sacristy door whilst he took the three into the sanctuary. They stood hangdog before him.

'Yes, you all look as if you are heading for the execution cart.'

Athelstan sat down on the altar steps and looked up at them.

'You know you can be hanged for helping a felon escape sanctuary?'

'But, Father, how could you . . .'

'Oh, very easily, Pike. I'll tell you how it was done, then I'll decide whether or not to inform the Judas Man. The Misericord has quick-silver wits, a nimble mind and a clever tongue. He knew all three of you before he ever took sanctuary here.'

The three stared at the paved floor as if they had never seen it before.

'Ranulf, where are your ferrets?'

'With God-Bless in the death house.'

'That's where you'll be, you stupid man. As I was saying, the Misericord is a merry rogue. He'd often leave the sacristy to relieve himself, and he secretly drew you three into conversation. I suspect he had silver coins hidden all over his person. He paid one of you to go across the river and tell his sister Edith, sheltering in the Minoresses, about his predicament. You all know she visited here last night, and one thing about a nun's robes is that you can hide an army beneath them. She brought a change of clothing, money, food, anything he might need to flee. She asked to speak with him alone and it would have been easy to hide a bundle in a darkened corner of the sanctuary. She left, I left, the posse outside settled down for the night. Somehow you three beauties managed to guard one part of the cemetery wall. You had arranged with the Misericord, in return for a pocketful of silver, to provide a signal when it was safe for him to slip out of the church.' Athelstan pointed down to the squint hole. 'And what better plan than to light a candle and place it at the squint hole, the sign that it was safe to leave? The Misericord was all ready, dressed in a wig, a dark cloak. Out of the sacristy he crept, across the cemetery and into the night.'

Watkin jumped in alarm as Bonaventure entered the church and sat next to his master, as if curious to discover what was happening.

'I may have some of the details wrong,' Athelstan whispered, 'but I think the story is true. Yes? How much did he pay you?'

'Ten marks,' Ranulf muttered. 'Three for each of us and one for the church.'

'I've got a better idea,' Athelstan retorted. 'You can

have one each and I'll keep seven for the church. Come on.'

The three quickly handed over the coins. Athelstan handed one back.

'Pike, give that to Pernel, and if I were you, I would keep out of the Judas Man's way.' He got to his feet. 'It's only a matter of time before his wits follow the same path as mine.'

Athelstan dismissed them and returned to his house. Malachi was fast asleep, head on his arm, so Athelstan left him, quietly going up to the bed loft, removing the warming pan and tidying things up. He heard shouting and went out to the cemetery, but it was only the Judas Man and his posse preparing to leave. Athelstan had returned and was banking the fire when Cranston swept through the door all abluster. Malachi started awake. Excusing himself, the Benedictine greeted Sir John but refused Athelstan's offer of food and said he would return to the tavern. Once he had gone, Sir John told Athelstan everything he'd learned in the Lamb of God. Athelstan listened quietly and hid his prickle of unease. He feared the Regent and wondered why a man like Matthias of Evesham should be so interested.

'It's not just the treasure, Sir John, it's something else.'

'And what about the excitement here?'

Cranston sat at the table mopping his brow, helping himself to a bowl of oatmeal mixed with honey. He stopped eating and listened with surprise as Athelstan informed him about the Misericord's disappearance.

'I'll tell that Judas Man to keep his hands—'

The coroner was interrupted by a furious pounding at the door. Athelstan answered it, and one of Master Rolles' tap boys burst into the room, red-faced, hair clammy with sweat.

'Sir John,' he gasped, fighting for breath, 'you've got to come. I've been across to Cheapside but couldn't find you. Sir Laurence Broomhill has been horribly wounded, he lies dying at the Night in Jerusalem.'

Athelstan made the boy calm down, giving him a small cup of buttermilk. With a little bit of coaxing, the boy described how, late last night, the tavern had been roused by a hideous screaming. How Master Rolles had gone into the cellar and found Sir Laurence Broomhill, awash with blood, his leg held fast in a mantrap which Rolles had kept in the cellar.

'Master Rolles sometimes uses them,' the boy explained. 'Places them in his garden against those who poach from the carp pond, or break into his stables or outhouses.'

Sir John nodded understandingly, though in truth he hated such devices, which were increasingly used by the powerful and wealthy to protect their gardens and orchards, and were so sharp and powerful they could sever a man's leg.

'Was it an accident?' Athelstan asked.

The boy shrugged.

'Master Rolles doesn't know. He thinks Sir Laurence

177

went down to the cellar for some wine; a jug was found nearby.'

'Why didn't they send for me immediately?' Cranston asked.

'Oh, Sir John,' the boy blustered, 'it was all dreadful, they had to free his leg, bind it and take him to his chamber. Master Stapleton the physician was sent for but there was nothing he could do. Sir Laurence now lies all sweaty and bloody. I saw him.' The boy imitated the dying knight's jerky movements.

'Yes, yes,' Cranston soothed, 'I know what happens. Brother Athelstan,' he pointed to the door, 'another day, another hunt.'

Chapter 7

They found the Night in Jerusalem eerily quiet. Rolles had kept the door shut, refusing to allow customers inside the stable yard. Ostlers and grooms lounged about, whispering amongst themselves. The passage ways and tap room lay silent. Sir Maurice Clinton and the rest were already waiting in the solar. Cranston and Athelstan greeted them and were halfway up the stairs when they met Rolles.

'You are too late, sir.' Rolles pointed back at the chamber. 'Broomhill's dead. Stapleton the physician has just left – there was nothing we could do.'

The taverner looked strangely agitated. Athelstan regarded him as a man with a soul as hard as flint, which not even the most dire of circumstances could weaken; now his fleshy face was pale and unshaven, eyes red-rimmed.

'I am not a well man, Brother.' The taverner

gestured at his clothes, which were soaked in blood. 'I am losing custom. I do not want these knights here ever again.'

He paused as Brother Malachi came up the stairs, a stole round his neck, in his right hand a phial of holy oils, in his left a beeswax candle.

'I must anoint him,' murmured the Benedictine.

They let him by. Rolles continued on his way down; Athelstan and Cranston went up on to the gallery and waited outside the Morte D'Arthur Chamber.

'You may come in.'

Brother Malachi was standing by the bed, the candle snuffed, the holy oil replaced in its small leather bag.

Cranston whistled as he looked round. 'It's like a battlefield!'

The bed drapes, linen, coverlets and rugs were drenched in blood. Bandages, linen pads, as well as the poultices Stapleton had used to try and staunch the bleeding lay everywhere. The corpse, its skin as white as a leper's, sprawled on the bed, naked from the waist down. Athelstan went across whilst Cranston, grasping his miraculous wine skin, turned away in disgust. Broomhill's right leg was shattered midway between knee and heel. The wound exposed raw flesh, muscle and vein, and, peering down, Athelstan could see even the bone beneath was gashed. The smell was offensive; infection had already set in.

'He must have been in agony,' Athelstan remarked, staring at the dead man's face, contorted by his last convulsions.

'Stapleton gave him an opiate,' Malachi replied.

'There was nothing we could do.' Rolles stood in the doorway like a prophet of doom. 'Nothing at all.'

'Did he say anything before he died?' Athelstan asked.

'He babbled about the past.' Rolles came into the chamber. 'He talked of a great river beast which could swoop up and gulp a man's body. He was feverish, he didn't know what he was saying.'

'What was he doing in the cellar?'

'He went down in the evening. I found a jug nearby; perhaps he was going to fill it from one of the vats?'

'Aren't there servants, scullions, tap boys?' Athelstan asked.

'Of course,' Rolles snapped, 'but sometimes the galleries are deserted, and I do not object to favoured customers helping themselves. The knights always pay well.'

'Pay well.' Athelstan echoed the words. 'Brother Malachi, what is the source of these knights' wealth?'

'Estates, some of the most fertile land in Kent, flocks of sheep, fishing rights. You could fill a charter with the sources of their profit.'

'But once they were poor.'

'Poor men become rich when their fathers die. Moreover, the knights brought plunder back from Egypt. They stormed palaces and treasures. Sir Maurice Clinton seized a box of mother-of-pearl, exquisite in their beauty, called the Pearls of Sheba; supposedly they once belonged to the great Solomon's lover.'

'And what happened to these?'

'On our way home, the fleet docked in Genoa. The Genoese were only too pleased to buy whatever treasure the Crusaders had seized.'

'Did you receive a portion of this wealth?'

'No,' Malachi smiled, 'but my order did.'

'Oh, for God's sake, let's leave here.' Cranston picked up a coverlet and draped it over the corpse. 'Master Rolles, I want to see where he was wounded.'

Malachi stayed in the chamber whilst Rolles took them down to the cellar, Athelstan gingerly following the coroner down the stone steps, where a few candles glowed in wall-niches. At the bottom they paused as Rolles lit lantern horns slung on hooks to reveal a long, low-ceilinged cavern with vats and barrels stacked down either side. In the corner, to Athelstan's right, were garden implements: mattocks, hoes and spades.

'I did my best to clean the blood,' Rolles muttered, and gestured at the great oval-shaped mantrap now resting against the wall. He pulled this out and prised apart the teeth.

'A simple contraption,' Athelstan conceded, 'yet so deadly.'

The trap opened up and was kept apart by a spring. When Rolles touched this with a stick, the teeth came together with such a clash Athelstan jumped.

'I need this,' Rolles explained, sensing Athelstan's horror. 'Brother, ask Sir John, anyone! I have carp ponds, stables and outhouses which must be protected. A gang of rifflers can take your livestock in a night. Just knowing the traps are here will keep them away.'

'You need a licence,' the coroner snapped.

'I have that. I know the law, Sir John, I can only use this when I can prove I am in danger of being robbed.'

'More importantly,' Athelstan crouched down, 'why was it left open down here last night? And why did Sir Laurence come down here?'

He picked up the metal jug.

'Was this from his chamber?'

'I don't know.'

Athelstan stared down the narrow passageway of this gloomy cellar, trying to imagine what had happened. Undoubtedly the Knights of the Golden Falcon would have been upset by Chandler's death, as well as their own forced confessions about consorting with prostitutes. They might have drunk deeply. Sir Laurence, eager for more wine, took a jug from his own chamber or the kitchen and came down here.

'This cellar is always in darkness, isn't it?'

'Of course,' the taverner replied. 'Candles are lit only when necessary.'

'What if Sir Laurence came down here expecting to see somebody. He didn't know this place. What do you do, Sir John, when you walk downstairs in the dark, particularly if you have been drinking?'

'Take great care; those small candles in the wall-niches provide scanty light.'

'And we don't know,' Athelstan mused, 'if Sir Laurence was carrying a lantern.'

He closed his eyes, trying to recall how he came down the steps of the bell tower at his church. He hated that spiral staircase; he was never too sure when he reached the bottom. Wouldn't Sir Laurence have felt the same? Athelstan got to his feet. The area around the steps stank of the brine and vinegar Rolles had used to clear up the blood; here and there splashes still stained the wall and the ground at the foot of the steps.

'Sir Laurence must have been distracted.'

Athelstan pulled the mantrap over, placing it closed at the bottom of the steps. He then walked down between the vats and barrels to the far wall. The brickwork here was uneven and Athelstan noticed, just above his own gaze, a rather large gap.

'Sister Wax,' he murmured, recalling his discovery at the squint hole at the church earlier that day. 'Sister Wax, you've helped me again!'

The wax on the brickwork was soft and clean, freshly formed.

'Master Rolles, come here.' The taverner came down to join him. 'Did you place a candle here?'

The taverner brushed the wax with his fingers.

'No, no, I didn't. By the amount of wax, a candle must have been burning here for some time.'

Athelstan asked Rolles to bring a tallow candle down. The taverner took one from the box beneath the staircase, lit it and placed it in the niche. The cellar lanterns were doused. Athelstan went back up the steps, ignoring Cranston's moans about the darkness, then turned and came slowly down again. Even though he was aware of the small lights in the wall-niches, he was still attracted by that solitary candle burning at the far end of the cellar. He reached the bottom step.

'Sir Laurence was murdered.' His voice echoed sombrely through the darkness. 'Master Rolles, please light the lanterns. Sir John, if you would . . .'

They left the cellar and walked out into the stable yard, well away from any eavesdropper.

'I'm sure Sir Laurence was murdered,' Athelstan repeated. 'That's how it was done. Somebody, somehow primed that trap and invited him down to the cellar. I wonder what the lure was? Perhaps a revelation about the mysteries now besetting us, or something else?'

'It was dangerous,' Cranston declared. 'Somebody else could have been killed.'

'I don't think the assassin cared. The real question is, who is it? The taverner? Any of those knights? And the Judas Man and Mother Veritable seem to be able to come and go as they wish.'

Athelstan stared across at the hay barn.

'Do we have one assassin, Sir John,' he asked, 'or two? Even more? Think of these mysteries as lines. We have the Misericord's strange doings; we have that infamous robbery twenty years ago; we have the death of those two young women; now we have the murder of two knights. It's a question of logic, Sir John. Do the lines run quite separate and parallel, or do they meet, tangled up with each other?'

He was about to continue when the Judas Man came swaggering through the gate, his face bright with pleasure.

'I've found him!' He clapped his leather-clad hands. 'Brother Athelstan, I apologise for my earlier rudeness, but the Misericord's been caught.'

'Whereabouts?'

'Just near Bishopsgate. I had men on the road leading out. They've sent a message; the Misericord is safely in Newgate and I shall visit him there.' Chuckling with glee, the Judas Man tapped Athelstan on the shoulder and entered the tavern.

'He'll find little comfort there,' Cranston murmured. 'Brother, where are you going?' Athelstan was already striding towards the gate.

'Why, Sir John, to Newgate. I want to question the Misericord before the Judas Man pays him a visit.'

This time Cranston found it difficult to keep up with Athelstan's pace as they threaded through the needle-thin alleyways down to the quayside. They were delayed for a short while, as bailiffs with staves and clubs were trying to break up a small but very noisy crowd shouting, 'Shovels and spades!' the usual cry which went up along the riverside whenever any private individual tried to take over a stretch of the Thames.

'It's happening along both banks of the river!'

Cranston exclaimed as they climbed into Moleskin's barge.

'That's right, Sir John,' Moleskin agreed. 'If the rich have their way they will buy up every plot of land along the Thames. I won't be able to moor my barge without paying a tax, whilst you, Sir John, won't be able to water your horse.'

'And the women of the parish,' Athelstan interrupted, 'won't have anywhere to wash their clothes. Water is a gift, Sir John; as the Gospel says, the Good Lord lets his rain fall on the just and the unjust.'

'But the unjust gets more,' Sir John quipped, 'because he owns a bigger barrel.'

'And has stolen the just man's,' Moleskin added, pulling back the oars and taking the boat out across the choppy tide.

While Cranston and Moleskin badgered and teased each other, Athelstan stared moodily across the river. A bank of mist still hovered mid-stream. Athelstan quietly prayed that Moleskin would have his wits about him, as well as a sharp eye for the various wherries, fishing boats and barges of every description going up and down the Thames. To his right he could make out the lines of London Bridge, including the poles bearing the severed heads of traitors. He wondered how Master Burdon, the Keeper of the Bridge, was doing. Burdon was a mannikin, very proud of the trust shown to him, an engaging little man if it wasn't for his rather macabre habit of combing the hair of the severed heads.

Athelstan, reflecting on the tumult behind him, wondered how the likes of Burdon, Moleskin, Pike the ditcher, Ranulf and the rest would cope when the great revolt occurred. He had listened most attentively to Sir John, he had witnessed first hand the soul-wrenching poverty of London's poor, aware of the stories flooding in from the countryside of how the peasants seethed at the taxes, levies and tolls imposed upon them. Would the revolt reach Southwark? Would his own parishioners join in? Would they achieve anything, or would it all end in murderous street fighting, and mass executions in Smithfield and elsewhere? He heard Moleskin mention the death of the two whores on the night of the Great Ratting, eager to find out if Cranston knew all the gory details. Was their journey across the Thames connected with this? Cranston replied evasively while Athelstan thought about the Misericord being trapped outside Bishopsgate.

'Have you taken anyone suspicious across?' he asked abruptly.

'I am suspicious about all my passengers, Father.' Moleskin nodded at Cranston.

'You've heard how the Misericord escaped?'

Moleskin shook his head, but his eyes betrayed him.

'If you were fleeing London?' Athelstan asked.

'I certainly wouldn't use the bridge or a barge,' Moleskin replied, 'but go south through the countryside.'

'That's what I thought.' Athelstan pointed at the

approaching bank. 'So he must have been going to meet someone, and I know who.'

Once they had landed at Queenhithe, Athelstan reminded Cranston about his previous night's visitor.

'So he was going to meet his sister?' Cranston asked.

'I think so. One last visit, perhaps,' Athelstan replied. 'He made a mistake; the Judas Man knew more about the Misericord than his victim realised.'

They walked up into Thames Street, making their way through the busy crowds. The thoroughfares and lanes were much broader here than in Southwark, the people better dressed in their fur-edged coats, mantles and ermine-lined hoods, the markets more prosperous, the stalls piled high. From the prices being bawled Athelstan understood how steeply the cost of everything had risen, be it cloths and leather goods from abroad, or vegetables from the garden estates outside the City. They passed the towering mass of St Paul's, up Dyer Lane and into the shambles, where the fleshers and butchers had their stalls. The broad cobble-lined lane had turned slippery with the offal and blood strewn about. Packs of dogs vied with beggars and the poor in snapping up these morsels. The air was rich with the odour of raw flesh; even the butchers and apprentices were drenched in blood, their stalls slippery with the juices dripping off. For the price of a penny, the poor were allowed to place pots and pans underneath to collect these drippings. Cranston was well known here; he was greeted noisily by the bailiffs and beadles as well as the officials who guarded the chain in front of Newgate, its forecourt stretching up to the prison's iron-barred black gates.

Athelstan always hated the place; it was a veritable pit of misery. Outside the gate, prisoners thronged, manacled together, sent out to collect alms by their gaolers for both themselves and other inmates. Relatives of those held in the pits and dungeons fought to bribe guards and turnkeys with messages and gifts for their beloved ones within. A woman shrieked that she had children to feed but how could she do so whilst her husband was in chains? Athelstan pressed a coin into her hand; only when they had passed through the gate and into the prison yard beyond did Cranston, with some exasperation, explain how the woman was a mummer who often preyed on passers-by. The prison yard itself was also noisy. Lines of prisoners, shivering in their rags and unshod feet, waited to be taken down to the cells, whilst a tired-looking bear sat chained in a corner. One of the gaolers explained how its keeper had become drunk and attacked a spectator.

'It seems a pity to punish the bear,' Athelstan murmured, 'it looks so tired and old.'

The gaoler followed his gaze, scratching the stubble on his cheek.

'What do you suggest, Brother, a blessing?'

'No.' Athelstan pressed a coin into the man's hand. 'Make sure it's fed and watered and looks a little happier before we leave.'

The gaoler agreed, then escorted them into the foul-smelling prison. They walked along narrow, badly lit passageways, down mildewed steps, into what the gaoler called the Netherworld, a narrow, sombre passageway with dungeons on either side. They were introduced to its keeper, a burly, thickset man with a leather apron around his waist. He recognised Sir John and swiftly handed back the coroner's seal of office which Cranston always carried to identify himself.

'The Misericord is along here.' He gestured with a sturdy finger. 'The Judas Man paid me well to keep him secure.'

He led them along the corridor. Occasionally Athelstan heard a groan, a scream, or raucous abuse hurled at them through the small grilles at the top of each door; occasionally he glimpsed mad, gleaming eyes staring out at them. The Misericord's cell was at the end, built into what used to be the foundations of the ancient Roman wall, one of the most secure cells in the prison, the keeper explained, inserting a key and scraping back the rusting bolts. The dungeon inside was small, with no window or gap for air or light. It reeked like a latrine and the rushes on the floor had turned to a muddy slime. The Misericord, sitting in a corner, sprang to his feet. The keeper beckoned Athelstan in and handed him the small tallow candle he was carrying.

'Brother, I thought . . .'

'You thought I was the Judas Man.'

191

The Misericord agreed and slunk back into the corner, gazing fearfully at Sir John.

'Let's make your guests as comfortable as possible.'

The keeper took the candle from Athelstan and placed it on a rusty iron spigot jutting out of the wall. He brought in two stools for Cranston and Athelstan, then closed the door, but not before explaining that he would keep it unlocked; if they needed help, he would be just outside.

'Why have you come?' the Misericord asked. 'Did my escape embarrass you?'

'I know how you escaped.' Athelstan sat down. 'Time is short, the Judas Man will be here soon.'

'He can't hurt me, he dare not.'

'He won't hurt you,' Cranston explained. 'He simply wants to see you hang.'

'I'll quote the Neck Verse.'

'Ah!' Athelstan replied. 'The first lines of Psalm 50. You'll claim Benefit of Clergy and demand to be handed over to the Church courts. The Judas Man will still hunt you down. So tell me,' Athelstan leaned forward, 'why is he hunting you so ruthlessly? Who hired him?'

'I don't know.'

'You're lying. You may be a felon, but London is full of Misericords.'

Athelstan noticed how the prisoner's face was bruised above his right cheek, whilst his jerkin was torn and rent.

'You were manhandled, weren't you?'

'The bailiffs certainly weren't Franciscans.' The Misericord smiled. 'But why are you here?'

'I could offer you a pardon.' Athelstan gently nudged Cranston's boot. 'The Regent could give you an amnesty for all crimes committed, on condition you leave London, and tell me everything you know.'

The change in the Misericord was remarkable. He stared open-mouthed at the coroner, who sat pinching his nostrils against the foul smell.

'You can really do that?'

'Of course. The Lord Coroner here will personally arrange it, full pardon and clemency. You'll be given a letter to show to all sheriffs, port reeves, bailiffs and mayors for safe passage.'

The Misericord put his face in his hands.

'The truth,' Cranston demanded. 'The full truth.'

'Who hired the Judas Man?'

The Misericord lifted his face. 'I don't know, Brother.' He raised his hands to plead as Cranston snorted in derision. 'I don't know. It may have been Mother Veritable, even the Judas Man doesn't know.'

'Why should Mother Veritable hire him?'

'For a number of reasons. As you know, Brother, I sold a potion, a powder, which I claimed could increase a man's potency between the sheets. Now, I often visited Mother Veritable's house. I became firm friends with Beatrice and Clarice. No, no, it's true, I enjoyed their company, they enjoyed mine.

193

They said I wasn't like the rest. I showed them dignity and treated them as ladies. They would tell me about their customers, their strange lusts and desires. They weren't supposed to. Mother Veritable keeps a strict house. They told me about the knights, particularly the small fat one who drank poison and died.'

'Sir Stephen Chandler?'

'Yes, the same. He visited the girls every time he came to London, not just when the Knights of the Golden Falcon met for their annual feasting. Sir Stephen had great ambition in matters of the bedchamber but not the potency to match it. I persuaded the girls to sell my miraculous powder to their lordly customer. They did, and made a pretty penny.'

'But it didn't work?'

'Of course not, Brother. The girls laughed, and I made up a poem about Sir Stephen.'

'I found that,' Athelstan exclaimed, 'amongst their few possessions. Something about a red crown, a cock, losing its power. I've seen such songs composed by scholars when they want to mock a master.'

'Why the red crown?' Cranston asked. 'I don't see the significance.'

'Chandler had red hair,' Athelstan replied, 'whilst Stephen, in Greek, means crown.'

'And cock,' the Misericord finished the explanation, 'was a nickname given to Chandler when he was young. He truly portrayed himself as a lady's man. Now, I gave my poem to the girls but I also sold copies in certain taverns in Kent. Somehow Sir Stephen discovered that. He complained to Mother Veritable. She beat the girls, took what gold they'd hidden and banned me from her house.'

'So Sir Stephen, as well as Mother Veritable, had great grievance against you? He too could have hired the Judas Man.'

'All things are possible, Sir John, especially with that cruel harridan.'

The Misericord fell silent, as if listening to the faint sounds in the rest of the prison, the muted cries and groans, the slamming of doors, the ominous rattling of chains.

Athelstan stared round the cell. In the poor light he saw how the walls were encrusted with dirt and slime. Here and there some prisoner had carved his name or a prayer, other times just a sign, a star, a woman's breasts or, more commonly, a gallows with a figure hanging from it.

'Why do you think it was Mother Veritable who hired the Judas Man?' Cranston asked. 'Why choose her rather than Sir Stephen?'

'I had interfered with her girls, mocked a powerful customer.'

'But there's something else. It involves your sister, doesn't it? Last night, in the church, I heard Mother Veritable's name mentioned.'

'Brother, your ears are as sharp as your wits. Two years ago I was still friends with Mother Veritable, she allowed me to shelter in her house. She met Edith and was much taken with her. She wanted me to entrust my sister to her.'

'To become a whore?' Cranston asked.

'I've heard of worse things happening,' the Misericord declared bitterly. 'Walk the streets of your city, Sir John, not every whore is plying for custom because she loves it. I, of course, refused. Mother Veritable offered me gold and silver. What she called pleasures beyond imagination. I still refused. I was banned from her house but, where possible, I would meet Beatrice and Clarice outside.'

'Did you invite them to the Night in Jerusalem for the Great Ratting?'

'No, Brother, I did not. It could have been Chandler. Remember, he did approach both girls. I think he was demanding satisfaction.'

'You said you met the girls?'

'Where possible, but I used their friend Donata as a messenger. One night, oh, it must have been about two months ago, they came to the Night in Jerusalem. Some customer had hired them and I met them out in the yard. They were both very excited. They claimed that they had some proof about what had happened to their mother and, perhaps, the truth behind the great robbery.'

'What!'

'Yes, my Lord Coroner. They didn't tell me much. I asked them, but they refused. They were giggling, and claimed that if they kept their wits they would possess a great treasure and be able to leave Mother Veritable for ever. Of course, I didn't believe them.'

'They must have offered you some proof?'

'They said my sister had it. She had it on her person. They were talking in riddles. They'd also confided in Donata. Donata said they didn't know whether to be happy or sad at discovering something which could prove the fate of their mother. I begged Donata to try her best to find out, but Beatrice and Clarice had not forgotten the beating Mother Veritable had given them over Sir Stephen. They kept their own counsel.'

'Do you think Chandler murdered them?'

'It's possible, Brother. On the night of the Great Ratting I was in the tap room. I wanted to be there, not only to lay my wager and collect my generous winnings, but to talk to Beatrice and Clarice. I knew the Judas Man was hunting me, following my tracks as carefully as any hound. I played that trick on poor Toadflax and kept in the shadows. When the fight broke out, Beatrice and Clarice had left the tap room for the hay barn. I was frightened. I knew the Judas Man would soon realise he had made a mistake and cast his net further. So I slipped into the kitchen, where Master Rolles was roaring at some poor cook who had made a mistake. I asked him for help as well as where the girls had gone. He replied that they were in the hay barn, that I should join them there and hide.'

'Did Master Rolles always offer such help?'

'Yes, I know him of old. He is very strict. I can only

enter his tavern with his permission and only hide when he tells me. You know how it is, Sir John, I have similar arrangements with innkeepers, hostellers and taverners the length and breadth of England.'

'Did you meet Beatrice and Clarice?'

'Brother, I was terrified out of my wits. My belly was full of ale and roast pork. I was going to meet them. I glimpsed a chink of light through the hay barn door, but I had to relieve myself. I dared not go to the latrines at the far side of the wall. I was frightened of being trapped there. So I ran outside. I was accosted by other people, who had also been at the Great Ratting. Men who had fled at the approach of the Judas Man, telling me about the fight which had begun in the tap room. Now, on any other night I would have run, put as much distance between myself and that tavern as possible.'

'But you wanted to meet Beatrice and Clarice?'

'Sir John, I was determined to. I had been in the hay barn before – it's a good place to hide. So I returned to the yard. I saw Sir Stephen, drunk as a sot, go staggering through the door. I waited awhile and then followed. I peered through.'

The Misericord's fingers went to his face.

'Both girls were dead. One of them may have been moaning a little, Beatrice with a dagger thrust in her. Clarice was certainly dead, a crossbow bolt high in her chest. She seemed to be awash with blood. Sir Stephen was kneeling beside the corpses. I'm sure I glimpsed an arbalest.'

'Did he kill them?'

'Brother, he could've done. In his drunken state he may have believed he had good cause. I ran back across the yard and hid in the shadows. Sir Stephen came out and closed the doors, replacing the bar.'

'Replacing the bar?' Athelstan asked. 'What do you mean?'

'Well, Brother, I'm sure that, just before I saw him entering the barn, Sir Stephen was holding the bar. He must have taken it off, and despite being drunk, he knew where it lay.'

'So,' Athelstan declared, 'either the girls went into the barn and someone barred the door from the outside, Sir Stephen goes across, removes the bar, enters the barn and kills them; or . . .' Athelstan tapped the writing satchel next to his leg. 'Or the killer, someone else, followed those girls into the barn, killed them and left, sealing them in. The lantern was still glowing?'

'Oh yes, Brother, I saw it, fastened to one of the hooks. By then I was truly frightened. I did not want to be accused of their murder, so I fled. I had drunk too much that night, my wits were blunted. The following morning the Judas Man picked up my trail, so I fled to your church for sanctuary.'

'And you don't know what the girls had discovered about their mother?'

'Brother, if I did I would tell you. Of course I wondered what their words meant.'

'Did you discuss it with Edith?' Athelstan asked.

'No, Brother. I never told her where the silver and gold I earned came from. Oh, I think she suspected. She did not like Mother Veritable and complained bitterly about how she looked at her. Edith said she would have nothing to do with her, the brothel or anyone who lived there. She would not even have her name mentioned unless it was necessary.'

'This morning . . .'

Cranston took a generous mouthful of claret from the miraculous wine skin; he offered it to Athelstan, who shook his head, and then to the Misericord, who snatched it and drank quickly.

'You were saying, Sir John, this morning?'

Cranston plucked the wine skin back.

'This morning, I discovered that, when you were a lad and not yet old enough in mischief to compose poems mocking old men, you served as a tap boy in Master Rolles' tavern?'

'Oh yes. He and my father were kinsmen, but distantly related. Even then, Sir John, I had a nose for mischief, and what better place than Master Rolles' tavern? I would serve as a tap boy, or in the kitchens. I loved to mix with the cunning men, the footpads, the charlatans, the quacks, and listen to their colourful tales of life on the highway, of whom they'd tricked and duped.'

'So, you knew the Knights of the Golden Falcon before they became Crusaders?'

'Oh yes, and Guinevere the Golden. Great days, Sir John! Master Rolles had recently purchased the tavern and was determined to make a name for himself. Those knights sheltered there when they were younger, more vigorous.'

'Do you recall the evening the Lombard treasure was stolen?'

'Of course, Sir John. The Fleet was preparing to sail. On that particular afternoon Richard Culpepper and Edward Mortimer were absent. I had seen them leave just before sunset. They wore quilted jerkins, sword belts fastened around their waists, they'd drunk and eaten sparsely. At the time I did not know what was happening. Around the same hour I'm sure I saw Guinevere, then she too disappeared. I never saw her again.'

'Now listen.' Athelstan held his hand up. 'You do recall that evening, I'm sure you haven't forgotten. Over the years you must have refreshed your memory. Yes?'

The Misericord nodded in agreement.

'And the recent revelations, by Beatrice and Clarice . . .'

Athelstan paused at a hideous scream from the passageway outside.

'You are not to be worried, Brother,' the Misericord murmured. 'That's a prisoner who thinks he is the Holy Spirit – he throws himself against the wall.'

'My question is this,' Athelstan continued. 'It is a most important one. Did you see Mother Veritable, Master Rolles or any, or all, of those knights leave the tavern the night the Lombard treasure was stolen?'

'No, Brother. Ask Master Rolles. They had hired a

private chamber. Mother Veritable entertained them. The revelry went on late into the night. They were much the worse for drink the next morning.'

'And afterwards?' Cranston asked.

The Misericord shrugged, spreading his hands. 'In a matter of days, Sir John, the Fleet had left. The hunt was on for the Lombard treasure. The rest of the story you know. The brave knights went on Crusade, and years later, returned to England. That is all I know! Will I have my pardon?'

'You'll be shown clemency,' Cranston got to his feet, 'but it will take time.'

'Will you bring me food and drink?'

'I'll do what I can,' Athelstan promised. 'For the moment, you must be patient.'

They left the Netherworld, Athelstan insisting Cranston accompany him to the convent of the Minoresses, which lay on the other side of the City, near Aldgate.

'I'm hungry,' the coroner protested.

'You are always hungry,' Athelstan remarked. He thanked the keeper as they walked back into the prison yard. 'Oh, I must see that bear.'

'Of course, the founder of your order loved animals.'

'Wrong order, Sir John, that was St Francis, although *Dominicanis* can be translated as "Hound of God"!'

In which case, Cranston reflected, as he watched Athelstan walk over to inspect the bear, apparently in a better mood judging from the rotten fruit strewn about it, 'Yes, in which case,' Cranston murmured to himself, 'you belong to the right order, Athelstan, God's hound and mine.'

Athelstan returned, satisfied that the bear was being looked after properly, at least for a while. They left the prison, forcing their way through the press and up past Cock Lane into Smithfield. Athelstan declared he preferred the fresh air beyond the City walls than the stink of Cheapside. Cranston could only agree. The day was still fine but beginning to cloud over, the breeze growing stronger, tugging at the coroner's hat. They took the road which snaked between the great carved mass of the Priory of St Bartholomew and the high red-brick wall of the hospital of the same name. Here the beggars and the infirm swarmed around the gates soliciting alms, or waiting impatiently to be seen by one of the good brothers. A few of these, rogues from the City, greeted Cranston's appearance in raucous fashion. The coroner replied with good-natured abuse whilst quietly wishing Athelstan wouldn't walk so fast. He tried to draw the Dominican into conversation, but Athelstan, cowl over his head, was more concerned about the heavy black smoke rolling in from the great City ditch, where the scavengers, masked and hooded like imps from hell against the fiery background, were busy burning the mounds of refuse. They turned the corner, passing Ramsey Inn, Cripplegate and on to the Moor. Athelstan paused, pushing back his cowl to savour the fresh breeze and watch the birds, great black-winged ravens, circle noisily above him.

'Well, Athelstan, what do you make of all that? Do you think the Misericord is telling the truth?'

'As much as he can, Sir John. He does deserve a pardon. I only hope the Judas Man does not take the law into his own hands. I've met his sort before; every grudge and grievance is personal, a source of animosity. He hates the Misericord, but whether it's because the rogue showed him a clean pair of heels, or for some other matter, I can't decide.'

'And Chandler murdered those two girls?'

'Did he, Sir John? One thing that intrigues me is the bar across the door to the hay barn. Whoever killed Beatrice and Clarice – why should they worry about locking the door? An assassin would flee. One thing is certain,' he continued, 'the Misericord may be a fugitive, a nimble-footed rogue but he would scarcely stand aside whilst two of his friends were murdered. As for their murderer? I don't know.' Athelstan shook his head. 'Mother Veritable is certainly a nightmare soul. She is wicked enough to have those girls killed as well as hunt down the Misericord.'

'And the murders of Sir Stephen and Sir Laurence?' Cranston asked.

'Ah now, that is a mystery!'

'Could the knights be responsible for all the deaths?' The coroner tugged at Athelstan's sleeve. 'Could they have killed Culpepper and Mortimer, murdered Guinevere the Golden, stolen the Lombard treasure and hidden it away until their return?'

'Sir John, continue.'

'They arrive back in England, laden with plunder which only increases their ill-gotten gains. They become landowners, lords of the shire. Every year they meet in London to celebrate their success. Recently they discover that not only is one of their number being tricked by the Misericord and mocked by two whores, but those two prostitutes have also stumbled on what happened twenty years ago.'

'And?' Athelstan asked, turning his face against the breeze.

'Well, they hire the Judas Man to track down the Misericord. They want to see him dance in the air at Smithfield. They persuade Chandler to hire those two girls, to wait in the hay barn on the night of the Great Ratting, where later he kills them. Or perhaps Sir Laurence Broomhill went out before him to commit the murderous deed?'

Athelstan changed his writing satchel from one hand to the other, carefully watching the path before him. The Moor was peppered with rabbit holes, a constant trap for the unwary.

'Sir John, I accept there's a certain logic behind what you say, but it's a dangerous path to follow. According to your theory, the knights are all thieves and murderers, vulnerable to betrayal. However, it doesn't explain how Sir Stephen was murdered, his wine so cunningly poisoned, or how Sir Laurence was enticed down to that cellar and into the hideous trap awaiting him. There are further problems. The Misericord has just informed us that the evening the Lombard treasure was robbed, all the knights, along with Master Rolles and Mother Veritable, were carousing in a chamber at the tavern, much the worse for drink. How did the murderers dispose of four bodies: Culpepper, Mortimer and the bargemen; five if we include Guinevere? Moreover, Culpepper and Mortimer were knights; they would not be easy victims.

'Next we come to the Lombard treasure. It disappeared without trace. If Sir Maurice and the rest stole it, surely they'd try and sell it? And yet.' Athelstan paused so abruptly Cranston bumped into him. 'I'm sorry, Sir John. There was undoubtedly mischief planned that night, some subtle plot. Remember what Mother Veritable told us, how Guinevere had hinted and boasted that one day she would escape her life of drudgery? I wonder what did happen to her? Is it possible Culpepper and Mortimer are still alive, lurking somewhere in the City, hiding behind different names? Then there's the business of the Regent. Why is he so interested in our investigation? Could the Judas Man be involved? Where was he twenty years ago? Is there any connection,' while Athelstan chattered on, Cranston stopped to drink from the miraculous wine skin, 'between a man who has no proper name and the conspiracy to steal the Lombard treasure?'

Athelstan paused whilst Cranston thrust back the stopper to his miraculous wine skin.

'I'm certainly going to ask him the next time we meet,' Cranston grumbled.

'There's one further problem, Sir John. If those knights stole that treasure but didn't try and sell it, where did they hide it whilst they were in Outremer? They could hardly conceal it on a war cog or some military camp!'

Athelstan returned to his reflections as they passed St Mary of Bethlehem and continued down Portsoken, to the limestone buildings of the Minoresses. A porter let them through a postern gate and took them across neatly laid-out gardens and herbers into the guesthouse, a long, whitewashed chamber, starkly empty except for a table, a high-backed bench, two chairs and a stool. At the far end was the Franciscan cross of San Damiano, with its richly coloured texture and finely etched images, each of which told a story. Whilst they waited, Athelstan described it to Cranston, explaining how it was the cross St Francis had prayed before when he received his mission to rebuild Christ's Church.

'Brother Athelstan?'

Athelstan turned. Edith, accompanied by Sister Catherine, stood in the doorway.

'Is everything well?' She hastened towards him. 'Is my brother safe?'

'No, he is not.' Brother Athelstan grasped her hands, moved by the stricken look on the young woman's face.

'Is he taken?' she gasped.

She had gone so pale Athelstan thought she was about to faint and guided her gently towards a chair.

He introduced Sir John and pulled up a stool to sit opposite her.

'Your brother has been captured and taken to Newgate. There is hope for him yet. He has told us certain things which may well earn him a pardon.'

Edith put her face in her hands as Sister Catherine hastened across the room, patting her gently on her head, murmuring how all would be well and that she would pray for it to be so.

'What you did last night,' Athelstan declared, 'was foolish.' He gestured to Sir John to sit in the other chair. 'You helped your brother to escape, didn't you? A change of clothing, money, even a weapon. He was captured trying to come here. I am sorry to bring you the ill news, but—'

'I had to help him,' Edith interrupted, glaring at Athelstan. 'You don't understand, Brother Athelstan, how much I hate that old bitch, that evil harridan.' She ignored Sister Catherine's glare of disapproval. 'If my brother had stayed in your church she would have had him murdered. She hates him for refusing to hand me over to her and her filthy ways.'

'Your brother was friendly with two of the girls who worked in Mother Veritable's house.' Athelstan grasped Edith's hands again. 'You may not know their story, about their mother disappearing so many years ago. They claimed that they stumbled on a secret, a clue to what had happened. When your brother asked them what it was, they replied that it could be found upon your person.'

Edith withdrew her hands, staring in disbelief.

'My brother once,' she whispered, 'came here and asked me a similar question. What of significance did I have upon my person. But,' she spread her hands out, 'I wear the brown robe and white wimple of a Franciscan novice, I have a troth ring on my finger,' she touched the Celtic cross hanging on a chain round her neck, 'and this is all. What on earth would I have in common with two prostitutes or their long-lost mother?'

'Is there anything,' Athelstan persisted, glancing quickly at Sir John, making sure he hadn't fallen asleep, 'you can tell us?'

Edith sat for a while, shaking her head. 'Ever since I came here this is all I have worn. Isn't that true, Sister Catherine?'

The old nun could offer no help, pointing out that she was dressed the same as Edith: a ring symbolising her union with Christ, the cross around her neck, and the girdle around her middle, one of the ends being tied with three knots symbolising her vows of poverty, obedience and chastity. Sister Catherine left them for a while and returned with a tray bearing a jug of buttermilk, four goblets, and a dish of marzipan. Sir John helped himself to the sweetmeats, but politely refused the buttermilk, claiming his miraculous wine skin was sufficient.

Suddenly there was a pounding on the door and one of the convent maidservants came in, shouting Athelstan's name. The Dominican followed her outside. He'd heard the sound of horses in the yard but was surprised to find the Keeper of the Netherworld from Newgate Prison, face soaked in sweat, leaning down from his saddle.

'Brother Athelstan, I had to come. I heard you say to Sir John that you were going to the Minoresses and so, when it happened, I had to tell you myself.'

'What is it?' Athelstan asked.

The keeper closed his eyes and drew a deep breath.

'The prisoner, the Misericord, he's dead! I found him poisoned in his cell.'

Chapter 8

Brother Malachi, of the Order of St Benedict, opened the door to St Erconwald's Church, closed it behind him and leaned back, staring up at the vaulted roof. Malachi was frightened. There was so much to think about, so much to do, yet dangers pressed on every side. He drew a deep breath and stared round the church. He needed to talk to Brother Athelstan, but the priest's house was locked up and the only inhabitants of God's consecrated ground were Bonaventure the cat, that old warhorse browsing in the stable, and Thaddeus, the mournful-looking goat, who was staring out across the cemetery. Thaddeus obviously missed its owner, God-Bless. The beggar man, fast as a rabbit, had joined the rest of Athelstan's parishioners in the Piebald tavern, summoned there by Pernel the Fleming, who seemed to have come into a mysterious inheritance. Crim the altar boy, playing on the lychgate, had told Malachi all this before running off to join the other children in the stable yard of the Piebald, where they too hoped to profit from the revelry with a slice of roast duck or a cup of mulled wine.

Malachi tapped his foot. He had come here many years ago with his beloved brother, Richard Culpepper. He closed his eyes. Even now, twenty years on, he still felt the heart-pulling pain, a deep sense of loss which haunted his soul, and beneath that, a seething anger, a curdling rage. Sometimes in his monastery Brother Malachi could not sleep; he'd go out and stare at the pale-faced moon and wonder, yet again, what had really happened. Richard must be dead, he had proof of that, unless something equally hideous had happened. Malachi opened his eyes. He tried not to remember the old days, the glory time when Richard's heart was full of passion, his tongue ever ready to chatter about the brave deeds of valiant knights. He still missed Richard. He cursed the day when that whore Guinevere the Golden had come into his life, pestering him for favours, hinting at what might be. Richard, gullible as ever, had thought a pretty face meant a fair heart. How wrong he had been!

Richard's fate vexed Brother Malachi, but two other questions dogged his soul. What was Richard planning the night he disappeared, and what did truly happen after darkness had fallen? Over the years Malachi had collected and sifted the information, yet the truth still remained hidden behind the blackness of that night twenty years ago.

'*Tenebrae facta est*,' he whispered to the gloomy nave. 'And darkness fell.' Wasn't that how the Gospel writers described the time of Judas' betrayal of Christ?

Malachi licked his dry lips. He had come here to think, as well as to see the ring he had given Athelstan. He wanted to draw strength from it. He did not want to think of the others, of Chandler lying like a stinking carp in his dirty bathwater or Broomhill jerking on the bed as the blood spilled out of him like claret from a cracked vat. He heard the squeak of mice and a dark shape shot across the ill-lit nave, scurrying from one transept to another. If Bonaventure was here, Malachi reflected wryly, there would be another death. But wasn't that how all life was? If he could only discover what Richard had truly planned . . . Malachi sighed in exasperation and walked up the nave, footsteps echoing hollow. He went to the rood screen and genuflected; he found it hard to look at the pyx hanging from its chain in the sanctuary. He stared round the sanctuary. No Miscricord now – he did feel sorry for that rogue. Didn't they say he was rotting in some cell at Newgate?

Malachi climbed the steps to the high altar. He lifted the heavy green gold-lined coverlet, pushed back the linen altar cloth and stared at the relic stone. In the poor light he glimpsed the red cross carved there and felt the rim of the stone. It was still firmly set, which meant that Athelstan had not yet removed it to insert the ring. Malachi replaced the cloths, and recalled the chantry chapel of St Erconwald's. A taper candle glowed in the Lady Chapel, so Malachi took this, lit another one, and carried both through the wooden partition door and placed them on the altar where he had celebrated Mass. The chantry chapel, despite the statue to St Erconwald, the candles and white linen cloth, did look rather bare and gaunt; no wonder Athelstan wished to furnish it more fittingly. Perhaps when all this was finished, Malachi promised himself, he would donate some money as reparation for what had happened.

Malachi moved across and stared up at the statue of St Erconwald, which gazed sightlessly back from its plinth. He didn't really have any special devotion to a Bishop of London who'd lived and died hundreds of years before the great Conqueror came. No, Malachi reflected, his devotion was more personal, stemming from those glory days when he and his brother Richard had come into Southwark with the rest. They had often come to this church and lounged in the long sweet grass, resting against the gravestones as they shared wine and food, before that great bitch Guinevere the Golden had swept into their lives and everything had changed. Richard no longer met his brother, he became closeted with his paramour, secretive and withdrawn, often being absent for days and returning without any excuse or explanation.

After the great robbery and Richard's disappearance, as the Fleet was about to leave, Malachi had come to this church and vowed to its patron saint that if he ever discovered the truth, he would make a special offering. Now he lifted the taper candle to study the relic statue more carefully, feeling beneath the linen cloths. He sighed with relief. Here, too, the relic stone held firm; Athelstan still had the ring in his possession. He was about to sit down on the small stool to continue his plotting when he heard a sound, a door opening or closing. He strained his ears. Was it the cat? He was sure he'd closed the door fully and leaned against it. Another sound, the slithering rasp of a soft boot. Malachi left the chantry chapel, holding up the taper light.

'Who's there?' he called. The murky light deepened the shadows in the corners and transepts. 'Who's there?' he repeated.

Malachi's skin went cold. Was he, too, to become a victim of brutal murder? Surely not! But someone was in the church, slinking through the darkness, watching him like some gargoyle of the night. Again, a sound. Malachi drew back just in time. Something hard and glittering spun through the gloom and embedded deep into the polished wood of the chapel screen. His heart skipped a beat at the sinister glitter of the blade, the dagger's dark brown handle. Another sound. He stepped back into the chapel, hastily dousing the taper lights. He felt beneath his robe and drew out his own small cutting knife. He didn't want to become trapped here. He stared across the nave and sighed in relief at the glint of daylight – the side door was off its latch! Malachi tried to control his breathing, the beating of blood in his ears and those trickles of fear which made him want to scratch his neck and back. He had to get out of here before whoever was hunting him trapped and killed him here where he had made his vow. For Richard's sake, he had to fulfil that vow!

Malachi's hand went across the altar and snatched up the calfskin-bound missal. He edged to the door of the chapel and hurled the book down the nave. Another dagger whistled through the air, but Malachi was already racing across, even as he heard a third dagger smash against a pillar. He reached the door, opened it and threw himself out. He pulled the door closed and ran across to the priest's house. The door was still locked and bolted. Malachi ran to the window. Thankfully, the two shutters were wide apart. Malachi quietly prayed to whoever was protecting him; the Dominican must have great trust in his parishioners. He slipped his knife through the slit, prising up the bar beyond. He heard it clatter to the floor, and gathering his black robe, clambered through the window, bruising elbow, arm and knees as he tumbled to the floor. Desperate to escape his pursuer, he forgot his pain as he pushed the shutters closed, seized the bar and replaced it in its iron clasps, wedging it tight with a horn spoon taken from the table.

For a while he stood listening. The silence was broken by the sound of voices of a woman and children approaching the church. Sweat-soaked, Malachi slid to the floor, trembling as the deep anger at what had happened overcame the fear seething within him.

'Death comes in many forms, yet terrifying all the same.'

Cranston, standing by Athelstan, stared down at the Misericord, his corpse sprawled on the muck-strewn cell floor. In the flickering light of the lantern horn the cunning man's face was truly ghastly, the eyes no longer merry but half shut in their glazed, sightless stare. The lips, once ever ready to laugh, were now a strange bluish colour, gaping to show the swollen tongue and the dribble of white saliva across the unshaven liverish skin. The cheeks looked puffy, as if swollen.

Athelstan had already performed the death rites; now he stood, as he always did on such occasions, fascinated by the dread of sudden death. He and Cranston had done their best to comfort Edith, taking her back up the very steep steps to her chamber on the third floor of the convent, and leaving her to the tender care of Sister Catherine before hurrying away. The keeper had left before them, riding back to the prison with Cranston's order ringing in his ears that nothing was to be disturbed or touched before they arrived. Yet what was there to see? How could they explain this?

Athelstan picked up the half-eaten pie. Its crust was thick and golden, the mortrews within glistening and rich. Athelstan recognised one of the famous delicious Newgate pies from the cookshops which bought their meat direct from the nearby flesher stalls. A delicacy of the area, the hard-baked crust enclosed a savoury stew of crushed beef and vegetables. He also picked up the linen cloth in which it had been bound, now muddied and soiled. He wrapped the pie in this, lifted it to his nose and sniffed carefully. He caught the aroma of the savoury meat, but something else, very sweet, as if sugar had been added. Was it some form of arsenic? Or the crushed juice of some deadly herb? He placed the napkin and pie on a ledge.

'Tell me,' he turned to the keeper, 'tell me again what happened.'

'Well, you left.' The keeper moved his bunch of keys from one hand to the other. 'In fact, you had hardly gone when one of my bailiffs entered. He had been given a pie for the prisoner, allegedly bought by Sir John himself.' The keeper pointed to the corpse. 'What was I to do? A gift from the Lord Coroner is not to be filched. Thank God it wasn't.' He squeezed his nose. 'Usually such gifts are taken by the gaolers, but as you had just left, Sir John, and had a special interest in this prisoner, we handed it over.'

The keeper walked to the door and shouted a man's name. A sound of running footsteps, and a small, thickset man, garbed in the soiled black and white livery of the prison, came into the cell. He stared mournfully at the corpse, wringing his hands.

'My Lord Coroner,' he swallowed hard, 'I didn't even know. I thought it was a gift from you. I brought it here still warm.'

'Who gave it to you?' Athelstan asked sharply.

'Brother,' the man sighed, 'I don't really know. I was on duty outside the gates, men and women pushing, beggars whining for alms, prisoners' wives screeching. All I remember is a black hood, the head turned to one side. The pie was thrust into my hand with a penny.'

'And the voice?' Cranston asked.

'I couldn't recognise it again, Sir John. Just a few words, "A present from the Lord Coroner to the prisoner known as the Misericord."'

The bailiff joined his hands together as if in prayer.

'Sir John, that's all I can tell you. For the life of me, even on oath, I would not be able to recognise or recall the look of that man or his voice.'

Athelstan dismissed him.

'So, Master Keeper, you brought the pie to the prisoner?'

'Yes, of course I did, Brother. I thought the same as the bailiff. A gift from the Lord Coroner is not to be interfered with.'

'What was he doing when you entered the cell?'

The keeper pointed towards the rusting manacles hanging from a clasp in the far corner. 'Like other prisoners, whiling his time away carving the wall. I've looked at it but can't make sense of it.'

Athelstan picked up the lantern horn, gave it to Cranston and went across. The Misericord's carvings were fresh, different from the rest. A Latin quotation, '*Quem quaeritis?*', and beneath it the numbers '1, 1, 2, 3, 5'.

'What does that mean?' Cranston asked. 'I understand the Latin – it's a question, "Whom do you seek?" But what does it mean? And the significance of the numbers?'

'God only knows,' Athelstan murmured, 'and the Misericord, but he too has gone to God. Remember, Sir John, the Misericord probably didn't tell us everything. He must have been holding something back.'

Athelstan returned to the keeper.

'So, then you left. What happened?'

'I went back down the passageway. Suddenly I heard this gut-wrenching screaming. Now I'm used to that. What happens, Brother, is that when prisoners are brought here, they often don't realise what is happening, then something occurs, and it can be something pleasant like food, a cup of wine or a visit, and they realise where they truly are and what has become of them.' The keeper looped his clutch of keys back on his belt. 'If I opened the door to every prisoner who screamed I would spend all day doing it. The screaming went on, then it began to fade.' He jabbed a finger at the wall to his left. 'Then the prisoner in the next cell, he's usually quiet, he began to shout that something was wrong.'

'Who's in there?' Cranston asked.

The keeper narrowed his eyes. 'Ah yes, that's it. Number 35, Spindleshanks.'

'Ah!' Sir John smiled. 'The relic-seller! Master Keeper, let's have a word with him.'

The gaoler led them out and opened the next door. A little man, sitting in the corner, sprang to his feet. He was so small and thin in his torn shirt, patched hose and boots apparently far too big for him that Athelstan could see why he was named Spindleshanks, for his legs were as thin as needles. The prisoner walked into the pool of light. A mournful face, even his eyes seemed to droop. He reminded Athelstan of a professional mourner; an impression heightened by the lank grey hair which hung down either side of his face.

'Oh, Sir John Cranston,' Spindleshanks whined with a gap-toothed smile. He clasped his hands together. 'What a great pleasure, what a great honour, a visit from the Lord Coroner.'

'Innocent or guilty?' Cranston barked.

'Oh, guilty, my Lord Coroner. I won't tell a lie. As felonious as Judas.'

'On what charge?'

'Oh, the usual, Sir John, relics, they'll be the death of me.'

'How many times is it now, Spindleshanks?'

The prisoner tapped his chin, staring up at the ceiling. 'My sixth, no, it's my seventh time, Sir John. It's bound to be a flogging this time,' his face grew more mournful, 'or my ears clipped.' His lower lip trembled as he fought back the tears. 'Maybe even a brand mark on my cheek.'

'What were you doing this time?'

'Dead dogs, Sir John.'

'Pardon?'

'Dead dogs. I was boiling their corpses, crushing their bones in a maer . . . a handmill.' Spindleshanks answered Athelstan's puzzled look. 'I ground the bones down, bought some little gilt cases and a roll of linen, which I cut into ever so small strips, and sold them as relics.'

'Whose?' Athelstan was genuinely intrigued by this funny little man.

'St Ursula and the eleven thousand virgins martyred by the devilish Huns.'

'And how were you caught?' Cranston asked.

'My neighbours, they alerted the watch complaining about the smell.'

'Well, at least it was only relics and not those potions you were selling. Why have they put you in the Netherworld?'

'Hermisimus!'

'What?' Athelstan asked.

'Have a smell, Brother.'

Spindleshanks drew closer to Athelstan, and the friar recoiled at the foul stench from the old man's clothing.

'Hermisimus, Brother,' Spindleshanks said proudly. 'Sweaty armpits.'

'Even the other prisoners object,' the keeper explained. 'We had to put him here for his own safety.'

'You should wash your armpits,' Athelstan declared. 'Use a mixture of mint and wild strawberries, it will help to clear up your condition.'

'Oh, that's a good idea, Brother. I'll be able to sell it as a genuine cure, won't I?'

'And if you are helpful,' Cranston stooped down, pinching his own nostrils, 'I'll set you free. I'll write a writ under my own seal.'

'Oh, Sir John,' Spindleshanks closed his eyes and moaned in pleasure, 'that would be most kind.'

'You'll give up the dog bones?'

'On my soul, Sir John.'

'Tell me then,' Cranston urged, 'what did you hear from the adjoining cell?'

'Oh, I heard the clank of the manacles, so I knew he was carving the wall.'

'Yes, yes,' Sir John urged, 'but what happened next?'

'I heard the door open, the keeper's voice, and then all went silent. Oh, it must have been some time, then low moans, followed by terrible screams. Sir John, they cut me to the heart. He was also shouting something.'

'What?'

Spindleshanks opened his eyes. 'I'll go free?'

'What?' Cranston persisted.

'He was shouting "Askit, Askit," or something like that. Sir John, that's all I can recall. I swear if I remember anything else, I'll visit you personally.'

'Only after you have washed your armpits!' Cranston dipped into his purse and thrust a coin into the prisoner's hand. 'Now go and wait in the press yard. I'll send a writ across to the keeper.'

'Oh, my Lord Coroner.'

Spindleshanks would have sunk to his knees, but Cranston gripped him by the shoulder and thrust him towards the half-open door.

'Oh, Sir John.'

'What?'

'Would you have any need for a thousand relic cases?'

'Bugger off.'

'Very good, Sir John,' and Spindleshanks scampered down the passageway.

'Have the corpse taken to Blackfriars,' Athelstan ordered. 'Put it in a proper brandeum . . . a shroud,' he explained. 'My good brothers will put him in a coffin until his sister decides where he should be buried.'

They left Newgate. The area outside the prison had now been turned into a makeshift fair, drawing in the crowds to watch a mummer's play, an old story, with two central characters wearing the mask and horns of a cow. First, Chivevache, a lean, ugly cow, who fed on patient women; consequently it was always thin and hungry. Next, Bicorne, a large fat cow, because it fed on patient husbands. In between these two danced a character dressed in a leather hood who assumed the role of the 'Digitus Infamus', the 'Middle Finger', who kept up lewd commentary on why these two cows existed and were so different. Of course, this provoked the ribald interest of the spectators, who quickly divided into male and female, hurling obscenities at each other as the Digitus Infamus explained why wives lacked patience whilst husbands were models of virtue. Every so often the mummer would break off from his commentary to sing an even more ribald song about a gentle cock residing in its lady's chamber. Naturally, when a boy in tattered rags ran round the crowd with a pannikin for pennies he received plenty of coins from the men and raucous refusal from the women.

'I've seen that play a hundred times,' Cranston murmured, as he led Athelstan through the milling crowd. 'The effect is always the same. The men relish the joke and pay the money; next week they'll return, and the lean, ugly cow will feed on patient husbands and consequently go famished, whilst the fat cow will be the result of patient wives. It's a clever way of drawing in money.'

They left the great forecourt, and the salacious mummer's play, and entered the dark coolness of an ale house, ducking to avoid the great green bush hanging above the doorway. Cranston took a window seat and immediately ordered two tankards of ale, while he dictated a letter on behalf of Spindleshanks to the Keeper of Newgate, and sent it back to the prison courtesy of a pot boy. When this was done he toasted Athelstan, took a deep draught and leaned back against the wall.

'Who killed the Misericord?' he asked.

'Somebody who followed us to Newgate and watched us leave,' the friar replied, 'and decided to act immediately. All these killings, Sir John, I am sure have their root in what happened twenty years ago. The Misericord discovered something, or was told something by those two girls. They had to die and so did he. But the question is what?'

'The Night in Jerusalem,' Cranston observed, 'lies in Southwark. Somebody must have crossed the river, walked up Cheapside, bought that pie, poisoned it, left it in Newgate and then returned. Hey, lad?' He called across to the pot boy, who had appeared in the doorway, still breathless after his errand to Newgate. 'Come here.' Cranston seized him by his thin arm and pressed a coin into the boy's dirty little hand. 'Here's a shilling, boy. Go to the tavern known as the Night in Jerusalem – it lies in Southwark, not far from the bridge. Tell mine host I wish to see him, all the knights and Mother Veritable, within the hour.'

The boy glanced across at the ale-wife, who stood near the barrels. She nodded.

'Repeat the message,' Sir John urged.

The boy, used to such tasks, closed his eyes, faithfully repeated what Cranston had told him, then hurried out into the street.

'One of those,' Cranston murmured, 'must have left Southwark.'

'One person whom we know little about,' Athelstan distractedly observed, 'is the man who was with

Culpepper the night the Lombard treasure was stolen – what was his name? Oh yes, Edward Mortimer. In fact, Sir John, we know very little about this treasure or its stay in the Tower. Could you make discreet enquiries?'

Cranston agreed.

'And I,' Athelstan offered, 'will find out more about the Lombards, the name of the banker responsible; I'll also ask Moleskin if he knows anything about the two bargemen who disappeared.'

Athelstan finished his ale and picked up his writing satchel, cradling it in his lap.

'I wonder what the Misericord meant,' he mused, 'about those numbers and that Latin tag. And what was he shouting? What did he mean by "Askit"? An educated man, Sir John, the Misericord was holding something back; perhaps he recognised that and left such a message on the wall just in case something happened.'

'Could the Judas Man have killed him?' Cranston drained his tankard.

'It's possible,' Athelstan agreed. 'He, too, is a man surrounded by mystery, gleeful at the Misericord's capture. He may have murdered him, fearful lest the Misericord's quick-silver wits allowed him to escape either Newgate or the hangman's noose. Which, in turn, provokes another question. Was the Judas Man hired by someone we've met, or by a complete stranger? And did that person, whoever it was, instruct the Judas Man to ensure the Misericord was not only captured but killed? Ah well, Sir John, the hour draws on.'

They left the ale house and, avoiding the crowd, went down Dean's Lane, past Athelstan's mother house of Blackfriars to East Watergate. The day was clouding over, the crowds intent on finishing trading and escaping the biting cold. The quayside was fairly deserted as it was too early for the fishing folk to prepare for the night's work. The barges had finished bringing their produce and now stood moored, waiting for the evening. Bailiffs and beadles patrolled the quayside, vigilant against any trader trying to sell or buy without the blessing of the Corporation or the guilds.

They hired a barge, Athelstan was disappointed that he couldn't find Moleskin, and went upriver, fighting the choppy current. A mist was creeping in. Athelstan huddled in the stern, his cowl pulled tightly about him, whilst Cranston, ever curious, kept up a constant commentary on which barges belonged to which noblemen, as well as those dignitaries of the city travelling to and from the Tower or Westminster.

'Thank God we don't have to go under London Bridge,' Cranston remarked. 'The river is running heavy and fast, and in this mist I can hardly make out the top of the bridge.'

Athelstan half listened as he closed his eyes and fingered his Ave beads. He was always wary of the river; a good portion of St Erconwald's cemetery was reserved for the corpses of poor souls who had drowned on the Southwark side . . .

'That's it!'

'What?' Cranston asked.

'Nothing, Sir John. It's just that . . . I wonder if the river was searched for the corpses of Culpepper and Mortimer, not to mention those bargemen. I mean properly searched by the Fisher of Men.'

'Was he here then?' Cranston asked.

He'd met the person Athelstan was referring to, a sinister, skull-faced man hired to search the river for the bodies of the drowned.

'I think he was,' Athelstan retorted, 'but we'll see.'

They landed near the Bishop of Winchester inn, a little further down from the infamous bath houses which Athelstan knew were a mask for prostitution and other secret sins. Once he was on the quayside he looked around for Moleskin, only to be informed by the boy guarding his barge that the boatman could be found in the cookshop next to the Piebald tavern, where he had business with Master Merrylegs, the owner. On the way to the Night in Jerusalem, Athelstan and Cranston stopped there. Moleskin was sitting in the far corner deep in conversation with Merrylegs, who supplemented his income with the sale of goods stolen by Athelstan's parishioners from the stalls in Cheapside. Once Cranston's huge form was seen bearing towards them, Merrylegs and Moleskin hastily drew apart, sweeping whatever was on the table before them into a leather bag.

229

'Oh! God bless you, Brother Athelstan.' Moleskin tried to hide his guilt behind a smile whilst Merrylegs hurried away. 'And you, Sir John, do you want some ale?'

'I would love to know what you have in that bag,' the coroner replied, 'but instead I'll give you a task. You recall the robbery of the Lombard treasure?'

'Of course, your grace,' Moleskin hastily replied. 'All the river people knew about it.'

'The boatmen, they left widows, families?'

'Just widows.' Moleskin pulled a face. 'And one of them has died too, drowned washing clothes! Silly woman, she always insisted on drinking ale.' He wagged a finger in the coroner's face. 'Ale and the river don't mix.'

'And the other widow?' Athelstan asked.

'Oh, that's fat Margot. She's left Southwark, sells fish in Billingsgate.'

'Tomorrow morning,' Athelstan declared, 'after Mass, bring fat Margot to see me.'

Moleskin agreed. Athelstan and Cranston continued their journey. When they arrived at the Night in Jerusalem, Master Rolles was acting all busy in the tap room. He was surly in his greeting, muttering under his breath at how busy he was.

'I have gathered the rest,' he declared, wiping his hands. 'They're in the solar. Sir John, what is this all about?'

The taverner's black eyes were almost hidden by creases of fat; his annoyance, however, was obvious,

in his petulant whine and the way he kept looking longingly towards the kitchen, where cooks and
scullions were busy preparing for the evening's entertainment.

'Why, Master Rolles, it's murder!'

'Nothing to do with me,' the taverner muttered.

'Mine host,' Cranston slapped him hard on the
shoulder, 'four corpses have been found in your tavern, whilst the Misericord is dead.'

Master Rolles gaped.

'Dead?' he spluttered. 'But he was taken safe to
Newgate.'

'He was safe,' Athelstan retorted, 'but now he is
dead! Poisoned in his cell.'

Rolles immediately ushered them into the solar.
The knights were there, surly-eyed and bitter-mouthed,
openly seething at Cranston's peremptory summons,
as was Mother Veritable, who made her annoyance
obvious by turning away, more interested in what
was happening in the garden beyond.

Cranston sat at the top of the table, Athelstan
beside him.

'You seem impatient with us,' the coroner began,
'so I'll be blunt. I'm in no mood for niceties. Where
were you all this afternoon?'

He paused while Athelstan undid his writing satchel
and laid out a piece of vellum on the table along with
his writing instruments.

'Well?' Cranston repeated. 'Where were you all?'

'We were all here,' Sir Maurice Clinton broke in.

'I can vouch for that, as can Master Rolles.' The knight gestured at the taverner. 'I can also vouch for him.'

'And you, Mother Veritable?' Cranston asked sweetly.

'Why, Sir Jack,' her voice was rich with sarcasm, 'I have been here since noon at Master Rolles' request. We were discussing the burial of poor Beatrice and Clarice.'

'And none of you left?' Athelstan asked.

'The gentlemen,' Master Rolles declared, 'rose late, broke their fast, and either stayed in their chambers, sat in the garden or, after noon, dined here. Ask any of the maids or scullions. You had best tell them, Sir John, what has really happened.'

'The Misericord is dead,' Cranston declared. 'He was kept safe in a cell at Newgate, but someone passed him a pie claiming it was a gift from me. The pie was poisoned . . .'

Athelstan watched their faces for any reaction. The knights seemed unconcerned, whilst Mother Veritable just shrugged, a bitter twist to her mouth.

'Look around you, Sir John,' Sir Maurice urged. 'Who is missing?'

'The Judas Man.' Sir Thomas Davenport spoke up. 'In fact, I haven't seen him since this morning. And where is Brother Malachi?'

'Why should we be interrogated,' Sir Reginald Branson coughed, 'because a rogue, undoubtedly bound for the hangman, had his pie laced with poison?'

232

His words provoked laughter, which Cranston stilled by banging on the table.

'The Judas Man,' Athelstan asked, 'is his horse still in the stable?'

'Yes,' Rolles replied, 'I saw it there myself. If you want, I'll check his chamber.'

They all waited as the taverner left the solar and, complaining loudly, stamped up the stairs. He returned a short while later.

'The door was off the latch,' he declared, retaking his seat, 'but the chamber is empty. All his goods, saddlebags,' he spread his hands, 'gone.'

'But not his horse?'

'No, Brother, neither his horse nor the harness. Perhaps the Judas Man has hired another chamber?'

'I wouldn't blame him,' Sir Thomas Davenport grumbled. 'Master Cranston, if we want to, we should be able to leave here.'

'Sir John, to you,' Cranston snapped, 'and I assure you, sir, that if you leave Southwark, I'll have you arrested and dragged back at my horse's tail.'

'Enough!' Athelstan's raised voice created a surprised silence. 'Why this hostility?' the Dominican continued. 'Five people have been foully murdered, their souls sent to God before their time. Beneath such murders the events of twenty years ago, the Lombard treasure being stolen, and again five souls disappeared. God knows if they were murdered or not.'

'Brother, that's a closed book,' Sir Maurice countered. 'The truth couldn't be established then.'

'Surely you know the proverb, Sir Maurice: truth is the daughter of time. If we resolve the mystery of twenty years ago, we shall be able to establish the truth now.' Athelstan glanced quickly at Cranston. 'So, none of you left the tavern this afternoon and, therefore, were probably not involved in the murder of the Misericord.'

'Probably?' Mother Veritable spat out.

'Well, mistress, you may not have left the tavern, but a man you hated lies murdered.'

Mother Veritable sneered, tapping her fingers on the table.

'Twenty years ago,' Athelstan continued blithely, 'the Lombard treasure was stolen. Master Rolles owned this tavern and the Knights of the Golden Falcon were staying here.'

They all agreed.

'On that particular night you gathered here. The only two persons missing were Richard Culpepper and Edward Mortimer.'

'Brother Malachi wasn't here.' Sir Maurice spoke up. 'He had been absent all day visiting Charterhouse and Clerkenwell. He didn't return until afterwards, when the news of the robbery was all over the city.'

'Very good.' Athelstan folded back the full sleeves of his gown. 'Whilst you stayed here, Richard Culpepper fell smitten with the courtesan known as Guinevere the Golden. That is correct?'

Sir Maurice agreed; Mother Veritable echoed the word 'smitten' under her breath.

234

'Mistress, you find this funny?'

'Yes, I do, Brother,' came the cool reply. 'Everybody was smitten with Guinevere, whilst she was smitten with anyone who had gold and silver.'

'Guinevere hinted,' Athelstan declared, 'that there was to be a change in her life. Do any of you know what she was referring to?'

'She was a whore!' Davenport shouted. 'We can't be held responsible for what went on in her pretty empty noddle.'

'So none of you were smitten with her?'

'Well of course not!' Branson spoke up, his face all aflush. 'Culpepper was our comrade; each to their own, I say.'

'Did Culpepper or Mortimer,' Athelstan continued, 'tell you why they had been chosen to receive the Lombard treasure and transport it to the flagship?'

'No.' Maurice shook his head. 'We only found that out later. Apparently, as I've said, Lord Belvers chose them especially, though rumour claimed His Grace the Regent was responsible.'

'Why?'

'They'd both fought in John of Gaunt's retinue. He was, I suppose, their liege lord.'

'Both of them?' Cranston queried. 'Culpepper is a Kentish name, but Mortimer, that's a name from South Wales, isn't it?'

'True, Sir John. Mortimer was Culpepper's friend and comrade – a mercenary who often frequented our company, a good swordsman and a master bowman.

Culpepper and Mortimer were like two peas in a pod. During the days before the great robbery they were often absent; they acted rather mysteriously, not telling us where they were going or what they were doing.'

'And you never questioned them?'

'Well, of course, Brother, we were curious, but those were very busy days: the fleet preparing to sail, men seeking out friends and comrades, and, of course, there was always the attraction of Guinevere the Golden.'

'So,' Athelstan summarised, 'you know nothing about the Lombard treasure or your two comrades being chosen to accept it; you spent that night here in the tavern, you have no knowledge of why Guinevere hinted that she should soon have a change in station, and you have no knowledge of what happened to the treasure, Culpepper and Mortimer?'

'I speak for us all,' Sir Maurice abruptly declared. 'We would also like to know why we are being kept here, and why,' he added, glaring bitterly at Cranston, 'two of our comrades, Sir Laurence and Sir Stephen, have been slain, yet their assassin has not been caught.'

'We are searching for the assassin,' Cranston stood, pushing back the chair, 'and until we find that person, everyone in this room, not to mention the Judas Man and Brother Malachi, is regarded as a suspect.'

Athelstan repacked his writing satchel, aware of the ominous silence. Once outside, Cranston put a finger to his lips. He crossed the stable yard and entered the street.

'Is it possible,' Athelstan pulled up his cowl, adjusting the strap of his writing satchel over his shoulder, 'that Culpepper or Mortimer, or indeed both of them, could still be alive, and be responsible for these murders? Where is the Judas Man, and Brother Malachi? They have questions to answer.'

'Oh, I forgot to ask them that.'

Cranston told Athelstan to wait, and strode back into the tavern. The friar waited impatiently, watching two boys play with an inflated pig's bladder, only to be distracted by two little girls chasing a rat they had disturbed in a rubbish heap. The sun had disappeared. Athelstan felt cold and hungry, and leaned against the gate post.

'It's time to pray,' he whispered. 'To eat and sleep.'

'Well,' Cranston came striding back through the gate, 'I asked my question and nobody could help.'

'Yes, Sir John?'

'Did any of them hire the Judas Man? They could tell me nothing, not even his true name. I wonder,' Cranston tapped his boot on the cobbles, 'I wonder if the Judas Man was hired, or does he have something to do with those events twenty years ago? I have checked the stables. His horse and harness are still there. I'll get my searchers out. If necessary I'll arrest him.'

'Very good, Sir John.'

'You look tired,' Cranston said kindly. 'Sufficient for the day is the evil thereof.' He patted Athelstan on the shoulder. 'Go back to your prayers, monk, I'll see what the Lady Maud has been doing.'

Cranston walked off down the street.

'Sir John?'

'Yes, Brother?' Cranston turned.

'I'm a friar.'

'And a very good one too. Good day to you, Brother.'

Athelstan returned to St Erconwald's. Some of the parish children were playing in the cemetery. He walked up the steps to the church and into the gloomy nave. He lit some tapers at the Lady Altar and, picking one up, walked round the sanctuary. He visited the chantry chapel and noticed the tapers lying on the floor. The missal was gone, and his curiosity deepened when he found it lying down the nave near a pillar. He hurried across to his house. Nothing seemed amiss, but as soon as he turned the key in the lock, he realised something was wrong, though the kitchen was swept and clean, and the fire built high.

'Brother Athelstan, I am sorry.'

The friar glanced up in surprise as Brother Malachi came down the ladder from the bed loft. The Benedictine looked as if he had been deeply asleep. Warming his hands over the fire, Malachi told Athelstan all about his visit to the church: how he had been attacked and fled to the house for safety.

'Strange,' he smiled, 'I never thought a church could be so dangerous. Brother, I had no choice, there was no one around. I forced the shutters and hid; I dared not go out.'

'I saw no sign of your attacker in the church or cemetery.'

'Once I was in here,' Brother Malachi declared, 'there was no further attack. I think my assailant fled.'

Athelstan reassured him that he had done the right thing, whilst trying to control his anger at the way the attacker had used his church for murder and sacrilege.

'He threw knives? You are sure of that?'

'Very sure, Brother. Two narrowly missed my face; they were long, thin and ugly. I thought I would die from fright. I went into the church to think, to make my devotions. I do not like that tavern. I am now highly distrustful of my companions. My days with them are ended.'

He held up his maimed hand.

'I have known them for longer than I care to think. I have eaten, drunk, lived, slept and fought with them.'

'Do you think one of them was your assailant?'

'Perhaps.' Malachi rubbed the side of his face. 'And yet, I know those knights. My assailant moved swiftly, a dagger man, and unless I am mistaken, that is not a skill shared by any of those knights.'

'Let us see, let us see.'

Athelstan took Malachi back into the church. They lit candles and carefully searched but, apart from the splintered wood in the entrance to the chantry chapel, Athelstan could find no sign of any knife.

'I'll get Crispin the carpenter to see to the wood.'
Athelstan patted Malachi on the arm. 'If you wish,
you can stay with me. You would feel safer, wouldn't
you?'

The Benedictine nodded. 'I'll go back later to collect my belongings. If you could shelter me, Brother,
when this is all over, before I leave,' he offered, 'I'll
make good any damage or inconvenience I may have
caused.'

Athelstan walked him back to the house, describing
what had happened that day. He talked whilst he
prepared the evening meal, laying out the tranchers.
From its hook in the buttery he brought a roll of cured
spiced ham, yesterday's bread, small pots of butter and
honey and a pitcher of ale. He recited the Benedicite
and sat down.

'Did you know the Misericord?' Athelstan asked.

'I remember him vaguely as a lad, a cheeky-faced
boy who had the run of Master Rolles' tavern,
nothing significant. I'm sorry for his death. God
assoil him and give him good rest. Brother, I was
not in Cheapside today.' Malachi grinned. 'I can
tell from your eyes you must be suspicious about
everyone.'

'The Judas Man?' Athelstan asked.

'Athelstan, I know nothing of him either, nor do I
know anything about Master Rolles or Mother Veritable. The knights? I thought they were honourable
men, boisterous when young, valiant warriors in war,
respectable and upright in their mature years.'

'Do you think they could have killed your brother and stolen the treasure?'

'How could they?' Malachi glanced away. 'On the night the treasure was taken, they were drunk. I was across the river visiting brethren at Charterhouse. The next morning I saw them; they were totally dispirited, indeed, irritable. Brother Athelstan, I went to Outremer with these men, I slept beside them on ship, on shore, in the desert. I fought with them before the walls of Alexandria. I heard their confessions. If they owned the treasure it would have been obvious. The mice in your church are richer than they were. They were pressed for money, even to eat and drink. When the ship docked at Genoa to take on supplies they had to pawn some of their own weapons and beg loans from their comrades.'

'But couldn't they have stolen the treasure and hidden it until their return?'

'It's possible.' The Benedictine pushed away his trancher, picked up a piece of cheese and chewed on it slowly. 'My order has houses the length and breadth of this kingdom, from Cornwall to the mountains of Scotland. I made enquiries through them; sometimes our abbots act as bankers. I have also circulated lists to the guilds of goldsmiths and jewellers in London, Bristol, Nottingham, Carlisle and even in the Cinque Ports. I promised rewards for any sign of the Lombard treasure being found.'

'How did you know the description of that treasure?'

'I went to see Teodoro Tonnelli, head of the Lombard

banking house in London. He still does business here. He gave me a complete list of what was stolen. He, too, offered a reward.'

Athelstan put his face in his hands. He tried to visualise the Oyster Wharf at night, the cresset torches burning, Culpepper and Mortimer, the two bargemen.

'How was the treasure transported?'

'According to Tonnelli, in an iron-bound coffer with three locks. The keys had been given to the captain of the flagship.'

'Ah!' Athelstan sighed. 'Further precaution, eh? I can't imagine someone trying to force that chest on the quayside or on a barge on the river at night.' He closed his eyes again. 'I'm trying to imagine, Malachi, how it happened? Did your brother and Mortimer kill the boatmen and disappear into the darkness with the treasure? Or did the boatmen help? If that was the case, surely someone would have seen them, two or four men staggering through the darkness with a heavy chest? Yet, if they were attacked, all four men were well armed; surely they would have defended themselves? The crash of swords, the yells, the cries. Someone must have heard! And how would they get so close?'

Athelstan rubbed his fingers around his lips, wiping away the crumbs.

'Of course, it is possible a master bowman, perhaps two skilled archers, slipping through the darkness, brought down all four men with well-aimed shafts. But there again, the treasure hasn't been found, nor the remains of any of the corpses. And if blood was shed . . .' He opened his eyes. 'The Oyster Wharf was inspected the following morning, wasn't it?'

Malachi nodded.

'I went down there myself, Brother, not a sign. My brother was a fighting man, he had been entrusted with an important task. He would be wary. How could his attackers even get close?'

'So you can tell me nothing about your brother?'

'What I know,' Malachi replied, crossing himself, 'is what you know.'

'Do you think your brother and Mortimer survived?'

'And attacked me in your church? No.' Malachi picked up a piece of cheese and broke it into two with his fingers. 'I believe my brother and Mortimer are dead.' He touched his chest. 'Just a feeling here.'

Athelstan studied the Benedictine carefully – Malachi seemed very agitated, as if trying to control his temper.

'No one left that tavern today.' Athelstan put his thoughts into words. 'Yet who murdered the Misericord? Who would want you dead?'

'There's the Judas Man.'

'Ah, yes.' Athelstan brushed the rest of the crumbs off and went to refill the ale jug. 'I'm afraid,' he called from the buttery, 'he's disappeared and is becoming the scapegoat for every awful act.'

'I know nothing of him,' Malachi called back. 'Why should he attack me?'

'Tell me about Mortimer,' Athelstan asked, coming back.

'A Welshman, related to the great family. You know the kind, the youngest son of the youngest brother; all Mortimer owned was a weapon and a horse. A dark, swarthy-faced man with raven-black hair down to his shoulders. A skilled dagger man, good with a bow. Mortimer and Richard met during the wars in France and became the closest of comrades. I felt as if Richard had acquired another brother.'

Athelstan sensed the hint of jealousy in Malachi's voice.

'I know what you are thinking: I'm jealous of Mortimer. Somehow he always made my brother laugh. Mortimer was close, secretive, he'd often disappear for days and nights, shifty-eyed but trustworthy enough. He had a sister, a quiet little mouse of a woman.'

Malachi rose from the table.

'It's growing dark, Brother, I can say no more. It's time for vespers, but I will not go alone into your church.'

'Let's pray together,' Athelstan murmured. 'For strength against the demon who prowls like a lion seeking whom he may devour.'

Chapter 9

The two knights were preparing to charge, a surging, united passion of man and horse eager to ride their opponent down. The herald, in the centre of the lists – a long stretch of multicoloured canvas just over a yard high down the centre of Smithfield – raised his white baton, hard to distinguish against the light blue morning sky. All eyes watched him, fascinated by this blue-, red- and gold-liveried herald who would begin the tournament. At either end of the lists trumpeters waited to give clarion blasts on their silver trumpets. Above them, stiffened pennants and loose-tied banners spread out in the early morning breeze. Vividly coloured cloths displayed the arms and heraldic devices of the two opponents: a silver half-moon above red gules and golden scallop shells; and a light grey boar ready to charge against a dark blue field, above that a strip of silver stars against a red background. The two knights waited at either end of the lists in their silver-edged armour, ready to joust; their war destriers, eager to charge, snorted and pawed the ground, resplendent in gorgeously caparisoned cloths and gleaming black harness. The knights sat, heads slightly down so that they could peer more clearly through their visor slits; from each helmet elegantly plumed feathers ruffled in the breeze. The noise of the horses, the creak of harness and the harsh clatter of armour carried across to the spectators, intensifying their excitement.

A drum began to beat, a striking hollow sound. The crowd fell silent, the course was ready. The knights, unable to control their restless horses, let them move forward a little to relieve the tension. All eyes watched their champions, visors down, sitting so immobile in the high horn saddles, shields up, blunted lances ready. The trumpets blasted, a carrying, ringing sound which sent birds in the nearby trees whirring up to the sky. The crowd moaned in pleasure. Another trumpet blast, followed by a third, and the jousters moved forward, a resplendent vision of moving, dazzling colour. The horses broke into a trot, the herald threw his baton down and stepped back even as the horses burst into a gallop, moving to a furious charge, the drumming of their hoofs drowning all sound. Lances came down, crossing over the horses' necks to meet their targets, shields slightly raised; a magnificent sight, man and horse, free as a bird, fast and furious as a falling falcon.

They met in a dramatic clash of steel. Each shattered their opponent's lance and shield. One knight swayed slightly in his saddle but managed to stay in his seat. They reached the end of the lists. Fresh lances were brought and the heart-throbbing music of battle began again as both knights moved into the charge, bearing furiously down upon each other. They met once again in the centre, lances shattering, horses neighing and rearing. The knight who fought under the banner of the Grey Boar swayed dangerously. He tried to right himself, his horse swerved, chain-mailed feet broke free of the stirrups and the knight tumbled to the ground with an almighty crash. His opponent reined in and turned round. The fallen knight tried to raise himself, struggled weakly and lay back as squires and pages, in tabards brightly coloured as a field of flowers, hurried across to help.

'Well I never! God and St George help us!' Sir John Cranston, Lord Coroner of the City, turned to the small, thin-as-a-beanpole man standing next to him. 'Well, Bohun, that was a mighty fight. Reminded me of my younger days.'

'Yes, Sir John, it did. But what was the tourney over?'

Cranston put his arm round his old comrade's shoulder.

'I asked you to meet me here, Bohun, as I knew you would be interested in it. The Knight of the Grey Boar is Sir William Stafford, his opponent Sir Humphrey Neville, both young bucks of the Court.

Now, a month ago, our noble Regent staged a *Bal des Ardents*.'

'What's one of them?' Bohun asked.

'A little conceit our Regent has imported from France, where the nobles of the Court, for God knows what reason, dress as wild men of the woods, their faces smeared with mud, their heads and bodies covered in coats of hay, straw and bracken. What happens is this . . .' Cranston kept his eyes on the hapless knight as he was lifted on to a stretcher. 'Oh good,' he murmured, 'it doesn't seem as if he was hurt too badly. What happens is this: the young bucks like to fight, to frighten the ladies, so all the candles are doused in the great hall. The wild men of the woods appear, carrying torches. The lady of their heart has to find which is her beloved. Anyway, to keep my tale brief and pointed, Sir Humphrey, whether by accident or design, let his torch slip and set fire to Sir William's coat. A lady doused it but Sir William was furious; he claimed it was no accident and challenged Sir Humphrey to a duel. It looks as though honour has been satisfied.'

'It's a pity both the stupid buggers weren't consumed by fire.'

Cranston laughed. 'Bohun, let's visit the glories of Smithfield.'

They walked across the open expanse which stretched in front of the great church of St Bartholomew's and its adjoining hospital, a favourite meeting place beyond the old City walls, with its makeshift stalls, the gathering point for petty tinkers and traders who sold a variety of goods. Most of the great field was dedicated to the horse fair, drawing in people of every kind and quality, from powerful nobles in their silks and ermine-lined capuchins, to travelling people in their sheepskin jackets and shaggy caps. All the entertainers of the City flocked here, not just the whores and the acrobats but the goliards, the storytellers and singers. Pedlars offered relics, cage-holders sold white birds which, if they looked directly at you – or so their owners bawled – could cure you of the malady known as yellow skin. Soldiers from the Tower in their brigadines brushed shoulders with archers from the garrison at Westminster, distinctive in their capeliens, their small iron scull caps, and brilliant blue and gold tabards. Beggars whined for alms from the pretty daughters of powerful merchants, who drew away in disgust. Cranston, one arm across his friend's shoulder, guided him through the swirling throng, eye ever keen for the rogues and pickpockets who swarmed as thick as crows on a dung hill.

'How are you, old comrade?' Cranston gave Bohun a squeeze.

'Happy as a hog's turd.'

'Thirsty?'

'Always!'

Cranston steered Bohun over to a makeshift ale shop set up under one of the trees, selling hot cups of posset, and tankards of lambswool, strong ale enriched with roasted apples, raw sugar, grated nutmeg and ginger, with tiny sweet cakes floating on the top. He ordered two of these, and he and his comrade sat on a nearby bench, sipping appreciatively at the rim of the leather blackjacks.

'I used to come here,' Cranston murmured, gesturing at the crowds. 'My father was a fearsome man, Keeper of the Horses at the Royal Stables, at Clerkenwell. He would collect me from St Paul's school and, if the master said I had done well, would bring me here to sip some lambswool. Fine days, eh, Bohun? I didn't become a philosopher or a lawyer,' he continued, 'but first and foremost a knight. I enjoyed the glory days.' He sipped from the tankard again.

'Sir John,' Bohun sighed, 'I have known you for many a year; our friendship runs deep.' He placed the blackjack on the ground between his feet and cocked his head, half listening to a group of scholars standing nearby, sweetly singing the hymn 'Alma Mater Dei'. 'I was Serjeant of the Tower, responsible for the Garde Manger and Garde Au Vin, supervisor of the food and wine. I suspect you have not brought me here to go back through the Gates of Ivory and Horn into the realm of dreams, of what might have been?'

'Sharp as ever.' Cranston plucked at the ganache, the over-robe Bohun wore, tied round the middle with a ribbon. 'You've lost weight?'

'*Bellum intestinum*,' Bohun whispered, picking up the tankard. 'War within! There's something wrong with my gut, Sir John. By noon I'm tired and the pain returns, that's why I'm impatient. So, why have you brought me here?'

Cranston stared at Bohun's sad face and pitied him. Some of his old friends had already gone; Cranston always feared that some day he would even lose the friendship of Athelstan, whose order could send him to any house in the kingdom.

'The Lombard treasure,' he began. 'Twenty years ago the bankers sent a casket of treasure into the Tower. It was meant for Peter of Cyprus' crusade against Alexandria. You remember? England had signed a peace treaty with France, so many knights and fighting men flocked to Lord Peter's banner. An English fleet assembled in the Thames. The bankers provided this treasure, which could later be exchanged for gold and silver, in return for which, as usual, they would receive their loan back with interest as well as a portion of all profits. The treasure was delivered to the Tower, a secure place where our noble Regent, John of Gaunt, was Keeper. He was fearful that it might be stolen if he sent it along the riverbank, or across London Bridge, so it was apparently taken from Tower Quay, across the river, along the south bank of the Thames, under London Bridge to the Oyster Wharf in Southwark. Here it was to be handed over to two knights, Richard Culpepper and Edward Mortimer. They, helped by two boatmen, were to take the treasure across to the Fleet's flagship, anchored mid-river somewhere between Queenhithe and Dowgate. The treasure was delivered, Culpepper sealed an indenture for it, but since that night, there's been no sight of the treasure, or those two knights or the boatmen they hired. Now, you were a Serjeant in the Tower at that time.'

'I suppose I haven't long left,' Bohun rubbed his hands together, 'and I'm not sure of the importance or truth of what I'm going to say, but,' he sipped at his drink, 'the Tower was full of Gaunt's men, archers, footmen and household knights. The Lombards brought their treasure in on a cart.'

'How big was the chest?'

'About a yard long, and a little more in height. A great black oaken chest, stiffened with iron bands. It had three locks and someone told me that the keys had already been given to the Admiral of the Fleet.' Bohun closed his eyes, eager to remember details. 'The chest was taken into the Norman Tower. The Lombards had pressed their seals on it, and so did John of Gaunt. I remember him, how can you forget that golden hair, those light blue eyes? I saw that chest because it was kept in the same cellar as the wine. Two days later it was gone, that's all I know. When the news came of the robbery Gaunt was beside himself with rage. He locked himself in the royal quarters, refusing to meet anybody, even messengers sent from his father the King.'

'And you know nothing?' Cranston showed surprise.

'Sir John, the treasure was meant to be a great secret. I don't know what happened to it or its guardians. But

I tell you this, Edward Mortimer was one of John of Gaunt's henchmen. Oh yes,' he smiled at Cranston's expression, 'Mortimer sealed indentures with him, fought in his retinue in Gascony; that's where he met Culpepper. And did you also know, Sir John, in the days preceding the Great Robbery, Culpepper and Mortimer were regular visitors to the Tower, met by no less a person than the Regent himself. Of course,' he shrugged, 'there's nothing wrong in that. They had been given a secret mission. Sometimes a woman came with them.'

'A woman with golden hair?'

'No, Sir John. This woman was small and dark. She often stayed in the refectory, being served by the pantry man.'

'Who was she?'

'At first I thought she was Mortimer's woman. In fact she was his sister Helena. Very close to her brother she was, owned a house in Poor Jewry.'

Cranston drained his tankard in one swallow and jumped up, ready to leave.

'Now to where, Sir John?'

'Helena Mortimer in Poor Jewry. Is she still alive?'

'God knows, Sir John.'

'Well, if she is, I'll find her.'

Cranston thanked his old friend profusely, said he would ask Brother Athelstan to say a Mass for him and hurried off towards Aldgate. He threaded his way through the back streets of the City, the alleyways which ran alongside the City ditch from St Giles to St Mary Axe Street, and into Poor Jewry. This was a broad thoroughfare, the houses on either side old and high, built on stone bases, the tops leaning over so dramatically they created a tunnel with only a strip of sky between them. A respectable although shabby quarter of the City, with garish signs hanging from hooks above shop doorways; a street where one could buy expensive leather goods and silver trinkets. Most of the houses were no longer owned by a single occupant, but each floor was leased out by absent landlords. Cranston made enquiries in a small ale shop at the corner of an alleyway.

'Helena Mortimer?' the ale-wife replied. 'What business do you have with her?'

She studied this large man with his beaver cap and fur-lined robe, who drank her ale, smacking his lips in appreciation. Cranston fished beneath his robe and brought out his seal of office.

'Sir John Cranston, Coroner of the City.'

The ale-wife became all flustered, snatched the tankard from his hand and almost hurried him out through the door, pointing him further down the street.

'The second house past the shop. You'll find the door open. Helena lives on the bottom floor.'

Cranston thanked her, and when he reached the place, almost collided with a small, swarthy woman, her black hair lined with grey, coming out of the door. She had a round, smiling face with smooth skin, and gracefully accepted, in a lilting voice, Cranston's apologies.

'Helena Mortimer?'

'The same.'

The woman stepped back in alarm; Cranston produced his seal.

'I must have words with you about your brother Edward.'

'Have you found him?'

'Not yet, mistress.'

Helena led him back into the house along a narrow, stone-flagged chamber carefully swept and washed. She unlocked a door and took him into a small chamber with a casement window which looked out on to a herber plot. The room was neatly furnished, coloured cloths hung against the white walls, the chairs and stools were of dark polished oak. She invited him to sit on one side of the mantle hearth while she took off her robe and perched herself on a high-legged stool, feet almost dangling. She reminded Cranston of a small, pretty bird, head to one side, eyes bright and watchful.

'What made you think we'd found your brother?'

'Just a moment, Sir John.'

Helena rose and, rubbing her hands, took a padded linen cloth and lifted across the small brazier to stand between them.

'Oh, he must still be alive.'

She got up again and went to a coffer, and with a jingle of keys opened the lock and threw back the lid. She brought across a white woollen pouch tied at the neck and stamped with the red lion rampant of the Mortimer family.

'Every quarter,' she announced proudly, 'at Easter, midsummer, Michaelmas and Christmas, I receive a pouch, like this,' she leaned forward, eyes gleaming, 'containing five pounds sterling.'

'A generous amount.'

She was intrigued by Cranston's disbelief.

'Honestly, Sir John. Every quarter Master James Lundy, Goldsmith of Cheapside, sends one of his apprentices with such a pouch. It's what Edward promised. You see,' she chatted on, 'we Mortimers are from Wales. We are related, very distantly, to the Mortimer family; our kinsman is the Earl of March. Well,' she warmed to her story, 'Edward and I were the youngest children of a third son . . .'

As she gabbled on about the family history, Cranston, totally bemused, continued to stare at her.

'I see, I see,' he interrupted kindly. 'So you, and your brother, left Wales? He was a master swordsman and archer?'

'He soon received preferment in the retinues of the great lords. He served Edward the Black Prince, Sir Walter Manny and John of Gaunt before moving to Kent, where I met Richard Culpepper. I truly loved Richard – no, not in the carnal sense, Sir John; he became like another brother. Edward and Richard were inseparable, two eyes in the same head I called them. Richard always looked after Edward. I wasn't too fond of Culpepper's brother Thomas, the Benedictine monk, too severe and pious for my liking.'

'And what about the others?' Cranston asked.

'Well, they were kind enough. One of them, Chandler, that's right, he had lecherous eyes and sweaty hands. Edward challenged him to a duel so he left me alone.'

'Have you been married, mistress?'

'Oh no, Sir John, spinster of the parish, though I have my admirers. There's Master Sturmy, he's a blacksmith, and John Roper, he's a—'

'Yes, yes,' Cranston intervened. 'Mistress, you heard about the great robbery of the Lombard treasure?'

The change in the woman was remarkable. Her face drained, her lips pursed. She looked at Sir John as if she should dismiss him from her house. 'My brother was guilty of no crime. Something must have happened.'

'Of course, mistress.' Cranston took off his gloves and warmed his fingers over the brazier. 'But it's a great mystery, isn't it? I know a great deal about your brother,' he continued. 'I realise he wasn't a thief.'

Helena's smile returned to her face, and she offered Sir John a cup of malmsey, which he gratefully accepted.

'Just tell me your story, mistress.'

'Twenty years ago,' she replied in that sing-song voice, 'around midsummer, we came into London. Edward and Richard were all excited about the great expedition to Outremer. Edward found me lodgings in Candlewick Street. I was left to my own devices, although he and Richard would often visit me on their way down to the Tower.'

'They often went there?' Cranston became aware of how quiet the house had fallen; he started at a sound from the passageway.

'Just mice,' Helena smiled, 'and yes, they often went to the Tower.' She leaned forward. 'Secret business, Sir John.'

'Which was?'

'I don't know, it was secret.'

'And Edward never told you?'

'Oh no, he told me how Richard had fallen in love. I was a little bit jealous and said how lonely I had become, so sometimes they took me to the Tower with them. I was all amazed, Sir John, not even the castles in Wales are like that.'

'Whom did they meet?'

'It must have been His Grace, John of Gaunt; both Edward and Richard were closeted with him. I was young and carefree and paid little attention. Edward did his best for me. He said he would buy me this house.'

'What?' Cranston almost dropped his cup of malmsey. 'I thought your brother was poor?'

'So did I, Sir John. One day he announced he had been given a commission, good gold and silver.'

'And Richard?'

'I don't know, perhaps he was given money too? But, knowing what I do, he probably gave it to his leman, the golden-haired one he often talked about. I chose this house. Poor Jewry is not too wealthy but not too poor. After the Great Plague, prices had fallen. It has five chambers above. I let these out to scholars from the Inns of Court. Edward promised he would bring back a treasure from Outremer, and every quarter I would receive five pounds sterling.'

'And when did these payments begin?'

'Well,' she glanced up at the ceiling, at the small Catherine wheel of candles dangling from its gleaming black chain, 'Edward's companions returned to England about two or three years afterwards. I hadn't heard from my brother, but it was around then that the payments began.'

'Now look, mistress.' Cranston put his cup on the floor and grasped her hand. Helena's smile widened. Cranston felt a deep sadness. This woman truly adored and loved her brother, she could believe no ill of him; for years she had refused to confront the truth. 'Mistress,' he repeated, 'here we have a great mystery. Your brother Edward disappeared, he did not go to Outremer. No one knows where he is, not even you, but four times a year for the last seventeen years you receive five pounds sterling, a goodly amount! Surely you must ask yourself where your brother is? Why doesn't he visit you? How does he send this money to the goldsmith? He was a landless swordman, what profits did he have?'

Helena blinked furiously, tears welling in her eyes. 'I don't know,' she stammered, 'Sir John, I don't really know. This is what I think. His Grace the Regent,

259

although he wasn't Regent then, also loved Edward and trusted him with the Lombard treasure. I believe something terrible happened on the river that night. Edward and Richard were attacked, perhaps Richard was killed and Edward had to flee, rather than face disgrace. Sir John, he would have been accused of robbery, he could have been hanged! I think he fled, he changed his name, and one day,' she added hopefully, 'he will return.'

'But why not now?' Cranston demanded.

'Sometimes, Sir John,' she pointed to the door, 'just occasionally, I feel as though I'm being watched. Perhaps Edward knows that, if he was caught here or elsewhere, and I was with him, I could be accused of being his accomplice.'

Cranston sat back in his chair and stared across at the tapestry picture hanging on the wall: Adam and Eve in the Garden of Eden under the Tree of Knowledge; a golden black-spotted serpent had wound itself around the trunk and the jaws of its great hydra head parted in a display of sharp teeth and thrusting tongue. I wonder, Cranston reflected, what was the serpent in Edward Mortimer's life? He accepted the logic of what Helena was saying; to a certain extent it possessed its own truth. But where had Mortimer, a poor knight, managed to secure such money, and was he in hiding, still looking after his sister?

'James Lundy, the goldsmith, surely you've gone to him?'

'Of course, Sir John, but you know goldsmiths.

Master Lundy is a kindly man but still a goldsmith. He will not reveal the secrets of his customers. "I don't tell people I give you the purse," he declares, "I don't tell anybody that I pass it on to you." All he will say is that at any hour of the day, though usually at night, a man hooded and visored, garbed like a monk, comes in, leaves the purse, receives Master Lundy's signature and leaves.'

'But Master Lundy must see the red lion emblem on the pouch. He's a goldsmith, he must remember the great robbery and realise that a Mortimer was involved in it.'

'I asked him the same.' Helena went and refilled her cup, bringing back the jug to fill Sir John's. 'He informed me that all he receives is a sealed black pouch. He doesn't know what is inside; that is what is passed on to me.'

Cranston sipped at the malmsey. The more he studied this mystery, the more perplexed he became. Perhaps he should have brought Athelstan here.

'Did your brother,' he made one last try, 'say anything, mistress? Something you have reflected on over the years, which could provide some clue as to what happened?'

Helena closed her eyes, face tight with concentration. 'Just one thing.' She opened her eyes. 'He told me I would never starve, and that perhaps, one day, I would be a great lady.'

'And that's what you are.'

Cranston drained the cup and got to his feet. He

grasped Helena's hands and kissed her fingertips, made his farewells and left. He was in the passageway smelling so sweetly of rosemary and rue when Helena came tripping behind him.

'Sir John,' she called breathlessly. 'You have been so gracious. There is one other matter.'

She asked him to stay whilst she went upstairs and brought down a small coffer with artificial jewels studded in the casing. She opened this and took out a gold cross on a silver chain.

'This was my mother's.'

'Very beautiful,' Cranston agreed. 'But what significance does it have?'

'On the day before Edward disappeared, he came to see me, looking rather pale and agitated, which was unusual. I asked him what the matter was but he wouldn't tell me. Now I know. Edward always wore this round his neck. He asked me to keep it safe but said that before he sailed for Outremer he would collect it again. Now isn't that strange, Sir John? Why didn't he wear it that night?'

'Perhaps he was afraid of losing it.'

'But the same could have happened on board ship or in the savage fighting before Alexandria. He always wore it.'

'Mistress, I truly do not know.'

'Now you must think I'm feckless,' Helena continued, 'that I live in a fool's paradise. I won't accept that my brother has died. The truth is, Sir John, as regards Edward I live in a fog of mystery. If he's alive, why doesn't he come and collect the cross, never mind see his beloved sister? Yet if he's dead, who is sending me that money?'

'I can't answer that,' Cranston replied, 'but I do have one final question for you. After your brother's disappearance, did anyone visit you?'

'Oh, John of Gaunt came to see me. He brought me gifts, he said if I was ever in distress I was to write to him.'

'Anyone else? Such as the knights, Culpepper's comrades?'

Helena shook her head. 'Only one, Richard's brother, Malachi the Benedictine. After the English fleet returned he often visited me for a while, asking questions, but I didn't tell him anything. He was so cold-eyed.'

'What sort of questions did he ask you?' Cranston asked.

'Oh, the same as you.' She pointed behind her. 'He sat in the chamber fingering his beads. One thing he did say was had I ever truly searched for my brother? I told him a little of what I had done, how I had written to friends in Wales. I even wrote to Sir Maurice Clinton, but he never replied. Then he said a strange thing. Had I thought of hiring a man-hunter?'

'Pardon?'

'A man-hunter. You know, Sir John, often former soldiers, they hunt down criminals. I replied no.'

'Did he now?' Cranston smiled. 'Mistress, I thank you!'

Cranston strode out of the house and left Poor Jewry, turning left into Aldgate, down past Leadenhall, the Tun and into Cornhill. He was so engrossed in his own thoughts that even the range of villains fastened in the Great Stocks opposite Walbrook failed to attract his attention with their raucous shouts and cries. Passers-by looked at him curiously as the large coroner, a well-known sight along this broad thoroughfare, seemed oblivious to their greetings and shouted questions. Cranston strode along the Mercery, thumbs pushed into his large war belt, only standing aside when the Cart of Shame, full of criminals bound for the stocks, forced him into a doorway. The late morning's cargo was a bevy of prostitutes caught soliciting outside their marked corner around Cock Lane. They all knew Sir John of old, and made rude jokes or gestured obscenely at him. This time they were disappointed. Cranston did not react but stared back stonily. He leaned against a door post and gazed across at the various stalls under their coloured awnings. This part of the market sold leather goods, pots and pans and finely textured tapestries from abroad. As he watched the swirl of colour, even the appearance of a famous pickpocket, nicknamed 'Golden Thumb', failed to provoke him.

Cranston was fascinated by what Helena had told him. Was Edward Mortimer still alive? Was he still sending money to his sister? But, more importantly, had Malachi the Benedictine hired the Judas Man? Was Athelstan correct? Had the Night in Jerusalem become a spiritual magnet drawing in all the sins from the past? Cranston recalled his own schooling along the chilly transepts of St Paul's Cathedral. His masters taught him about the Furies of Ancient Greece who pursued criminals down the tunnel of the years and always caught their victim. Everyone who had gathered at the Night in Jerusalem, as well as those who hadn't, such as old Bohun and Helena, was linked mysteriously to that great robbery twenty years ago. Except one: the Judas Man hunting the Misericord, yet he had never made any reference to Mortimer or Culpepper. Had Malachi been searching for the Misericord because that rogue, now dead and rotting in a casket, did possess some knowledge about the Lombard treasure and the men who stole it? Yet there seemed to be no tie between Malachi and the Judas Man. He had never even seen them speak together. Cranston cursed his own memory, though he was certain Malachi had denied any knowledge of that ruthless hunter of men.

'Don't lurk here!'

Cranston whirled round and quickly apologised to the fierce-eyed old lady who had appeared in the doorway resting on a cane. He remembered why he was here and continued his journey to West Cheap and the shop of the goldsmith Master James Lundy. Two beautiful blonde-haired girls were playing outside, well dressed in their smocks of fustian. They announced that they were Master James' daughters and pointed through the doorway where their father was instructing apprentices who manned the stalls outside. Cranston walked in. James Lundy was small, his black hair swept back. He looked up as Cranston entered, and his gentle face creased into a smile.

'Well I never, Sir John!'

They clasped hands and Lundy took him into the counting office at the back of the shop, a small, lime-washed chamber, its heavy oaken doors bound with steel and its only window a fortified hole. Chests and coffers, all neatly labelled, were grouped against the wall or on the heavy wooden shelves higher up. Lundy waved him to a stool.

'Sir John, to what do I owe this pleasure?'

'Helena Mortimer.' Cranston decided to ignore the niceties. 'I respect you, Master James, but my business is urgent. Every quarter you send a pouch to her house in Poor Jewry.'

'To be just as blunt, Sir John, I don't know what's in that pouch or why it is sent. I am a banker, a goldsmith. People trust me with their valuables and their secrets.'

'How is the man dressed?'

Lundy smiled. 'You've visited Mistress Helena, haven't you? Otherwise you wouldn't know it's a man. Sir John, he comes to my shop cowled and masked. He gives me the purse and coins for my trouble. I give him a receipt and he leaves.'

'Aren't you suspicious?'

'What he does is not a crime. People make repara-tion, pay compensation; if they want to keep their faces and motives hidden, who am I to insist? That's all I can say.'

Cranston thanked him and left, fully determined to pay a visit to the Lamb of God and then return to Southwark to question Brother Malachi.

Chapter 10

Athelstan had risen early and roused Malachi from the makeshift truckle bed he'd set up under the bed loft. They had both prepared for Mass, celebrating it just after dawn, before returning to the priest's house. Malachi was profuse in his gratitude, fearful, as he said, about returning to the Night in Jerusalem. Athelstan kept insisting that he could stay at St Erconwald's as long as he liked. He repeated his promise over bowls of steaming oatmeal laced with honey, followed by rather stale bread, salted bacon, and the dark brown ale Athelstan had warmed over the fire as Cranston had taught him. Malachi now felt more at ease since his assault and Athelstan easily understood the horror the Benedictine had been through. The fresh light of day illuminated the marks in the church where the assassin's daggers had smashed into the walls. The Benedictine had recovered his poise and

269

ate hungrily. He accepted Athelstan's hospitality and said he would return to the Night in Jerusalem to collect his belongings, as well as buy provisions for the pantry and buttery.

'I'll send Crim down,' Athelstan offered. 'I'll tell him to wait for you. He's skilled with a wheelbarrow and you can pile your possessions on that.'

'One final favour, Brother.' Malachi put his horn spoon down. 'I told you last night how I had come to St Erconwald's to pray; I also came to see the ring I had given you, just once more, before it is sealed under the relic stone.'

'Of course!'

Athelstan went across to the parish chest, unlocked it and took the ring from its small coffer. He handed it to Malachi, who took it over to the window and, still examining it, brought it back to Athelstan.

'I'm glad we brought this ring here. It's the least we could do for the trouble and inconvenience caused.'

Athelstan turned the ring over, looking at those strange crosses carved on the inside.

'It's rather small,' the Dominican declared. 'More like a woman's ring. The good bishop must have worn it on his little finger, as we would a friendship ring.'

'Athelstan,' Malachi rose, 'I must go.'

He collected his cloak and left. The Dominican heard him greet the parishioners already congregating outside for another meeting of the parish council. Athelstan put his face in his hands and groaned; as if he didn't already face a sea of troubles. Bonaventure came through the half-open shutters, dropping softly to the floor. As usual, he went round the table and then sprawled in front of the fire. When Athelstan didn't bring his bowl of milk, he lifted his head, staring fiercely with his one good eye.

'*Concedo, concedo,*' Athelstan said. 'You remind me of Cranston when he is eager for claret!'

He gave the great tomcat his drink and sat hunched on the stool by the fire. Last night he and Malachi had chanted both vespers and compline, standing in that shadowy church, their voices ringing out, *Exsurge Domine, Exsurge Domine.* Athelstan recalled the words of that psalm: 'Arise O Lord, Arise and Judge my Cause, for a band of wicked men have beset me and wish to take my soul as low as Hell.' The problem was, Athelstan mused, who were the wicked men? Who had killed the Misericord and launched that vicious attack on a poor unarmed Benedictine monk? What did the Misericord mean by those strange markings on the wall? Or those two dead women, Beatrice and Clarice, by their veiled references to the Misericord's sister Edith having upon her person the possible solution to their own mother's disappearance? Athelstan recalled Edith's tear-streaked face, and felt a pang of compassion and guilt. He must go and visit the poor woman. He had tried to talk to Malachi the previous night but the Benedictine was tired and, as he confessed, had drunk one pot of ale too many, so he had retired early. Athelstan had secured the church, made sure God-Bless had eaten and was warm enough in the death house before retiring himself. He had spent an uneasy night, a sleep plagued by dreams. For some strange reason he dreamed that he was celebrating Mass, and when he turned to lift the Host, a pack of weasels was kneeling before him. He didn't like such dreams or thoughts.

Athelstan started at the knock on the door. Benedicta came in, her head and shoulders hidden by a thick woollen shawl, beautiful eyes glistening in the cold.

'Brother, we are ready,' she exclaimed.

'Oh, God!' Athelstan replied, quoting from the psalm, '"Come quickly to my aid, make haste to help me." You are well, Benedicta? I saw you at Malachi's Mass.'

'I decided to go to the chantry chapel. I had to get away from Pernel and those gloves she's bought.'

Athelstan put on his cloak. 'The troubles of the day are only just beginning.'

He left the house, looked in on Philomel, and followed Benedicta round, up the steps and into the church, closing the door behind him. The parish council was ready in all its glory. Watkin had brought down the sanctuary chair, as well as a smaller one for himself, so that as leader of the council he could sit on Athelstan's right. The rest perched on benches or stools. From their angry faces and stony silence it was obvious battle was about to begin. Watkin the dung collector was glowering at the floor, his fat, unshaven face mottled with fury. Pike the ditcher looked rather smug. Beside him, sharp-tongued Imelda

leaned forward like a cat ready to pounce, eyes glaring at Cecily the courtesan, who looked fresh as
a buttercup, her golden hair like a nimbus around
her pretty face. She sat all coy and demure in a new
dark blue smock with a white petticoat beneath. She
had hoisted both up to give Pike a generous view of
her delicate ankles. Ursula's sow was stretched in
the middle of it all, fat flanks quivering, fast asleep.
Ranulf cradled his ferret box whilst Pernel, her hair
freshly dyed, kept admiring the dark red gloves she'd
bought, daggered and slashed: their backs, studded
with pieces of glass, had little bells fastened to them.
She kept shaking these and the tinkling was a further
source of vexation to the parishioners. Only Moleskin
was missing; Athelstan recalled his meeting with the
boatman the previous afternoon.

'Well, Father, are we to begin?' Watkin rose.

'Yes, we are. First bring down the hour candle.'

'Oh no!' Basil the blacksmith moaned. 'Father,
you're not angry with us?'

'No, I'm not,' Athelstan replied, 'but I can see you
are angry with each other. The clouds are gathering,
the anger will come, the lightning will flash!'

Watkin brought the hour candle and placed it next
to Ursula's sow, whilst Crim the altar boy scampered
off to bring a taper from the Lady Chapel.

'I've lit the candle,' Athelstan said, taking his seat.
'This meeting will certainly end when the flame
reaches the next red circle.'

He nodded at Mugwort the bell clerk, who was

sitting on his stool, his crude writing tray on his lap.

'Only take down the important decisions; afterwards, put that ledger back in the sacristy. Right, the preparations for Advent. Watkin, you will have to take your cart and go out to the wasteland to collect as much greenery as possible . . .'

'You haven't said a prayer.' Pernel lifted one gloved hand and shook it vigorously.

'No, we haven't,' Athelstan confessed, 'and I think we need one.' He closed his eyes and, in a powerful, carrying voice, sang the first three verses of the Veni Creator Spiritus. The parish council sat transfixed. Brother Athelstan had a rich, vibrant voice, and when he sang with his eyes closed, they recognised that he was not in the best of humours. He had taught them the translation of these words and he always emphasised the same verses: 'Oh come you Father of the poor, Oh come with riches which endure.'

'You know what I'm talking about.' Athelstan opened his eyes. 'We've asked God to warm our hearts of snow and make us bend our stiff necks. Now, Watkin, the greenery . . .'

The parish council went through each item, but as soon as they reached the Christmas play, the Holy Spirit was forgotten as the intense bitter rivalry resurfaced. Athelstan shouted for silence but, as he quietly whispered to Benedicta, he was 'a voice crying in the wilderness'. Nevertheless, he was given a sharp schooling in the language of the alleyways, as Imelda and the rest hurled abuse at each other. Athelstan decided to weather the storm out, keeping one eye on the greedy candle flame. He soon learned that coylums were testicles, a cokeny was a homosexual, a gong was a prostitute, a Jordan was a chamber pot whilst a mamzer was a bastard. For a while he let his parishioners shout themselves into exhaustion, and when they looked to him for direction, turned immediately to Huddle the painter.

'What is glair?' he asked. 'You mentioned it a week ago when you proposed to paint the great Chain of Being in one of the transepts.'

The parishioners stared in disbelief at their priest. He hadn't answered their question but simply moved on, and of course, once Huddle was asked about paint, there was no stopping him. He immediately began a lecture on how glair was beaten egg white used for binding paint but that it must be mixed with red arsenic to prevent a foul odour and corruption. Athelstan let him talk, and as soon as the red ring on the candle disappeared, he shot to his feet, made a sign of the Cross, and walked up into the sanctuary to pray.

He knelt in the rood screen, eyes closed. The parish council came to an abrupt ending and the members unanimously decided to continue their argument outside.

'Brother Athelstan.'

The friar turned. Moleskin stood halfway down the nave, his hand on the arm of an old woman garbed completely in black. Athelstan rose and went down to meet them.

'This is Margot.' Moleskin stumbled over the name.

'Mistress, you're welcome.' Athelstan took her vein-streaked hand; it was icy cold. 'You had best sit down.'

Margot, rheumy-eyed, peered up at him. 'I've seen you say Mass, Father. I come here sometimes on the Great Feasts. Moleskin here nearly called me "Fat Margot".' She tapped her bony cheeks and moved a wisp of white hair from her brow, tucking it under her black hat. 'But that was years ago; now I'm as thin as a wand.'

Athelstan took her back to where the parish council had met and let the old woman warm her fingers over the brazier.

'Margot,' Athelstan opened his purse, took out a coin and dropped it gently into the old woman's hand, 'that's for your trouble. You're the widow of one of the boatmen who disappeared on the night of the great robbery.'

The old woman's eyes filled with tears as she sat down on a stool.

'Godric was his name, a fine man, Brother. He left that afternoon. I've never seen him since, though we found his boat further down the river, caught in some reeds, it was.'

'In Southwark?' Athelstan asked.

'No, no, where the river bends, going down to Westminster. Just the barge, Father. No pole, nothing.

It was as if the hand of some ghostly giant had picked it up and emptied men and goods into the river.'

'Was there any mark of violence – a bloodstain?'

Margot shook her head. 'A long, low craft, Brother, built of fine wood, with benches and a small locker at each end for Godric and his partner to store their goods. Painted black, it was, with a high prow and stern. Godric called it the *Glory of the Thames*.'

'Did your man ever tell you,' Athelstan asked, 'why he had been hired that day?'

'He wasn't hired, Father.'

'Pardon? I thought he was.'

'No, no.' Margot shook her head fiercely. 'Godric had been paid well by those two knights. All he told me was that the barge had been hired, but not him.'

'Oh, so they were to bring their barge to the Oyster Wharf and hand it over?'

'I think so. I'm not sure where the knights took it, but Godric was to remain at the wharf until they returned. He didn't know why, but the knights were respectable so he trusted them. They'd also paid him good silver.'

She paused as Malachi came through the side door of the church. He raised his hand at Athelstan and walked across to the Lady Chapel.

'Continue,' Athelstan asked.

'I've told you all I know, Brother. My man was paid good silver, he was to hire out his barge and wait at the Oyster Wharf. He left just before sunset; I've never seen or heard from him again.'

Athelstan thanked Moleskin and Margot, and when they'd left, he sat down in the sanctuary chair. What Margot had told him possessed a logic of its own. Culpepper and Mortimer would never tell anyone what they were doing. And the money given to the bargemen? That must have come from either the Admiral of the Fleet, or perhaps from John of Gaunt himself. Athelstan rose and was about to walk across to the Lady Chapel when the door crashed open and Cranston came in.

'Brother, I have news.'

Athelstan put a finger to his lips and gestured with his head toward the Lady Chapel.

Cranston peered through the murky light. 'Just the person!' he exclaimed. 'Brother Malachi, a word.'

The Benedictine crossed himself and came down.

'Brother Malachi,' Cranston gestured to the stool, 'I'll come swiftly to the point. I've just visited Helena Mortimer in Poor Jewry.'

'And, Sir John?'

'You've visited her as well. You could have told me!'

'Why, of course, her brother was a close comrade of Richard. It's logical, isn't it, to seek such a woman out? Yet, she knows nothing—'

'Did you hire the Judas Man?'

'Don't be ridiculous. Yes, I did discuss such a possibility with Mistress Mortimer. Again, it's a matter of logic, Sir John. I mean, to hire a man hunter to find a man.' He spread his hands. 'My Lord Coroner, what I have done, to quote Holy Scripture, has been done in the full light of day.'

Cranston's shoulders slumped. He could tell from the Benedictine's composure that he wasn't hiding anything.

'Did you know,' Cranston sat down on a stool, 'that Mortimer was a henchman of John of Gaunt?'

'A retainer, perhaps, but there was nothing significant in that. His Grace was deeply upset by my brother's disappearance, as well as that of Edward Mortimer. Perhaps Sir Maurice hasn't told you, but John of Gaunt instigated the most thorough search for the missing knights. He alerted every sheriff, bailiff, mayor and port reeve throughout the kingdom. If he could have no success, why should I? I'm not lying. Ask His Grace yourself. The letters and writs ordering such a search are still enrolled in the Chancery, I've seen them with my own eyes. Now,' Malachi got to his feet, 'Brother Athelstan, I've brought down my possessions, I need to store them in your house.' Malachi nodded at Athelstan, sketched a blessing in Cranston's direction and left.

'Is he staying here? Why?' Cranston mopped his face on the edge of his gown.

Athelstan told him in short sharp sentences everything that had happened since they'd parted the previous day. Cranston held his peace, then he, in turn, related all he had discovered. For a while both sat in silence.

'Oh, by the way,' Cranston shuffled his feet, 'on

my short but very cold journey across the Thames, I met Master Flaxwith. The Judas Man seems to have disappeared. I only wish I knew who had hired him.'

'We keep asking the same questions,' Athelstan replied, 'and receive the same answers. The mystery always deepens. I have a special cask of the best Bordeaux hidden in my buttery. I can't take you there because of Malachi. So, like Melchisedech of old, if you sit there, I will bring you gifts of bread and wine and, here, in the presence of God, we shall sit like master and scholar and dispute what we've found.'

Cranston readily agreed. Athelstan brought across a small jug of claret, two pewter goblets and a trancher of buttered bread smeared with honey. While Cranston ate, Athelstan prepared his writing tray, and made himself comfortable on Mugwort's stool.

'So, let's list the mysteries.'

Item Sir Edward Mortimer and Sir Richard Culpepper disappear with the Lombard treasure from Oyster Wharf twenty years ago. At the same time, Guinevere the Golden is seen no more.

Item The two boatmen also disappear, but they were only supposed to bring the barge to Culpepper and later meet them at the Oyster Wharf, yet they too vanished, their barge found floating downriver near Westminster.

Item Despite a scrupulous search, by His Grace

John of Gaunt, as well as Brother Malachi, no trace of the missing persons, or the Lombard treasure, has ever been found.

Item There is no doubt that Culpepper and Mortimer received monies for the secret task assigned to them. I thought this was just to pay for the boatmen and barge but there was considerable wealth. Mortimer could give gifts to his sister and buy her a narrow house in Poor Jewry.

Item The Lombard treasure was held in trust by His Grace, John of Gaunt, who hired these two knights so that the movements of this treasure could not be traced. No one, apart from Gaunt and the two knights, knew when, where and how the treasure was being transported.

Item Although Mortimer and Culpepper disappeared, Helena Mortimer receives, every quarter, five pounds sterling in a little pouch bearing the Mortimer crest. This is delivered to the goldsmith Lundy, who has no knowledge of who or why such a request is made. Again, that's logical. There is no crime in giving a lonely spinster the means for a comfortable life. We also know that Guinevere the Golden was boasting of some unexpected wealth which would transform her life, but she too has gone into the dark.

Athelstan paused, and sipped at the claret. 'Now, Sir

John, we move forward twenty years.' He continued his writing.

Item Who murdered those two unfortunates in the hay barn? Probably the same person who hired them. Was it Chandler, or did that dead fat knight merely stumble on the corpses? There is no proof of anyone else approaching the hay barn on that murderous occasion.

Item Who hired the Judas Man? Who is the Judas Man?

Athelstan glanced up. 'We don't even know his name. He was given the task of hunting down the Misericord. Why?' He kept writing as he .talked. 'Because the Misericord was a rogue who had deceived Sir Stephen and composed a poem about him?' He shook his head. 'Definitely not.'

Item The Misericord was a frequenter of the tavern the Night in Jerusalem. Twenty years ago, when the great robbery occurred, he vouched that all the others concerned, apart from Malachi, stayed in that tavern carousing all night. Again that is logical. Culpepper's companions, not to mention Master Rolles and Mother Veritable, did not even know that the Lombard treasure was being transported along the Thames. There is no evidence whatsoever that the knights, Rolles or that Witch Queen ever came into any unexpected wealth.

Item A relationship did exist between the Misericord and the two sisters, Beatrice and Clarice. They too began to hint of unexpected wealth, of transforming their lives, of knowing what had happened to their mother. The only clue they would give was a veiled allusion to something Edith, the Misericord's sister, wore upon her person. I cannot discover that.

Item Mother Veritable had good reason, therefore, like Sir Stephen Chandler, to hate the Misericord, who may have been plotting to take away two of her favourite girls. All three of them had mocked a very valuable customer. Yet there is no evidence whatsoever that Mother Veritable, or indeed anyone else, went to Cheapside to deliver that poison pie to silence the Misericord. Of course the Judas Man has disappeared, except for his horse and harness. He may have killed the Misericord and returned to attack Malachi in the church. But why?

Item What did the Misericord mean by shouting 'Askit, Askit' before he died? And what were those strange etchings on the prison wall? The quotation '*Quem quaeritis*', not to mention the numbers 1, 1, 2, 3, 5?

Athelstan paused in his writing and carefully scrutinised his conclusions. Cranston, who had listened as he finished off the bread and wine, came over and sat next to him. He studied the clerkly abbreviations Athelstan had made in listing all his points.

'In the end,' Cranston muttered, 'we come back to the great robbery.'

'There are two people,' Athelstan replied, 'we haven't questioned. And we should, sooner or later. His Grace, John of Gaunt, and Signor Teodoro Tonnelli.'

Athelstan stared across at the glorious red rooster Huddle the painter had begun to depict on one of the pillars. It was supposed to represent the cock which crowed three times, marking Peter's denial of Christ during the Lord's Passion. On the other pillar an elegant pelican stabbed its own breast to feed its young, a symbol of Christ giving His Body and Blood to the world. The friar realised only now, sitting here, how he had underestimated Huddle's consummate skill in bringing these two symbols to life, and he felt a pang of regret at not congratulating that dreamy-eyed painter more forcefully.

'Brother?'

'Yes, yes,' Athelstan replied, 'we should do it now. But Tonnelli won't see us without John of Gaunt's permission, he'll act the cautious banker.'

'I'll send the letter myself,' Cranston offered. 'His Grace the Regent is at his palace in the Savoy.'

Athelstan became busy, hurrying across to his house for a sheet of better vellum, a sander of pounce and a slice of sealing wax. Sir John dictated the letter. Athelstan melted the wax and used the sander to sprinkle the very fine dust, so that the ink wouldn't blur. The letter was sealed by Sir John, and sealed again when Athelstan folded it.

'Benedicta's in the house,' Athelstan declared. 'I think Malachi is getting under her feet. She'll take this over to the Savoy.'

He hurried off and came back to find Cranston beating his boot on the paved floor.

'There's the other mysteries,' the coroner declared mournfully. 'In God's name, Athelstan, how was Chandler poisoned? And that psalter of his, what great wrongs had he done to keep begging forgiveness?'

'He was a soldier, and only the mind of God knows what horrors he committed in Outremer whilst his lust for soft flesh must have been a canker in his soul. But for his murder? I can't say, Sir John, and the same for Broomhill. Oh, he was lured into that cellar, but by whom, how and why remain a mystery.'

Athelstan sat on his stool, head in his hands. Cranston stared at him out of the corner of his eye. Such mysteries often perplexed him; he was more concerned that Athelstan, this little dark-faced friar, was mystified. Time was slipping away like sand in a glass. How long could he detain those knights? Sooner or later they would assert themselves and seek the writ of the Chancellor or a Justice of the Bench at Westminster, and he would have to let them go. Athelstan lifted his face and smiled.

'Now I know,' he sighed, 'what the ancients meant by psychomachia.'

'Pardon?'

'A Greek term, Sir John, signifying war in the mind or the soul, the conflict of different ideas. Contradictions impede any progress,' he tapped the side of his head, 'in all this confusion.'

'So?'

'Well, I'll quote the great Archimedes, and his famous phrase, *"Pou-sto"*; it means "I act from where I stand". Archimedes meant that if you stand in the right place with the right instruments, no problem is impossible.' He gestured round the sombre church. 'This is where we begin, Sir John, this is our place.'

'And the right instruments?'

'Well, I recall my studies of that brilliant Dominican Thomas Aquinas, and his *quinque viae*.'

'Oh no,' Cranston groaned.

'No, Sir John, Aquinas had to study a more complex problem than the one facing us – the existence of God. He established what he termed the *quinque viae*, the five ways. To summarise, Sir John, everything must have a cause. So let's look at the cause of all this, and the place where it all began. Well, my Lord Coroner?'

'Why, the robbery of the Lombard treasure, twenty years ago on the Oyster Wharf.'

'Right, let's start there. We are told the treasure was brought to the wharf.'

'Yes,' Sir John grunted.

'Why?' Athelstan asked.

'Well, because it was away from the City but near the Crusaders' fleet.'

'How do we know that?'

'Well,' Cranston spread his hands, 'it's the accepted story.'

'Yes, that's what intrigues me. Indeed, old Margot was less specific. Would you send treasure to a quayside in Southwark? What guarantee would you have that the quayside would be safe, that footpads and outlaws weren't sheltering there? The Good Lord knows Southwark has enough of those, and always has. And if you are going to rob it, would you launch an attack on four strong men and just hope that there would be no witnesses? No beggar loitering in the shadows, no footpad sheltering from the law, no lovers locked in close embrace? If you had planned such a robbery you would be taking a terrible risk. After all, you didn't know John of Gaunt wasn't sending a company of archers with it.'

'But that proves Culpepper and Mortimer are guilty,' Sir John retorted. 'We now know they were by themselves.'

'No we don't. The boatmen must have been accomplices because they have disappeared as well. I know what you are thinking, Sir John, but your hypothesis is weak. I find it difficult to accept that Culpepper and Mortimer received the treasure chest, loaded the barge, persuaded two honest boatmen to go out on the river with them, journeyed to some lonely place, broke the chest open and disappeared into the night for ever. I don't think, Sir John, that Culpepper and Mortimer stole the treasure, which means others did, which in turn brings us back to the problem of how the attackers felt so secure in robbing a valuable treasure on one of the well-known quaysides of Southwark. Remember, Sir John, the Oyster Wharf is mentioned in all accounts, but according to old Margot, that was only the place her husband was to reclaim his barge. Did he take it there or somewhere else?'

Sir John's lower lip came out, a sign that he was seriously considering Athelstan's theory. He held the friar's bright-eyed gaze and winked.

'You're correct, little monk.'

'Friar, Sir John.'

'Whatever, you're still right. I wonder what Moleskin would think of your theory?'

'*Res ipsa loquitur* – the matter speaks for itself. Now let's look for the proof. I know Moleskin is not far, he'll be plotting with Merrylegs.'

Athelstan hurried out through the main door and down the steps. Cranston heard him shouting at Crim, who was playing hodman in the cemetery. When the friar returned, Cranston was pleased at Athelstan's ill-concealed excitement. He started walking up and down, fingering the vow knots on the cord round his waist.

'It can't be the Oyster Wharf,' he kept exclaiming, 'it just can't be, not with a parish like this nearby.'

So distracted, Athelstan ignored Cranston's questions about Moleskin and went off to fill the situla with holy water. Only then did he return to sit opposite Sir John.

'Benedicta has left to deliver the letter,' he declared. 'We must question the Regent whether he likes it or not.'

'Is he behind this mystery? Oh, *Jesu miserere,* I hope not.' Cranston lowered his voice. 'He's a veritable salamander. Everything he touches becomes tainted.'

'Salamander or not,' Athelstan retorted, 'he has a finger in this pie.'

Athelstan was about to go and trim the candles on the high altar when Moleskin, garbed in sajreen green, the coat of his guild, fashioned out of the untanned skin of a horse and dyed a rich hue, came running through the door.

'Oh, Brother,' he gasped, 'I was with Merrylegs. He's a marvellous cook and had some pastry to sell to my wife . . .'

'Never mind.' Athelstan was unusually sharp. 'Moleskin, you've heard the rumours about the great robbery? I ask you in confidence, would you bring a treasure, even in the dead of night, to the Oyster Wharf in Southwark?'

'No, Father, I wouldn't, and I've often thought about that—'

'Twenty years ago,' Athelstan continued, 'who would be found at the Oyster Wharf at the dead of night?'

'Well, Father, the usual, whores, a few fishermen, beggars looking for scraps or a place to sleep. Oh!' Moleskin's fingers went to his lips. 'This was twenty years ago?'

'Yes.'

'The year of our Lord 1360 – the thirty-third year of the old King's reign?'

'Yes,' Cranston barked.

'Ah!' Moleskin blithely ignored the coroner's anger. 'That would be three years after the year of the Great Stink.'

'The what?' Athelstan asked.

'The Great Stink,' Cranston explained, 'occurred in the summer of 1357, after a very dry, hot summer. There was no rainfall, the brooks and the canals of the Thames became polluted and full of rubbish. The smell carried as far north as the great forest of Epping.' He wagged a finger at Moleskin. 'I know what you are going to say.'

'That's right, Sir John, the Stink lasted for years – at least two, I think. Many pious old ladies thought the Second Coming was due and the Seventh Seal on the Judgment Book of God about to be removed, so they formed the Vespertines. Every night after vespers, these pious old creatures would form a torchlight procession, whilst their husbands would carry statues of the plague saints; you know, Sebastian and the rest. They walked along the quaysides of Southwark, praying that God would send fresh rain and a cleaning wind. I was a young man then but I'm sure the Vespertines were still busy about the same time as the great robbery. I can still remember their chanting and prayers, asking God to repel the demons and the foul airs and vapours they'd brought up from hell.'

'Thank you, thank you.'

Athelstan dismissed Moleskin and slowly began to put away his writing implements.

'So, it wasn't the Oyster Wharf after all, Sir John. I want to visit the Chancery room in the Tower. I want to see what the documents published at the time actually said. I'll tell Malachi where we are going . . .'

Rosamund Clifford, she called herself. Of course, when they had held her over the font in St Mary-le-Bow Church, she'd been given another name, Mathilda, but that wasn't a name used by the troubadours or minstrels. Rosamund Clifford had a romantic ring about it; she'd heard the legends, how once an English king had a mistress of the same name who was later foully poisoned at the centre of a maze. Well, that would not be her fate, she thought as she left Mother Veritable's house and turned into a needle-thin alleyway. Rosamund: Mother Veritable said it came from *rosa mundi* – rose of the world. That was flattering, even though her rivals, who also knew a little Latin, called her 'Rosa Munda', the cankered rose. She would ignore such taunts! After the deaths of Beatrice and Clarice, as well as the sudden and mysterious disappearance of Donata, she was now Mother Veritable's principal lady of the bedchamber.

Rosamund hunched her pretty shoulders in glee; she had received a message from what Mother Veritable called the Castle of Love at the Night in Jerusalem. Sir Thomas Davenport needed her services. Rosamund was delighted at the news, and had decked herself out in all her glory. Her fiery red hair was scooped up in an embroidered net, or reticule, whilst her low-cut gown, loaned by Mother Veritable, was of costly pers, a rich blue fabric from Provence. Beneath it, white lace-edged petticoats and stockings of dark blue with silver stars, on her feet Spanish pattens, and thick-soled high-heeled shoes over soft woollen slippers. Rosamund had visited Sir Thomas before; he always liked to see her in these. She fingered the silver brooch on her cloak, carved in the shape of a pear, a blatant symbol of sexual desire. She tripped down the alleyway oblivious to the lecherous glances and whispers; she was well protected by two of Master Rolles' bully boys, armed with cudgels, only a shadow-length behind her. Rosamund felt hungry and her mouth was watering as she entered the Night in Jerusalem. Perhaps Master Rolles would give her a bowl of rapes and lentils mashed with a mortar along with breadcrumbs, spices and herbs, or perhaps a dish of pain-pour dieu, circlets of bread soaked in egg yolks, salted till golden and sprinkled with cinnamon and sugar. She was soon disappointed.

'He's upstairs.' Rolles broke her reverie. The tavern keeper was standing at the entrance to the tap room. He certainly didn't look well, Rosamund reflected. She climbed the stairs; he hadn't even offered her a goblet of wine! She'd been informed that Sir Thomas was waiting for her in the Galahad Chamber and had to walk into the adjoining gallery before she spelled out the words painted in gold above the great oaken door.

'Sir Thomas.'

No answer. Probably maudlin, she thought, as he did like his wine.

'Sir Thomas!'

She knocked hard, and pressed her ear against the door. She tried the latch but the door held firm. She picked up a jug from the floor outside the room and used this to bang noisily.

'What's the matter?' Sir Maurice Clinton, his thin face all cross, came out of the room next door, pulling a fur-edged cloak around him. 'What's the matter, girl, can't you rouse Sir Thomas?'

'No, sir, I cannot.'

Fair Rosamund would never forget what happened next. Master Rolles, also alerted by the noise, came thundering up the stairs. They were joined by Sir Reginald Branson as well as servants and other maids. Sir Thomas Davenport still could not be roused, and their agitation deepened as people recalled the brutal murders of Chandler and Broomhill. At last the door was forced, broken off its hinges, the locks and bolts snapping free. It fell back with a crash like a draw-bridge going down, revealing a gruesome sight. Sir Thomas lay stretched on the floor with a pricket, a pointed candlestick, thrust deep into his heart. The floor around him glistened with blood, still curling and running, as it found its way through the turkey carpets. Nobody told Rosamund to stand back and, fascinated by the horror, she followed the rest into the room.

'He's been murdered,' the head ostler whispered.

Rosamund gazed at the frightful sight. Sir Thomas lay crumpled, slightly to one side, as if he had fallen from the soft-backed chair beside him, face all pale, but the look on his face! As if his sightless eyes were about to blink and those gaping lips about to talk! Rosamund watched Sir Maurice pick up a solace stone, semi precious, its flashing rubies oval cut and polished, and place it on the table. He crouched down beside the corpse, turning it over gently.

'We had best leave him,' Rolles whispered. 'That fat coroner and his snooping friar have to be called. No, don't,' he intervened as Sir Maurice went to pluck the pricket from Sir Thomas' flesh.

'Yes, leave it,' Sir Reginald urged. 'We should clear the room, leave everything until Cranston comes.'

Chapter 11

Athelstan and Cranston sat blowing on their fingers in the freezing Chancery room of the Tower. Athelstan's throat felt slightly sore and his back sweaty and cold. He wondered if he was about to suffer an attack of the rheums. He quietly promised himself a boiling cup of posset before he retired that day and tried to forget the symptoms. He stared round the circular room high in one of the towers, just a short walk from the Norman Keep. The lancet windows had been boarded up, a fire burned in the cavernous hearth, braziers crackled and glowed, yet the chamber was still freezing cold. Colebrook, the surly lieutenant, with whom Cranston and Athelstan had done business before, had greeted them at the Lion Gate, and taken them immediately up to the Chancery room. Hubert, the chief clerk, had reluctantly left his beloved filing and recording of memoranda, writs, letters and proclamations. A small, curiously bird-like man, in both appearance and movement, Hubert had gestured at the various great coffers and chests arranged neatly around the room by regnal year. At first he gave Cranston a lecture on the storage, preservation and filing of parchment and, ignoring their interruptions, insisted on showing them how documents were recorded and stored. He then proudly demonstrated the new invention he had found in Hainault, what he termed a 'Rotulus', a small wheel with a handle on the side. The roll of vellum was attached to a clasp on the rim and the wheel cranked round so that a searcher could scrutinise the different membranes twined to each other.

'If a letter is sealed by the Great or Privy Seal,' Hubert pompously announced, 'it is copied and brought here. Oh, I heard you before, Sir John, I remember the year of the Great Stink, and who can forget the robbery of the Lombard treasure?' He creased his face into a look of sharp condemnation. 'I was in the Chancery at that time; letters of proclamation were issued, north, south, east and west. Come, I'll show you.'

He searched amongst the coffers and brought out a small roll of parchment, its contents summarised in Latin shorthand on the back. He inserted this on the Rotulus and Athelstan began his search.

'Very curious,' Athelstan remarked, turning the wooden handle. 'There's no doubt His Grace the Regent,' he nodded at Hubert, 'although he wasn't that then, there's no doubt about his rage.'

'Oh, very true,' the clerk intoned. 'Brother, I saw

him the day after the robbery. Raging like a panther he was. Eyes bright with anger, he lashed out with his tongue.'

'You're sure of that?' Athelstan asked.

'Brother, I'm a skilled clerk. I have inscribed the letters of the old King, when he was lying in bed, ill with myriad ailments. On that day His Grace was angry. If he had caught the perpetrators he would have hoist them from the highest gallows.'

Athelstan, Cranston standing beside him, continued the search.

'Most remarkable.' Sir John pointed to one document. 'The ships weren't riding at anchor off Southwark but between the river fleet and St Paul's Wharf.'

'And look,' Athelstan pointed to a line, 'there's no reference, well at first, to the Oyster Wharf. Simply to a great robbery along the river.' He turned the handle again, moving the document forward. 'Only a month after the crime is the Oyster Wharf mentioned. Remember what I said, Sir John, about Archimedes. We must go to the right place, and now we have it.'

He paused as Cranston took a deep draught from the miraculous wine skin, offered it to Athelstan, who shook his head, and then to Hubert who, despite his size, surprised Cranston with the generous swig he took.

'What it means, Sir John,' Athelstan continued, 'and we shall have to ask His Grace this question, is why was the Oyster Wharf mentioned, when all the evidence indicates that the robbery took place on the south bank of the river, but much further down? Imagine, Sir John, if you can, the Southwark bank. You pass the Bishop of Winchester's inn, the stews, the washing places, and then what?'

Cranston closed his eyes. 'Muddy banks,' he replied, 'marshy fields, giving way to mud and shale. Lonely places.' He opened his eyes. 'The ideal spot.'

'Exactly, Sir John, I think that's where the robbery took place.'

Hubert the clerk was listening intently.

'Ah, I see what you mean,' he muttered. 'By St Mary and all the angels, this is interesting.'

'It will become common knowledge soon enough.' Athelstan stood back. 'Right, Sir John, in that fertile mind of yours, imagine the treasure barge, leaving the Tower. It goes directly across the river, following the bank along the Southwark side, past the Oyster Wharf, down to this lonely spot. Culpepper and Mortimer are waiting with their own barge. They use lanterns or torches to bring the party from the Tower in to where they are waiting. The treasure is exchanged. In the flickering light of the torches, Culpepper hastily signs the indenture.'

Athelstan returned to the Rotulus and found the indenture. 'Only one word, *thesaurum*, the Latin word for treasure, indicated the great wealth he received. The document had been drawn up by some clerk. The party from the Tower probably took writing implements with them. Culpepper scrawled his name, "Ricardus Culpepper", with a cross beside it, and beneath that,

"Edwardus Mortimer", who drew a roughly etched lion, his family symbol.' Athelstan stared at the signatures. Something about them pricked his memory, but for the life of him, he couldn't place it. 'Anyway,' he continued, 'the treasure is exchanged, the Tower barge leaves. I'm not too sure when the bargemen arrived, but there, on that dark lonely bank, the demon struck. Whatever people say, I truly believe four souls were sent into eternal night. The treasure chest is stolen, the barge is ransacked and pushed out into the river, where the tide takes it down to some reeds near Westminster.'

'And the corpses of the four men?' Cranston asked.

'I don't know, Sir John, I truly don't.'

'But why all this mention of the Oyster Wharf?'

Athelstan was about to answer when there was a knock on the door. Colebrook entered, grasping a tap boy from the Night in Jerusalem by the scruff of his neck. The lad broke free and hurtled towards Athelstan, almost colliding with him.

'Brother,' he gasped. 'You have to come.' He swallowed hard. 'Sir Domus—'

'Sir Thomas,' Athelstan corrected.

'Well, he's dead,' the boy retorted, 'stabbed through the heart with a pricket. Master Rolles is fair raging like a hungry dog on a leash.'

'When did this happen?' Cranston asked.

'This morning,' the boy declared, eyes riveted on the coin in Athelstan's hand. 'A real mystery,' he whispered. 'The windows all shuttered, the chamber doors all locked and barred. Master Rolles wasn't pleased with that either.' His little eyes didn't leave the coin. 'A good door to the Galahad Chamber broken down, bolts and hinges all destroyed. Sir Thomas lying in his own blood like a duck on a stall, fair swimming in blood he was—'

'Thank you,' Athelstan interrupted, pressing the coin into the child's hand. 'Now lead on, Gabriel.'

'My name is not Gabriel.'

'It is today,' Athelstan smiled.

They thanked Hubert and Colebrook and, with the lad scampering ahead like a monkey released from its chain, left the Lion Gate, up Thames Street and into Billingsgate. They pushed their way through the fish market, thrusting aside the sharp-eyed apprentices eager to sell them the fresh catch of the day. The boy moved like a coursed hare, dodging round the stalls, making obscene gestures at anyone trying to stop him. On the approaches to London Bridge, Cranston had to roar at him to halt whilst he and Athelstan paused to catch their breath.

'Another murder, Brother,' the coroner gasped, 'and it looks as mysterious as the last.'

And they were off again, threading their way through the narrow thoroughfare. They passed the shops and houses built on either side of the bridge, the gaps where the great laystalls stood, full of reeking rubbish from the midden heaps, wary of the makeshift sewer coursing down the centre of the thoroughfare. The stench was sickening. Athelstan hated the place. From the bridge rails soared the long ash poles bearing the severed heads of traitors and criminals. The boy had to slow down here, as the crowds thronged, to look over the side and watch the water rushing through, gape up at the severed heads, visit the shops and stalls, or pray in the cold darkness of St Thomas' Chapel, built in the middle of the bridge directly above the rushing torrent. Athelstan crossed himself as he passed the half-open door. He sketched a blessing in the direction of Bourdon, the diminutive Keeper of the Bridge, who was sitting on the steps of the chapel, between his feet a bucket of brine in which he was washing the severed head of a criminal. Athelstan kept his eyes on the ground. Such sights were offensive, and the dizzying height over the rushing water always made him feel nervous. He was pleased to be off the bridge and hurrying down the lanes and alleyways and into the courtyard of the Night in Jerusalem.

Rolles met them at the door and, like a prophet come to judgement, mournfully took them up the polished oaken staircase into the Galahad Chamber.

'I told people not to move anything.'

'Has Brother Malachi been sent for?' Athelstan asked, staring down at the blood-soaked corpse.

'He was here much earlier this morning,' Rolles replied. 'Then left with his belongings. Good riddance, say I.'

'Did he come up here? Did he visit Sir Thomas?' Cranston asked.

'No, his chamber is on the other side. Anyway, at

that time Sir Thomas wasn't in his chamber but sitting in the garden. He came in, took a cup of malmsey and returned to his chamber. He'd hired the services of one of Mother Veritable's girls, a whore called Rosamund. I've put her in the garden arbour.'

Athelstan turned and looked at the door. The lintel had been ruined; the leather hinges, bolts and locks had torn away huge strips of wood as they were forced.

'The door was fully secured?'

'See for yourself, Brother.'

Cranston went across to the window. This was still shuttered, the bar down. The room was very warm, and beneath the faint fragrance of perfume he smelt something else, the tang of blood, of something unwholesome. He opened the shutters and stared at the window with its small latch door which looked as though it hadn't been opened for days, whilst it was too small for a man to force his way through. He turned back to the corpse, lying slightly on one side, mouth and eyes open, the skin a dirty white. He could tell from the arms and hands that the muscles were stiffening, and reckoned Sir Thomas must have been dead for at least two hours.

Athelstan took napkins from the lavarium and used them as a kneeler beside the corpse. Removing the small wooden cross he wore around his neck, he performed the rites of the dead, blessing the man's brow, eyes, nose and bloodied mouth, sketching with his thumb as he quickly recited the words of absolution and invited the powers of heaven to go out and meet this soul, to protect him against the hands of the enemy. Athelstan secretly wondered if it was too late. Perhaps the soul had already left the body, its fate resting with the mercy of God. Once finished, he turned the corpse over and, using both hands, pulled out the pricket, an ugly-looking weapon with its broad base, the point as sharp and deadly as any slitting knife. It came out with a gentle plop, and more blood dripped. Athelstan handed the pricket to Cranston and carefully scrutinised the corpse. The flesh was cold and clammy, the muscles hard. He noticed how most of the blood stained the stomach and the lap of the gown. He could detect no other bruise or mark, and when he sniffed the goblet of wine standing on the table, as well as the plate of sweetmeats beside it, no malevolent odour. He picked up a solace stone and felt how it fitted snugly into the palm of his hand.

'Sir Thomas often used that.' Clinton stood in the doorway, Branson behind him. 'He would often use that stone, flexing his fingers to comfort himself.'

'Did he need comforting?' Athelstan asked.

Sir Maurice shrugged.

'And you, sir,' Cranston pointed to Sir Reginald Branson, 'do you know anything about this man's death?'

'Only what you see,' Branson retorted tersely, 'and all I can add, Lord Coroner, is that good men, knights of the Crown, are being foully murdered, but no one is brought to justice. He was murdered.' Branson advanced into the room. 'Look, Sir John, at the corpse, search this chamber. Sir Thomas liked life and all its comforts. He brought up a goblet of wine, a dish of sweetmeats. He had invited a young lady to share his company; that was all cut short! Someone came into this chamber and stabbed him to the heart.'

Athelstan, still kneeling down, picked up Davenport's right hand, slightly blood-splashed, the skin clean and smooth, the nails neatly cut. He sighed and got to his feet and, ignoring Clinton's protests, began to search the chamber with Cranston's assistance. He found nothing significant: personal treasures, a prayer book, clothing, documents, purses of silver. Everything was neat and tidy. The bed curtains of the tester bed had already been folded back, as if Sir Thomas was preparing for his visitor. Athelstan could find nothing of significance, no sign of a struggle.

'Is this how the room was?' he asked.

Sir Maurice nodded.

'But how,' Athelstan asked, 'can a man be stabbed to the heart when the door is locked and bolted, the windows shuttered, with no other entrance? There isn't one, Master Rolles, is there?'

The taverner shook his head.

'Yet someone came in here,' Athelstan insisted, 'a friend who was allowed to get very close, snatch up that pricket and stab Sir Thomas through the heart. Had he drunk much claret today?'

'A fair bit,' Sir Maurice replied. 'He was sitting out

in the garden for most of the morning, enjoying the sunlight, watching the carp in the pond.'

'He then came in.' Rolles picked up the story. 'He was in excellent humour. He demanded a goblet and a plate of sweetmeats to be sent up to his chamber and asked me to send for Rosamund.'

'So he didn't use the Castle of Love? The pocket in the tapestry.'

'Oh yes, Brother, but I'd failed to check it. What with all these troubles, and so early in the day . . . When I did look I found the small roll of parchment. Sir Thomas was very eager. I asked if he wanted Rosamund to come after dark. He replied no. When the wench arrived, that's how we found him, dead.'

Athelstan asked Cranston to clear the room. The coroner politely told Rolles and the two knights to wait downstairs. Athelstan went to the high wooden settle. He sat, arms crossed, staring down at the corpse and the blood pools all about it.

'Sir John,' he whispered, 'in God's good name, what is happening here? Here is a man hale and hearty, more interested in his claret and his wench than anything else, but he is found stabbed to death in a locked chamber.'

'He had drunk heavily, Brother. Perhaps more deeply than we thought, which would make him weak and vulnerable.'

'To whom?' Athelstan lifted his head. 'There's only one explanation, Sir John; the only logical explanation is that the assassin crept in here, stabbed Sir Thomas, and hid until the door was broken down, but even then . . .' He got to his feet. 'I must see this fair Rosamund.'

They went down the stairs. Athelstan told Sir Maurice he could see to the corpse of his comrade. Rolles took him out into the garden, where Rosamund, wrapped in her cloak, was sitting in a flower arbour, cradling a cup of posset and chewing rather noisily from a bowl of grapes.

Athelstan introduced himself and Cranston and sat down beside the young woman. Despite her fiery red hair, laughing mouth and merry eyes, Rosamund reminded Athelstan of Cecily the courtesan. For a while, he just sat staring out across the garden, admiring the small lawns, the raised herbers, the vegetable plots, separated from the herb garden by a small trellised walk over which rose bushes now grew. To his right, screening off the high-bricked curtain wall, broken by a small postern gate, was a line of trees. In the centre of the garden, with coloured stone edging, glittered a broad carp pond.

'I always love gardens,' he began, 'especially ones like this, laid out to catch the sun.'

'Mother Veritable has a garden.'

Rosamund smiled at Sir John, who stood outside the arbour, glancing admiringly down at her. She crossed her legs, swinging a foot backwards and forwards, plucking at a red tendril of hair, turning her face, only too eager to flirt with this powerful Lord Coroner.

'The ostler brought me out here. I am sitting in

the very place Sir Thomas did before he went up to his chamber. Oh, Brother Athelstan, what a hideous sight. I'm only too pleased to be sitting here. Master Rolles' garden is famous. They say, when he bought the tavern, he laid it out himself.'

'You saw Davenport's corpse?' Cranston asked.

'Oh yes, like a lump of meat on a flesher's stall, blood everywhere, and that pricket, sticking out like a demon's knife.'

'And there was no one in the room?' Athelstan asked. 'I mean, besides the corpse.'

'Of course not.'

Rosamund chatted on and, without being invited, smiling flirtatiously at Cranston, recited everything which had happened that day, from the moment she had been summoned by Mother Veritable, to finding the corpse of Sir Thomas. She then finished the bowl of grapes, drained the cup of posset and jumped to her feet.

'I must go now,' she said softly, her eyes never leaving Cranston. 'I've been a good girl.'

Cranston opened his purse and thrust a silver piece into her hand. Standing on tiptoe, Rosamund kissed him on each cheek and, hips swaying, walked up the path back into the tavern. Cranston sat down next to Athelstan.

'Beautiful garden,' he agreed. 'I wish I could have the same, but the dogs would eat the carp and the poppets would fall in the pond. What do you make of all this, Athelstan? Who could have killed Sir Thomas?'

'Shifting mists. Shifting mists,' Athelstan repeated. 'Sometimes, Sir John, I get a glimpse of the truth. These murders, are they in a logical line – I've talked about this before – or are there two lines? Different assassins, working on their own evil affairs? I'm sure that those good knights, and Master Rolles, and everyone else in the tavern, can account for their movements. Brother Malachi was apparently back in St Erconwald's. It's the Judas Man who concerns me.'

He rose to his feet, followed by Cranston, and walked over to the carp pond, watching the great golden fish swimming lazily amongst the reeds. Athelstan tried to hide the flutter of excitement in his stomach. He had seen something today, small items glimpsed and then dismissed. He wished he could go back to St Erconwald's, sit down and reflect on what he had learned. Lost in his thoughts, he re-entered the tavern. Rolles was in the tap room, supervising the slatterns and the cooks. Athelstan, uninvited, walked into the kitchen. Through the clouds of steam billowing across from the ovens and the two great blandreths hung above the fire, he studied the open windows and the side door.

'Can I help you?' Rolles, wiping bloodied fingers on his apron, stood in the doorway.

'Yes, sir. Have you had sight of the Judas Man?'

'Not a glimpse, but his horse and harness remain in the stables.'

'I would like to see his chamber.'

Rolles shrugged and ordered a tap boy to take

Athelstan up. Cranston decided he would stay and sample the tavern ale. The boy, armed with a bunch of keys, took him on to the second gallery and unlocked the door to the Judas Man's chamber. The friar closed this and leaned against it, staring around. There was nothing much: a truckle bed, a few sticks of furniture, a lavarium, the chest at the foot of the bed was empty, as was a small coffer on the table. Athelstan noticed the fresh ink stains on the table and wondered what the Judas Man had been writing. He was about to leave when he changed his mind and began to search the room more thoroughly, lifting stools, moving the bench, pulling the bed away from the wall. He exclaimed in pleasure at a small screwed-up piece of parchment lying on the floor. He unrolled it and took it over to the small window to obtain a better view. On one side was a list of supplies, but on the other the Judas Man had written, time and again, '1, 2, 3, 4, 5, 1, 2, 3, 4, 5, 1, 2, 3, 4, 5, 1, 2, 3, 4, 5, 4 not 5, 4 not 5 . . .' He had underscored these columns. What on earth did that mean? 4 not 5?

Athelstan heard voices from the yard below and, standing on tiptoe, stared out of the window. Henry Flaxwith, his two hounds of hell beside him, was arguing with an ostler. Athelstan folded the piece of paper up, slipped it into his wallet and went downstairs. Cranston was sitting in the tap room, Flaxwith whispering in his ear. The coroner beckoned the friar over.

'I do not want to drink, Sir John.'

'What a pity,' Cranston smiled. 'I think you are going to need one.' He patted Flaxwith's burly hand. 'Henry's been a good hound. He has been out along the river and visited the Fisher of Men.' He lowered his voice and leaned closer. 'He's found the Judas Man, naked as he was born.' Cranston tapped his chest. 'Dead as a stone. A terrible wound to his chest. The Fisher of Men found his corpse trapped amongst weeds under London Bridge.'

'You are sure?' Athelstan asked. 'Henry, how did you know?'

'I have just come from there. I asked the Fisher of Men to view his corpses. I would recognise that man anyway, drenched with river water, his skin slimed green. Brother, it was the Judas Man, and he is dead . . .'

Cranston and Athelstan stood at the entrance to the Barque of St Peter which stood set back from the quayside near La Reole. The air reeked of tar from the nets and cordage drying in the weak sun; a sombre place, especially now in the early afternoon as the sun began to wane and the mist to boil in from the Thames. Even on a sunny day this was not a place frequented by many. People called it 'the House of the Drowned Man', or 'the Mortuary of the Sea'. The Barque of St Peter was a single-storey building fashioned out of grey stone, with a steep red-tiled roof, built by the fathers of the city as a death house for corpses dragged from the Thames: a primitive chapel where the bodies of the drowned could be laid out for inspection and either collected by grieving relatives or, if not, buried at very little cost to the Corporation in one of the poor man's plots in the City cemeteries.

The main door of this macabre chapel fronted the quayside, all about it clustered the wattle-and-daub cottages of those who served there under the careful guidance of the Fisher of Men. Above the wooden porch was a roughly carved tympanum showing the dead rising from choppy waves to be greeted by the Angels of God or the Demons of Hell. Beneath it were scrawled the words 'And the sea shall give up its dead'. On the right side of the door, near the net slung on a hook which the Fisher of Men's company used to bring in bodies, were inscribed the words 'The Deep shall be harvested'. On the left side of the door a garish notice proclaimed the prices for recovering a corpse: 'The mad and insane, 6d.; Suicides, 10d.; Accidents, 8d.; Those Fleeing from the Law, 14d.; Animals, 2d.; Goods to the value of 5 pounds, 10 shillings; Goods over the value of 5 pounds, one-third of their market value.'

'It's good to see you, Sir John, Brother Athelstan.'

The Fisher of Men never seemed to age. He always looked the same, with his cadaverous face, his bald head protected from the cold by a shroud-like cowl made out of leather, and lined with costly ermine. Athelstan could never discover the true antecedents of this enigmatic individual. Stories abounded of how he had once been a soldier, but others claimed he was a scholar who had contracted leprosy, been cured and so dedicated his life to harvesting the river. He was definitely cultured and educated, with more than a passing knowledge of scripture, as well as being able to talk in both Norman French and Latin. Beside the Fisher of Men stood his chief swimmer, the young man known as Icthus the Fish. He certainly looked like one, with his pointed face, protuberant eyes and mouth; he was bald as an egg and totally devoid of eyebrows, his long bony body hidden beneath a simple but costly woollen tunic, good leather sandals on his long feet. Nearby, sitting on a bench, were the rest of what the Londoners called the Grotesques, all shrouded in robes to hide their disabilities.

'May we go in?' Athelstan asked. The Fisher of Men always demanded that courtesy and etiquette be observed.

'Well,' the Fisher of Men smiled, blood-filled lips parted to show perfect teeth, 'Brother, you may claim what you wish from our chapel. Sir John, there is no fee for you. However, now you are here, Brother, would you first shrive us, hear our confessions?'

Athelstan looked at him in surprise, whilst Sir John stamped his foot in annoyance.

'While you wait, my Lord Coroner,' the Fisher of Men added tactfully, 'perhaps you would like to savour a generous cup of Bordeaux from a new cask, a personal gift from a vintner . . .'

Cranston was immediately converted. He sat on a bench outside, cradling a deep-bowled cup, whilst

Athelstan, a little bemused, agreed to the request. He was escorted like a prince to the Fisher of Men's chancery, a small, opulently furnished chamber built at the rear of the barque. The friar sat on a throne-like chair whilst the Fisher of Men and his company trooped in one after the other to confess their sins and be absolved. Athelstan's exasperation gave way to compassion as he listened to these men, outcasts of society, with their disfigured faces. He was touched by their striking humility as they listed sins such as drunkenness, frequenting Mother Harrowtooth's house on the bridge, cursing and swearing, not attending Sunday Mass. He tried to reassure each one, asking what good they had done, before imposing a small penance of one Paternoster and three Ave Marias.

After an hour, he was finished, and with Cranston standing next to him, still sipping at the claret, Athelstan led the assembled company in prayer. Standing on that shabby quayside, he intoned the lovely hymn to the Virgin Mary, 'Ave Maris Stella' – 'Hail Star of the Sea' – accompanied by Icthus on pipe and drum. Once this was done, the Fisher of Men and Icthus escorted Cranston and Athelstan into the Sanctuary of Souls, a long chamber with a makeshift altar at the far end under a stark Crucifix fashioned out of wood from a royal boat, so the Fisher of Men informed Cranston, which had sunk in the Thames, drowning a party of revelling courtiers. On wooden planks before the altar was a line of corpses laid out on trestle boards, each covered by a death cloth, a pot of incense glowing beside it to drive off the dreadful stench of the river in which all these corpses, at varying degrees of putrefaction, had been found.

'We try to keep things neat and wholesome,' the Fisher of Men informed Athelstan. 'Death may be stinking, but life is fragrant.'

The Fisher of Men led them down the line of the dead, describing the various corpses. 'This was a maid who committed suicide near Queenhithe. Oh, and this one,' he pointed to one bundle where a clawed hand hung from beneath its cover, 'this is Sigbert, who thought he was a swan and tried to fly from the bridge. But this,' he added triumphantly, 'is what you are looking for.' He pulled back the cover to expose the Judas Man, naked except for a cloth over his groin, still drenched in river water and covered in green slime. Despite the liverish skin, the changes brought by death and the river, Athelstan immediately recognised the hunter of men. He lay, eyes half closed as if asleep, lower lip jutting out, the pallid white flesh slightly swollen.

'That's caused by the river,' Icthus explained in his high-pitched voice. 'The body always swells.'

Athelstan was more concerned by the dreadful black-red wound high in the man's chest, and the feathered crossbow bolt embedded deep.

'Do you want me to remove that?' the Fisher of Men said.

'No, no.' Athelstan lifted a hand.

For a while, his companions remained silent as he quickly performed the rites for the dead.

'He was a soldier,' Cranston observed. 'You can tell that from the wounds on his body – look at the cuts.'

'A fighting man,' Icthus agreed. 'The muscles on his arms and shoulders are strong.'

'If he *was* a fighting man,' Cranston declared, 'how was he killed like that? Whoever held that crossbow must have been very close. Where did you find him?'

'Beneath London Bridge,' Icthus replied. 'We were out this morning looking for Sigbert. I saw him, floating near the starlings, the wooden supports. A great deal of rubbish is dumped there, the reeds cluster thick and rich. He was trapped by it, floating face down, pushed up by the reeds underneath, as well as the refuse.'

'If he was there,' Athelstan asked, getting to his feet, 'where was he thrown into the river?'

'He was found just under the bridge,' the Fisher of Men replied, 'almost beneath the chapel of St Thomas, so I would guess he was thrown directly over.'

'But,' Athelstan gestured at the corpse, 'he's stark naked. Even at night the bridge is busy. How does a fighting man allow an enemy to get so close and release that deadly crossbow? If he was killed on the bridge and fell over, then he would still be in his clothes, sword belt on. I find it hard to imagine someone meeting the Judas Man in the centre of London Bridge, killing him with a crossbow, stripping his corpse and throwing it over, without being observed. Are you sure he wasn't killed elsewhere on the river?'

'Brother, you know religion,' the Fisher of Men replied, 'and I know the Thames. I can't give you all the answers, but this man was thrown over London Bridge and his corpse trapped in the reeds below.'

Athelstan examined the corpse but could find no other wound, no blow to the head or stab wound to the back. He crossed himself and walked out of the barque, plucking at the Fisher of Men's sleeve.

'Tell me now,' he said, 'another matter. How many years have you worked here?'

'I know what you are asking.' The Fisher of Men shaded his eyes against the bright glow of the setting sun. 'It's my business to know everything which goes on along the river. The robbery of the Lombard treasure? I was here then. I and my company.' He made a face. 'Though it was different then. Icthus was yet to be born, but his father was just as good. Well, we were paid to comb this river for the treasure. I swear the only thing we found was that barge, many miles downstream, trapped in the reeds where it is very marshy, few people go there.'

'So do you think the attack took place at the Oyster Wharf?' Athelstan asked.

'No, I don't. I never did. Quaysides are busy places.'

'So why do you think you were told to look there?'

'I don't know. Our orders were to comb both sides of the river as far down as Westminster. Apart from that barge there was nothing else.'

'And the barge?' Cranston asked.

'Empty, nothing but a floating piece of wood.'

'Tell me,' Athelstan asked, 'you know the Thames. If you had to wait at night to take possession of a treasure chest, without others knowing or being seen?'

The Fisher of Men pointed south-east across the river.

'Somewhere between Southwark and Westminster, where the banks are flat and firm, and you can see both the river and the land behind you.'

'Is it possible,' Athelstan asked, 'for four men to be killed and their bodies to be—'

'Hidden? Weighted down?' the Fisher of Men asked. 'I doubt it. Perhaps one corpse, but four? I know the story, Brother. If those four men were attacked at the dead of night, their assailants would be moving quickly, clumsily. You can tie rocks to a corpse, weigh down its clothes, but time and the river will take care of that. I've always said this, and I'll say it again: if those men were killed by the riverside, their corpses were taken elsewhere.'

'Buried along the banks?' Cranston asked.

'But that would take time,' Athelstan remarked. 'You're not talking of a shallow grave, but a burial pit. I know enough about the river. Earth and soil are shifted; eventually their bodies would be uncovered.'

The Fisher of Men clasped Athelstan's shoulder. 'If you ever wish to become our chaplain, Brother, you are most welcome. You are correct. If those men were killed, their corpses must have been taken away. Is there anything more I can do to help?'

Athelstan shook his head, clasped the man's hand and made their farewells to Icthus and the rest of the company.

'Where to now?' Cranston asked as Athelstan walked up an alleyway leading from the quayside.

'Why, Sir John, the bridge.'

Athelstan kept to the alleyways as he and Cranston discussed what they had seen and heard at the Barque of St Peter. The coroner was full of observations. Athelstan, half distracted, kept thinking about what the Fisher of Men had said. How could four strong men be attacked at the dead of night, so swiftly, so deadly, their corpses removed, as well as the treasure?

He was still thinking about this when they reached the bridge and walked along its thoroughfare, stopping every so often to examine the gaps between the houses and shops built on either side. Some of these places were nothing more than short, thin alleyways leading down to the high rails overlooking the gushing water. Athelstan went into the Chapel of St Thomas, but quickly realised no one could bring a corpse in there. He went out, further down, until they came to the great refuse mound, piled high between two wooden slats with a third behind; this served as a drawbridge. Cranston explained how, when the cords were released, the slat would fall, and the refuse be tipped into the river. The front of the lay stall was a high wooden board. Two young boys, pushing a wheelbarrow, loosened the pegs, pulled the board down and, wheeling their barrow in, tipped the rubbish out. The arca around the lay stall was free of any encumbrance and the passers-by hurried along, clutching their noses, pulling cloaks up or using pomanders against the awful stench. The rubbish was a dark slimy mass: broken pots, scraps of clothing, the refuse of citizens, piled high to be fought over by rats, cats, and the gulls which wheeled screaming above them, angry at being disturbed from their feasting.

'Must we stay here, Brother?'

'That's where the Judas Man was tossed,' Athelstan declared, 'I'm sure of that. Buried deep in the rubbish. When that trap door was lowered, his corpse fell, into the river. Sir John, I've seen enough.'

They hurried across the bridge. Athelstan agreed with Sir John to stop at a small ale house to wash, as the coroner put it, the dirt and smell from their noses and mouths. Cranston persisted in questioning Athelstan about the lay stall on London Bridge, but the friar sat on a stool as if fascinated by the chickens pecking in the dust just outside the ale-house door. He seemed particularly interested in the carts which passed, and although Sir John asked him questions, Athelstan replied absent-mindedly; he even began to hum the 'Ave Maris Stella' under his breath.

'I think the Archangel Gabriel is outside the door, don't you?'

'I think you're right, Sir John,' Athelstan replied dreamily.

'Brother, you are not listening to a word I am saying.'

'I would like to go to the Night in Jerusalem.'

Athelstan put his tankard down and, like a sleep-walker, left the inn, leaving Cranston to drain his blackjack.

They made their way through the streets and into the tavern yard. Athelstan looked into the hay barn, then visited the stables, asking the ostlers which was the Judas Man's horse. He patted this distractedly on the flanks and left, walking across the yard, stopping now and again, trying to memorise every detail before following Sir John into the tavern. Being mid-afternoon, the tap room was busy with all the traders and pedlars chewing on roasted pork from tranchers at the communal table and warming their fingers over the chafing dishes. There was no sign of the knights or Brother Malachi. Master Rolles came bustling up.

'You've a visitor!' He pointed to the far corner.

'Oh yes.'

Athelstan went across and stared down at Ranulf the rat-catcher, the ferrets scratching in the box by his feet.

'Ranulf?'

'Brother, I have come as a messenger from the parish council.'

'What's the matter?' Cranston asked, coming up behind.

320

'Hush now,' Athelstan replied. 'Ranulf,' he warned, 'I'm busy. I'll take no nonsense.'

'Oh no, peace has been made.'

'*Deo gratias*.'

'Oh no, Brother, not that!' Ranulf had misunderstood the Latin. 'We all put it to the vote,' he smiled triumphantly, 'on one condition: that everybody agreed to abide by the majority decision. Cecily the courtesan will be the Virgin Mary.'

'Good.' Athelstan sat down on the stool opposite. 'Can I buy you a pot of ale?'

'No, no.' Ranulf seized his precious box and kissed the small bars through which the ferrets pushed their pink snouts. 'We're all going to celebrate at the Pie-bald tavern. Oh, Brother, by the way,' Ranulf sat down again, 'Benedicta decided to clean the church. She found this.' Ranulf undid his leather jerkin, took out a piece of rolled cloth, put it on the table and left, eager to join the celebrations at the Piebald tavern. Cranston took his seat whilst Athelstan unrolled the cloth. He stared down at the thin, wicked-looking dagger.

'One of those used against Malachi.' Athelstan quickly put it into his leather writing satchel.

'I've seen that before.' Cranston leaned across the table. 'It belonged to the Judas Man.'

Athelstan was about to reply when the tap room fell strangely silent. He glanced across; mailed men-at-arms wearing the royal livery thronged in the doorway behind a dark cowled figure.

'Sir John Cranston, Brother Athelstan?'

The cowled figure came forward. Master Rolles pointed to the corner and Matthias of Evesham strolled across, a beaming smile on his face.

'Well, Sir Jack,' he gave a mocking bow, 'Brother Athelstan. As Scripture says, you have appealed to Caesar, and to Caesar you will go. His Grace, the Regent, awaits you at his Palace of the Savoy.'

Chapter 12

The journey to the Savoy Palace was solemn and silent. Matthias of Evesham led the way as men-at-arms garbed in the royal livery grouped around Athelstan and Cranston under standards and pennants displaying the lions of England and the fleur-de-lys of France: thirty soldiers in all, the sight of their drawn swords clearing the streets as they marched down to the quayside and the awaiting royal barge. They clambered in, Matthias in the prow, Cranston and Athelstan sitting under an awning in the stern. The order was given to cast off. The barge drifted away, the rowers lowered their oars, cutting through the icy, misty river. They had hardly reached mid-stream when other boats grouped around them; these were full of royal archers in their brown and green padded jerkins, across their chests the personal escutcheon of John of Gaunt – displaying the arms of France, England

and Castile. Athelstan pulled his cloak around him, took out his Ave beads and tried to calm his mind by reciting the Ave Maria.

Cranston sat strangely silent. Usually he would take a swig from the sacred wine skin, or engage in friendly banter with those about him. The coroner did not like His Grace the Regent and had often clashed with him. Despite his bonhomie, Sir John refused to sell his soul; he obeyed the law and pursued justice without fear or favour. Now Cranston sat like some great surly bear, cape close about him, his beaver hat low on his head, glowering at the various craft, quietly muttering under his breath. The day was dying, the river freezing cold. Occasionally the bank of mist shifted to reveal the spires of St Paul or the crenellated walls of mansions along the north bank of the Thames. Now and again a herald on the prow gave a long, shrill blast on the trumpet, a warning to other craft to pull away. The barge swept past the Fleet river and down towards the quayside of the Savoy Palace. It slipped easily alongside, servants hurrying up to catch the mooring ropes. Cranston and Athelstan were helped ashore; their escort ringed them and led them into the palace proper.

Athelstan was aware of crossing cobbled yards where the stink of horse muck mingled with more savoury smells from bakehouses and kitchens. On one occasion he glimpsed two pages carrying across a peacock on a platter which had been de-feathered, roasted and then feathered again, its claws and beak being gilded in gold, so lifelike that Athelstan expected it to rise and give its flesh-tingling scream. A gate opened; they were walking through gardens, their beauty hidden by the mist and cold frost, along a colonnaded walk and into the corridors of the palace. The opulent beauty of this place was famous. Athelstan felt that he was entering a world far different from the poverty and grime of his own parish. The floors were a shiny mosaic of black, white and red lozenge-shaped tiles, rich oaken wainscoting gleamed in the light of countless beeswax candles. Above these glowed tapestries, the work of the best craftsmen in Europe, displaying scenes from the classics, the Bible and Arthurian legend. One in particular caught Athelstan's eye and made him smile: the 'Great Beast of Time', part wolf, which devoured the past, part lion, displaying courage to face the present, part dog, faithful enough to accept the future. Inscriptions carved in gold gleamed above doorways. The Latin poet Terence's famous quote 'Without wine and food, Love dies,' symbolised the life of the palace. The courtiers they passed were dressed in the latest attire from France, the men in doublets and elaborately pointed shoes, the ladies in the finest gowns with lacy bodices, low-slung girdles, their fashionable cloaks inlaid with embroidered silk. They reminded Athelstan of lovely butterflies in a gorgeous garden.

Matthias of Evesham first took them to a buttery in one of the main halls, a comfortable chamber with polished walnut furniture and tiled floors, linen panelling covering most of the walls. Edible bread platters of delicate red rose, tinged with the green of parsley, were placed before them, on which a scullion served a ladle of spicy lamb, accompanied by the finest wastel bread and goblets of cool white wine. The coroner regained his good humour and did not take long to finish the bread and wine. Matthias had to hurry his own food before leading them into the gorgeous meeting chamber, its walls decorated with resplendent samite cloths, each displaying the six principal colours of heraldry. They were told to sit together on a cushioned settle, to the right of the mantled hearth; they had hardly done so when the far door opened and two men entered. The first, John of Gaunt, the Regent, was easily recognisable in his gold and red silk and soft boots. His narrow, intelligent face with its sharp nose and flinty blue eyes was a sharp contrast to his soft silver-blond hair and neatly clipped moustache and beard.

'Your Grace.' Cranston and Athelstan went to kneel.

'Oh, sit down,' Gaunt declared wearily. 'I'm tired of bobbing courtiers.'

He grasped a stool, brought it forward and sat down in front of them, one elbow on his thigh, chin cupped in his hand. He gestured with his other hand for his companion to do likewise. Now, up close, Athelstan could clearly study the other man's swarthy face, fringed by long dark hair. He was not as relaxed as the Regent; his large soulful eyes were watchful, one beringed finger scratching at a bead of sweat which ran down into the close-cut moustache and beard. He was dressed soberly in a dark blue cotehardie; rings glistened on his fingers, a single gem dazzled on the gold chain around his neck. A secretive man, Athelstan thought, who kept his own counsel, but the way that he sat next to John of Gaunt, and the look which passed between them, showed intimacy and affection.

'Signor Teodoro Tonnelli, may I present Sir John Cranston, Coroner to the City, and his secretarius, Brother Athelstan, parish priest of St Erconwald's in Southwark.' Gaunt smiled. 'You all know who I am.'

Athelstan gazed steadily back at this scion of Edward III, regent of the kingdom during the minority of his nephew Richard, son of the Black Prince. A man many called the Viper, who was feared by the Church and loathed by the peasants and their secret society, The Great Community of the Realm. Nevertheless, Gaunt was also personable, capable of dazzling charm and extraordinary generosity.

'Well, Brother,' Gaunt studiously ignored Cranston, 'you and the Lord Coroner have questions for us?'

'The Lombard treasure, a chest of jewellery worth at least ten thousand pounds,' Athelstan replied.

'Double that,' Gaunt whispered, 'double that, and half as much again.'

Cranston whistled under his breath.

'There are dreadful murders at the tavern the Night in Jerusalem,' Athelstan declared.

'I have heard of them.' Gaunt looked at Cranston.

'Is it not time, my Lord Coroner, that you arrested someone?'

'The treasure,' Athelstan insisted, 'how was it composed? What happened to it? I mean, before it was stolen?'

'I have brought a list.' Tonnelli's English had only a tinge of an accent. 'You may study it, you may keep it.' He pulled a scroll from his sleeve and handed it to Athelstan, who unrolled it. The jewellery was very carefully listed.

Item 1 A pelican brooch: the pelican stands on a scroll, on the breast of the golden pelican lies a ruby and on the scroll a glowing amethyst.
Item 2 The Swan Jewel: the swan is of gold and studded with precious gems.
Item 3 A silver Cross studded with rubies and amethyst . . .

Athelstan moved the document so that Cranston could also study it. A hundred items were listed there, as well as pouches of silver and gold minted in Genoa, Pavia and Milan. The jewellery was of every type imaginable: rings, crosses, brooches, chains, pendants, bracelets and even precious buttons taken from robes of gold.

'I collected this jewellery,' Tonnelli explained, 'from our banking houses in England, France, Italy and the cities of the Rhine. It was supposed to be part of the Crusaders' war chest to buy weapons, supplies and animals, as well as bribe officials. The treasure was placed in a chest, what I called a chest of steel, protected by bands of iron with three different locks. Twenty years ago I brought the chest down to the Tower whilst I sent the keys to the Admiral of the Fleet. He in turn shared these with trusted officers.'

'This was a loan?' Cranston asked.

'Yes,' Tonnelli agreed. 'The Crusader leaders had agreed to pay it back at a fixed term of interest and give my banking house a percentage of whatever profits they earned. We considered it a sensible venture.' Tonnelli allowed himself a smile. 'The cities of North Africa are fabulously wealthy; the plunder from even one would settle such a debt ten times over.'

'And why did you take it to the Tower?' Athelstan asked. 'Why not hand it over to the Admiral of the Fleet immediately?'

'Oh, little friar,' teased the Regent, 'do not act the innocent! London is full of thieves at the best of times, and many of them live in Southwark. The war with France was over. There was no plunder to be had, or profits to be made from fat ransoms. The city was swollen with desperate soldiers, camped along both banks of the Thames, men of every kind, from a dozen kingdoms, whilst the sailors of the fleet were the riff-raff from every port in Christendom. They'd all heard about the treasure, so Master Tonnelli approached me. The chest of steel would be hidden in the Tower and secretly conveyed to the Fleet at night shortly before it sailed. Once it was aboard, the Admiral, who didn't trust his own crews, would have the chest opened and the contents distributed amongst captains and masters he could trust.'

Gaunt tapped Athelstan on the knee.

'I understand you have been to see Master Hubert in the Tower? Go back there and search amongst the records. Did you know that every gang of outlaws in London, and beyond, had an interest in that treasure? Take a walk along the quayside near London Bridge; you'll see the river pirates hanging from their gibbets for three turns of the tide. London was full of such men who feared neither God or the law.'

Athelstan nodded in agreement. The Regent's reasoning was logical, yet he detected a glibness like the patter of some subtle lawyer presenting his case.

'Why didn't you have the treasure conveyed by your own armed retainers, or even the garrison in the Tower?'

'I didn't trust them. Once they knew the secret, they would know everything, wouldn't they? When and where and to whom it was to be given. Once people know the times and seasons, Brother Athelstan, it is easy for them to plot. I wanted as few people as possible – so did the Admiral, not to mention Signor Tonnelli – to know about the treasure's whereabouts, even when it came aboard ship.' He shrugged. 'Even my captain of the guard, who took the treasure to Culpepper, was told the chest was empty, a diversion to distract certain people I couldn't name.' Gaunt paused. 'The problem was twofold. We didn't want anyone seeing such a barge go directly from the Tower to the flagship; any would-be thief would be watching for that. More importantly, and remember this, we wanted as few people as possible to know when or where the treasure was taken aboard. The design was mine—'

'So, it was you who chose Mortimer and Culpepper?'

'Yes. Mortimer was my henchman, a man who was mine both body and soul, as I was his,' Gaunt added sadly. 'In France, Mortimer saved my life on at least two occasions during sudden ambuscade. I talked to him and swore him to secrecy, and asked him to find one man he could trust. He brought along Culpepper, whom I also liked. I paid them for their needs, good silver to ease their path.'

Gaunt's strange blue eyes held Athelstan's gaze. The friar wondered how much this cunning nobleman knew about the searches by both himself and Cranston. He recalled the whisperings of his own parishioners, how Gaunt had more spies in London than the city had dogs.

'We decided,' Gaunt continued, 'to transport the gold on the Eve of St Matthew, the twentieth of September. My boatmen were told to take the chest across the Thames. They would pause for a while at the Oyster Wharf, where my agents would ensure that all was well, before continuing further south. They did so. Mortimer and Culpepper had not even told me the precise location, except that it was a lonely stretch on the south bank of the Thames, near to where the river turns down towards Westminster.' Gaunt paused, sucking on his teeth. 'According to my men, everything went according to plan. My agents on the Oyster Wharf were satisfied that everything was well and the barge continued. You see, Brother, boats and barges go up the Thames every day and every night; those who lusted after the treasure expected it to be moved with great pomp and ceremony from the City to the Admiral's flagship. They would hardly be looking for a simple barge with a crew of two. My men had been told to look for a lantern light, one which would swing and clearly flash, and they found it.'

'Who was there?' Cranston asked.

'According to my men, Mortimer and Culpepper, still waiting for their barge from Southwark. They handed the treasure over, Culpepper and Mortimer signed the indenture. My men withdrew and that was it.'

'And there was nothing wrong?'

Gaunt pulled a face. 'Mortimer was deeply uneasy, he kept looking back into the darkness. Culpepper too was suspicious and a little wary. Mortimer comforted him and teased him that he would soon lie with the love of his life amongst the dead.'

'Amongst the dead?' Athelstan exclaimed, and immediately thought of the cemetery of St Erconwald, the grass growing long and thick amongst the tombs and crosses.

'My retainers left,' Gaunt continued. 'I thought all was safe. Just before dawn the Admiral sent a message that the treasure had not arrived. I immediately ordered both banks of the Thames to be scoured. I instructed every official in the kingdom to search for the treasure, and gave a description of it and its keepers to every reeve and harbour master.'

'Nothing,' Tonnelli almost shouted, 'nothing at all in either this kingdom or any other; no sign of Culpepper and Mortimer.'

Cranston recalled Helena Mortimer's gentle face, but held his peace. He glanced quickly at Athelstan. The friar was a closed book when it came to thoughts and emotions. Nevertheless, Cranston had studied Athelstan most closely, and something about the way he sat, tapping his foot against the tiled floor, the gentle shaking of his head, followed by an abrupt glance at Tonnelli, showed that the Dominican was not satisfied. The Regent was glib because he had been through this story time and again, but he was still cunning enough to sense Athelstan's reservations.

'What is wrong, Brother? You act as if something is amiss. Don't you believe me?'

Gaunt pointed to a lectern on the far corner.

'A book of the Gospels lies over there. I, Regent of England, uncle to the King, will take the most solemn oath. I loved Mortimer as a brother, I owed him my life, a blood debt. I have searched and I have scoured but I have found no trace of him.'

'Do you suspect anyone?' Athelstan asked.

'I suspect everyone, Brother. Where are the corpses, where is the treasure?'

'You think that Mortimer is dead?'

'Yes, I do. I would take another oath, regretting I ever drew him into this business. I know as much now as I did the morning after the great robbery. Now, these murders in the Night in Jerusalem . . .'

Athelstan described what had happened; John of Gaunt sat shaking his head, keeping his face down, and the friar's unease deepened. Gaunt wasn't telling a lie, but was he withholding something? He looked guilty; why?

Athelstan asked the same question as he and Cranston, after being dismissed by the Regent, made their way up into Fleet Street and through Bowyers Row into the City. The day was now drawing on, lanterns and torches spluttered against the misty, murky nightfall; the market horn had sounded, a sign that the day's trading was ending. The bells of the city tolled, booming across the rooftops, reminding the citizens of evening prayer. They went up past the soaring mass of St Paul's. A group of the sheriff's men had ringed the cathedral cemetery, shaking their fists and shouting curses at the wolfsheads who had taken sanctuary beyond the cemetery wall and so could not be touched. The criminals and felons answered with a hail of rocks and mud. One scoundrel recognised Cranston and started shouting a litany of abuse, brought to an abrupt end by the appearance of a funeral party. A Carmelite, face hidden in his cowl, chanted the prayers of the dead as he led the procession from the cathedral towards the main gate of the cemetery.

He was followed by a cross bearer, and a little boy who carried a lantern in one hand and a bell in the other which he shook vigorously. The mourners carried the cathedral coffin chest covered by black and gold pall. On either side acolytes swung censers; their perfumed smoke billowing out did something to hide the pungent stench, whilst the lowing sound of the funeral bell stilled the clamour. Athelstan used the occasion to hurry Sir John on up into Cheapside.

'Sir John, His Grace the Regent could tell us little.' He smiled mischievously at the coroner. 'His silence told us much more.'

'Like what?' Cranston glared across Cheapside at the stocks filled full of pilferers caught during the day's trading

'I truly don't know, Sir John. Gaunt regrets Mortimer's death, and I agree with him: those two knights and the boatmen were foully murdered, though how and why?' He caught the coroner's arm. 'Now I'll stay here. You must visit that goldsmith, the one who helped Helena Mortimer; goldsmiths are very scrupulous, they keep excellent records. I want you to ask him two things.'

Athelstan tapped his wallet and remembered how the ring of St Erconwald was safely hidden away in the parish church.

'Ask the goldsmith if he has the list of the Lombard treasure distributed by John of Gaunt and that Italian banker.'

'Why? Don't you think that they did?'

'Oh yes, Sir John, I believe him. Ask him also if he

has a second list, distributed by the Benedictine monk Malachi.'

Cranston made to protest.

'Please, Sir John, it's very important! If he doesn't have it we will have to try elsewhere. I know, I know,' Athelstan declared, 'I already have a list from Tonnelli, but I have to be sure.'

Cranston, grumbling under his breath, strode across Cheapside. Athelstan found a plinth and sat down. He pulled up his cowl and, as the bells tolled for vespers, quietly recited the opening psalm of the divine office.

'Oh Lord, come to my aid, make haste to help me.'

He was halfway through the third psalm when Cranston returned brandishing two lists, both written on good vellum. Athelstan took them over to a lantern on a door-post hook, then turned, smiling brilliantly at Cranston.

'I have found it, Sir John!'

Athelstan left a bemused Cranston and hurried down to the riverside, along Thames Street into the Vintry, and took a barge from Dowgate across to Southwark. Night was falling, growing colder by the moment, so he was pleased to find that Malachi had built up the fire in the priest's house. The Benedictine was sitting at a table reading the treatise Athelstan had borrowed from the library at Blackfriars. The friar did his best to be pleasant, but found the pretence difficult, so he immersed himself in a whole series of petty tasks. He went backwards and forwards to the church, taking across his writing satchel, pots of ink and fresh sheets of vellum, as well as a small desk he kept stored under the bed loft. When he moved the truckle bed across and informed Malachi that tonight he would be sleeping in the church, the Benedictine glanced up sharply.

'What is wrong, Brother? You have work to do? You seem agitated.'

'That's because I am.' Athelstan shook his head. 'So much to do,' he murmured, 'so little time to do it. Brother Malachi, you must excuse me, I have accounts to finish, certain business of Sir John's, and of course,' he forced a smile, 'there's always my parish council.'

Athelstan continued going backwards and forwards, praying quietly that Brother Malachi would not question him any further. He turned the chantry chapel into a small chamber, with writing desk, chair, bed; it even included a tray bearing a jug of watered wine and three goblets. Malachi, as if he sensed Athelstan's growing agitation, politely excused himself and said he would go down and sample the ale at the Piebald tavern. Once he had gone, Athelstan immediately relaxed, feeling the tension drain from his back and legs. Bonaventure appeared, following the friar like a shadow, getting under his feet and making himself a genuine nuisance. Only when the cat heard the scurry of mice in the far transept did he decide his bowl of milk could wait, as he loped across to investigate.

Athelstan wheeled out two cupped braziers from the church tower and filled each with a small sack of charcoal.

'Can I help, Father?'

Benedicta had appeared suddenly in the doorway. Athelstan clutched his stomach.

'Benedicta, you made me jump! If I had been drinking, I would have thought I was having a vision.'

'You don't have visions, Brother!'

Benedicta pulled back her hood. Her black hair hung loose to her shoulders.

'And don't try to distract me; the bells will soon ring for vespers. The hour is growing late. Why are you lighting two braziers? You intend to spend the night here, don't you? You are not going to study the stars? And don't tell me,' Benedicta drew close, 'you are going to lie in front of the high altar and pray for our parish council.'

Athelstan went over and closed the church door. 'No, Benedicta, I'll tell you the truth. I am hunting the sons of Cain. I want to trap men who have done great evil, who believe that they can wipe their mouths on the back of their hands and face God as if they were innocent.' He walked out of the shadows and grasped her cold hands.

'Why, Brother Athelstan?' Benedicta kept her face serious, but her beautiful eyes smiled.

'You're cold.' Athelstan let her hands slip.

'I'll help you light the braziers.'

He brought out the tinder box and a bundle of

dry bracken, which they pushed into the small gap under the charcoal. Benedicta found the bellows in the church storeroom. For a while, laughing and chattering, they attempted to fire the braziers, at first unsuccessfully, but eventually the charcoal caught and began to glow, as Athelstan remarked, 'like the fires of hell'. Benedicta went out and brought back sweet-smelling weeds which she sprinkled on top, then helped Athelstan wheel the braziers up the nave and into the chantry chapel. She insisted that they dine together and hurried off to Merrylegs' cookshop. On the way she met Crim and persuaded the altar boy to help her, and together they brought back a large meat pie.

'Freshly baked,' Benedicta announced. 'Merrylegs went on oath to tell me the meat was no more than a month old. I also stopped at the Piebald.' She gestured at Crim. 'Jocelyn sent that free of charge, and Crim hasn't spilt a drop, have you?'

The altar boy, holding the beer jug as he would the sacred pyx, shook his head.

All three sat at the entrance to the sanctuary, Athelstan sharing out the pie and ale, regaling Crim with stories about how the ghost of the leper woman had helped him solve a recent mystery. Crim sat round-eyed, and once the meal was finished, left, taking the jug back to the Piebald and the cookshop's bowl for Merrylegs.

Athelstan washed his hands and face in the small lavarium in the sacristy.

'You were talking about the sons of Cain?' Benedicta stood in the doorway.

'He killed his brother, Benedicta, and when God questioned him, shouted back a question which has rung down the ages: "Am I my brother's keeper?" Like Pilate he didn't wait for an answer, but, also like Pilate, received one whether he liked it or not. God hunted Cain down, seized him and marked his head. Tomorrow,' Athelstan sighed, 'God willing, I am going to see that sign myself.'

'Can I help?' Benedicta offered.

Athelstan folded his napkin and put it over the arm of the lavarium.

'Not now, but tomorrow. I'll celebrate Mass just after dawn. I'll ring the bell so you will know. I want you to bring Cecily here. Oh, and tell Pike the ditcher not to drink too much tonight, I also want him at Mass. He must take certain messages for me.'

Benedicta left, and Athelstan returned to the house. Thankfully Malachi hadn't returned. Athelstan quickly unlocked the chest, took out the casket and St Erconwald's ring. He banked the fire, made sure that everything was in order and left for the church, where he locked and bolted the doors behind him. Then he prepared himself, laying out the parchment, quills, ink horn and other writing materials. Going into the sanctuary, he prostrated himself before the high altar. He quietly recited the Veni Creator Spiritus, but stumbled on the words, so he recalled the famous hymn 'In Laudem Spiritus Sancti': *Spiritus Sancte, pie Paraclete, Amor Patris e Filii, Nexus gignentis et geniti'*, O Holy Ghost, O faithful Paraclete, Love of the Father and the Son . . .

Once he had finished, Athelstan lit more candles around the chantry chapel and concentrated on his task. Slowly but surely he teased out the facts, listing the various killings one after the other, trying to find a pattern, basing his theory on the hypothesis that one person, and one person alone, was responsible for the murders, only to quickly realise that that was futile. He then tried various combinations, listing the incidents in different categories, but eventually he changed this to three: the great robbery; the murder of the knights, Chandler, Broomhill and Davenport; and finally, the murder of the rest. The great robbery he ignored, and concentrated on the latter two, but the problem became even more vexatious, particularly Davenport's death. For a while Athelstan concentrated on that blood-soaked corpse, until eventually he closed his eyes and whispered, *'Deo Gratias!'* At last he was able to impose some order, a harmony on these apparently disjointed facts, before returning to the great robbery.

'The *radix malorum*, the root of all evil,' Athelstan whispered. He left the desk, warmed his hands over the brazier and walked up and down the nave, turning the problem over and over in his mind, looking for the weakness, preparing what he called his bill of indictment. He could see the logic of what he proposed, but where was the evidence? He had very little except for that ring, the casket and those two lists of jewellery. He returned to his writing desk and re-examined the evidence. He now understood the Misericord's scratchings on the wall of his Newgate Prison cell, what he was truly shouting as he died, as well as the veiled allusion that the clue to Guinevere the Golden's death was something which could be found on his sister's person. It all made sense. He also understood the Judas Man's strange scribblings, which, in turn, took him back to the night of the Great Ratting.

Athelstan sifted amongst the evidence he had collected; what else was there? He picked up his quill and wrote a few words. The real problem was the Lombard treasure. Where had it gone? And those four men who'd disappeared off the face of the earth twenty years ago? Athelstan closed his eyes. He thought of the desolate stretch of bank south of the Thames, the dark, lonely night. Other images came to haunt him: John of Gaunt, with his glib tongue and sharp eyes; Sir Stephen Chandler's pitiful prayer for mercy; Rolles the taverner, a knife in one hand, in the other a letter from the Castle of Love; the hay barn; the great cart standing in the tavern yard; Davenport sitting all alone in that garden. Athelstan felt thirsty, so he took a gulp of watered wine. If he could only make sense of the robbery. He recalled the axiom of one of his masters: *Nihil ex Nihilo*, 'Nothing comes from Nothing'. He paused in his pacing, so surprised by his conclusion he threw his head back and guffawed in laughter. He had his proof; the hypothesis was firm, the bill of indictment was ready!

Athelstan went across to the side door, unbolted it and peered out. The priest's house was shrouded in darkness. Malachi must have retired, so Athelstan vowed to do the same. For a short while he knelt in front of the high altar and gave thanks for the help he had received. As he stared up at the Crucifix, the words of the old Crusader song came drifting back:

They have crucified their Lord of flesh
Upon another Cross
His wounds are new again
The tree of life is lost.

He sighed, blessed himself and, extinguishing all the tapers except one, lay down on the narrow cot bed and drifted off to sleep.

He woke before dawn with Bonaventure nuzzling his ear. 'I know, I know,' Athelstan murmured, and, picking the cat up, staggered across to the corpse door to let Bonaventure go hunting in the cemetery. Athelstan then stripped, washed himself at the lavarium in the sacristy and put on a new robe. He tidied the chantry chapel, preparing the high altar for morning Mass. At the first streak of light he tolled the bell three times, and by the time he had vested and knelt before the high altar, Benedicta and Cecily, the latter as fresh and pert as a sparrow, had come into the sanctuary, followed by a rather disgruntled Pike. The ditcher spent most of the Mass scratching himself and yawning loudly, grumbling under his breath. He soon cheered up when Athelstan met him in the sacristy afterwards, and gave him a silver coin and a message which Pike had to learn by rote.

'Go to the Lord Coroner's house,' Athelstan warned, 'and tell him he must be at the Night in Jerusalem by the ninth hour. He is to bring Master Flaxwith and all his bailiffs. Oh yes, and some guards from the Guildhall. Mark me now, you are to go directly to the Lord Coroner's. Only afterwards visit a tavern.' He made sure the ditcher had memorised the message, then Pike left, as swift as a whippet, and Athelstan took the two women down towards the main door of the church.

'I want you to help me,' he began. 'Cecily, you know Mistress Veritable?'

'Whore Queen!' Cecily spat back. 'A bitch steeped in villainy. She tried to get me into her house.' She shook her head, blonde curls dancing, blue eyes angry.

'Hush now,' Athelstan warned. 'Today you and Benedicta must pretend to be her friends. This is what you must do. You are to go to the Friar Minoresses near Aldgate and speak to a novice called Edith Travisa. You are to tell her to meet Mother Veritable and pretend to accede to all her demands. Tell her to negotiate to make it believable.'

'Brother, what are you doing?' Benedicta exclaimed. 'I know Mother Veritable by reputation, a most unsavoury woman.'

'And so does Edith,' Athelstan replied. 'She knows it's only pretence, but she must be convincing. Once you have done that, you must return to Southwark. Act as though you are the Lady Edith's messengers. You must tell Mother Veritable how Edith Travisa, now bereft of her brother, is seriously considering entering Mother Veritable's house. You must pretend, you must convince that hideous woman. You must also persuade her to come back with you across the river this very morning to meet Edith to negotiate certain matters. She'll ask you who you are. For the sake of the truth you must tell her you are Edith's friends, and that you support her decision. Garnish your tale as you would a meal; emphasise Edith's poverty, her lack of family; but one thing you must achieve is Mother Veritable's departure from Southwark, before the ninth hour.'

Both women agreed and left. Athelstan continued with his cleaning of the church, interrupted now and again as parishioners drifted in. Satisfied, he went across to the priest's house, where Malachi had just risen and was praying from his psalter before celebrating Mass.

'Brother Athelstan, you have been up early?'

'I have celebrated my Mass, Malachi. Now I have business to do.' Athelstan kept his face impassive, closing his mind to what he now knew, as well as what he planned to happen before this day finished. 'Once you have celebrated Mass,' he continued, 'I must insist you go back to the Night in Jerusalem.

No, no, you will be safe. You must inform Master Rolles, Sir Maurice and Sir Reginald that I, and the Lord Coroner, must have words with them in the solar just after the ninth hour. If they are not there, Sir John will issue warrants for their arrest. I'm sorry, Brother, I cannot tell you the reason why, but all four of you have to be there.'

The Benedictine, mystified, left for the church. Athelstan finished his preparations. He donned his cloak, put the casket in a leather bag, collected his writing satchel and walked down through the early morning streets. He paused outside Merrylegs' cookshop to eat one of the cook's specialities, a sweet pie of apple and raisins. He stopped at the Piebald for a mug of ale, then continued down to the riverside to watch the mist lift and the fishing fleets come in. People passed him, Athelstan smiled or raised his hand in blessing, yet he was still very distracted. He kept turning over in his mind what he had planned for that meeting in the solar at the Night in Jerusalem. Church bells chimed, drowning the scream of the hunting gulls. Athelstan felt the cold seep through his heavy robe, and turning round, he walked up to the tavern.

Master Rolles greeted him in the doorway. Athelstan was equally courteous in reply.

'I have received your message, Brother.'

'Thank you, thank you. Master Rolles, do you have spades and mattocks? I would like to borrow them for my church field.'

'Of course, quite a few.'

'Good.' Athelstan answered absent-mindedly, patting him on the arm. 'I need to see you this morning, I assure you it won't take long.'

Athelstan warmed himself in front of the tap room fire, listening to the chatter of the spit boy, who questioned the friar closely on how much he ate, and did he have a spit? Was it true that friars were forbidden to eat? Athelstan laughed and gave the boy a penny. The lad was still chattering when Athelstan heard a clamour outside, and Sir John, with his retinue of bailiffs and serjeants-at-arms, strode into the tap room.

'Brother, good morrow, what's this all about?'

Athelstan took him into a far corner, whispering what he had planned and what Sir John must do. The coroner loosened his cloak, took off his beaver hat, scratched his head and whistled under his breath.

'Little friar, you have been busy!' He nodded at the doorway. 'As I came in, they were gathering in the solar.'

'So, we must join them. There must be a guard in the room and one outside.'

'And the bailiffs?'

'Oh, they'll be busy. They have a garden to dig!'

Athelstan, clutching his writing satchel and leather bag, left the tap room, followed by a mystified Cranston. The others were already grouped either side of the solar table. Athelstan sat at one end with his back to the window, Sir John at the other.

'Good morning, gentlemen.'

The knights grunted a reply as if bored by the proceedings. Rolles, however, was clearly agitated by the presence of the guards and so many bailiffs.

'Ah, Henry.' Athelstan pointed at Flaxwith, who was standing behind Cranston. 'I must ask you to leave. I have a very important task for you. In the outhouse, across the stable yard, you will find spades, mattocks and hoes. No, keep still, Master Rolles.' Athelstan spoke as the taverner scraped back his chair. 'I want you to collect them, go into the garden behind me and start digging.'

Athelstan glanced quickly at the knights, gratified at the shock in their faces. Rolles was so agitated he couldn't keep still.

'Brother Athelstan,' Flaxwith retorted, 'Master Rolles' garden is beautiful.'

'Master Rolles, you will keep seated,' Athelstan repeated, 'or I will ask you to be bound. Henry, the garden behind me is not beautiful. It houses the mortal remains of five poor souls, murdered by the men who are now seated around this table.'

The knights jumped to their feet, followed by Rolles. Cranston banged the table, shouting that they would be arrested if they moved three paces from their chairs. Once silence was imposed, Cranston looked over his shoulder and nodded at Flaxwith.

'Do it!' he ordered. 'And dig deep. Brother Athelstan?' He turned back.

'Thank you, Sir John. I will repeat what I've said. Each of you seated at this table, all four of you, is guilty of the most hideous homicide.' Athelstan paused. 'One is missing. You may have made enquiries about her, Mother Veritable. She has been taken by two friends of mine across the river. She has confessed, and will do so again, to the murderous events of twenty years ago.'

Chapter 13

'It is an unassailable theory,' Athelstan began, 'that murder, like charity, always begins at home. In this case, home was the Night in Jerusalem, where a group of young knights, brothers-in-arms, assembled over twenty years ago to take part in the Great Crusade of Lord Peter of Cyprus. Eager, hungry young men, raised in the House of War, who saw their fortunes threatened by the recent peace treaty with France. A group of such knights from the shire of Kent assembled here with their chaplain Brother Malachi.' Athelstan glanced quickly at the Benedictine. 'Only one was an outsider: Edward Mortimer, a landless knight who'd become the handfast friend of Culpepper, so close they were like peas in a pod.'

Athelstan moved his chair sideways so he could stare out of the window to where Flaxwith and the others were busy digging up Master Rolles' garden.

'You didn't have much money.' He was aware how quiet the solar had become; the ghosts were now gathering. 'You came up to London,' he continued, 'and took lodgings in this tavern, recently purchased by Master Rolles with the plunder and the ransoms he had earned in France. Through Master Rolles you became acquainted with Mother Veritable, who owned a pleasure house down near the stews. Now, Culpepper fell in love with one of the ladies of the night, who rejoiced in the name of Guinevere the Golden, a beautiful woman, fair of face but fickle of heart. You all enjoyed yourselves while the crusading army gathered and the cogs of war assembled in the Thames.'

'What does all this mean?' Sir Maurice Clinton spoke up, his face ashen and sweat-stained.

'God knows the true reason,' Athelstan ignored the interruption, 'but His Grace John of Gaunt, together with the Lombard banker Teodoro Tonnelli, decided that part of the war chest, the loan raised by the Crusader commanders, should be transported secretly, by night, to the Admiral's flagship waiting in the Thames. His Grace wished to avoid any public show, so as not to attract the attention of the outlaw gangs or mob of river pirates which crowded along the Thames like flies on a dung heap. To make a long story brief, on the Eve of St Matthew, the Year of Our Lord 1360, the treasure barge left the Tower, crossed the Thames and went along the south bank, past the Oyster Wharf to a secret location. His Grace had decided that the treasure would be taken out to the Fleet by his trusted retainer Edward Mortimer, who'd also brought Richard Culpepper into the secret design. Both knights were well rewarded by His Grace. They were to attract the treasure barge in, by lantern or torchlight, and the chest would be moved to an ordinary barge specially hired for that occasion. The treasure duly arrived. The two knights, waiting on the river bank, took charge of it, and brought their own barge in. They were to pay the boatmen off and take the treasure to the flagship.'

Cranston played with the edge of his cloak. He didn't know what path Athelstan was following, but he understood why the little friar was talking so slowly, keeping a watchful eye on what was going on in the garden. Cranston was also vigilant. The two knights sat like carved statues as their mask of respectability was slowly peeled away. Cranston was more wary of Rolles, who seemed to have recovered his wits. One hand had already slipped beneath the table. Cranston remembered how this dagger man had a knife in a sheath on his belt, as well as another in the top of his boot. His fingers slipped to the hilt of his own knife. He would watch Master Rolles.

'Imagine the scene,' Athelstan continued, 'a fairly cloudless sky, the moon riding high, the Thames quiet and sluggish, the silence broken by the cries of the night, creatures hunting their prey. Culpepper and Mortimer talking to the bargemen, eager to be away, unaware that more deadly hunters were loose along the river that night.'

353

'But, but,' Sir Reginald Branson intervened, 'no one knew of this.'

'Nonsense!' Athelstan scoffed. 'No one, apart from those two knights, was supposed to know; they didn't even tell the boatmen why they needed their barge. Culpepper, however, had made a dreadful mistake. He truly loved Guinevere the Golden. He had shown her the money he had earned, and whispered about how there would be more. Guinevere was the last person he should have told, and he did tell her everything: the treasure, the secret place along the Thames, the arrangements, even the hour. Guinevere was fickle of heart. Culpepper may have loved her, but her attentions were already wandering. Unbeknown to Culpepper, she was also bestowing her favours on one of the other knights. I don't know who. Perhaps you, Sir Maurice? Sir Thomas Davenport, or Sir Laurence Broomhill? She told one and he told the rest. Were you poor, penniless knights already resentful of the fortune and favour shown to Culpepper and this relative newcomer Mortimer? So, you hatched a plot to steal the treasure, and you enlisted the help of Master Rolles and Mother Veritable.'

'I didn't . . .' Master Rolles raised a hand. 'Sir John,' he gasped, 'this is nonsense.'

'Hush now,' Athelstan soothed. 'On the night in question you pretended you were all revelling and carousing in a chamber here at the Night in Jerusalem. No one would mark the hours, not even the Misericord, who was serving as a pot boy, or the other heavy-eyed servants and maids, only too eager to slip exhausted into their narrow beds. Now, Master Rolles, you owned a great high-sided cart, the perfect place to hide a group of men under a leather awning. You had the cart hitched, its wheels covered in straw and sacking to hide the sound, and slipped away, leaving probably only two of the knights to continue the sound of revelling and carousing so as to distract the attention of others. You knew, thanks to Guinevere, where Culpepper and Mortimer would be waiting for the treasure. You came upon them suddenly and silently. All of you are trained bowmen, skilled archers. You arrived at the moment Culpepper and Mortimer took possession of the barge.'

Athelstan paused.

'The attack would be swift, the shafts hissing through air.' The friar glanced quickly at Malachi, now so pale his eyes seemed like dark pools, his lips thin, bloodless lines. 'Four corpses,' Athelstan continued, 'transfixed by arrows. You quickly carried them to the waiting cart, together with the treasure chest. The location was secret. The river water would soon wash away any signs of violence. You pushed the barge out into mid-stream, having cleared it of any possessions.'

'And Guinevere the Golden?' Cranston asked, his gaze still intent on Master Rolles.

'Ah, Guinevere the Golden,' Athelstan sighed. 'She whom fortune didn't favour. Poor Culpepper died thinking she loved him and him only. The men she betrayed him to encouraged her to maintain this illusion. I suppose she was told to wait for Culpepper somewhere lonely and dark; what better place than their usual love tryst, the cemetery at St Erconwald's, near to the river but far enough away from the Night in Jerusalem. She was to wait there until it was all over. Of course, if you betray one person, it's only a matter of time before you betray someone else. Guinevere had to be silenced. I have no proof that it was at St Erconwald's, but I do know that Mother Veritable took care of her. The cart containing the four other corpses would stop to pick up her body as well. In the dead of night that cart, its wheels muffled, slipped back into the Night in Jerusalem.'

'Master Rolles on his cart,' Cranston intervened, 'was a common enough sight at all hours of the day and night. Slatterns and servants, the Misericord included, slept in the tap room, under the tables. There'd be enough of you to keep watch in the dead of night . . .'

'There was also another way in.' Athelstan spoke quickly, fearful lest Cranston be carried away by his excitement at what was being revealed. 'The small postern gate to the garden.' The friar stared down the table. 'Master Rolles, I must study your accounts. I believe you were having the garden laid out then, weren't you? The ground all dug up? A beautiful place now, but an ideal one at the time for hiding five corpses and all their possessions. They were brought through the postern gate that night.' Athelstan gestured at the window. 'No wonder you had mantraps to protect such a place.'

'This is preposterous,' Sir Maurice broke in. 'You have no proof.'

'You don't deny it,' Cranston barked, 'you simply ask for evidence.'

'I'll supply that soon enough.' Athelstan pointed to the window. 'We'll find the corpses, then there's Mother Veritable: she'll be about to take the oath now, provide the Crown and its lawyers with all the proof they need.'

'But this treasure . . .' Sir Reginald Branson spoke up.

'You know the answer to that,' Athelstan retorted. 'We'll come to it by and by. What were you planning to do with that treasure? Break it up, hide it away until you returned?' Athelstan's face creased into a smile. 'But you couldn't do that, could you? In the end all you had to do was hide the corpses, and let those poor men take the blame. The perfect crime, except for Mother Veritable. She has already confessed to killing Guinevere the Golden. She was supposed to destroy all that poor woman's possessions, make it look as though she had packed all her bags and vanished without a trace, but she was greedy. She kept a small coffer owned by Guinevere.' Athelstan leaned under the table, brought out the small casket and placed it carefully in front of him. 'The years passed, the casket became tawdry. Mother Veritable grew careless or her conscience pricked her. She gave the casket to Beatrice and Clarice, not realising the terrible mistake she was making.' Athelstan tapped the broken clasps. 'Look at that, gentlemen, do you see the insignia? Dark blue Celtic crosses on a tawny background. Don't you remember whose insignia it was?'

'In God's name!' Sir Maurice leaned forward, hands shaking.

'Ah, Sir Maurice, you have reached the same conclusion as I have, hasn't he, Brother Malachi?' Athelstan glanced quickly at the Benedictine. 'Aren't those the personal insignia of your brother, as opposed to your family escutcheon? A dark blue Celtic cross on a tawny background. I noticed that in the Tower when I scrutinised the indenture. Your brother Richard always signed a cross like this next to his name, while Mortimer used a lion, the heraldic device of his family. You had forgotten that, but the Misericord didn't. He became very friendly with Beatrice and Clarice. One day he saw this coffer and, being keen of eye and sharp of wit, realised it must have been a personal gift from Sir Richard, a fact Mother Veritable had overlooked. The Misericord would wonder why their mother Guinevere, supposedly so devoted to Sir Richard, would vanish but leave that here. He began to reflect, racking his memory, recalling the events of that night. Did he remember something amiss? An item he had glimpsed? Did he grow suspicious of the accepted story? Eventually he shared his secret with Beatrice and Clarice whilst enigmatically hinting to his own sister what he had found. Something which could also be found on Edith's person, namely a Celtic cross. When I visited Edith at the convent of the Minoresses she was wearing a cross similar to this one.' Athelstan tapped the casket. 'The Misericord must have told those two young women to be careful, to entrust the casket to someone else, which they did, their friend Donata. After their murder, Donata suspected something was wrong and decided to flee Mother Veritable's, entrusting this to me.'

'Is this true?' Sir Reginald Branson shouted, glaring at Brother Malachi.

'You know it is,' the Benedictine spat back.

'Of course you do,' Athelstan declared, pushing the casket further down the table.

Malachi's hand went out, as if by caressing it he could somehow touch his dead brother.

'Let me continue my story,' Athelstan continued. 'Once the vile deed was done, you warriors of Christ went to Outremer, Master Rolles returned to looking after his tavern, whilst Mother Veritable followed her own evil path. But sin, like a beast at the door, crouches and waits, doesn't it, Brother Malachi? You see,' Athelstan chose his words carefully, 'Brother Malachi was very anxious about his brother. For a while he believed the accepted story, that his brother, with Mortimer, had stolen the Lombard treasure, and disappeared with his leman, Guinevere the Golden. Now the Crown, not to mention the Lombard bankers, had circulated a list of the missing treasure to the goldsmiths' guilds in all the principal cities of the kingdom. Brother Malachi did likewise.'

Athelstan opened his writing satchel and took out the two documents Cranston had given him the night before.

'There are two lists here, one circulated by the Crown, the other by Brother Malachi. There's one difference. On yours, Malachi, you added an item not found on the other.' Athelstan undid his wallet and brought out the small velvet-lined box which held the Erconwald ring. 'Your brother owned this. It may be Saxon but I suspect he bought it because the crosses inside the ring are very similar to those of his personal insignia. Did he buy it in London, Brother Malachi? He certainly showed it to you before he gave it to Guinevere the Golden as a token of his love.' Athelstan paused. The silence now weighed so heavily that every sound from the garden echoed through to the solar. 'None of the treasure ever reappeared,' Athelstan continued, 'but this ring did. A goldsmith contacted Brother Malachi. Once he saw the ring, he realised that Guinevere was dead, and so was his brother. When Mother Veritable killed Guinevere, greedy as ever and disappointed at what was found in the Lombard treasure chest, she kept the casket, but sold the ring. It was only a matter of time before some goldsmith recognised it and, hoping to claim the reward, wrote to Brother Malachi. This ring has already made Mother Veritable confess.'

'I told you!'

Master Rolles' outburst surprised even Cranston. The taverner leaped to his feet, dagger already drawn, and lunged across the table, the point of the blade narrowly missing Sir Maurice's face. The knight pushed his chair back, hand going to his own dagger, but Rolles, face white and tight, eyes glaring, now lunged at Athelstan, his tormentor. Cranston, even swifter, lashed out with his hand and knocked Rolles' wrist, sending the dagger flying. Athelstan could only sit as the taverner, backing away, drew the evil-looking Welsh dagger from the top of his boot. He turned on Cranston, lips moving soundlessly, one hand going to brush the sweat from his cheek.

'Don't be stupid.' Cranston rose, drawing his own sword in a hiss of steel, his other hand expertly plucking a dagger from its sheath. 'Come, Master Rolles, this is no way forward, whatever charges you face.'

'Charges?'

Rolles wiped his face with the back of his hand. He had lost all sense of where he was and what was happening, trapped by the mistakes of the past.

'You stupid bastard.' Rolles turned on Sir Maurice. 'It was your scheme from the start. I should have known better. And what for? All that blood, for what? And that stupid bitch Veritable, greedy as a jackdaw.'

Sir Maurice still sat in his chair, slightly pushed back from the table. Sir Reginald's hand edged slowly towards his own dagger.

'All this,' Rolles shouted so loudly the guards outside became alarmed and burst in, only to be waved away by Cranston, 'all this,' he screamed again, a white froth appearing at the corner of his mouth, 'lost because of you.'

'Master Rolles,' Cranston warned, 'put down your knife.'

'And you,' Rolles took a step forward, 'fat Jack Cranston, come to take my profits, have you? I never did like you, with your prying eyes, all bluff and merry, ever righteous.'

Cranston took a step back, raising both sword and dagger. Rolles was lost in his own fury, mad with rage at what was about to be revealed. Athelstan had calculated that the disappearance of Mother Veritable would disconcert Rolles, but not to this extent.

Suddenly there was a tap on the window. Flaxwith, alarmed, was peering through. Cranston lowered his sword; Rolles seized the opportunity, turning slightly sideways like the fighting man he was, and lunged, his dagger making a feint for Cranston's face, but moving just as quickly, he brought the dagger down, aiming for his true mark, the coroner's broad chest. Cranston, despite his bulk, acted even more swiftly. Instead of retreating, he moved to the right. His dagger hand blocked Rolles' blow, whilst he thrust his sword deep into the soft flesh where stomach and chest met. The force of Rolles' lunge made him take the blade deeper, and for a while he just rocked backwards and forwards on his feet, a look of pained surprise on his face as he dropped his dagger.

Sir John pulled his sword out. Rolles tried to speak,

moving forward even as the blood frothed between his lips. He made one last effort, then fell to his knees, gave a sigh and collapsed to the floor. Flaxwith threw open the door, others of his company thronging in behind, Cranston roared at them to withdraw.

'But Sir John, I've—'

'Never mind,' Cranston retorted. 'You saw it all, Henry. I had no choice.'

Flaxwith nodded. 'It's treason, Sir John, to draw a weapon on a King's officer who is about to make an arrest.'

'Thank you, Henry.'

Cranston gestured to the door. The bailiff withdrew, and Cranston ordered the rest to stay where they were and keep their hands on the tabletop. He knelt down, pressing his fingers against Rolles' neck. Athelstan joined him. By now the blood was gushing out of Rolles' mouth and the gaping wound in his chest, forming a dark red puddle on the floor. Neither Cranston nor Athelstan could find the life beat. The friar whispered a prayer, but Cranston was more practical.

'He'll have to wait. Let his corpse sprawl there and his soul can hear our judgement.'

'Are you sure?' Athelstan asked.

'Sit down, Brother,' Cranston ordered.

The friar returned reluctantly to his chair. Malachi was smiling to himself, as if savouring the moment.

'You celebrated Mass in my church,' Athelstan accused. 'You condemned these men because they

363

consorted with whores, yet you smile because an enemy lies dead a few paces in front of you.'

Malachi's response was to turn and spit at the corpse. 'He was an assassin,' the Benedictine replied. 'You know that and so do I. He was lawfully executed by a King's officer in pursuit of his duty. Rolles had a hand in the murder of my brother.'

'Aye, and others.'

Athelstan stared across at the two knights. Both men looked beaten, faces grey with fear.

'And so we come to the night of the Great Ratting,' Athelstan continued. 'All of you, the knights, Master Rolles and Mother Veritable, had decided that the Misericord was too great a danger to ignore; his friendship with Beatrice and Clarice posed a threat, whilst the knights, especially Chandler, had other grievances against him. Mother Veritable had heard rumours, and God knows what questions the Misericord may have been asking. The Misericord moved about in the twilight of the law; he could piece information together, reaching the conclusion that you, Malachi, were innocent but the rest were a coven of assassins. He would keep such knowledge close, fearful of reprisal, unable to approach the law but greedy for what wealth blackmail might bring. He wouldn't have learned everything, but enough to feed suspicions. Once this were known, his death, and those of the two women, was decided upon. Beatrice and Clarice were easy prey; it was just a matter of time, of waiting for a suitable occasion. The Misericord was different; a man of keen wit, he would have to be hunted down, so the Judas Man was called in. He was, in fact, hired by all the assassins.

'On the night of the Great Ratting, Beatrice and Clarice were lured here and sent to the hay barn. The Misericord was to be killed by the Judas Man, but he escaped and fled to the last man he should have approached, Master Rolles. The taverner sent him to the hay barn, either to be killed with Beatrice and Clarice or trapped and depicted as their assassin. The cunning man's stomach saved him: he was desperate for the privy. He was fortunate, blessed by that luck which had always kept him one step ahead of the law. He wasn't there when the assassin entered the hay barn.'

'Who was it?' Brother Malachi asked.

'Oh, I suspect Master Rolles. He had sent both the girls and the Misericord to the hay barn. He must have known that the Judas Man had trapped the wrong felon, but he didn't really care. He pretended to be busy in the kitchen to distract the likes of harassed Tobias, then slipped through a side door, out across the yard. Sir Stephen Chandler was waiting in the shadows. He would act as sentry, whilst Rolles committed the deed. Broomhill also came down to keep an eye on matters.' Athelstan paused. 'Rolles crept into the hay barn, killed those two women, but realised what Chandler may have told him, that the Misericord wasn't there. He bars the hay barn door and returns to the kitchen. Chandler, drunk and maudlin, goes into the barn to view the corpses before staggering back to the tavern. If anything went wrong, Chandler and Rolles could vouch for each other. The Misericord had escaped, but he could wait for another day, and that day came sooner than he thought.

'The Misericord is arrested and taken to Newgate. He now realises what the deaths of Beatrice and Clarice mean. Whilst locked in Newgate, he leaves further clues about what he suspects. He scratches on the wall "*Quem quaeritis*", "Whom do you seek?" It comes from the Gospel at Easter; when the women arrived at Christ's tomb to anoint His Body they met angels who asked the same question. It's a reference to the Crusaders, soldiers who vow to fight for the sepulchre of Christ. In a subtle way the Misericord was naming those knights who, twenty years earlier, had robbed the treasure intended for that crusading fleet. Such an allusion would appeal to the Misericord, with his knowledge of music and liturgy, as did the second clue, the reference to numbers – 1, 1, 2, 3, 5. He was actually numbering the assassins – the five knights staying at this tavern. In fact he was doing more than this. The numbers 1, 1, 2, 3, 5 come from Signor Fibonacci's work on geometry, *Practica Geometriae*. The writer demonstrated a sequence of numbers, each of which, after the first, is the sum of the two previous. The Misericord, a scholar, had to show off: he was not only listing you knights, but demonstrating how you were all bound up in one murderous coven. Finally,' Athelstan sighed, 'as he died, the Misericord became more explicit. He tried to scream the source of his suspicions. The prisoner in the adjoining cell thought he was shouting "Askit". In truth, it was "casket".'

Athelstan stretched out and brought the casket towards him.

'You had decided on his death, hadn't you, Sir Maurice? You and your companions, Master Rolles and Mother Veritable. You were a coven of conspirators, who could vouch for each other whatever pretended quarrels occurred between you. When Sir John came with his questions, you could act all innocent, and claim that no one left the tavern, but one or more of you certainly did slip across to Cheapside and, cowled and cloaked, arrange for that poison pie to be sent in to the Misericord. I suspect two of you went. Mother Veritable bought it, and one of your company gave it to the keeper. You knew we were going there. You simply watched and waited for us to leave, then carried out your murderous design. You must have known a gift from the Lord Coroner to a prisoner in Newgate would be handed over immediately.'

Athelstan paused. In the garden outside the window the bailiffs were gathering around a deep pit, talking excitedly at each other, pointing down to something. Athelstan half rose to get a better view, and realised that the bailiffs had been digging near the small flower arbour where he and Rosamund had sat.

'In a while,' he murmured, 'all will be revealed. By now . . .' he continued. Sir Maurice seemed not to be listening, leaning on the table, head in hands, whilst Branson gazed at the wall like a man who had taken a blow to the head. 'By now you had decided on other deaths. The Judas Man was a danger, narrow of soul but with a razor-sharp wit. He grew suspicious; indeed, anyone would have. During those long hours in St Erconwald's cemetery, he would ask himself questions like, why the Misericord? Who had hired him? Why the great secrecy? He would learn about the Lombard treasure and the mysterious events of twenty years ago, and, of course, he was a suspect over the killings of Beatrice and Clarice, even though he was involved in a brawl on the night they were murdered. I searched his chamber and found a scrap of parchment where he had written "4 not 5".'

'He was talking about this present company, wasn't he?' Cranston asked.

'Yes, he was,' Athelstan agreed.

'He had met you, hadn't he, Sir Maurice? He knew all about the five knights and their chaplain. He was keen-eyed, and on the night of the Great Ratting, he came down into the tap room. He must have met you, did he not?'

Sir Maurice refused to look up.

'He noticed one of you was missing around the very time that those two young women were murdered. He noticed Chandler wasn't there. This is pure deduction,' Athelstan conceded, 'but the Judas Man would be intrigued: what important event occurred where only four of the knights, not five, were present? The only significant occasion, the only murders which occurred when he was close by, were those of Beatrice and Clarice. He must have heard the gossip about Sir Stephen quarrelling with those women as well as being seen in the yard afterwards. Above all,' Athelstan glanced quickly at the corpse stiffening beside him, 'he wondered why Master Rolles never interfered with his confrontation with that poor miscreant Toadflax. Was Rolles so busy in the kitchen he couldn't come out? The Judas Man started asking questions, so one of you killed him, very close, with a crossbow bolt. The Judas Man was a soldier, a hunter; he would have to be caught unawares. I could imagine Master Rolles tapping on his door, the primed arbalest well concealed. The Judas Man flings the door open, and in a few heartbeats he is dead.'

Athelstan glanced at Malachi, lost in his own thoughts, beating his fingers against the table edge.

'Master Rolles must have been involved. You would need his cart. The Judas Man's corpse, stripped naked, was concealed under mounds of rubbish. At dusk Master Rolles took it out to the lay stall, the great refuse mound on London Bridge. Nobody lingers to watch refuse, ordure and other unmentionables be unloaded. The Judas Man's corpse became part of the midden heap, and along with the rest was tipped into the Thames.'

He paused at the furious knocking at the door, and

Flaxwith came in. The bailiff stood fascinated by the corpse sprawled on the floor.

'What is it, Henry?' Cranston asked.

Flaxwith whispered hoarsely in the coroner's ear. Athelstan overheard a few words: something had been found in the garden.

'Let it wait, Sir John.'

Cranston agreed, but ordered Flaxwith to remove the taverner's corpse. A sheet was hastily brought, the body rolled in it, and taken out into the passageway. Athelstan heard the cries and groans of the servants and maids, now gathering, horrorstruck at what was happening. He rose and closed the door firmly against the noise.

'Brother Malachi, we come to you. You were attacked in my church by a dagger man. One of the knives used belonged to the Judas Man, but of course, that was just to muddy the water. That poor unfortunate had already gone to God. Master Rolles, a prime mover in all these matters, was your assailant.' Athelstan pointed at the coroner. 'When Sir John first described Rolles, he called him a sicarius, "dagger man"; the knights sent him to silence you.'

'And why should they do that?' Malachi's voice was rich with sarcasm.

'You know why.' Athelstan held the Benedictine's gaze. 'Once you had that ring,' he continued, 'you realised your brother was dead. On the day of the great robbery you had been absent across the river; for all I know, that may have been arranged by Rolles, Sir

Maurice and the other conspirators. You returned and, like the rest, were mystified at what had happened. In the end you reluctantly accepted that your brother was a thief and a fugitive. You had no reason to suspect otherwise. The crusading fleet left the Thames; never once did you see or hear anything to arouse your suspicions, until that ring came into your possession. It was a matter of logic. Who else would have known about that treasure? Who else had the means to carry out the deed? Did you reflect upon Guinevere the Golden, on the possibility that she may not have loved your brother as he loved her? And, of course, the treasure. Have you been to see His Grace, John of Gaunt?'

Malachi gazed coolly back.

'What was it, Brother?' Athelstan urged. 'What made you decide to carry out God's judgement on these murderers?'

'Did I?' Malachi taunted back. He scraped back his chair, smiling to himself. 'Tell Sir Maurice how I did it, Athelstan.'

'You decided Chandler should die first,' Athelstan replied. 'That fat knight was all a-quiver, still disturbed by the events of the previous night, hot and sweaty and agitated. He wanted to sip at claret and soothe himself in a hot tub. You saw the taverner take it up. You waited until he had gone and then, carrying an identical cup, of claret, tapped on Sir Stephen's door. The knight, all in a fluster, admitted you. He was in a state of undress, and when he realised that you had come to talk about nothing of significance, he wanted you to go.'

'But only after Malachi had exchanged one cup for another,' Cranston replied.

'Oh yes,' Athelstan agreed. 'The goblet Malachi brought was heavily laced with poison. How many times do we put a cup down and pick up the wrong one? Chandler didn't even notice. He let Malachi out, placed his boots to be cleaned, locked and barred the door, climbed into that hot bath and swallowed his own death. The rheums in his nose would dull the taste of poison.'

'And Sir Laurence Broomhill?' Cranston asked. 'You lured him into that cellar, lit the candle at the far end and he stumbled into that repulsive mantrap.'

'God knows,' Athelstan added, 'how you did it. A message that Broomhill was to come alone to learn something? You know all about this tavern, the cellar and what it holds.'

'I now realise,' Cranston tapped the table, 'why we were not summoned when Broomhill was first found. You, Sir Maurice, delayed, you didn't want us to hear the dangerous babbling of a dying man who might ask Athelstan to shrive him.'

'You are truly evil men,' Athelstan accused. 'You didn't give a fig for Broomhill's soul or Chandler's reputation. If matters were pressed, Chandler could be blamed for the deaths in the hay barn, the result of too much wine and hot lust. After all, he'd touched the corpses and bloodied his hands. You claimed

Chandler's crossbow was missing, I doubt very much if he had one. You were more concerned about your chaplain being your nemesis.'

'And you accuse me of Davenport's death?' Malachi asked.

'I do!' Sir Maurice seemed to have recovered his wits. He tried to shake Branson from his reverie, but Sir Reginald turned away like a frightened child. 'I do!' Clinton repeated, pushing back his long grey hair. 'Whatever he says.' He pointed at Athelstan.

'Are you confessing, Sir Maurice?' Cranston asked.

'I'll confess to nothing until I have a meeting with His Grace.'

'Oh, I'm sure you will,' Athelstan retorted. 'Yet no one killed Sir Thomas Davenport. He committed suicide. You, Sir Maurice, lied about him, you tried to depict Davenport as a jovial, merry man, eager for a goblet of wine and the sweet embraces of the fair Rosamund. It was you or Master Rolles who sent for her to divert Sir Thomas. He had lived with his sin for twenty years; every time he came here was a sharp reminder. Indeed, it was the real reason you gathered here every year. Under the pretext of celebrating a past triumph, the conspirators met to reaffirm their loyalty to each other. That's why Chandler brought his chancery coffer with him. I don't think any of you feared God or man. Sir Thomas may have been different. He realised that one sin begets another. The murders of Beatrice and Clarice, the Misericord, the Judas Man, and of course when you sent Master Rolles to dispose of Brother Malachi . . . Sir Thomas realised that the conspiracy was crumbling away. The Beast of Sin no longer lurked by the door; it was hunting him. Davenport went out in the garden and, like Sir Stephen Chandler, begged God to forgive him. He asked for pardon but, like Judas Iscariot, guilt consumed him. He sat in that garden and thought of the corpses mouldering there, the other victims, their blood shrieking for God's vengeance. He could take no more. He returned to his chamber, locked himself in and died in the Roman fashion. He took the candle pricket and thrust it up into his own heart.'

'How did you know that?' the Benedictine intervened. 'I thought you'd lay his death at my door.'

'No, no, Malachi. You knew what had happened. The knights, Master Rolles and Mother Veritable had taken careful counsel over the murders of Chandler and Broomhill. If one of them was not responsible, and the Judas Man was elsewhere hunting the Misericord, it must have been another of their number. The logical conclusion was the pious Brother Malachi, so devoted to the memory of his brother. Rolles tried to kill you in St Erconwald's. You realised that, so you fled this tavern and sheltered with me. Your departure so frightened Davenport, terrifying him out of his wits, that he took his own life.'

'I danced when I heard the news,' Malachi jibed.

'Undoubtedly,' Athelstan retorted. 'But suicide is the only logical solution. Sir Thomas was sealed in that chamber. He ate the sweetmeats, drank some wine, then drove the pricket in whilst seated in the chair, which is why the blood splashed out on to his lap. Rolles and Clinton didn't want me to discover the truth, so they confused matters to make it look like murder. Why not? We hadn't resolved the killings of Chandler or Broomhill; Davenport's supposed murder not only removed the suspicion of suicide but tangled matters further. Naturally they could only go so far, as the chamber had been visited by the fair Rosamund, whom I later questioned. You made one mistake, Sir Maurice. When Davenport drove that pricket into his heart, he must have kept his hands clenched on it. His fingers, sticky from the sweetmeat, would have been drenched in blood. You or Rolles wiped both the blood and the sugar off. Sir Thomas went to God with clean hands but a stained soul.'

'If it had been suicide,' Cranston spoke up, 'if we had established that immediately, we would have wondered what could have frightened Sir Thomas Davenport so much that he took his own life.'

'How did you,' Athelstan pointed at Malachi, 'eventually realise what truly happened twenty years ago?'

'How did I realise?' the Benedictine mimicked. 'How does anyone know? Oh, it was the passing of the years, a crumb here, a crumb there. My brother would never have disappeared, not like that.' He shook his head. 'Not like smoke on a spring day, and the same goes for Mortimer. He truly loved his sister. I heard reports about Guinevere being seen here or there, but I dismissed them as lies. Then these,' he gestured around, 'these reunions, every year. Why were five knights of Kent, powerful Lords of the Soil, so eager to meet up with the likes of Master Rolles and Mother Veritable? Every year they came together, and I began to wonder. It was like the weather, little signs, but you know there's a change. I used to wander this tavern, that's how I discovered the mantrap. Like you, Brother Athelstan, I noticed the high-backed cart, the tavern's many entrances, then the ring was found.' He smiled dreamily at Athelstan. 'I showed it to them and they didn't even recognise it. The only thing I had from my brother; that's why I gave it to you, in fulfilment of a vow. I wanted it to be kept in a sacred place.'

He leaned over and pulled the small coffer closer to him, gently caressing the top.

'On the night of the Great Ratting, when those two whores were killed and the Misericord was being hunted, I made my decision. Oh yes, I had been to see His Grace the Regent. I wanted to clarify something. He knew who I was. Perhaps he suspected what I planned. He didn't call me by my monkish name, but "Master Culpepper". What passed between us is a matter for you and Sir John to find out. Yes, I did what I did, because I was compelled to. Innocent blood demands justice.' He scraped back his chair. 'No, Sir John, I'm not leaving. I want to view my dead.'

Cranston and Athelstan followed him out of the solar. The coroner ordered the two knights to be guarded and shouted at the throng of servants and maids to stay in the tap room. They all retreated fearfully, stepping around the gruesome remains of their former master wrapped in their blood-stained cloth. Followed by Brother Malachi, Cranston and Athelstan went out into the garden, now ruined by the digging of the bailiffs: mounds of hard clay where the lawn had been ripped apart, flower beds and herb patches roughly dug up. To the left of the arbour stretched a long, deep pit. Flaxwith went over and pointed into it. Athelstan gazed down and closed his eyes at the pitiful scene.

'The corpses must have been stripped,' Cranston whispered. 'Not even a burial shroud.'

The skeletons lay like a collection of bones in a charnel house, one tossed on another, all flesh and hair rotted away. Athelstan could see no trace of clothing belt or boot, nothing to distinguish these five people sent to their deaths in such a hideous fashion.

'I'll make a full confession.' Brother Malachi knelt down beside the pit, hands clasped. 'I know my brother; whatever they have done, I'll still know my brother.'

He lifted his head, tears spilling down his cheeks, an old man stricken to the heart by what he had seen and heard, no longer any smiles or taunting, just the heart-stopping pain of loss and grief.

'In a way I thank you, Brother Athelstan. God's judgement has been done. Don't worry about me, I won't flee. I am a priest. I will demand to be handed over to the church courts. Until then I will mourn for my brother.'

Athelstan quickly blessed the pit and stepped away. Cranston ordered Flaxwith and his bailiffs to remove the skeletons and have them coffined.

'Take them to St Mary-le-Bow,' he ordered, and gestured at the Benedictine. 'He may go with you but under strict guard. Brother Athelstan?'

They returned to the solar. Sir Maurice and Sir Reginald had demanded a jug of wine and now sat cradling their goblets. Branson looked as if he was ill, but Sir Maurice was steely-eyed and determined.

'You and Rolles,' Athelstan reflected, studying that grim face. 'You and Rolles must have been the prime movers. You have no pity, no conscience.'

'I demand my rights.' Sir Maurice spoke up. 'Both Sir Reginald and I are knights of the shire. We demand to see His Grace the Regent.'

Athelstan paused as he heard the sound of a horse leaving the stable yard. Going to the door, he asked what had happened, only to discover the head ostler had left on some urgent errand. Athelstan smiled to himself and came back into the room.

'You have no authority!' Sir Maurice yelled at Sir John.

'I have every authority.' Cranston walked down the room. He gripped Clinton's shoulder and forced him back in his seat. 'Sir Maurice Clinton, Sir Reginald Branson, I arrest you for high treason, for foul murder, for robbery, for breaking the King's peace. You are my prisoners and will await the King's pleasure.' He prised the goblets from their hands, throwing each to the floor, allowing the metal cups to spill their contents and roll into a corner, then he walked to the door, gesturing for Athelstan to join him. He ushered the friar out and closed the door behind him, shouting for more guards. He ordered two to go into the room and told the others to allow no one in or out. Then he took Athelstan by the shoulder and led him into the great tap room, now deserted.

'Well, well, little friar. You had scant proof. Clinton and Branson will not confess. They'll try to pass the blame on to Rolles and others, whilst Brother Malachi will plead Benefit of Clergy. How did you know?'

Athelstan led him across to a table and sat down. 'Straws in the wind, Sir John, straws in the wind! As Brother Malachi said, it was like watching the weather changing.'

He paused as one of Sir John's bailiffs brought in both his writing satchel and the small casket he had left in the solar.

'Think, Sir John,' he continued, 'of all these vile deeds being held in a basket. Time passes, the basket begins to rot, one or two strands break free: the ring, the casket, Brother Malachi. I used to wonder whether it was one or more murderers, and I eventually decided it must have been two.' He used his hands to emphasise his point. 'On the one hand we have Chandler and Broomhill, murdered secretly. I deduced there was only one assassin at work behind those deaths.

But the others, the Misericord, the Judas Man, Beatrice and Clarice, as well as the attack on Brother Malachi, all pointed to a conspiracy. What we had to decide was who was part of that conspiracy? I concluded that all of them were, except Malachi. Davenport's death, and the way it was twisted to look like some mysterious murder, convinced me. In the end it was merely a question of breaking the conspirators up and presenting them with the evidence I had gathered. And there's one left. Oh no, Sir John.' Athelstan got to his feet and smiled as he recalled the head ostler riding so swiftly out of the stable yard. 'There are in fact three, with one more guilty than the others.'

'Athelstan?'

The friar handed Sir John the coffer. 'Tell your men to keep this safe, place a close guard on those two knights and Brother Malachi and let's hasten across the bridge. We have business with Mother Veritable. I knew her absence would unsettle Rolles.'

During their swift walk through Southwark and across London Bridge, Athelstan tried to placate Sir John, whilst at the same time keeping his own counsel.

'One thing I cannot understand, Brother Athelstan, is the treasure! If the knights stole it, then what became of it? According to all the evidence you have collected, it was not the source of their wealth. Indeed, it has never been traced.'

'Hasn't it?'

Athelstan paused in front of the House of the

Crutched Friars. Both men seemed unaware of the crowd milling around them and the strange glances they received from tradesmen in the stalls either side of the thoroughfare. Only a cart packed with prisoners heading up towards Newgate forced them to step aside.

'Don't talk in riddles, friar.'

'I'm not, Sir John. When did you last lose something precious?'

'Oh, about three years ago; a medallion.'

'And did you find it?'

'No, I didn't.'

'And are you still looking for it?'

'Of course not!'

'Precisely.' Athelstan smiled. 'But come, Mother Veritable awaits.'

They were hardly through the gate of the Minoresses when they became aware that something was wrong. A cluster of brown-robed nuns greeted them excitedly; led by Sister Catherine, they gathered round Sir John.

'Oh, my Lord Coroner, an accident! A terrible accident!'

Athelstan's heart skipped a beat. 'Oh no, not Edith?' he whispered.

'Oh no,' Sister Catherine answered, 'her visitor, Mother Veritable.'

She pointed across the courtyard towards the very steep steps running up one side of the convent building.

'A strange one her, Brother.'

381

Athelstan gazed across the courtyard and felt a chill of fear. A dark stain blotched the bottom step and the cobbled yard beneath. Cranston was trying to placate the rest of the nuns.

'She fell, didn't she? Edith agreed to meet her there, in her chamber, on the top floor.'

'What was that?' Cranston turned.

'Young Edith,' Athelstan repeated, 'she agreed to meet Mother Veritable in her chamber at the top of the stairs, and when they'd finished talking they came out, didn't they?'

Sister Catherine nodded.

'And something happened, didn't it?'

'Oh, yes,' the nun gabbled. 'Mother Veritable must have missed her footing. We were in the refectory at the time and heard the scream. Her body bounced down the steps, that's how Edith described it, her head sliced open. Our infirmarian said she had broken her neck. Edith is now in the guest house, with the two visitors you sent.'

She led Cranston and Athelstan across the yard. The friar glanced quickly at the pool of blood, the dark red stain, slowly drying, which marked the end of that wicked woman. Inside the guest house they found pale-faced Edith cradling a posset of wine, Benedicta and Cecily sitting either side of her.

'I wish to speak to Brother Athelstan alone,' Edith called out. The friar nodded at Cranston.

'I'll stay outside with these two beauties.' The coroner coughed abruptly as he remembered Sister

Catherine. 'I mean three. Sister, you wouldn't have some bread and a jug of Bordeaux for a hungry, thirsty coroner?'

'Of course, Sir John.'

Grabbing the coroner by the arm as if they were long-time friends, Sister Catherine led him out, Cecily, grasping his other arm, tripped cheekily alongside. At the doorway, Benedicta came back. She gripped Athelstan by the shoulder and gave him the kiss of peace on each cheek.

'They say it was an accident, but . . .'

Then she was gone. Athelstan sat next to Edith on the bench.

'I came to thank you for what you did. You intimated to Mother Veritable that you wished to join her house.'

'I promised her the world and everything in it,' Edith replied quietly, 'and the old bitch preened herself as if she was Queen of the Night. I kept her for as long as I could, Brother. I tolerated her smell, her presence. This woman who, I knew, had a hand in my brother's death, who certainly was responsible for hunting him like a dog the length and breadth of this City. She assured me of a fine time, of beautiful clothing, jewellery, the favour of the great and good.' She leaned her head back against the wall. 'I could tolerate her no more and said she should rejoin her companions. We left my chamber and reached the top of the stairs. Then she tripped.' Edith turned her head, her sea-grey eyes all innocent. 'The Lord works in wondrous ways, Brother, his wonders to behold! That's my confession and all I will ever say. Eye for eye, Brother, tooth for tooth, life for life.'

Edith sat for a while, eyes half closed as if praying.

'Whatever you think, Brother,' she whispered, 'whatever you say, I truly believe that God had decided to call that wicked woman to Him.'

Athelstan patted her on the shoulder.

'What will be, shall be,' he murmured, 'so come, let's join the rest.'

They found Sir John in fine fettle, seated at the high table in the refectory, a goblet of claret in one hand, a small manchet loaf in the other. He was busy regaling Benedicta, Cecily and what appeared to be the entire convent with his exploits at Najera in northern Spain. He hardly broke off to greet Athelstan and Edith, but ceremoniously waved them to a seat further down the table. Cranston knew what had truly happened to Mother Veritable but he decided to leave that with Athelstan. As he refilled his goblet, he wryly reflected, before continuing his description of the battle, that the deaths of Rolles and Mother Veritable had saved the City the expense of a hanging. He winked at the friar and continued his graphic description of how the English archers had deployed in a series of wedges to defend themselves. The nuns hung on his every word. Cranston grew suspicious. Athelstan, too, listened attentively, as if he had decided to stay the entire day in the convent. The coroner was about to bring his story to a close when the sound of horses and the jingle of harness echoed through the cavern-ous, low-beamed refectory, followed shortly by an old porter hobbling in, cane rapping on the paving stones. He breathlessly announced that His Grace, John of Gaunt had arrived!

Athelstan rose swiftly to his feet and Cranston quietly cursed. Now he realised why Athelstan had been waiting, even as he recalled the head ostler riding so swiftly from the tavern in Southwark. He and the friar courteously excused themselves and walked out of the refectory. Cranston stopped on the top step. The convent yard milled with armed men, all wearing gorgeous livery displaying the arms of England, France and Castile. Banners and pennants fluttered in the breeze. Knights of the royal household gathered round Mother Superior and other officials of the convent, placating them and offering the Regent's excuses for this sudden visit.

'Satan's buttocks!' Cranston whispered. 'I wonder what the royal serpent wants.'

Athelstan felt a chill as he noticed that each gateway and entrance was guarded by archers, bows unslung, quivers hanging by their sides. A knight banneret, in half armour, his ruddy face gleaming with sweat under a mop of close-cropped blond hair, broke away from the group around Mother Superior and came striding across.

'Sir John, Brother Athelstan, His Grace waits for you.'

He led them across to the guest house, opened the

door and ushered them in. John of Gaunt, dressed in a simple leather jerkin, open at the neck to reveal the golden double S collar of Lancaster, had already made himself comfortable, war belt slung on the floor, his long legs and booted feet up on the table, gauntlets stripped off. He was enjoying a small jug of beer at the far end of the table. Signor Tonnelli and Matthias of Evesham did not look so relaxed as their master.

'My Lord Coroner, Brother Athelstan, come here!'

The Regent gestured at the stools on the other side of the table. Cranston and Athelstan went over, bowed and took their seats. The coroner stared pointedly at the Regent's boots. Gaunt smiled apologetically, swung his feet off the table, and leaned across, hand extended so that Cranston and Athelstan could kiss the ring on his middle finger.

'Now we have dispensed with ceremony, let us get to the heart of the matter.'

'The heart of the matter?' Athelstan retorted. 'You mean the truth, your Grace. Well, I shall tell you the truth. No Lombard treasure was ever put on that barge. Oh, it may have arrived in the Tower, but it was never sent downriver.'

Cranston gasped and put his hands to his face, peering through his fingers. Gaunt seemed unperturbed, playing with the ring, watching Athelstan as he would a fellow gambler reach for the next throw. Tonnelli and Matthias of Evesham went to protest, but Gaunt waved his hand.

'An interesting theory, Brother.'

'The truth usually is, your Grace. You took the treasure, and concocted that farrago of nonsense about outlaws and river pirates. Oh, it was true enough, but it only served as the spice for the meal you cooked. Edward Mortimer was your man, body and soul, a knight who would have gone down to hell for you. He brought Richard Culpepper into your plot. You took the treasure, opened the chest, removed the precious hoard and filled it with bricks and stones, or whatever came to hand. It was then locked and resealed, the keys sent to the Admiral of the Fleet. Mortimer and Culpepper were to take possession of it and, in midstream, would tip it overboard, where it would sink to the bottom of the river. They would then tear their clothes, inflict minor wounds and bruises on themselves, and arrive at the Admiral's ship with a story about how they were attacked by a group of river pirates. Mortimer prepared for that by giving his sister a cross he did not wish to lose in the darkness on the river. They would be believed. After all, where was the treasure? And they bore wounds to prove their resolute defence. The Fleet would sail. Later on, Mortimer and Culpepper would receive their reward. Nobody was to be really hurt. The Lombard treasure was only a part of the Crusaders' war chest; they would claim that they could not pay back what they didn't receive. The Lombard bankers might cry piteously in public, but in private, Signor Tonnelli was part of the plot, as were you.'

Gaunt clapped his hands together quietly.

'Very good, Brother,' he murmured.

'But then something went wrong,' Athelstan continued. 'You and Mortimer made one mistake, as did Richard Culpepper. He had fallen in love with Guinevere, a courtesan who sold her favours to the highest bidder. She betrayed him to what I call the company at the Night in Jerusalem. You never knew that. In the end, as in a game of chequers, everyone's move was blocked. The Crusaders had lost their treasure, but there was more to be had from the Lombards, not to mention the profits of the war. The bankers hadn't really lost their money and stood to gain more. The Keeper of the Tower was the secret recipient of fresh wealth, whilst the true thieves were the proud owners of a mere midden heap. The real victims were Mortimer, Culpepper and those two innocent boatmen. You knew Mortimer and Culpepper must be dead, but, of course, you couldn't reveal that without telling the truth, for why should two knights abscond with a chest full of rocks and bricks? Oh, you would make a careful search, but the game was played, there was nothing to be done. All you could do was sit, wait and watch. Only one person warranted sympathy, poor Helena Mortimer, still hoping, still trusting that her brother would return. You took pity on her. You made sure that every quarter your comrade here, Signor Tonnelli, handed a pension to a London goldsmith for her. This kept Helena's dreams alive and made sure she didn't fall into poverty; it was the least you could do to honour Edward's memory.'

Athelstan's gaze never left the Regent's face. Handsome as an angel, he reflected, his light skin burned dark by the Castilian sun. The silver-blond hair, beard and moustache so neatly trimmed, those beautiful blue eyes so frank and direct, except for the glint of mischief; only this time Gaunt looked genuinely sad. For a moment Athelstan caught this powerful man's deep regret and sorrow at what had happened.

'Do you believe this, my Lord Coroner?' Gaunt glanced at Cranston.

'I have always admired both your courage and your cunning, your Grace. A source of wonderment for me, as it was for your blessed father and elder brother.'

Gaunt laughed quietly to himself.

'You may have suspected the other knights,' Athelstan declared, 'but you could never prove the truth, which hangs in a delicate balance and, as I have said, like a two-edged sword, cuts both ways. You kept the treasure, the years passed, Signor Tonnelli would arrange for it to be broken up and sold elsewhere in the cities along the Rhine or even in the lands of the Great Turk. One person remained keen in the hunt for the truth: Brother Malachi, a Benedictine monk, Sir Richard Culpepper's brother. He approached you, didn't he? Asking questions, some of which you could answer, others you had to ignore. Malachi was dangerous, an intelligent man, a scholar and, above all, a Benedictine monk. I do wonder,' Athelstan deliberately picked up the Regent's goblet and sipped from it; Gaunt did not object, 'I do wonder what he said to you.'

Gaunt leaned his elbows on the table and cupped his face in his hands, tapping his boot against the floor as he scrutinised this friar.

'You're a very dangerous man, Athelstan.'

'Is that why you have spies in my parish?'

Gaunt smiled.

'You do have spies in the Night in Jerusalem. The head groom, for one.'

'True, true,' Gaunt quipped. 'I have a legion of spies in Southwark. I watched the Night in Jerusalem like a hawk surveys a field.'

'You know what happened there today?'

'Of course, but I would like to hear it from you, Brother.'

Athelstan quickly described the events of the last few days and the violent, bloody confrontation in the tavern solar. Gaunt listened, eyes closed, now and again interrupting with a short sharp question. At the end he turned to Matthias of Evesham.

'Tell the good sisters to bring some wine, nothing too heavy, the juice of the Rhineland, so we can all slake our thirsts.'

Matthias hurried off. He brought back a tray of mugs and cups and Gaunt insisted on serving everyone. He then retook his seat, lifted his goblet and toasted both Athelstan and Cranston.

'*Tu dixisti*, you have said it, Brother. Twenty years ago I was Keeper of the Tower. I had barely reached my twenty-first year. As Jack Cranston knows, I'd campaigned in France, but not long enough to harvest any wealth. In the May of that year the Treaty of Bretigny was signed. There would be,' Gaunt sighed, 'for the foreseeable future, no more armies in France, no more ransoms or plunder. My father and elder brother kept me on a tight rein. To put it bluntly, I hadn't two sous to rub together. Then the crusading fleet arrived and Signor Tonnelli collected the Lombard treasure; the rest you know. I would take the treasure and return it to Signor Tonnelli for a secret loan, the bankers would take the treasure elsewhere, and nobody was to be really hurt. Signor Tonnelli considered it was a good business agreement. We advanced monies to Mortimer and Culpepper. They were sworn to silence and promised, in time, a lavish reward. My friends the Lombards would not lose their treasure, the crusading fleet wouldn't have to repay a loan they had never received, but they would still give their bankers a percentage of their profits, whilst I, and Culpepper and Mortimer, became richer men. On the morning of the twenty-first of September 1360, the Feast of St Matthew, I accepted that something dreadful had happened. As God is my witness, Brother, I didn't care about the treasure, but I scoured the City and the kingdom for Mortimer and Culpepper, even though I was forced to accept both were dead. I kept my vow and looked after Helena. The years passed, times changed and the Lombard treasure was forgotten.'

'Until Brother Malachi appeared.'

'Yes, he came to my palace at Sheen, and later to the Tower. He never dressed as a Benedictine but in the robes of a clerk; he always insisted that I call him by his family name, Master Thomas Culpepper. He told me about the ring, and questioned me most closely. He pricked my suspicions and, I think, suspected the truth. I told him to do what he had to and let me know the outcome.'

'But you must have been concerned?'

'Of course I was. If Culpepper's comrades were guilty, they might, in court, describe what they found when they opened that chest.'

Gaunt laughed abruptly.

'That must have been a soul-chilling shock for them. Oh, I knew about the knights gathering every year. I decided I would watch the events in the Night in Jerusalem very carefully. I heard about the murders.' He shrugged. 'Well, you know how it is, Brother? The names Cranston and Athelstan appeared. There, I thought, now the hawk will fly.'

'And so it did,' Cranston remarked. 'What will you do, your Grace? You have two knights of the shire guilty of the most heinous crimes. If you bring them to trial before the King's Bench at Westminster, they will hang, but they will also confess to what they found in that treasure chest.'

Gaunt stared up at the black rafters. 'Do you know, Sir John, Brother Athelstan, we live in very strange times. They say great armies are moving in the east. Some people claim the Church has lost its mission; there are even people,' his eyes rounded in mock innocence, 'who claim that all men are equal, that

Watkin the dung collector and Moleskin the boatman should enjoy the same rights as John of Gaunt.'

'Jesus said the same, your Grace, and was crucified for it.'

'True, but as you know, my relationship with the Spanish kingdoms is very close. They dream a great dream, of becoming united, of driving the Moors out of Spain, and in their conversations, the princes of Aragon, Castille and Portugal talk of sending ships into the great unknown seas down the west coast of Africa. Some people claim there are lost kingdoms, full of gold and silver. Anyway,' Gaunt drained his cup, 'I shall have Sir Maurice and Sir Reginald brought to the Office of the Night in the Tower, where we shall reach an agreement. I am going to send them as envoys to the Court of Lisbon. They are to join an expedition, a seaborne expedition, to charter unknown lands. They will, in fact, be given a choice: to go to Portugal under strict guard, or wait for trial at Westminster.' Gaunt steepled his fingers. 'I shall remind them about how many people die of prison fever, or even eating poisoned pies.'

'And Brother Malachi?'

'He doesn't know the full truth about the treasure. I understand that the Order of St Benedict have a monastery, a small community, outside St Ives in Cornwall. I will personally ensure that he spends the rest of his days there. Holy Mother Church owes me a favour or two.'

He got to his feet, scraping back his chair, gesturing at Tonnelli and Matthias of Evesham to follow.

'Sir John, Brother Athelstan, a good day's work. The Night in Jerusalem will be sold by the Crown; after all, Master Rolles was a traitor and a thief, so all his property is forfeit. I think I will give it to the chief ostler on a lease. I will ensure that some of the profits go to the chantry chapel at St Erconwald's.'

He bowed to both of them and swept through the door. Matthias of Evesham patted Athelstan's and Cranston's shoulders as he passed.

For a while, the friar just sat staring at the wall.

'Do you know, Sir John, one of the great differences between good and evil is that good is so necessary and evil isn't. Look at those assassins. When did they make the decision to rob and kill their friends? An afternoon? An evening over their cups? And when they did, they planted an evil, a malevolent shrub which took root and spread out to blight so many lives. Yet it was so unnecessary. They never got the treasure, and within a few years they were all rich, powerful knights of the shire.' He crossed himself quickly. 'All those hideous deaths for nothing.'

'Come on, Brother.' Cranston rose to his feet. 'I'll treat you to a pie and a blackjack of London ale in the Lamb of God, and we'll take those two beautiful women for company.'

'Why, Sir John, are you leading me into temptation?'

'No, Brother, just delivering you from evil.'

Author's Note

The character of John of Gaunt is, I believe, accurately depicted in this novel. A man of great cunning, Gaunt was regent of the kingdom during the 1380s. The repressive policies of his government did eventually lead to a great revolt and the rebels burned down his beautiful palace at Savoy. A Crusade under Lord Peter of Cyprus did sail into the Mediterranean and meet with varying success, and although the great robbery is a matter of fiction, such outrageous crimes were not uncommon in medieval London. Many of the street scenes and the infringements of the law described in the novel spring directly from primary sources. The role of the Night in Jerusalem characterises the activity of many London taverns, which were often the centre of a great deal of law-breaking. Little wonder that, until the late twentieth century, the taverns, inns and pubs of England were constantly under the close scrutiny of magistrates. The Misericord reflects the myriad confidence tricksters who through the centuries have made London their home, whilst the bounty hunter (true historical characters like Giles of Spain) was as common in medieval England as in the Wild West.

One final note, about John of Gaunt's declaration about sea voyages along the west coast of Africa. In the nineteenth century, British troops entered the West African kingdom of the Ashanti and found a jug which had actually been made in London during the fourteenth century (it can still be viewed in the excellent London Museum). How it got there, of course, is a matter of speculation!

Headline hopes you have enjoyed THE HOUSE
OF SHADOWS, and invites you to sample
THE ASSASSINS OF ISIS, Paul Doherty's new
mystery set in Ancient Egypt, out now from
Headline.

Prologue

The violaters of the Houses of a Million Years could not believe their luck. They had swept into the Valley of the Nobles, a deep gully to the right of the soaring peak of Meretseger, the Silent One, which overlooked the Necropolis on the west bank of the Nile, opposite the temple complex of Karnak. The tomb guards had posed little problem, nothing which a silent knife thrust or the tight cord of a garrotte string couldn't resolve. Their leader had given them precise details regarding the princely tomb they were to ransack. Once inside the valley, garbed in black from head to toe, they had swept like ants along the branching trackways. None of them knew or recognised any of his companions. They were united by one stark purpose: the pillaging of a tomb, the rifling of treasures of the ages from a House of Eternity whose owner had long gone across the Far Horizon into the Eternal West.

Now they were finished, sweeping up the moon-washed valley. They had enough light to see their way, a long line of fast-moving figures laden down with booty, so excited they were oblivious to the roars, grunts and growls of the night prowlers, the lions, the hyaenas and jackals which lurked on that broad wasteland between the City of the Dead and the scorching desert which stretched like an eternity. They'd thought their night's task was finished when their leader paused, holding up his dagger. Abruptly he left the narrow track, plunging down the shale and sand, sending dust flying as he moved between two jutting crags on to an unseen ledge and a carefully masked cleft which concealed the door to another tomb. The leader gestured for the rest to follow, calling them down by imitating the 'yip, yip' of a night fox. The violaters, who took the name of the demon Sebaus, would never have dreamed of searching for such a place.

The group gathered in the small porchway and quickly dug away at the plaster-covered entrance. Once inside, the pot of fire was brought, pitch torches, taken from a sack, quickly lit and pushed into crevices along the wall. The Sebaus had long lost their fear of the Kingdom of the Dead. They glanced around, realising that the tomb consisted of four roughly hewn chambers, a main one with three storerooms leading off. The tomb had been hastily prepared. No paintings on the wall, no dried-out baskets of flowers, whilst the plaster coating hadn't been properly finished or smoothed down. Nevertheless the burial chamber and adjoining storerooms were full of costly artefacts: precious game boards, ivory shabtis, mother-of-pearl boxes, chairs and stools of the finest wood inlaid with precious metals, boxes of precious oils, caskets of brilliant jewels, trinkets, bracelets and floral collarettes. In the far corner a collection of costly weapons lay heaped: knives and swords in jewelled scabbards, a magnificent bow of honour. Next to this was an exquisitely carved wooden casket containing the canopic jars, but the real prize was the red quartzite sarcophagus with the wadjet, the Eye of Horus, painted on each corner. The Sebaus' leader, a former scribe, crouched down and read the hieroglyphs.

'Rahimere,' his muffled voice grated, 'former Grand Vizier of Egypt. Well, let's see what this lordly one holds.'

Using crowbars and mallets they prised the lid loose, letting it fall to the ground with a crash, ignoring the great crack which appeared along the side. They climbed up on to the side, staring down at the luxuriously painted coffin casket within. Tools were hastily brought, the lid wrenched off and the casket inside brought out and thrown unceremoniously to the ground. The Sebaus leader wrenched off the beautiful face mask, ordering one of his men to break it up while the rest began to plunder the mummy, unwinding the bandages, fingers probing and searching for the sacred jewels and amulets.

The leader returned to the sarcophagus. He swung

himself up, lowered himself gently down and searched around. His hand grasped a costly leather case. He picked this up, opened it and took out a book wrapped in the finest linen. He had been expressly ordered to look for this and leave the case deliberately on the floor. He climbed out and gazed round the burial chamber. His companions, faces and heads masked and hooded, were now seizing whatever they could carry. Baskets were emptied, chests and coffers kicked over, sacks and pouches hurriedly filled. The leader of the Sebaus wiped the sweat from his brow and smiled contentedly. He knew none of his companions; he had simply been given his orders, precise directions, where to go and what to do, and had memorised every detail. He rejoiced in the great honour shown to him. Just before midnight he had gone out to the Dried Oasis to the north of the valley and met the Khetra, their silent, secretive master. The Khetra had stood hidden in the shadows, as he had done when the Sebaus leader had last met him, on that desolate island of Khnum to the north of Thebes. As usual, he had relayed his orders through another, so softly the leader couldn't decide whether the Khetra was man or woman. He could detect nothing but moving shadows and that pervasive smell of jasmine. Was the Khetra a woman? In the past the Sebaus leader would have found this disturbing, yet didn't Egypt have its own Pharaoh Queen? Wasn't the Khetra a deep fountain of knowledge about the Valley of the Kings and all its treasures? What did it matter! He or she was making all of them rich beyond their wildest dreams.

The Sebaus leader, cradling the book wrapped in linen, wondered where the Khetra could have acquired his knowledge about a hidden tomb like this. How could he have possibly known? Yet the orders had been quite precise, to follow the trackway above the two crags, reach the middle point and plunge down to the waiting ledge. The leader watched one of his gang empty a pure alabaster oil jar which had been filled with pearls. The wealth of this tomb spoke for itself. He recalled what he knew of Rahimere. Hadn't he once been the Grand Vizier who'd opposed Pharaoh Hatusu and been given no choice but to drink poisoned wine? His family had been disgraced and must have chosen this lonely, hidden spot to protect Rahimere in the afterlife. There were scores of such tombs; some were discovered by accident, but others would remain as they were, a hidden horde of treasures.

The Sebaus leader, cradling the linen parcel, walked over to the wall and unwrapped it. The book itself was composed of papyrus sheets sewn together with a strong twine; the writing was that of a learned scribe. The Sebaus leader, who had knowledge of such writing, began to read carefully, and as he did so, his heart skipped a beat. He hastily closed the book and rewrapped it in its linen sheet. The pitch torches were burning down and, going to the entrance of this man-made cave, the leader peered out. He glimpsed the stars low against the blackness of the heavens.

His orders had been quite precise: to ransack this tomb and return to the Dried Oasis, where the Khetra would be waiting.

'Enough!' He turned to his companions. 'Take what you have.' He held up a hand, his wrist bracelet glistening in the light. 'Remember, nothing must be withheld, nothing taken. Theft by one of us is a danger to all.'

The gang nodded in understanding. The Khetra was ruthless; any theft meant instant death.

They left the tomb, slipping and slithering up the shale. A number of objects were dropped, but the leader, distracted by what he had read in the book, ordered them to be left. Speed was the order of the night; although it was still dark, they had to reach the oasis before dawn. They left the lonely valley, climbing over the limestone gullies, sinister shapes, the only sound their grunts and groans as they carried their heavy burdens. To their left glowed the lights of the Necropolis, and across the river was the shadowy mass of Thebes.

The Sebaus leader urged his men on, although he remained distracted. He was frightened, for deeper fears had now been stirred. The robbing of the royal tombs had already caused scandal in the city. The Medjay police and the chariot squadrons were being deployed, and troops would soon be dispatched. The situation was growing more fraught by the day. The leader climbed a rocky outcrop, skirting the tall posts driven into the ground bearing impaled corpses, now only tattered remains after the vultures and desert prowlers had taken their share. The lights of the city had disappeared. They were now on the borders of the Red Lands, yet they moved carefully, wary of foot patrols or chariot squadrons camped in some ravine. On the night air throbbed the heart-chilling roars of the night creatures.

The rest of the gang were climbing the rocky escarpment now, fanning out and peering down at the Dried Oasis below. The fire bowl was brought; a light flared, which was answered from the oasis, its bent, twisted trees black against the starlit sky. The Sebaus moved down the rocky outcrop and across to the oasis, where they squatted in a semi-circle, as they had been ordered to, around the crumbling wall of the old well. On the far side of this lurked other Sebaus who had not taken part in the raid, and somewhere in the trees beyond them was the Khetra. Orders were issued, the plunder collected, men were beckoned forward to be rigorously searched, the choice being indiscriminate. Once the Khetra was satisfied, rewards were distributed, the profits from previous raids, now converted into gold, silver and precious stones. Some of the robbers were selected to take the new plunder to certain places in Thebes. No home or person was named, only this pleasure house or that beer shop, or some other anonymous location. All they had to do was leave the treasure; it would be collected, and sometime in the future the price would be paid.

At last the Sebaus dispersed and the oasis fell silent. The leader of the tomb robbers had been given strict instructions to remain. He did so, still cradling the book wrapped in its linen shawl.

'Come!' whispered a voice through the darkness.

The Sebaus leader moved around the well.

'Kneel.'

The tomb robber did so. He was aware of dark shadows coming towards him; the smell of jasmine was very strong.

'You have what I told you to find?'

'Yes, master.'

A pair of hands abruptly plucked the book away.

'Did you read it?'

'No, master.'

'You lie. You opened it when you should have been watching those who were with you.'

'Master, I—'

The Sebaus leader heard a faint sound, followed by the twang of a horn bow. The arrow took him deep in the chest, loosed so close it flung him back to lie coughing and kicking in the sand. The last words he heard, as he choked on his own blood, were the order for his corpse to be taken and buried deep in the desert.

Three days later a sweat-soaked runner raced up the Avenue of Sphinxes towards the soaring pylons of the Divine House, the Palace of Hatusu, Pharaoh Queen of Egypt. The runner, the swiftest in the imperial corps, was covered in dirt. He had to wash and purify himself before being allowed into the entrance porch, where he was anointed and perfumed in preparation for being taken into the Kingfisher Chamber – a beautiful room with light-green-painted walls. The kingfisher bird was everywhere, its vivid plumage accurately depicted in a number of scenes, perched above ever-blue water or plunging life-like into some reed-ringed pool.

Inside the door the messenger knelt. The man squatting on cushions on the dais at the far end of the room ordered gauze linen curtains to be pulled aside to reveal a strong man, his balding head glistening with oil. He had a soldier's face, with hard eyes and harsh mouth, and he was dressed in a simple white tunic, although costly rings glittered on his fingers. The messenger, beckoned forward, nosed the ground before the dais, then, grasping the step before him, gasped out his message to Lord Senenmut, Grand Vizier of Egypt, First Minister and, some claimed, lover of the Pharaoh Queen.

Senenmut threw down the map he was studying, hiding his alarm as he listened intently to the message. Once the runner had been rewarded and dismissed, he rose to his feet and strode through open acacia doors on to the balcony where Hatusu lay on a silver couch under a perfume-soaked awning. She was laughing and chattering with her maids, but broke off as Senenmut came across, catching his glance, and dismissed the maids.

'My lord?'

'They have found the tomb. Rahimere's. It has been robbed and the coffin opened.'

The lovely faience goblet slipped from Hatusu's fingers as she stared in horror.

'It can't have been,' she whispered.

'The tomb was robbed,' Senenmut confirmed. 'A leather case was found which must have contained the book. There's no mistake. Rahimere died and took his secrets with him; now they're in the hands of some tomb robber.'

'So the Temple of Isis was right, the information they gave us.'

Hatusu crunched the broken glass under her sandal.

'Enough is enough!' she whispered. 'Ask Lord Amerotke to be here by dusk. I'll instruct him to root these robbers out. Somewhere in this city is a merchant or official who's helped them; he can be easily broken . . .'